EXTREME DIVORCE

Gazing out the window at the shades of gold that edged the sky across the sound, Judith sensed movement on the Belmont Hotel's roof directly below her.

A dark-haired woman in a wedding dress and a bearded man in a tuxedo were standing by one of the big air vents. Judith was intrigued.

Then, to her horror, the man grabbed the woman by the shoulders and threw her off the roof. Judith let out a little cry.

"Joe," she whispered in an urgent voice. "Joe!"

With a small quiver, Joe swerved to look at Judith. "Mmm?" he said with what Judith considered a silly smile on his face. "What is it?"

Trying to refrain from frantic gestures, Judith pointed to the Belmont. "A man just pushed a woman off the roof! Look!"

Joe complied. But when Judith turned again, the roof was empty.

Bed-and-Breakfast Mysteries by
Mary Daheim
from Avon Books

MARY DAHEIM

Wed
and
Buried

A BED-AND-BREAKFAST MYSTERY

AVON BOOKS
An Imprint of HarperCollinsPublishers

AVON BOOKS
An Imprint of HarperCollins*Publishers*
10 East 53rd Street
New York, New York 10022-5299

Copyright © 1998 by Mary Daheim
ISBN: 0-380-78520-X
www.avonmystery.com

First Avon Books paperback printing: February 1998

Avon Trademark Reg. U.S. Pat. Off. and in Other Countries, Marca Registrada, Hecho en U.S.A.
HarperCollins® is a trademark of HarperCollins Publishers Inc.

Printed in the U.S.A.

10 9 8 7

ONE

JUDITH McMONIGLE FLYNN tripped over the silver bells on the silver box, fell against the oak banister, and landed on her knees atop something odd from Aunt Ellen. Cursing under her breath, Judith sat on the next to the bottom stair and tried to figure out what her aunt in Beatrice, Nebraska had sent Mike and Kristin for a wedding present. Was it a wall plaque? Was it a clock? Was it a hat? Unable to make heads nor tails nor anything else out of the jumbled corn husks, Judith rubbed her sore knees and called for Joe.

"Your aunt gives some weird gifts," Joe Flynn remarked around the cigar he held between his teeth. "Is she nuts or just cheap?"

"Neither," Judith replied a bit testily. "You met Aunt Ellen and Uncle Win when they came to our wedding five years ago. Aunt Ellen is the sanest person I know, but she is a bit . . . um . . . thrifty. Plus, she does crafts." Judith lifted the cluster of corn husks. "Maybe it's a wreath for the front door."

Joe's round face registered mild interest. He picked up the object of conjecture, experimented with setting it on his thinning red hair, and finally brandished it like a shield. "I think it's a toilet seat cover. You'd have

to be careful, though.'' His green eyes sparkled with mis-
chief.

Judith stood up. She was almost as tall as Joe, who
fudged a little when listing his height at six feet. ''I'll let
Mike and Kristin deal with it,'' she said. ''I've got other
things to worry about before the wedding.''

It was Thursday morning, and the ceremony was set for
Saturday at eleven A.M. Between now and then, Judith had
a long list of things to do. As the mother of an only child
who was male, she had never expected to shoulder the
lion's share of putting on a wedding. That was usually up
to the bride's family, but Kristin Rundberg's parents lived
on a wheat ranch in the eastern part of the state, a remote
locale that wasn't conducive to hosting large celebrations.
Thus, Mike had asked his mother if he and Kristin could
be married in the city, at the parish church on Heraldsgate
Hill. Euphoric over the news that her son and his long-
time fiancée had finally set a date and were actually going
to become man and wife, Judith readily agreed.

But that was almost eight months ago, at Thanksgiving.
Now it was late June, and Judith was wondering why
she'd been so accommodating. Kristin's relatives were
coming, not only from the wheat country, but from Idaho
and Montana. Most were arriving in a few hours, and
some would stay at Hillside Manor. Judith would be out
of pocket in more ways than one, since she would have
to give up at least three nights of paying guests at the bed
and breakfast. There would be meals to provide for the
visitors, including those who were checking into motels
or camping in their RVs. Judith wasn't looking forward
to the descent of the Rundbergs.

The phone rang as Judith was carrying some of the
presents from the hallway into the front parlor. Joe picked
up the cordless phone from where Judith had left it at the
bottom of the staircase.

''It's Renie,'' he called. ''What should she do with the
lutefisk?''

"Ask her if it smells bad yet," Judith shouted back. "If it does, it's ready to eat."

There was a pause, then Judith heard Joe's mellow voice speaking into the phone. She loved that voice, which sounded like honey on warm toast. It wasn't a cop's voice, though it served Joe well. Those soft, ripe tones had deceived many a perp in the interrogation room. Of course Joe could also yell, which he proceeded to do just as Judith came out of the front parlor.

"She says it smells like a Metro bus on a hot afternoon, and if you don't get it out of her . . . oh." Joe's voice dropped several notches as he saw his wife come into the entry hall. "Renie's kind of mad," he said, putting his hand over the mouthpiece.

Judith took the phone from her husband. "What's wrong?" she demanded.

Renie told her cousin exactly what was wrong, which was just about everything. "It's not *my* sons that are getting married," Renie snarled. "They'll never marry, nor will our daughter. They will drift in and out of this house and that college and this job and that relationship until Bill and I are in some pest house, putting spaghetti in what's left of our hair. William and Serena Jones are doomed. Meanwhile, your son is taking a fine, buxom young woman to wife and will produce grandchildren for your posterity. And all I have is this *stupid stinking lutefisk*. The lye it's soaking in has eaten through my new kitchen counter. I'm bringing it over now and throwing it on your front porch. Good-bye." Renie hung up.

"You're right," Judith said to Joe. "Renie's mad. Where's Mike?"

"He took your car to the airport to collect the Montana contingent, remember?" Joe replied mildly. "He and Kristin were going to stop at Nottingham Florists to check the flowers."

Judith ran a hand through her shoulder-length salt-and-pepper hair. "Oh. That's right, I forgot. Do you need the

MG? I was thinking of going over to Renie's and rescuing the lutefisk.''

Joe's green eyes regarded Judith with something akin to pity. "Jude-girl," he said, using the nickname that his wife had once despised, but had gotten used to since their marriage, "I'm taking two days off from chasing murderers and other bad guys to play designated driver, remember? I'm heading for the bus depot and the train station in about twenty minutes.''

"Oh," Judith repeated. "I forgot." Renie would have to deliver the lutefisk, but hopefully not in the manner she had threatened. "Do I have time to run up to Falstaff's and get the pork roast for tonight?''

Joe glanced at the grandfather clock in the living room. "If you hurry."

Judith grabbed her purse from off the marble-topped table in the entry hall. "I'm on my way."

But she wasn't. Upon reaching the back door, she saw the nose of Renie's big blue Chevrolet pull into the drive. Renie flew out of the car, and raced around to the trunk. A moment later, she was staggering under the weight of a huge white carton.

"Here's your damned fish," she shouted. "I hope those crazy Norwegians or whatever they are eat until they puke."

Judith hurried to take the carton from Renie. One whiff of the lutefisk sent her reeling backwards. "Ooof! You're right, it doesn't smell so good. I'll put it in the basement."

A small, hunched figure appeared in the backyard, squinting against the midday sun. "Who's that? Serena? What stinks? Don't you ever bathe, kiddo?"

Judith ignored her mother and headed back into the house with the carton. Renie could handle Gertrude. Sometimes it was easier for a niece to deal with an aunt than a daughter with a mother. Judith edged her way downstairs and settled the carton on the basement floor next to Joe's fishing tackle. The odor wafted after her up the stairwell. At the back door, Sweetums was poised, ready to investigate.

"Don't even think about it," Judith murmured to the cat. "You wouldn't like it. You're part Persian, not Norwegian."

Sweetums shook his orange and white fur, a gesture of disdain for human opinion. Swishing his plumelike tale, he sauntered into the kitchen. Judith wasn't fooled. But she had no time to waste on the cat. Outside, she found her mother and Renie engaged in one of their usual arguments. Judith waved as she headed for the garage and Joe's MG.

"Knucklehead!" Gertrude yelled. "*You* tell her!"

Judith halted in midstep. "Tell her what?"

"That I'm not going to any wedding this weekend." Gertrude had clumped forward on her walker, thrusting out her chin and assuming a defensive attitude under the baggy blue cardigan and black- and green-striped housedress. "What would I go to a wedding for? I don't know anybody who's getting married." The old woman shot Renie a fierce, obstinate look.

Judith and Renie exchanged quick glances. Gertrude's memory had been slipping for some time, slowly but surely sinking into a morass of advancing age and increasing self-absorption. As her physical world grew smaller, so did Gertrude's perception of what went on around her.

"Mother . . ." Judith began with what she hoped was patience and understanding. "Of course you're going to a wedding. Mike's wedding. He's getting married Saturday at Our Lady, Star of the Sea."

Gertrude's small face puckered. "Mike?" She gazed up at the cloudless blue sky. It was hot for June in the Pacific Northwest. "Oh. Mike." A twitch of her nose seemed to dismiss her grandson. Then she tipped her head to one side and regarded her daughter and her niece with small, shrewd eyes. "It's about time," she declared and turned back to the converted toolshed where she made her home.

Judith sighed. "I don't know when she really forgets and when she's trying to annoy me. Did I tell you what she said on Mother's Day?"

Judith had told Renie. Twice. "You're getting as goofy as she is," Renie chided gently. Now that she had rid herself of the lutefisk, her good humor seemed restored. "She asked if she had any children. You said yes, she had you. Your mother said, 'You're it?' and acted disgusted."

"See what I mean?" Judith said, her patience eroding as she watched her mother disappear inside the toolshed. "Was she kidding then? Is she kidding now? I never know anymore."

Renie gave a little shake of her chestnut curls. "My mother remembers too much. If I'm five minutes late getting to her apartment, she brings up the latest abduction from the local news. If Bill and I are going to spend a weekend in Port Royal, she recalls seeing that they had a hepatitis outbreak six months ago. If one of our kids is off sailing, she reminds me that somebody drowned two weeks ago off Cape Whazzits. She's still got a mind like a steel trap, and everything in it is scary."

"They're a pair, all right," Judith lamented. "I don't know which is worse. Hey, thanks for taking care of that lutefisk. I'm sorry I bothered you with it."

Renie shrugged. "It's okay. I volunteered, didn't I? I just didn't realize how it smelled. Anne and I will have the groom's cakes ready by tonight. She's working on them now," Renie noted, referring to the Jones's only daughter. "What else do you need?"

Judith considered. Her neighbor and partner in catering, Arlene Rankers, was handling the reception, which would be held at Hillside Manor. Judith and Arlene had put on many a wedding reception over the years, so both women knew the drill. The rehearsal was set for Friday, with dinner to follow at the Naples Hotel, a refurbished landmark overlooking downtown. The details at the church—music, flowers, guest book, and the service itself—had already been worked out. It would be an ecumenical ceremony, with Kristin's Lutheran pastor joining Father Francis Xavier Hoyle.

"I can't think of anything at this point," Judith said a bit wearily. "I've worked my tail off for the past two months. Probably I've missed something, but I don't know what."

Renie's gaze was sympathetic. "Trust me, it won't matter. They'll still get married." She hesitated, her sandal-shod foot tracing a circle in the lush green grass. "Um . . . Have you made up your mind about . . . You know." Renie's loss of words was uncharacteristic.

Judith's dark eyes grew troubled. "No. Not yet. I've talked to Joe, but he refuses to give me any advice. It's between Mike and me, he says. I suppose he's right."

Renie grimaced. "I suppose."

The cousins stood in silence for several moments. For over fifty years, they had been as close as sisters. They could say anything to each other—or nothing at all. So close was their communion that they could virtually read each other's minds.

"Talk about being damned if you do and damned if you don't," Judith finally murmured. "Is honesty always kind? Does Mike need to know after all these years? Is it fair to Joe to go on keeping a secret?" Judith made a desperate little gesture with her hands. "My problem is that I can see both sides."

Renie's smile was wry. "That's always been your problem. You're too blasted fair. It's enough to make me believe in that astrology stuff. Libras are like that. Scorpios aren't. We not only aren't fair, we bend the rules."

"I already did," Judith gulped. "That's why I'm in this quandary."

Renie held up a hand. "It's too late to give yourself a

bad time over *that*. Besides, it all worked out. It just took twenty-five years to get there.''

Judith offered Renie a small smile. ''But I haven't dealt with it where Mike's concerned. I've played ostrich, and buried my head in the sand.''

''You tend to do that,'' Renie said, not unkindly. ''Hey, I've got to run, coz. My mother needs a few things at the drug store. You know what happens if I'm not on time. An APB goes out.''

''Right,'' Judith nodded. ''I merely get called a lot of awful names, like chowderhead and moron and Big Stoop. That is, if Mother remembers I left in the first place.''

Renie drove away, but before Judith could get into the MG, Joe appeared in the driveway. The twenty minutes were up; he had to leave for the bus depot and the train station. Judith was stuck waiting for Mike and Kristin to return from the airport.

Fortunately, they did, less than ten minutes later. The relatives they'd picked up had been delivered to the Naples Hotel. They'd arrive at Hillside Manor around six, after they'd ''freshened up.''

Thoughtfully, Judith watched Mike and Kristin head into the house. At twenty-eight, her son was a fine specimen of young manhood, tall, broad-shouldered, and extremely fit. As a park ranger, his deep tan was almost permanent, obscuring the smattering of freckles that went with his dark red hair. Judith swelled with pride as she watched his easy, long-legged stride.

Should she tell him? Was it fair not to? Did it really matter? Judith wrung her hands. She'd never been good at making hard decisions. That was why she'd stayed with Dan McMonigle for eighteen years. Despite Dan's verbal abuse, his gluttony, his drinking, and his refusal to work, it had *seemed* easier to keep the marriage intact. It had been a delusion, of course. Or was it cowardice that had kept her shackled to Dan? Had she been afraid of Dan's reaction, afraid of the unknown, afraid to act? Maybe she had feared all those things. Once Judith put down roots, she pulled them up only when forced by circumstances.

Such circumstances had changed her life when Dan's four-hundred-pound body gave out at the age of forty-nine. Or, as Judith sometimes put it less delicately, Dan had blown up. However his demise could be described, it had spelled freedom for Judith, at least of a sort. She and Mike had moved home to the old Edwardian house on Heraldsgate Hill. There Gertrude had held sway, giving grudging consent to the reinvention of the Grover house as a bed and breakfast establishment.

Judith spared a fond look for the old, solid three-story structure that had been home to four generations of Grovers. Nine years had passed since Judith had begun the major renovation. Hillside Manor's green-on-green exterior had faded in the rain and damp of those gray Pacific Northwest seasons. Maybe it was time for a paint job come the fall. It wasn't a smart idea to take on any big projects during the height of the tourist season.

Fleetingly, Judith glanced in the direction of the bay where the water sparkled like diamonds and the mountains to the west stood out against an almost flawless sky. The vista never palled: Even in a downpour of autumn rain or thick winter fog or what sometimes seemed like perpetual drizzle, Judith found something that caught her eye. Perhaps it was a ship riding at anchor in the harbor or the sleek glass and steel structures of downtown or merely the changing play of light and shadow. She had grown up with that view, and while many things had changed including herself, certain elements remained constant. Judith smiled as she hurried into the house.

Mike and Kristin were foraging in the refrigerator. "Hey, Mom," Mike asked, "is Grams making her killer potato salad for the reception?"

Gertrude's potato salad was famous. "She'll supervise Arlene," Judith replied. "It's too big a job for Grams to do alone. I need the car keys. I've got to run up to the store.''

Holding a twenty-pound ham in one hand, Kristin closed the refrigerator door with her hip. She was a big girl, a tall girl, a Valkyrie of a girl. Her long blond hair was more or less tamed into a single braid, and her flawless skin was almost as tanned as Mike's. She wasn't exactly pretty, but neither was she plain. Judith usually settled for ''striking'' when describing her daughter-in-law to-be.

''Aunt Leah and Uncle Tank had a little trouble checking in at the Naples Hotel,'' Kristin said in her low, calm voice. ''There was some confusion about their reservation, but they got it straightened out after Uncle Tank threatened to shoot the desk clerk.''

Startled, Judith glanced at Mike. Her son, however, showed no unusual reaction as he opened a loaf of rye bread. Kristin placidly began carving ham.

''You're kidding?'' Judith sounded dubious.

''In a way,'' Kristin replied matter-of-factly. ''The airlines don't allow guns in the passenger cabin. Uncle Tank left his at home where they live in Deep Denial.''

Judith's dark eyebrows arched. ''Deep denial? Of what?''

With only the faintest hint of a smile, Kristin shook her head. ''They live in Deep Denial, Idaho. It's a place, not a state of mind.''

I wonder, thought Judith. She knew little about Kristin's extended family. Maybe that was just as well. Mr. and Mrs. Rundberg seemed like sensible people, but that didn't mean that their shirttail relations were. Judith knew that too well from her own sometimes peculiar relatives.

But there was no time to discuss family eccentricities. Judith was off to Falstaff's Market. As she turned on the ignition of her Subaru, the radio also came on. Judith winced. Mike and Kristin had been listening to a young adult music station.

"Ya-a-a-h!" the DJ shouted. "Turn up the volume and tear off the knob! It's rockin'-sockin'-slammin'-jammin'-rappin'-slappin' tunes right here on KRAS-FM, with your freedom-lovin'-gun-totin'-butt-kickin' Harley Davidson, bringing you all the . . ."

"No, you aren't," Judith said quietly but firmly, and tuned the dial to a station that featured hits from the fifties and sixties. Andy Williams and "Moon River" caressed her ears as she drove up the steep hill to the neighborhood's main shopping area. Judith smiled and relaxed behind the wheel. The song had been one of her favorites when she was dating Joe over thirty years ago. They had danced to it, hummed to it, made love to it. And then Joe had eloped with another woman. Judith had never wanted to hear "Moon River" again, refused to watch *Breakfast at Tiffany's*, despised Andy Williams, and had secretly admired his ex-wife, Claudine Longet, for shooting her lover, Spider Sabich, in a fit of jealous rage. She would have liked to have done the same thing to Joe. Judith hadn't known then that Joe had gotten drunk after his rookie encounter with teenaged OD fatalities, and been lured onto a Las Vegas–bound plane by the woman known as Herself. Nor had Judith realized that while she suffered in her rebound union with Dan McMonigle, Joe had done penance of his own as the husband of a dedicated alcoholic. It was only when one of Judith's guests was murdered at the B&B that the erstwhile lovers were reunited. Joe had been assigned to break the case; his marriage was already broken. After all was explained, much was forgiven. Judith and Joe had taken up more or less where they had left off, and five years later, life was usually good. There were minor problems, of course. Gertrude had loathed Dan, but she'd never liked Joe much, either. After Judith and Joe had gotten married, Gertrude had steadfastly refused to share a roof with her new son-in-law. The move to the converted toolshed ensued, though Judith's mother never ceased to complain about being thrown out of her own house. There was some truth to the charge, but Judith had been forced into a corner. Gertrude had to go, if only about twenty yards.

Then, just as Judith foolishly thought life was moving on a fairly smooth course, Herself—or Vivian, as was her real name—returned from Florida. To Judith's horror and Joe's dismay, she purchased a house in the cul-de-sac just two doors down from Hillside Manor. While Herself hadn't quit drinking, she apparently had stopped making passes at her former husband. Judith did her best to accept the other Mrs. Flynn as nothing more than a slightly eccentric neighbor. Most of the time, the approach worked.

"Moon River" ended as Judith pulled into the grocery store parking lot. She had ordered a very large pork roast, since at least two dozen guests would be on hand for dinner. Maybe, she reflected as she waited for Harold, the butcher, to bring her order, she should get a second, smaller roast. It wouldn't go to waste; she could always use the meat for sandwiches. Gertrude loved pork sandwiches.

"I'm not cooking," said a voice at Judith's ear. She turned to see Renie, looking resolute. "It's too hot. We're getting a couple of pizzas."

"So why are you here if you're not making dinner?" Judith inquired.

Renie made a face. "It turned out that my mother also needed a few things at the grocery store." She waved a lengthy list in front of Judith. "I've got coupons, too. She can save twenty cents on toilet paper, thirty on flour, fifty on coffee, and a whole dollar off an oilskin tablecloth. Why does my mother need an oilskin tablecloth? She's been using plastic table covers for twenty years."

Judith made sympathetic noises. "She probably wants to save it for good. My mother has eight slips that have never been out of their gift boxes."

"So what?" Renie snorted. "My mother has ten old

girdles in her closet. The last time she wore one of them, a stay popped up and cut her chin.''

Harold presented the pork roast with a flourish. Judith gaped at the price, recovered herself, and thanked the butcher. A second roast was beyond her budget. The cousins continued down the aisle, toward dairy.

"At least you won't have to cook tomorrow night," Renie pointed out. "The food at the Naples Hotel should be quite good. They've had an outstanding restaurant ever since they remodeled a few years back.''

"I wish you and Bill were coming," Judith said with fervor. "I really don't know any of these people. It's going to be dull.''

Renie, who drove a grocery cart almost as erratically as she handled a car, knocked over a papier-mâché pineapple that was part of Falstaff's "Hawaii Days" display. "You do very well with strangers. That's why you're such a success as a B&B hostess. Besides, you'll get to know most of the in-laws tonight. By the rehearsal dinner, they'll all be your new best friends.''

"I don't know," Judith said in an uncertain voice as they passed into housewares. "They sound kind of . . . odd.''

Renie got tangled up in an orchid lei. "Ooops! Hey, they can't be any odder than some of our shirttail relations.'' The lei came apart, spilling purple petals all over Aisle B.

"I don't think they're used to the city," Judith remarked as she paused to pick up a box of laundry detergent. "They're basically small-town folks.''

"Then they're probably thrilled to be in a big city," Renie asserted. "I'll bet the ones who have already arrived are having a great time sightseeing.''

"Mmm, maybe." Judith waited for Renie to choose an oilskin tablecloth. "I'll be relieved when this weekend is over.''

Renie smiled at her cousin. "I don't blame you—weddings are stressful. Not that I'd know,'' she added archly, mowing down a plastic pig. ''But when you think about it, what can really go wrong?''

Judith admitted she didn't know. Indeed, she couldn't begin to guess.

TWO

BY THE TIME the pork roast had been reduced to cat scraps, the dinner party seemed somewhat awkward to Judith. Sig and Merle Rundberg provided pleasant conversation, but the other relatives tended to retreat into themselves. Judith thought they wore an air of suspicion. She said as much to Joe when they were in the kitchen, readying the strawberry parfaits.

"You bet they're suspicious," Joe replied in a low voice. "I'm guessing they're a bunch of survivalists. Did you look up Deep Denial, Idaho and Trenchant, Montana on a map?"

Judith shook her head. "I didn't have time."

"You'd have wasted it. Neither one shows up. I figure they're up north, in the Idaho panhandle, or near the Montana–British Columbia border. These people have a real isolationist mentality. Did you hear them say one word about going outside their motels or hotels?"

"No," Judith admitted. The Rundbergs had driven four hundred miles from the eastern part of the state and had been understandably tired. Still, Sig and Merle were more outgoing, and seemingly at ease in a social situation. They were staying at the B&B, along with Kristin's brother, Norm, and his wife, Jewel, Merle's brother and his wife, Sig's two widowed sisters, and a

curmudgeon called Uncle Gurd. While various other relatives camped out in their RVs and holed up in nearby
motels, only Aunt Leah and Uncle Tank had joined the
Hillside Manor contingent for dinner. Since Judith had
expected to feed another half-dozen, she had urged her
mother to join them at table. Joe had invited Herself. To
Judith's surprise, her husband's ex had dressed decorously, imbibed moderately, and conversed minimally.

As Judith carried in the dessert tray, there appeared to
be a lull in the conversation. Gertrude abhorred a vacuum,
and proceeded to fill it: "I'm a lifelong Democrat. Voted
for FDR four times—all in the same election." She
chuckled at her own wit. "What about you folks?"

Glances were exchanged around the table, most of them
hostile. "The eastern part of the state is more conservative," Merle Rundberg said in her quiet, yet forthright
manner. She was a raw-boned woman who looked as if
she could sit a tractor or a horse with the same ease. "We
tend to cast our ballots on farm issues."

"Democrats!" Uncle Gurd, who had not spoken until
now, practically spat into his parfait. "Crackpot do-good
Commies!"

"Hey, Buster," rasped Gertrude, "you some kind of
nut case?"

Uncle Gurd glared, but said nothing more.

"There's coffee," Judith put in hastily. "Or tea. Would
anyone prefer tea?"

"Politicians are all crooks," declared Uncle Tank,
whose graying brown hair was cut very short and whose
tattoos evoked the Third Reich. Judith found the heart
surrounding the SS runes particularly offensive. "Just today I heard this guy on the radio, Harley Davidson, he
called himself, who said we got too many politicians and
too many damn fools and they were one and the same.
Why can't the government leave us alone?"

"Kyle died too young," lamented Aunt Tilda, one of
the widows. "Why'd he have to do that?"

"I'll have coffee," Sig Rundberg said with a tight little smile for Judith. "The wife here kind of likes tea. Don't you, Merle honey?" He put a big paw on his spouse's shoulder.

"Marv was younger," declared Aunt Leota, the other widow. "Kyle was no good anyway."

"Tea's fine," Merle agreed. "What about you, Kristin?"

"Marv was shot by the sheriff," Aunt Tilda said, making a gesture that looked like pulling a trigger. "Gunned down while trying to get away during a bank robbery. There were so many bullet holes, he looked like Swiss cheese."

Kristin was sitting between Mike and her brother, Norm. "Tea's great," she said, sounding strained. "Are any of you going to the center tomorrow? There's so much to do. I think you'd all enjoy the exhibits."

"Kyle's best friend was a goat," Aunt Leota said, making a face at her sister. "Goats stink. So did Kyle. You're better off without him."

"What're they exhibiting, political prisoners?" growled Uncle Tank. "It's probably put on by the frigging FBI. Do you know what FBI really stands for? Well, I'll tell you . . ."

"I'm a lifelong Democrat," said Gertrude in a chipper voice. "I voted for FDR . . ."

"I could make lattes," Judith put in. "Would anyone like a latte?"

"Too many breeds," Uncle Gurd muttered. "That's why I hate cities. Yep, everybody's all mixed up, just like mongrel dogs. Shoot 'em."

"What's a latte?" asked Aunt Leah.

"Sounds foreign," Uncle Tank muttered.

Joe had reentered the dining room. "Let's go outside," he suggested. "It's kind of warm in here tonight. We can sit in the backyard and cool off."

Judith noticed the veiled threat in her husband's voice

but she doubted that anyone else did. "What a good idea," she enthused. "Maybe our neighbors, the Rank-erses, will be outside, too. I'd love to have you meet them. Arlene is putting on the reception."

Nobody budged. To Judith's surprise and relief, Herself finally stood up. She gazed down at Uncle Gurd, giving him a flutter of false eyelashes. "You look like the out-door type to me, Gourd. Let's slip out beneath the trees and let the wind play through our . . ." She paused, apparently noting that Uncle Gurd was completely bald, ". . . fingers."

"It's Gurd, not Gourd," the curmudgeon insisted. But he rose, and followed Herself like a gnarled lamb.

The rest joined them. Judith watched Mike help Gertrude make her way through the kitchen to the back door. "Say, Mike," Gertrude was saying as they headed into the narrow hallway, "did I ever tell you about Harry Truman coming through here back in . . ."

Judith sighed and slipped her arm through Joe's. "You're right, I think this bunch is extremely right-wing. Mike says they've asked him all sorts of questions about his background. Being Catholic is definitely strange. I wonder how Kristin turned out so well?"

Joe shrugged. "Her parents seem okay. But I don't think we should talk about politics any more." He held back, stopping by the sink. "I also don't think we should let them know I'm a cop."

That, Judith decided, was good thinking.

The evening had wound down without further mishap, though Uncle Gurd had insisted on sleeping under the Rankers's hedge. Small rooms confined him, he asserted. He preferred the open air, the stars above, the bugs in his pants.

That was fine with Judith. Friday was going to be a busy day, with last-minute details and final preparations for the rehearsal dinner. Judith's cleaning woman, Phyliss

Rackley, arrived promptly at nine. As usual, she first headed upstairs to strip the guest beds. Judith stopped her on the landing.

"I'm afraid the guests are still in their rooms," Judith said apologetically. "They've had breakfast, but they don't seem inclined to leave."

Phyliss's fluffy white eyebrows lifted. "These are the in-laws? Can't your roust 'em?"

Judith grimaced. "I don't think so. Kristin's parents are going off with her and Mike to check on the hotel dining room in a little while, but the rest of them seem to enjoy just sitting up there." Judith gestured towards the second floor. "They're from rural areas. They don't care for cities."

Phyliss snorted. "Didn't the good Lord preach in cities? He wasn't put off by people. Maybe I should have a little chin-wag with them." The cleaning woman patted the small Bible she kept in her apron pocket. "I'll bet they don't know Scripture. Let me give 'em a few good words."

"I wouldn't be too sure of that," Judith said, recalling from recent news items that survivalists were often knee-deep in Old Testament references. Indeed, Phyliss's fundamentalist credo might be right up the in-laws' alley. "Do what you like, Phyliss. Just try to get them out of the way so we can clean this place."

Fired with missionary zeal, Phyliss's squat figure thudded up the stairs. Judith retreated into the kitchen where she began wading through her list of phone calls. The one she dreaded most was to Artemis Bohl, the local fashion designer who had created Kristin's gown. Bohl was brilliant, expensive, and temperamental. Kristin's choice had struck Judith as uncharacteristic. But Bohl sold his exclusive designs through I. Magnifique, the city's most prestigious apparel store. Sig and Merle Rundberg wanted the best for their baby girl, and as wheat ranchers, they could

afford it. Kristin's gown was simple, almost austere, but
it suited her perfectly.

"Mr. Bohl," Judith began nervously when the designer
finally came on the line, "this is Mrs. Flynn. We were
wondering what time we could pick up . . ."

"Mr. *Artemis*," the faintly accented nasal voice cut in.
"To my public, I am always Mr. Artemis."

"Oh. Sorry. Well, Mr. Artemis, I know there were
some final alterations on . . ."

"Not alterations! Never alterations! *Enhancements!* Mr.
Artemis does not alter, he *enhances*! One cannot alter—
or change—perfection. One can only *enhance* it."

"Okay, enhancements." Judith muffled a sigh as an
unusually listless Sweetums entered the kitchen. "Are the
enhancements done yet? The bride would like to pick up
the gown and veil this morning while she's in the downtown . . ."

"I must go. I have a fashion show to mount. All is
chaos. All is confusion." Artemis Bohl hung up.

Annoyed, Judith clicked off. Kristin would have to take
her chances. Sweetums laid down at Judith's feet. Puzzled, Judith reached out a hand to pet the cat. To her
surprise, he didn't balk at the affectionate gesture. Perhaps
Sweetums wasn't feeling well. Judith tried to put the cat
out of her mind as she dialed Nottingham Florists. The
table arrangements for the rehearsal dinner would be delivered at five. The wedding flowers would be at the
church by ten, the reception bouquets would arrive at Hillside Manor before noon. Judith said thank you and hung
up just as tramping feet resounded overhead and the
strains of "Onward Christian Soldiers" floated down the
backstairs.

"What the hell is that?" demanded Joe Flynn who was
coming in the back door.

"Phyliss," Judith replied weakly. "She's bonding with
the in-laws."

"Great," Joe groaned. "It sounds like they're all being tortured."

"I don't think so," Judith said, now forced to shout as the din grew louder. "Joe, would you take the summer wreath down from the front door and pull the planters over to the far side of the porch? Nottingham's is going to bring a theme wreath and some wedding trees tomorrow."

"Nottingham's is going to get rich," Joe retorted, but he headed for the front entrance. Phyliss descended into the kitchen hallway, still singing her head off.

"Now there's some fine Christian folks," she declared, her gray sausage curls bobbing. "Not a queer one in the bunch. They don't mind me cleaning their rooms with them in it. It's not like regular guests, after all. They aren't paying."

"Don't remind me," Judith said as the stamping and the singing died away. "Go ahead, I've already put in a load from the third-floor family quarters. It should be ready for the dryer by now."

As Phyliss would have put it, she was happy as a pig in slop as she marched off on her rounds. Sweetums still lay on the kitchen floor, chin on paws. His yellow eyes blinked with effort. Maybe a call to the vet was in order. Judith leaned against the counter, trying to tell herself it was too early to have a headache. She was losing the argument even as she heard shouts from the front of the house. Hurrying outside, she saw the neighborhood patrol car with the familiar faces of Corazon Perez and Ted Doyle. Between them, they held onto a frantic, struggling, doubled-over figure. Joe had gone to the curb of the cul-de-sac and was waving his arms.

"Goon squad! Pigs! Stooges!" cried the flailing figure. "Shoot me! Why not? You'll whitewash it, like everything else!"

"Hold it!" Joe shouted. "That's Uncle Gurd!"

Corazon Perez's limpid brown eyes widened as she

loosened her hold on the suspect. "You know this guy? Somebody called about a bum sleeping in the Rankers's hedge."

Ted Doyle also slackened his grip. "Are you sure? He seems kind of loco to me."

"That doesn't mean he isn't Uncle Gurd," Joe said dryly, making enigmatic hand gestures at the officers. "I know *you police personnel* have to do your duty, but I assure you, he's just an average citizen *like me*."

Perez and Doyle both blinked at Joe, then exchanged swift glances. "Oh," said Perez, finally letting go of Uncle Gurd who fell onto the pavement and rolled up in a ball, "I understand. We're sorry to have bothered you. But further trouble could be avoided if you told the other neighbors that you've got a guest sleeping in the hedge."

"We'll do that," Joe said, motioning vigorously for Perez and Doyle to take off. "Trust us. We don't want any trouble around here."

Silently, Judith agreed. On the day before her son's wedding, she certainly wasn't looking for trouble.

But trouble had already found her. Phyliss erupted from the house, screaming. "Pestilence! Boils! A plague of locusts! It's Armageddon!"

Joe and the patrol officers turned, but Uncle Gurd remained on the ground in a fetal position. Judith staggered as Phyliss fell into her arms.

"Death everywhere!" shrieked the cleaning woman. "Entrails! Decay! Stench! Save me from the fiery furnace!"

Now Perez and Doyle looked alarmed. It wouldn't be the first time that a corpse had turned up in the cul-de-sac. Murder might be Joe Flynn's profession, but sometimes it seemed like it was also Judith's middle name. Over the years, she had often found herself involved in homicide investigations, most of which had nothing to do with her husband's job.

"Calm down!" Judith ordered, giving Phyliss a shake.

"Take a deep breath and tell me what's happened."

Nose to chin with Judith, Phyliss's eyes crossed. Then her stocky body shuddered and she seemed to relax a bit. "Your basement," she gasped. "It's filled with . . . flesh . . . *stinking white flesh*. It's as if the hounds of hell had gotten loose and torn apart the . . ."

Judith let go of Phyliss so abruptly that the cleaning woman almost fell down on top of Uncle Gurd. "Hounds of hell, my foot!" Judith shouted, racing for the house. "It's Sweetums! He must have gotten into the lutefisk! Damn!"

An hour later, Judith had the dreadful mess cleaned up. She did the task alone, unable to convince Phyliss that lutefisk might be smelly, but it wasn't ungodly. Or maybe it was, but by eleven o'clock, it was all in the dumpster. Meanwhile, Sweetums had begun to stir, his upset stomach on the mend. Judith felt like giving the cat a swift kick, but refrained. She had more pressing matters at hand, including another quick trip to Falstaff's to pick up a couple of overlooked items for Gertrude's supper.

Mike and Kristin and the Rundbergs had borrowed the Subaru for their errands, so Judith climbed into Joe's aging but much-loved MG. To calm her ruffled spirits, she turned on the radio.

"Party down, party on!" screamed a voice from the dashboard. "Party twenty-four-seven! Party with Harley on KRAS—we're the bomb! Freedom's my middle name! Don't eat! Don't sleep! This is Harley Davidson, saying party til you . . ."

Judith hurriedly turned the dial to another station, any station not intent on deafening her. Mike and Kristin had borrowed the MG after dinner last night. Obviously, they'd tuned to the same wretched wavelength that had blared forth from the Subaru. It seemed to Judith that her son and his future wife were a bit old for such raucous radio listening. Surely the approaching-thirty set should have more sedate musical tastes.

But maybe Judith was out of touch. Mike had lived away from home for several years. She had to admit that she was no longer familiar with his every whim and want, as in the days before he left for college. That, of course, was what wives were for; they leaped into the breach that mothers relinquished by default. Judith still thought of Mike as a boy, not a man. The boy might not have understood what she wanted to tell him. Surely the man would be more kindly disposed. *If* she told him. Time was running out.

Half-panicked and half-relieved, Judith turned into Falstaff's parking lot. It was better to do than to think. For the rest of the day, Judith kept very busy.

In its previous incarnation, the Naples Hotel had been a favorite late-night rendezvous for Judith and Joe. The paneled downstairs bar had provided a cozy trysting nook for the young lovers in the days of button-down collars, bouffant hairdos, and cars that were bigger than some Third World countries.

Thirty years later, the bar and the brick and sandstone exterior were all that was still recognizable about the Naples. For a decade or two, the hotel had slid into genteel decay. But ten years earlier, it had been rescued and revamped. Reining proudly over the downtown area, the Naples was now one of the city's premier hostelries.

There were almost thirty people gathered in the penthouse dining room. The tables formed a U-shape, with Mike, Kristin, Judith, Joe, the Rundbergs, and Gertrude in the places of honor. Mike's best man and former college roommate, Nick Satayama, appeared oblivious to the curious, even malevolent, stares of Uncle Tank and a few other in-laws. Kristin's maid of honor, Chandra Smith-Washington, seemed used to the hostile gazes. Judith realized that as Kristin's best friend, she probably understood the clan only too well. Asian-Americans and African-Americans were inimical to survivalist mentality.

Despite it all, the rehearsal at Our Lady, Star of the Sea Catholic Church had gone smoothly. Uncle Gurd had refused to go inside, but had finally been coaxed by Herself, who somehow had finagled an invitation. Judith suspected that Vivian had presumed upon her former husband. At first, Judith had inwardly bristled, but decided that Herself's ability to keep Uncle Gurd in tow was worth a free meal.

Now, deep into the cocktail hour with the open bar set up in a corner of the room, the guests were beginning to relax. Morris Mitchell, the flamboyant photographer who had been hired to film all the wedding events, was slipping in and out, clicking his camera and making hissing noises. No one paid much attention, which, Judith reflected, was the sign of a good photographer. Yes, the guests were definitely oblivious to everything but food and drink. Away from a church atmosphere, they were unwinding in a strange and wondrous way. More than unwinding, Judith noted, as Kristin's brother Norm put a cluster of white and yellow roses on his head and began to dance the hula. Great whoops of laughter followed, along with Cousin Thorald's playing of the paper comb. Thorald's wife, Gitti, sidled up to Judith and announced that they were staying near the zoo in their RV. Judith thought that figured.

Sipping her Scotch, Judith turned to enjoy the view which was similar, but at a different angle from that of Hillside Manor's. The dining room actually looked out over a corner of the bay as well as downtown, but also took in Heraldsgate Hill. If Judith studied the rows of dwellings that marched up to the crest, she could pick out her beloved B&B.

As the entree carts were rolled into the dining room, Joe caught his wife peering through the big plate glass window directly behind them. ''Are you wishing we were home in bed?'' he asked out of the corner of his mouth.

"What?" Judith turned to smile at her husband. "Oh.
Yes. Always."

Uncle Tank was eating filet mignon with his hands.
Actually, Judith realized with a startled look, he was eating three filets. She wondered where he'd gotten the other
two. Cousin Thorald's paper comb wheezed to the tune
of "Swanee River."

"The darkies are gay!" shouted Uncle Gurd.
"Wouldn't you know it?"

Judith shot Chandra a commiserating look. Chandra
laughed and shook her head. Judith knew that Kristin's
maid of honor was interning as a pediatrician. No doubt
she had enough understanding—and self-confidence—not
to be bothered by bigoted boobs whose IQs were lower
than their body temperatures.

While Norm and Jewel flipped French peas at each
other, Judith resolutely turned back to the plate-glass window. Directly below her was the roof of another, far less
elegant hotel. The Belmont, Judith recalled. It had once
been as grand as the Naples, but not now. Drapes were
pulled at all of the windows, a thick patina of grime covered the exterior, and the roof's tar paper was peeling
away to reveal dingy concrete.

An argument had broken out at the end of the table on
Judith's left. The widowed sisters were in the thick of
things, hurling rolls and potatoes at each other and whoever else came within range. Aunt Leah got smacked in
the chops and began throttling Aunt Tilda. Joe started to
rise from his chair, but Herself was already on top of the
table.

"Love is in the air," she asserted, making a minor,
sensual adjustment to her skin-tight red dress. To dis-
pute the point, Aunt Leota smashed a plate over Aunt
Tilda's head. Herself was undaunted. "Mike and Kristin symbolize young love. S'wonderful, s'amorous,
s'marvelous." She leaned down—*way* down—to exhibit
her cleavage to Uncle Gurd. "But not everyone has some-

one. For example . . .'' She nodded to Cousin Thorald. ''A-one and a-two . . . I ain't got nobody . . .''

The diners seemed transfixed. Aunt Tilda picked the shards of china from her gray hair and Cousin Thorald labored through the accompaniment. Norm was so awe-struck that he didn't notice several peas rolling down his arm. Morris Mitchell clicked away with his various cameras.

Judith touched Joe's sleeve. ''Your ex can be very helpful.''

''Former lounge singers have a way with them,'' Joe murmured, patting Judith's hand. ''We may get out of this without any fatalities.''

Herself crooned on. Judith's gratitude ebbed a little as she recalled how her former rival had sung her torch songs to Joe on the night they had eloped to Vegas. Try as she might, the memory could still rankle Judith. She shifted in her chair, gazing out at the shades of gold that edged the sky across the sound. It was well after eight, and the waiters were bringing on dessert. Soon they could all go home. Judith couldn't wait.

Herself had launched into ''Bewitched, Bothered, and Bewildered.'' Judith allowed her dinner plate to be removed, and just as she was turning to face the table, she sensed movement on the Belmont Hotel's roof. Curious, she swiveled around again. A dark-haired woman in a wedding dress and a bearded man in a tuxedo were standing by one of the big air vents. Judith was intrigued.

But she was interrupted when dessert arrived in the form of an elegant meringue topped with chocolate and raspberries. Herself kept singing, Morris kept clicking, Thorald kept tootling on the paper comb. Judith glanced behind her to check out the couple on the hotel roof. They had now moved to the opposite edge and appeared to be engaged in a heated discussion. Judith leaned sideways in her chair, craning her neck.

Then, to her horror, the man grabbed the woman by

the shoulders and threw her off the roof. Judith let out a little cry. On her left, Sig Rundberg swung around to see what was wrong. Joe, however, appeared transfixed by Herself's hip-swinging rendition of the "St. Louis Blues."

Judith shook her husband's arm. "Joe!" she whispered in an urgent voice. "Joe!"

With a small quiver, Joe swerved to look at Judith. "Mmm?" he said with what Judith considered a silly-assed smile on his face. "What is it?"

Trying to refrain from frantic gestures, Judith pointed to the Belmont. "A man just pushed a woman off the roof! Look!"

Joe complied. But when Judith turned again, the roof was empty. Joe frowned. "What are you talking about? I don't see anything except bird poop and garbage." He glanced suspiciously at Judith's empty cocktail glass.

"I'm not drunk!" she asserted in a low but angry voice. "Just now I saw a man push a woman off that roof! Go check on it. There must be a body in the street. Hurry!"

Herself had finished her set and finally climbed down from the table. Uncle Gurd was holding both hands over his heart and appeared to be hyperventilating. With an air of reluctance, Joe got up and left the dining room.

Judith toyed with her dessert and tried to keep up an intelligent conversation with Sig Rundberg. Yes, traffic in the city was terrible. No, Judith never felt hemmed in by the tall buildings. The rain didn't bother her, the freeway wasn't intimidating, the steep hills weren't the least bit frightening, except when it snowed. Which, Judith acknowledged, trying to cast a discreet backward glance at the Belmont roof, it didn't do very often.

"In our part of the state," Sig noted, then paused to put a sugar cube in his mouth and drink his coffee through it, "we have snow several months out of the year. It never ceases to amaze me how the mountains divide us and make two entirely different kinds of climate and geography.''

"Me neither," Judith replied vaguely. The roof was still empty. She switched her gaze to the private dining room entrance. Joe had not yet returned, nor had Judith heard the sound of sirens. Hadn't her husband summoned emergency personnel?

"Then there are all those panhandlers," Sig was saying as he returned to his litany of complaints about city life. "It looks to me as if a lot of able-bodied people are sitting around with their hands out. Why can't they do an honest day's work like the rest of us? Oh, I'll give a buck to somebody like that blind guy with the harmonica who was sitting outside the hotel. I don't mind when somebody's really handicapped. That's different."

"Billy Big Horn," Judith murmured. The bearded Montanan with the sweet songs was something of a local legend, though his usual post was outside of Donner & Blitzen department store. But Judith's compassion for the less fortunate was temporarily diluted. If Joe didn't show up in two minutes, she was going after him.

"Hey, Siggy," Gertrude called from her place next to Mike, "what's that trick with the sugar cubes?"

Sig held up his coffee cup. "It's an old Norwegian custom. You put the sugar in your mouth, not in your coffee."

Gertrude looked impressed. "Think I could manage it with my dentures?"

Sig chuckled. "Are you Norwegian?"

"Nope," Gertrude replied. "Not that I can remember." Her wrinkled face fell as she looked at Judith. "Am I?"

"No, Mother," Judith answered, standing up and going over to the window. From that angle, she could see nothing past the top three floors of the Belmont. "You're English and German, just like my father was."

"Your father?" Gertrude seemed puzzled. "Who's he?"

The return of Joe Flynn spared Judith an explanation. To Judith's consternation, her husband seemed more annoyed than upset. He spoke out of the corner of his mouth:

"Nothing. Zip. Zero. Sit down, eat your meringue, and keep your eyes to the front."

Bewildered, Judith hesitated, then obeyed. "But . . . I saw the woman go over the edge," she whispered. "The man pushed her."

"Uh-huh." Joe lapped up his dessert.

"Joe . . ." Judith sounded miserable.

"Forget it," Joe ordered tersely.

With great reluctance, Judith tried to concentrate on her food. But it wasn't easy. She'd had only two drinks, she'd eaten in the meantime, she was a mere thirty yards away from the man and woman who had been standing on the Belmont roof.

"This is the back of the hotel," Judith said in a low, determined voice as she gestured behind her chair. "The front of the hotel is on the other side, facing the opposite street. That's where the woman fell. Did you look there?"

Joe refused to answer. Judith pinched him, hard.

Joe scowled. "I went all around the damned block. There's no sign of anything unusual, let alone a dead body. I checked with Kobe, the parking valet who took our car. He and the other valets are moving cars along the street and into the garage next to the Belmont all the time. They didn't see anything, but Kobe gave me a cigar." Joe pulled the object out of his pocket. "It smells terrific. I'm going to smoke it in about four minutes."

Judith ignored the cigar. "Was anyone else around? Guests, passersby?"

Joe sighed. "Plenty of them, but they were all coming and going. I did ask Billy Big Horn if he'd noticed anything unusual. He hadn't."

"Billy Big Horn is blind," Judith pointed out with some asperity.

"I know that," Joe retorted, putting aside his empty dessert dish and lighting the cigar. "But Billy's hearing is extraordinary. No screams, no thuds. Come on, Jude-Girl, put it out of your mind. The sun's going down, it was probably in your eyes."

"No, it wasn't." Judith folded her arms and stuck out her lower lip. "I know what I saw."

"What you saw," Joe said, trying to sound reasonable, "didn't produce a corpse. *Ergo*, I can't investigate a crime. Finish your dessert, and let's get the hell out of here."

But Judith had lost her appetite. She was beginning to wonder if she'd also lost her mind.

THREE

JUDITH COULDN'T HELP it. She cried at Mike's wedding. The tears trickled down her cheeks as a bemused Joe stood at her side. When Father Francis Xavier Hoyle and the Reverend Harald Bjornstad proclaimed Michael Donald McMonigle and Kristin Ingrid Rundberg man and wife, Judith blubbered out loud.

From behind, Renie poked her cousin. "I could cry, too, but for different reasons," Renie murmured. "Put a sock in it, coz."

After the service, Morris Mitchell insisted on taking photographs both inside the church and out on the lawn. The session went on for over half an hour, and Judith was getting nervous. Arlene would be waiting at Hillside Manor, trying to keep the food both fresh and hot.

"Morris," Judith finally said in a tentative voice, "could we take some of these pictures back at home?"

Morris Mitchell was a tall, gangly young man who looked no more than twenty-five, but was probably ten years older. He had established his reputation in various fields of photography, including portraits, fashion, and commercial advertising. But he had originally made his name with wedding pictures.

"Do you want your money's worth of memories?"

Morris asked, loading yet another camera. "You don't get to come back later and do this over."

The phrase "money's worth" sunk in. Judith knew Morris Mitchell was expensive. Indeed, his schedule was such that he probably wouldn't have condescended to shoot the McMonigle wedding if Renie hadn't exerted her influence. In the world of graphic design, Judith's cousin came into contact with all sorts of photographers. Renie considered Morris the best.

At last, a few minutes after one, the bridal party made the short trip to Hillside Manor. By then, the majority of the guests had arrived, and Arlene had the situation well in hand.

"Wasn't it a beautiful wedding?" Arlene sighed after Judith had sought her out in the kitchen. "Carl and I were so happy for them. We remembered being like that, right up until our honeymoon, when Carl called me 'Darlene' and I tried to kill him."

The remark was typical, sentimental, contradictory, and good-hearted, with a dash of domestic violence thrown in. The Rankerses were a big, loving family who never seemed happier than when they were chasing each other around the house with large rubber spatulas.

"The food looks wonderful," Judith declared. "I was so nervous before the wedding that I didn't think I could eat, but now that it's over, I'm ravenous."

"Everything seems to have turned out all right," Arlene said modestly. "Except for the lutefisk. I couldn't find it."

"Oh." Judith put a hand to her cheek. "Yes, well, the lutefisk came a cropper. I hope nobody misses it."

Renie entered the kitchen and grabbed an apron. "Hey, Arlene, I'm here to help." She gave Judith a push. "Get out there and mingle. Everyone wants to talk to the mother of the groom."

Judith looked uncertain. "I don't know . . . I hate to leave you and Arlene to do all the . . ."

Renie pushed again, much harder, until Judith was forced out through the swinging doors into the dining room. Several guests were proceeding around the big oak table, sampling German sausages, salmon finger sandwiches, teriyaki chicken wings, sliced turkey, and four kinds of salads. Judith noted that none of the congenial buffet-goers belonged to the Rundberg contingent.

"Did you tell him?" Renie hissed in Judith's ear.

Judith jumped. "Huh? Ah . . . no. There wasn't a good time to catch Mike alone. Maybe I'll have a chance when they get back from their honeymoon."

"Chicken," Renie muttered, then reversed into the kitchen.

Judith edged around the line of guests and stood under the archway between the crowded dining room and the long living room. Garlands of white and yellow roses entwined with daisies and lilies and baby's breath decorated the walls. At the far end of the living room, one of Mike's friends was playing the baby grand piano. Kristin, who looked more than striking in her Artemis Bohl wedding gown, was chatting with Renie's husband, Bill, and the Joneses' sons, Tom and Tony. Mike had a glass of champagne in each hand, and was trying to foist one of them off on Uncle Corky, who preferred straight shots of Scotch. Uncle Al was making hand gestures that looked like a basketball set-shot, Auntie Vance was trying to awaken Uncle Vince, who was snoring peacefully on the window seat, and Anne Jones was tucked away by the bookcases with Nick Satayama. Renie's mother, Aunt Deb, was holding court in her wheelchair, allowing various family friends to wait on her hand and foot. Gertrude used her walker to bar their way when they approached with yet another morsel for Deb. The two sisters-in-law claimed to love each other dearly, but it seldom showed in public.

Most of the Rundbergs were clustered together between the matching sofas that flanked the fireplace. Their gazes were typically wary. Uncle Gurd, however, had attached himself to Herself, who was resplendent in gold lamé. By comparison, Judith felt dowdy in her simple mint-green silk sheath.

"It's all very lovely," Merle Rundberg said as she came to stand beside Judith. "Sig and I are so appreciative of everything you've done for Mike and Kristin."

Judith smiled at Merle. "It was a big job, but it seems to have turned out fine. Let's hope this is just the first of many happy moments for them."

Merle nodded as both mothers' gazes moved from Kristin to Mike and back again. "Marriage is a hard job. But Kristin is a hard worker. I think Mike is, too."

Mike was now talking to Joe. Judith felt a surge of pride. They looked so handsome in their tuxedos. "Certainly Mike and Kristin have known each other long enough to be aware of each other's flaws," Judith said, accepting a glass of champagne from Renie, who was coming through with a tray. "That's so important. Surprises aren't good for a marriage."

"True." Merle sipped from her punch cup as she continued to watch Joe and Mike. "It was different in our day. Nobody lived together before they got married, and engagements were usually short." She sighed, apparently awash with memories, not all of them good. "Mike's such a nice-looking young man. Seeing Mike and Joe together, I realize I've never noticed how much your son looks like his father."

Judith choked on her champagne.

By five o'clock, the newlyweds were off to the airport, the wedding guests had begun to disperse, and the Rundberg contingent had retired to their various lodgings. They would all depart the following morning, which caused Judith an anticipatory sigh of relief.

"Well, I guess that's it," Joe said, loosening his tie and cummerbund.

Judith nodded slowly. "I guess." The house suddenly seemed empty, despite the debris left by two hundred guests. "I'd better change and get this place cleaned up."

Arlene burst out through the dining room. "No, you don't! Carl and I'll take care of that. Carl!"

Carl appeared, his craggy, handsome face bemused. "Yes, Lamb-chop. Where's your broom?"

"Now, Arlene . . ." Judith began.

Arlene Rankers held her ground, pretty features set in a familiar stubborn line. "You know the catering business, Judith Flynn. Good caterers don't walk away from a mess. You go upstairs and relax."

"But . . ." Judith protested.

Joe took his wife by the arm. However, he led her not to the stairs but to the front door. A small suitcase sat next to the Victorian hat rack. Judith gaped.

"Five years ago, almost to the day," Joe said, his face very close to Judith's. "How about a second honeymoon?"

"Oh, Joe!" Judith melted into his arms.

Thirty minutes later they were in the bridal suite at the Naples Hotel. The floral motif wasn't the white and yellow of Kristin's choosing, but the more vibrant orange and lavender hues that Judith had chosen for her wedding to Joe Flynn. Champagne had been replaced by an eighteen-year-old Scotch from a deep Highland glen. The view wasn't of a smooth, sandy beach in Mexico, but of the glistening hometown harbor and the snow-capped mountains to the west. Judith was ecstatic.

It was only later, much later, that she realized she couldn't see the Belmont Hotel from their rooms. Then, as she snuggled next to Joe in the big canopied bed, she wondered why she cared.

But she did.

Everyone was gone by Monday morning. Everyone except Uncle Gurd. He had remained under the hedge Sunday night, apparently waiting to be awakened by his fairy princess, Vivian Flynn.

"What are we going to do with him?" Judith asked Joe over their second cup of coffee.

Joe shrugged. "He's an adult. So's Vivian. They'll have to work it out. If I know her, she'll send him on his way, and he'll feel good about it."

Ordinarily, Judith would have asked Joe exactly what he meant by such a comment. But she was still feeling euphoric after their stay at the Naples Hotel. Joe was right: Uncle Gurd wasn't her responsibility. But she certainly didn't want him sleeping all summer under Carl and Arlene's shrubbery.

Joe went off to work, and Phyliss Rackley showed up promptly at nine. "Where are all those good Christian people?" the cleaning woman demanded. "They were my kind of folks. I hoped they'd stay long enough to sit down and have a real good talk about Judgment Day."

"They went back into Deep Denial," Judith answered absently. She was checking her calendar for the rest of the week. The B&B was booked solid through early August.

"That's too bad," Phyliss said, trying to stare down Sweetums, who was sitting on her shoes. "Did you know that your cat is a limb of Satan?"

"Yes, Phyliss, you've told me that many times." Judith shut off the computer that Joe had given her for Christmas a year and a half ago.

"Well, you don't do anything about it," Phyliss asserted. "Why don't you get this place exercised?"

"You mean exorcised?" Judith sighed. She didn't feel like dealing with Phyliss's peculiar religious beliefs this morning. "Sweetums is a cat. No more, no less. Are you going to do the second floor first?"

Phyliss took the hint, though with ill grace. Judith went over to the refrigerator and began taking inventory. Hillside Manor's supplies were definitely depleted. A trip to

Falstaff's was in order. Judith headed out the back way and got into the Subaru.

Heavy metal assaulted her ears, followed by a local grunge group gone global, and then a raucous rap song. Judith drew the line at the fourth recording, which sounded like someone dying during surgery. The thumping bass made her chest hurt.

Judith turned the dial. On a muggy Monday morning in June, she couldn't stand listening to Harley Davidson's program another second. Assuming, of course, that Mike had switched back to the station that broadcast the ear-shattering DJ. Judith hardly needed to hear him shout at her to know that it was his show. Mike had driven the Subaru to the wedding while Judith and Joe had traveled in the MG. But Mike was gone now. He wouldn't be switching radio stations anymore in his mother's car. Judith suddenly felt sad, but she still didn't want to listen to Harley Davidson.

It was after ten when she returned home with six sacks of groceries. Judith wasn't ready to dive back into her regular routine. She was at loose ends, a natural reaction after such a major life change. Halfway through putting the victuals away, she stopped and called Renie.

"What are you doing, coz?"

"Huh?" Renie never completely woke up until ten. At ten-eighteen, she still sounded foggy. "I'm staring at a mug of coffee and wondering where I am. Morning is a stupid concept."

"Would you go downtown with me?" Judith asked in an unusually humble voice.

"Can't," Renie replied. "I mean, I have an appointment downtown at the Belle Epoch at one. I'm working on their fall catalogue. We see page proofs today."

"Could you go early and I'll wait for you?" Judith still sounded meek. "We could have lunch." Any task involving food usually got Renie's attention.

"Lunch?" Renie's voice brightened. "Now that's a *good* concept. Where are we going?"

Judith hadn't yet had an opportunity to tell Renie all the details about the man and woman on the Belmont roof. Now she related the incident in full. By the time Judith finished, Renie sounded completely alert.

"That's really weird," Renie declared. "Especially the part about Joe not finding any sign of them."

"He sure didn't," Judith replied. "And he looked all around the hotel block. I finally got him to 'fess up yesterday."

"So what do you want to do?" Renie inquired.

"See for myself," Judith answered, no longer meek. "I couldn't do much Saturday night when Joe and I stayed at the Naples. It hardly seemed the time to act like I don't trust him. And I really do, but I know what I saw. I don't think he believes me. I guess I want to make sure there's nothing he missed."

"He's a cop, he wouldn't miss anything," Renie said, though there was a hint of doubt in her tone. "Okay, pick me up in half an hour. But I warn you, I'll be wearing my uniform."

Judith understood that her cousin was referring to her professional wardrobe, which was a collection of eight-hundred-dollar designer suits. When Renie wasn't working in public, she wore clothes that looked as if they'd been rejected by the homeless. Judith somewhat reluctantly exchanged her cotton T-shirt and slacks for a navy summer suit. It was going to be too warm for long sleeves, but she didn't want to look like a bum next to Renie.

"If we eat at the Naples, we can get free parking," Judith pointed out as they drove through the neighborhood that boasted not only a few hotels, but most of the city's hospitals and a number of older, elegant apartment houses. As Judith drove south through traffic, she could glimpse the downtown towers and the sparkling bay. A century ago, the city's most affluent residents had lived in mansions on this hill. Only a handful remained, inexorably replaced by more modern, commercial enterprises. As the city swept upward from the harbor, the number of sky-scrapers diminished, but this adjunct to the heart of town was an intriguing blend of old and new and somewhere in between. To Judith, it was a neighborhood that visibly marked time, from the late Victorian era to the high-tech glitz of the waning twentieth century.

The courtyard of the Naples was one of the landmarks that hadn't changed over the years. Indeed, the circular, narrow driveway had been built not for cars but to ac-commodate horse-drawn carriages. Judith gingerly eased the Subaru past the Italian fountain. As the valet parking attendant opened the door for her, she noticed that his nametag identified him as "Kobe."

"You parked our car Friday night," Judith said with a friendly smile. "It was a very old, very well kept red MG."

Kobe, who was young, outgoing, and a second- or third-generation Japanese-American, grinned in recollec-tion. "That's one sweet set of wheels. You don't see too many like that any more."

"My husband came down later to ask if you'd heard or seen anything odd," Judith said. "He told me you hadn't, but I was wondering if since then, you might have remembered at least some small detail that was unusual."

Kobe laughed. "I see lots of unusual stuff this time of year. First come the proms, then the weddings, next all the tourists. I've only worked here since the end of April, but every time I turn around, a limo pulls up or a bride and groom arrive or a bunch of people want me to help them spring a surprise party on their friends or relatives. It's kind of a fun job, and it helps pay my tuition."

"Yes, it sounds very nice," Judith said resignedly. Ap-parently, Joe was right—Kobe hadn't noticed anything peculiar. Judith explained that she and Renie would be lunching in the hotel, but had an errand to run first. Care-fully walking downhill in their high heels, the cousins passed the Naples, then turned towards the Belmont. To their astonishment, the old hostelry was a beehive of activity.

Workmen were piling trash into two big dumpsters, a huge truck blocked the side street and was being loaded with furnishings, and a foreman was on a bullhorn, shouting orders to his men. Near the hotel entrance, a sign was being put up. Judith and Renie moved closer, to read the black-on-white lettering:

DANGER—DEMOLITION SITE!!!
This structure will be demolished Friday, June 30.

The notice went on to quote city codes and other details of the project. Apparently, the hotel site was going to be used for an addition to St. Fabiola's Hospital, which was located on the opposite corner from the Naples. Judith took a deep breath and approached the foreman.

"When was the hotel officially closed?" she asked.

The man was wearing a nametag that said "Hector Pasqual." His black eyes regarded Judith with vexation. "January first. The place was a fleabag." He put the bullhorn to his mouth and shouted another order.

The cousins tried to get out of the way, but it wasn't easy with all the activity going on. Under the warm sun, clouds of dust swirled around the sidewalk. The noise was deafening, and Judith didn't blame Renie for trying to drag her away by the sleeve of her navy suit.

But Judith wasn't quite ready to leave. "This is the front of the hotel," she said, raising her voice over the din. "See the main entrance?"

"Yeah, right, very nice," Renie responded, choking a bit on the dust. "See the cousin? She's getting hungry."

Judith counted the floors. There were ten in all. Certainly anyone who fell from the roof would be seriously injured and most likely killed. "There's not much of a guardrail on the roof," Judith shouted. "See that low wall? It's probably only about knee-high. The woman in the bride's dress went right over and . . .'' Judith stopped. Now that some of the dust had cleared, she noticed a small balcony jutting out from the top story. It was about six feet wide, serving what looked like French doors. "Coz!" Judith cried. "Look! What if the woman landed on that balcony? She would only have fallen about eight feet. She might not have gotten more than a few bruises."

With a tortured sigh, Renie gazed upward. "Okay, I see it. Is that the part of the roof where she went over?"

Judith tried to picture the scene from Friday night. "I think so . . . It was more or less the middle part, so it could have been. It all happened so fast."

"And where did Tux Boy go after that?" Renie asked, brushing dust from her lavender designer suit.

"I don't know," Judith admitted. "I turned around to tell Joe what had happened, and when I looked back, the roof was empty."

"Hmmm." Renie now seemed intrigued. "So he could have jumped onto the balcony, too, or gone back into the hotel the same way they got onto the roof."

"Right." Judith's excitement was still palpable. "That might explain everything. But why do such a thing?"

The foreman was now at Judith's side. "Look," said Hector Pasqual in an impatient tone, "you're gonna have to get outta here. This is a construction zone. We can't have gawkers."

Frowning, Judith took a couple of backward steps. Renie was already halfway to the corner. But just as Judith started to turn around, a workman came running out of the building, waving his arms and shouting.

"We got a stiff on ten! Somebody call the cops!"

Judith froze. Hector Pasqual grabbed the newcomer by the arm. "What the hell? Keep it down, Louie!"

Louie yanked off his hardhat and rubbed his curly blond hair. "I'm telling you, it's a stiff! And whoever it is has been dead for awhile. Jeez, I feel sick!"

Some of the other workmen had now begun to congregate around Hector and Louie. Their voices were lost in the tight little knot of burly, sweaty laborers. Then Hector apparently signaled for quiet as he summoned help on his cell phone.

Judith beckoned to Renie who was slowly, if reluctantly, walking back toward the Belmont. "Louie found a body," Judith said, both fearful and excited. "What do you suppose? I'll bet it's the woman in the bridal gown."

Renie's brown eyes widened. "You mean—you were right?"

Judith glared at Renie. "Don't tell me you thought I was nuts, too?"

"Ah . . ." Renie grimaced. "Not nuts, just . . . embroidering? I mean, sometimes you come up with some pretty big fibs, coz."

"Only when I have to," Judith retorted, keeping one eye on the ever-growing cluster of workmen in front of the hotel. "But I never make things up just for the sake of invention."

Renie gave a little shrug. "Okay, I guess not." Seeing the fire in Judith's black eyes, Renie hastily corrected herself. "I mean, of course you don't. So why are we standing here under the noonday sun? You've proved your point. Can't we eat lunch?"

"Coz!" Judith was appalled. "How can you think of *lunch* when some poor woman is lying dead in that hotel?"

"Well . . ." Renie was only marginally chagrined. "It's not going to bother her if I have a small steak sandwich and some fries and maybe a salad with . . ."

"Oh!" Judith spun around on her high heels. "You can contain yourself for a few minutes while we find out what happened to her. Just stand there and try to act like a normal, sensitive human being. It won't be long—I hear sirens."

Sure enough, two patrol cars pulled up. One of them blocked the intersection, though there was no need, since the big van already barred the way. Judith stared at the four police officers as they hurried by, but didn't recognize any of them. After a quick exchange of information, the patrolmen escorted Hector and Louie into the old hotel. The rest of the work force began milling around, talking animatedly, rummaging in lunch pails, drinking from Thermoses and plastic water bottles. Judith and Renie propped themselves against a low stone wall and waited.

"It's noon," Renie announced ten minutes later. "I have a one o'clock appointment. If I don't eat right now, they'll need two ambulances. Or should I just walk over to St. Fabiola's emergency room while I still have the strength?"

As the minutes ticked away, Judith wasn't unsympathetic to Renie's predicament, but she knew from experience that it might be some time before she could find out any details of the woman's death. "I'll tell you what," she said. "You go to the Naples and order for both of us. I'll be there as soon as I can."

Renie didn't require coaxing. She hadn't been gone more than a minute when two of the four policemen reappeared and an ambulance pulled up at the intersection. Right behind it, Judith spotted an unmarked city car, just like the kind Joe drove when he was on duty. It shouldn't have surprised Judith to see her husband get out of the car—but it did. With his partner Woody Price at his heels, he moved swiftly through the growing crowd of onlookers. Judith shrank back against the low stone wall. She wasn't anxious to have Joe find her at the site of another disaster.

Joe and Woody went inside the Belmont. Judith shielded her eyes from the sun and felt perspiration trickle down her neck and back. It was a temptation to join Renie inside the cool confines of the Naples Hotel. But she had to stay put; she had to vindicate herself.

Ten minutes later, another city car pulled up. This time Judith did recognize at least one of the passengers, Waldo

Chinn, an experienced medical examiner. The woman with the official camera gear also looked familiar, but Judith couldn't recall her name. If further proof were necessary, it arrived a moment later when two of the patrol officers began affixing crime scene tape to the Belmont's entrance. Judith realized that the law enforcement officials were acknowledging that a murder had been committed.

The discovery might have come as a surprise to Joe and Woody, but in a tragic, perverse way, Judith felt vindicated.

It was going on one o'clock when Joe and Woody emerged from the hotel. By then, Judith was not only hot, but hungry. Just as she spotted her husband in the hotel entryway, Renie poked her in the arm.

"I've called a cab," Renie announced, apparently not noticing Joe and his partner. "I figured you'd stick around until your rampant curiosity was satisfied. Give me a buzz when you get home. I should be back by four." Renie returned to the intersection to wait for her taxi.

Judith had removed her high heels and was standing in her stocking feet. Joe was talking and nodding to Hector Pasqual. Hector seemed upset.

A gurney was being wheeled out of the Belmont. The workmen had been dispersed, and the path to the ambulance was clear. Judith grabbed her shoes and ran, heedless of the havoc she was wreaking on her good pantyhose.

"Joe!" Judith cried, no longer able to conceal her presence. "Is it her? Is she wearing a wedding dress?"

Startled, Joe stared at Judith from behind dark glasses. "What the . . . ? Jude-girl!" He didn't sound pleased to see his wife.

Woody, however, nodded pleasantly. Joe's partner was in his mid-thirties, with brown skin the color of polished mahogany, a walrus mustache, and deep brown eyes that could convey both heart-wrenching melancholy and an unexpected puckish humor. He said nothing, however; nor did Joe. The ambulance attendants started to roll the gurney into their emergency vehicle.

It was then that Joe held up a reluctant hand. "Just a minute, guys," he said. "We may have a witness." The dark glasses turned in Judith's direction. "It won't be a positive ID, but it may give us . . . a clue."

Judith moved forward, edging past Dr. Chinn, Hector Pasqual, the medical personnel, and the patrolmen. "Renie and I were going to have lunch at . . ." she began in a small voice.

Joe didn't seem to hear her. With an impatient hand, he unzipped the body bag. Judith took a deep breath and steeled herself. She didn't know what ghastly sight to expect: If the woman in the bridal gown had fallen any distance, she might be mangled, disfigured, crushed. Judith felt her teeth clench and her knees turn to water. But she took a final step, and gazed down at the gurney.

It wasn't the woman she had seen on the Belmont's roof.

It was the man.

FOUR

GERTRUDE REFUSED TO eat the salmon quiche that Judith had prepared for dinner. Or, as Gertrude preferred to call the evening meal, "supper."

"It's fish slop," Judith's mother declared. "Feed it to your awful cat. I want ribs."

"It's too late to fix ribs, Mother," Judith protested. "And it's too hot to turn on the oven. I heated the quiche in the microwave."

"You should have put the cat in the microwave," Gertrude grumbled, eyeing her plate with disgust. Abruptly, she looked up. "Where's Mike?"

Judith gave a little start. "In Mexico, on his honeymoon. They'll be gone ten days."

Gertrude snorted. "Very funny. Where is he? On his paper route?"

Judith gnawed on her forefinger. Had her mother really forgotten how old Mike was? Was she unable to recall the wedding from two days ago? Did she truly picture Mike as a twelve-year-old boy?

"Mother, Mike and Kristin had a lovely . . ."

Gertrude shoved her plate at Judith. "Give me some wienies. You can boil wienies without having the vapors, can't you? It's not hot in here. In fact, I need my

47

sweater.'' She hunkered down in her baggy orange cardigan.

It was useless to argue. It was also depressing. Maybe
Gertrude's mind really was going. Certainly her circula-
tion wasn't very good. Judith trudged back to the house,
hoping that her mother would at least eat the spinach salad
that accompanied the quiche. It was almost six, and Hillside Manor's guests would expect their appetizers and
punch in a few minutes. Judith felt hot, tired, and frazzled.
It had been a trying day.

In the next half-hour, Judith managed to feed Gertrude
and the full house of guests. Joe still hadn't arrived home
from work. For once, Judith wasn't anxious to greet him.
He had not been pleased to find her at the Belmont, he
had insisted that she go straight home after viewing the
body, and he had refused to share any information with
her at the site. By the time the ambulance had pulled away
and the police personnel had departed, Judith had lost her
appetite. The bearded man on the gurney was no longer
an ephemeral figure on the roof of the Belmont, but a
lifeless corpse, drained of color, shrunken inside the deb-
onair tuxedo, another sad statistic headed for the morgue.
Feeling desolate, Judith had returned to the Naples to
claim her car, tipped the parking lot attendant lavishly,
and headed downtown to the Belle Epoch in search of
Renie. But Renie was not available. Apparently, there had
been some glitches in the printing job, and Judith's cousin
was tied up making artistic adjustments. In a glum mood,
Judith went home.

There, she had found the first of the wedding-related
bills in the mail. The understanding between the Flynns
and the Rundbergs was that Kristin's family would pay
for all of the bride's traditional expenses. Nottingham Florists' invoice came to over two thousand dollars. After a
big gulp, Judith copied it on her small scanner and readied
it for mailing to Sig and Merle.

In the living room, Judith could hear the guests laughing and talking. In the kitchen, she was nursing a gin and tonic. She hadn't eaten since breakfast, and the alcohol seemed to be going to her head. Judith was humming to herself when Uncle Gurd came into the kitchen.

"What's for dinner?" he asked, plucking a dried laurel leaf from his short-sleeved combat shirt.

Judith sat up with a start. She had forgotten about Uncle Gurd. "Uh . . . quiche." Fortunately, there was Gertrude's portion. "Salmon quiche and spinach salad."

"*Quiche*?" Uncle Gurd looked puzzled. "What the hell is *that*?"

Judith was annoyed. Was there no one over sixty-five who liked quiche? "It's a kind of casserole," she said, trying not to show her pique. "It's very good. Let me fix a plate. Do you want to eat it here or in the hedge?"

"The hedge is fine. But I'd rather have ribs."

"I don't have any ribs," Judith lied. In truth, she had about ten pounds of them in the freezer. "How about wienies?"

Uncle Gurd's thick lower lip protruded. "Well . . . wienies are okay. You got sauerkraut?"

Judith did, in a can. Hurriedly, she boiled wienies and heated sauerkraut. The brief euphoria of the gin and tonic had already faded. "Are you enjoying your stay?" she asked, hoping to feign polite interest rather than the more gnawing need to know when he might be leaving.

"Yep, this is okay," Gurd replied, leaning against the counter. "You got trees around here, and a view of the water and the mountains. It's not as bad as some city places. Now if you could only get rid of them cars that keep whizzing by. Yep, I could get used to this. Yep, I could."

"Well now." Judith felt a little breathless. "It rains a lot, you know. I mean, you can't spend the cooler months in the hedge."

Gurd hitched up his pants. "We'll see about that. I'm a hardy sort."

Her back turned, Judith rolled her eyes. "How's Vivian?" she inquired, trying another tactic.

Uncle Gurd chuckled. "She's just fine and dandy. But you know," he continued, assuming a conspiratorial air, "she's kind of a tease. Likes to play hard to get. That's fine with me. At my age, I've got nothing but time." He paused, his high forehead crinkling. "Or do I?"

Judith dished up wienies, sauerkraut, and a small portion of salad. "Here you go. Enjoy."

Uncle Gurd took the plate, but disdained Judith's offer of silverware. He went out the back door just as Joe was coming in. The two men acknowledged each other in the monosyllabic manner that passed for male greetings. Judith retrieved her gin and tonic.

Like Judith, Joe was a native Pacific Northwestern who despised hot weather. Furthermore, his rubicund complexion lent itself to sunburn. He had arrived home in a bad mood.

"What's for dinner?" he demanded, making only a desultory attempt to brush Judith's cheek with his lips.

"Quiche," Judith gulped.

Joe recoiled. "Quiche? That's ladies' luncheon food. Whatever happened to broiled salmon steaks and baked potatoes?"

Judith sucked at the ice cubes in her glass. "Well, there was leftover salmon from the reception, so I had to use it up, and quiche seemed like a good . . ."

Joe yanked off his holster and threw it over the back of one of the captain's chairs. "Toss the damned stuff out. We're not paying for it, the Rundbergs are. Fish doesn't keep in this weather."

"It's only been two days . . ."

"You got any ribs? I could eat ribs."

"Ohhhh . . ." Judith twirled around the kitchen, then slammed her hand against the counter. "I'm not cooking ribs in this weather! I refuse to turn on the oven! If you'd told me you wanted ribs, I could have fired up the barbecue. But it's too late now."

Husband and wife glared at each other. Both were angry and out of sorts. Neither seemed willing to give in. From the other side of the kitchen wall, the guests' laughter rose to semihysterical proportions. Fleetingly, Judith wondered if she'd put too much rum in the punch bowl.

"Let's eat out," Judith said at last. "We can go to the pub on top of the hill."

Joe's shoulders slumped under his summer-weight dress shirt. "Okay. I'll go change."

Judith went into the living room, a phony smile plastered on her face. The laughter had ebbed, and it appeared that the guests were getting ready to go out on their evening rounds. Judith chatted briefly with each one, then waved them off in a variety of conveyances, from rented cars to taxi cabs. The last couple had just departed on foot when Joe came down the stairs.

"Uncle Gurd's nude," he remarked. "Do you think Carl and Arlene will mind?"

Judith's hands flew to her head. "Yes! No. Why is he nude?"

Joe shrugged. "I guess they have a different dress code in Deep Denial, Idaho. Or no code at all. I suppose I should talk to him. I am an officer of the law, after all."

Judith stayed inside the house while Joe conversed with their quasiguest. It turned out that Gurd had been romping through the Rankerses' sprinkler. Where else could he bathe? There wasn't a creek for miles, as far as he could tell.

"I hope you impressed on him that he mustn't prance around in the altogether on Heraldsgate Hill," Judith said in a prim, uncompromising tone.

Joe tossed the car keys into the air and caught them with one hand. "He was wearing a shower cap."

Judith paused with her hand on the passenger door. "What for? Uncle Gurd is bald."

Joe's green eyes twinkled. "I didn't say he was wearing it on his head."

"Oh." With a weary sigh, Judith got into the car.

As the MG purred up the steep hill, she tried to unwind. But her brain was jumbled with all sorts of distracting thoughts: Mike was a married man; Gertrude was losing her mind; Joe was annoyed; the body on the gurney was a man, not a woman; the bills were starting to pour in; the weather was unseasonably warm; Uncle Gurd was running amok in the altogether.

"I feel awful," Judith declared after they had driven around the block four times to find a parking place and waited ten minutes for a table. "I think it's the heat."

Joe was scanning the long list of microbrews that were written in various shades of colored chalk above the bar. The Heraldsgate Pub was crowded as usual, but Judith and Joe had been lucky—their table was at the far end of the long, narrow establishment, and, thus, not quite in the center of noise and bombast.

"The heat?" Joe replied rather absently. "Maybe." The green eyes finally made contact with Judith. "How about the corpse? You pegged the wrong one, Jude-girl." A faint smile touched Joe's mouth as he started to reach for her hands.

Abruptly, Judith pulled back. "Hey! I pegged *some-body*! You're ticked off because I knew there was a dead person at that hotel. You thought I was hallucinating."

Joe's grin was off-center. "You're having one of your fantasies. Nobody was pushed off a roof. The dead man didn't die from a fall. He was stabbed."

Judith gaped. "Stabbed? With a knife?"

Joe was noncommittal. " 'With a sharp instrument' is the way we put it. No weapon was found. Dr. Chinn says he'd been dead about forty-eight hours. He'll know more after the formal autopsy."

"Stabbed," Judith echoed. Then the rest of what Joe had said sank in. "What do you mean? 'Whoever he is'?"

Joe shrugged. "Just that. The guy had no ID. He looked to be about thirty, just under six feet, a hundred and forty pounds, not in the best of health, signs of poor nutrition. But you're right about one thing—he was wearing a tuxedo."

Judith's eyes sparkled. "So he was the man I saw on the roof."

Joe's gaze narrowed. "You didn't recognize him?"

"I didn't really see his face. I mean, he was several yards away. I doubt that I would recognize the woman, either. It all happened so fast, and there was so much distraction during the dinner. I hardly expected a crime to be committed."

Joe signaled to their server, a young man who looked like a college student. "No crime was committed—not then," Joe said after he had given their orders. "This guy was found in a room on the top floor. There was quite a bit of blood, but it was confined to the room itself. We asked Pasqual if anybody could get into the hotel after they stopped work on Friday afternoon. He admitted they were kind of careless about locking up, despite the fact that some homeless folks had gotten in there to spend the night. A watchman was on duty but I gathered he was fairly lax. Everything in the hotel was old and crummy, so theft wasn't a big problem. It was all going into the dumpster in the next few days anyway."

Resting her chin on her hand, Judith was thoughtful. "Do you mean the Belmont could have been full of transients?"

But Joe shook his head. "Nothing as rampant as that. One or two or three, maybe. Or souvenir-seekers or just plain curious folks. I know, it seems half-assed, but Pasqual and his crew are in demolition, not security."

Judith was silent until their microbrews arrived. "And nobody knows who the dead man is?"

"His pockets were empty," Joe replied, moving his chair a bit to allow the group at the next table to leave.

"The tux's labels had been cut out. But eventually, we'll be able to trace it. It's just a matter of time."

The beer that Joe had chosen for them was deep amber, thick and fruity. Judith sipped slowly. "Now why," she asked, more of herself than of her husband, "would a man and a woman who were wearing wedding attire show up on the roof of the Belmont?"

To her surprise, Joe began ticking off reasons on his fingers: "They were getting married and wanted to have their wedding night at a really secluded place. They're performers from some local production. They're acting out a sexual fantasy. They're . . ."

Judith waved a hand in Joe's face. "Okay, okay. People do all sorts of strange things for even stranger reasons, but they do not shove one another off of tall buildings just for the fun of it. That's the part that I don't get."

Joe didn't either. "Something went wrong," he finally said, raising his voice above the sudden din of crashing crockery that emanated from the vicinity of the kitchen. "They quarreled. They were drunk or on drugs. They . . ." The noise level subsided; so did Joe's voice. ". . . didn't know what they were doing."

Judith shook her head. "Whoever stabbed the man knew what he—or she—was doing. Was it a big knife?"

Joe's expression turned blank. "I didn't say it was a knife."

"Oh, come on, Joe," Judith said impatiently. "Your forensics experts can tell what kind of weapon was used. What did Dr. Chinn say?"

Joe sighed. "Basically, that it was a penetrating puncture wound to the chest, made by a sharp instrument about an inch wide and at least six inches long. Yes, it sounds like a knife. But it could be a spear, a sword, a scissors, or a saber."

Judith looked up as her pot pie and Joe's burger arrived. "She didn't have a saber or a spear," Judith said after their server had left.

"Huh?" Joe paused in the act of piling onion, tomato, and lettuce on his burger. "Who, the bride?"

Judith nodded, then frowned. "I hadn't thought of her as 'the bride' until now. Only as the woman in the wedding dress. I wonder . . ."

"What?" Joe's expression was skeptical.

Judith frowned. "I don't know. Something flitted through my brain, but now it's gone. Tell me more about the wound."

There wasn't much to tell. In any event, Joe was tired of talking shop. "Let it go, Jude-Girl. I'll keep you up to speed. It's my case, after all."

"I know." Judith smiled at her husband.

Joe smiled back. He knew that Judith knew the homicide investigation was his responsibility. He also knew that it didn't faze Judith in the least.

There were times when Joe understood why a man might want to push a woman off the roof of a ten-story hotel.

FIVE

PHYLISS RACKLEY WAS praising the Lord. As she dusted the living room, the cleaning woman turned up the volume on a religious radio station and chimed right in with her own hallelujah chorus. Judith was used to Phyliss's fundamentalist programs, but on this muggy Tuesday morning in June, the hymns and the witnesses and the so-called miracles were too much.

"Phyliss," Judith called over the racket, "I have a terrible headache. Can you turn down God's Army?"

"A headache?" Phyliss popped up from under the glass-topped coffee table. "Pray on it. The Reverend Crump can make you whole again in no time. Ever seen him on TV?"

"No." Judith leaned against the archway between the dining room and the living room. "Just a notch, Phyliss. Turn it down. Please."

Phyliss trudged over to the radio that was embedded in the tall bookcases that flanked the big bay window. "I don't know how," she admitted. "I can turn it on, but that's it. Which knob do I use?"

Judith let out a sharp sigh of exasperation. "If you can turn it on, you can turn it off." But before she could reach the radio controls, Phyliss had started pushing buttons and pounding on speakers. The radio squawked, squeaked, and squealed. Suddenly, a deep, rich, and somehow familiar voice filled the living room.

"This is Revolution Man, filling in for Harley Davidson on KRAS-FM. Stay tuned for news, sports, and weather . . ."

Phyliss hit something which plunged the entire system into silence. She glared at Judith. "Now see what you made me do. How do you expect to get healed?"

"I know that voice," Judith murmured. "It's Bill Jones's nephew, Kip Sherman."

With an angry shake of the dustcloth, Phyliss snorted. "I don't expect this Kip person has healing powers. Just last week my lumbago was acting up something fierce, and I put my hand on the radio when Reverend Crump said . . ."

Judith, however, had hurried over to the telephone, which sat on a small round pedestal table near the grandfather clock. "Coz?" said Judith when Renie answered as the clock chimed ten. "Are you awake?"

"Sort of," Renie replied with a yawn. "What's up? Besides me, though I don't know why."

Judith explained about hearing Kip's voice on KRAS-FM. "I thought he was a country and western DJ."

"He is." Renie yawned again. "He's been working for KRAS-FM's affiliate, KORN-AM. But after seven years he wanted a change, so he quit a couple of weeks ago. I don't think he's made up his mind about a new job yet. I suppose he's filling in for somebody who's sick."

"Oh. Yes," Judith added quickly. "He said he was subbing for that loud-mouthed Harley Davidson."

Renie chuckled. "I've accidentally heard Harley Davidson a couple of times. The kids love him, but he gets on my nerves. Kip's a lot more mellow. I should tune him in—if I can stand the music he's playing. Maybe I'll give Bill's niece, Kerri, a call about doing lunch. *She* actually sits down with me when we eat together." Renie's implication was clear.

"Sorry, coz," Judith said in an abject tone. "I thought you'd understand. You know how distracted I get around dead bodies."

"Right, sure, I guess." Renie had stopped yawning, but she seemed tired of Judith's excuses. Or perhaps she, too, was distracted: Judith could hear a voice in the background.

"Have you got a man there?" Judith inquired.

"My husband," Renie answered dryly. "He doesn't teach summer quarter, as you know perfectly well." She paused; the masculine voice was still speaking. "But that wasn't Bill," Renie finally said. "That was the news on KRAS-FM. I turned the radio on while we were talking. They just mentioned your favorite stiff. No ID yet—but you must know that."

"I knew it as of seven-thirty when Joe left for work. Did they say anything else?" Judith asked, moving out of Phyliss's way as the cleaning woman dusted the grandfather clock.

"Not that I could tell," Renie replied. "The announcer—Kip goes on break during the news—said that the body found stabbed to death in the condemned Belmont Hotel hadn't yet been officially identified, but police were investigating. No mention of the woman, no mention of the body being attired in a tux. Your husband is playing this one close to his chest."

"He usually does," Judith sighed, then went on in a more obsequious tone. "Do you want to go to lunch today? I could spare some time."

Renie, however, could not. She had more page proofs to check at the Belle Epoch. "I should be done around three, though," Renie added. "I. Magnifique is having a big sale of spring clothes. Do you want to meet me there and have a drink afterwards?"

Judith drummed her nails on the cherrywood tabletop. "Well . . . if I could get home before five so I have time to do the hors d'oeuvres . . ."

"We could skip the drinks—if we find anything worth trying on," Renie noted. "See you at three, third-floor salon?"

Judith gulped. The salon fashions were out of her price range. They were out of Renie's, too, but she somehow managed to scrimp on her everyday ragamuffin wardrobe which allowed her an occasional extravagance. "Okay," Judith finally agreed. "But I may go down to sportswear on two."

After hanging up, Judith heard the mailman arrive on the front porch. His name was Cecil, and he hadn't been on the route very long. By the time Judith stepped outside, Cecil was being accosted by Uncle Gurd.

"You oughtta be ashamed, wearing a uniform that represents a no-good government like that passel of crooks in Washington, D.C.!" Gurd raged. "What kinda trash are you delivering here anyways? Commie crap, I'll bet, and propaganda from big business!"

Cecil, who was young, black, and burly, eyed Uncle Gurd with disdain. "I just deliver the mail," he said quietly.

"Government tool! Political stooge! Bureaucratic lackey! Pshaw!" Uncle Gurd hopped up and down. Fortunately, Judith noted, he was clothed this morning.

"Excuse me," Cecil said with considerable patience, "I've got to go to the Rankers's house . . ."

"Good morning!" Judith called with forced cheer. "How are you, Cecil? Say, Uncle Gurd, have you had breakfast?"

Gurd stopped hopping, which allowed Cecil to cross the cul-de-sac. "I already ate," the old man replied. "Vivian cooked me breakfast. We had French toast."

According to Joe, Vivian Flynn wasn't much of a cook. But maybe Uncle Gurd didn't know the difference. "How nice," Judith said, still cheerful. "Say," she continued, coming off the porch onto the walkway, "wouldn't you be more comfortable in a *motel*?"

Uncle Gurd looked at Judith as if she were ranting. "Now why would I want to stay in one of them phony places? What's wrong with this hedge?"

"Well . . ." Judith's gaze traveled to the Rankers's house. "It's just that my neighbors might . . . ah . . . um . . . feel uncomfortable after awhile with somebody staying on what's actually their property."

Gurd hitched up his pants and eyed Judith with something akin to pity. "A lot you know. The missus over here likes me. Yep, she's making me lunch today."

"Oh." Judith's smile tightened and died. It appeared that the neighbors in the cul-de-sac were conspiring against her. It was bad enough that Herself had befriended Uncle Gurd, but now it seemed that Arlene, in her typical good-hearted manner, was also encouraging the old man to remain on the premises. "Okay," Judith sighed, "but it's going to rain. Eventually."

Uncle Gurd seemed unintimidated by the prediction. With a small chuckle, he wandered back to the hedge. Judith returned indoors, sorting the mail as she headed for the kitchen.

There were three deposits from upcoming guests, several advertising circulars, a thank-you note from a grateful couple who had spent a full week at Hillside Manor, and five more bills. One was from I. Magnifique, for Kristin's wedding dress. Judith was preparing it for forwarding to the Rundbergs when she thought of something that had been eluding her: Hurriedly, she picked up the phone and dialed Renie's number.

Renie's machine played a message recorded by one of the Jones boys. Judith would have to save her little idea until she saw her cousin at I. Magnifique. Meanwhile, she finished going through the rest of the mail. The last piece was addressed not to her or Joe or Gertrude, but Phyliss. It was postmarked Deep Denial, Idaho.

"Phyliss," she called from the top of the basement

stairs. "You've got a letter here. I'll put it on the counter by the computer."

Phyliss bobbed up like a cork, sausage curls bouncing. "Lord be praised! Them good Christian people kept their word! I told 'em to write me once they got home."

Judith fingered the plain white envelope. "Then this *is* from Kristin's relatives? Why did they send the letter here?"

" 'Cause I forgot to give 'em my home address," Phyliss replied, snatching the envelope from Judith. "But that's okay—they knew how to find me." Eagerly, she ripped the letter open. "Now let's see what they have to say for themselves about following the righteous pathways of the Lord."

Judith left Phyliss to her letter. If she never heard from any of the Rundbergs again—except Kristin's parents—it would be too soon. But of course one of them was still in the hedge. Judith fervently wished Uncle Gurd would leave.

Three hours later, Judith left for downtown. She had plenty of time to spare, and couldn't resist a short side trip past the Belmont Hotel. The street was still blocked off by the demolition crew, but the crime scene tape was gone. Joe and Woody must have finished their on-site investigation.

Judith was tempted to talk to Hector Pasqual, but she couldn't find any on-street parking. Disappointed, she headed down the steep hill to the business district and I. Magnifique. The thought that had been triggered by the store's bill had been festering for three hours, and Judith was anxious to try out her theory on Renie.

Renie was already deep into the sale racks when Judith arrived in the third-floor salon. The designer room exuded an aura of elegance, wealth, and the subtlest of French perfumes. Plush beige carpets, flowing beige draperies, pristine beige walls, and muted sounds encouraged a leisurely pace. Customers spoke in hushed tones, behaving with a reverence more suited to a church. Then again, Judith realized, for some, shopping was a religion, and an act of faith.

"Look," Renie said excitedly, not quite as low key as the other dozen would-be buyers who calmly sorted through two long racks of sale garments, "half price! I can save three hundred dollars on this green silk and two-fifty on that . . ."

"Coz," Judith interrupted, "do you have a regular sales clerk here?" Renie blinked. "Right, Portia, the platinum blond over there with the fat French roll." Renie nodded towards a sleek saleswoman who was engaged in very serious conversation with a large middle-aged woman whose hands glittered with diamonds.

Swiftly, Judith flipped through the size fourteen models and pulled out a lime-colored pantsuit. "I'll try this on. Can you get her for me?"

But Renie hesitated, tipping her head to one side and studying the pantsuit critically. "I don't know—that color's not you, coz. Plus, the jacket's too short. It'll cut you off at . . ."

Judith shook her head impatiently. "I don't want to buy the thing, I just want to try it on."

Renie reached for an off-white jacket and matching skirt in Judith's size. "This is much more suitable. Look, you can save a hundred and . . ."

Judith grabbed Renie's wrist. "Skip it. I know what I'm doing," Judith declared, black eyes boring into her cousin's puzzled face. "I'm not buying, I'm sleuthing. I think I know how the bride and groom got on the Belmont Roof. Go get Portia, and we'll find out who got killed in the old hotel."

To Judith's shock, Renie laughed. "Oh, that! I know who it was. I meant to tell you, but I got so excited over all these sale items." She held up a sleeveless navy dress with buttons from collar to hem. "What do you think of this?"

In reply, Judith punched Renie in the stomach.

"That was mean," Renie said in annoyance as two of the other would-be bargain-hunters turned to stare. "Besides, I don't know for sure."

"We're going into a dressing room right now," Judith asserted between taut lips. "You're going to unload. And then I'll talk to Portia. I think you're full of it."

Renie made one last grab for another garment. "Okay, okay, I'm going." She half-stumbled between the racks, then led the way into the dressing room area off the main salon. "Kerri, our niece, Kip's wife, told me about that disc jockey," Renie began, speaking quickly as she noted that the fire was still banked in Judith's eyes. "I called her right after I talked to you. She said Kip was filling in for Harley Davidson—which of course isn't his real name. It wasn't because he—Harley—was sick, but because he was missing. Which, frankly, isn't all that unusual in radio. Some of the on-air personalities are sort of unreliable. On Monday, they were caught short when Harley didn't show, so they ran a tape, and interspersed it with commercials."

Recalling the nonstop playing of songs she'd heard in the car Monday morning, Judith gave a slight nod. "That explains why I didn't actually hear Harley on the air."

"Right," Renie agreed, hanging her selections on round wooden pegs. "Anyway, Kerri said Kip told her that nobody has seen or heard from Harley since he took part in a fashion show Friday afternoon for"—Renie stopped to take a deep, meaningful breath—"I. Magnifique."

"Ah!" Judith felt her cheeks grow warm with excitement. "That's what I figured. Not about Harley, because I didn't know that part—but about the fashion show. When I got the bill for Kristin's dress this morning, I remembered that Artemis Bohl said he was putting on a show. Last night at dinner, Joe referred to the woman on the roof as 'the bride.' It occurred to me that all major fashion shows end with a bridal gown. That's when I realized there might be a connection. I. Magnifique is only a few blocks from the Belmont. That's why I wanted to talk to Portia. She could find out who modeled the wedding attire.''

Renie was wrestling the navy dress over her head. ''Wouldn't it be something if Harley is in fact the dead guy?'' Her voice was muffled under the fabric.

''Do you know Harley's real name?'' Judith asked, peeking out into the corridor to see if Portia was in sight.

Renie emerged through the neck of the dress. ''Kerri told me it was John Smith. I'm not sure if she was kidding.''

Judith made a little face. ''Let's hope so. But the station would have all his bona fides, wouldn't they?''

''Oh, sure.'' Renie fastened several buttons, then posed in front of the long, three-sided mirror. ''Some of the DJs may be nuts, but KRAS and KORN are owned by Esperanza Highcastle. She's all business.''

Judith gazed at Renie's reflection. ''Highcastle? As in Highcastle Hot Dogs?''

''The very same. Also sausages and baloney. Old money, old family, old meat.'' Renie twirled. ''What do you think?''

The dress was well cut, but almost reached Renie's ankles. The collar came right up under her chin. To Judith, her rather short, small cousin looked as if she were wearing a tent.

''We-ll . . . if you had it shortened . . .''

Portia announced her presence with a discreet knock. Before she could begin gushing, Judith went straight to the point and asked who had been the models for Artemis Bohl's Friday fashion show.

Portia smoothed her already-perfect blond hair. ''It was a benefit, so some local celebrities took part,'' the saleswoman replied, ''but Mr. Artemis also used his regular model, Tara Novotny. I'm sure you'd recognize her. She's internationally known."

Judith hadn't recognized the woman on the roof, but that wasn't surprising. Between running a B&B and playing the triple roles of wife, mother, and daughter, Judith didn't have much time to spare for high fashion magazines. Besides, the couple had been too far away to identify.

Renie, however, pointed to the cover of a designer catalogue that sat on a small side table. "That's her. Tall, dark, very handsome. Great cheekbones. No shape."

Portia laughed, a throaty, yet musical sound. "Tara's shape isn't as important as the way she wears clothes. Mr. Artemis isn't one for curves, just wonderful fluid lines."

Renie jiggled inside the dress. "I have curves. Lumps and the occasional bulge as well. Does this work for me?"

Judith gritted her teeth. "About the groom . . ."

Portia put a well-manicured index finger to her cheek and studied Renie closely. "It's very smart. Perhaps if we turned up the hem about two inches, and took a tuck under the arms . . . Yes, that would make it perfect, especially for travel."

"You mean she'd look better in it out of town?" Judith snapped. "Who modeled the groom's tux?"

Portia looked startled. "What? Oh—it was some radio person. I don't recall his name." She turned back to Renie. "If you need a dress that will carry you right into fall, we just got a new—"

"Who'd know?" Judith interjected.

Portia's professional patience was beginning to erode. "Ask the salon manager, Daphne DeVries. You'll find her at the desk by evening wear."

Judith abandoned Portia, Renie, and the voluminous dress. If possible, Daphne was even more sleek than Portia. Her raven hair was pulled into a tight chignon, her ebony skin was flawless, and her bearing indicated that she had probably started in the business as a model. Judith groveled and inquired after the man who had modeled the bridegroom's tuxedo.

Daphne did not take the question well. "He wasn't an agency person, nor is he under contract to Mr. Artemis. I'm sorry, I can't help you."

"He was—I mean, he is—a radio personality. A disc jockey," Judith clarified. "At least I'm sure he was. *Is.* I'm just trying to make sure he's the one I'm thinking of." She gave Daphne her most engaging smile.

"We had several radio personalities modeling on Friday." Daphne seemed bored as she fiddled with an armload of silver bangles.

Judith was momentarily stymied. Then her eye was caught by a diaphanous lavender evening gown floating around a mannequin in a recess just beyond Daphne's chair.

"Does that come in a size fourteen?" Judith asked, trying to achieve an expression of extreme desire.

Daphne swiveled slightly. "No, but the twelve is very generous." Her dark eyes raked Judith's statuesque figure. "Very."

"I'd like to try it on," Judith declared, her voice breaking only slightly. "Now about the bridegroom . . ."

Daphne had opened a drawer in the small Louis XIV desk. "One moment. I'll find out for you." She looked up as another saleswoman glided into view. "Clemence, could you take this customer back to a fitting room and get her Mr. Artemis's Lavender Dreams in a twelve?"

Clemence could and did. By the time that Judith rejoined Renie thirty minutes later, she had verified that Harley Davidson had indeed modeled the tux. The bride had been Tara Novotny. The lavender Artemis gown cost twenty-five hundred dollars, which was the price that Judith had paid for her information.

It was way too much.

*   *   *

"I'll take it back in a couple of days," Judith vowed as the cousins marched off to Ron's Bar and Grill, just around the corner from I. Magnifique. "Even if I could afford it, where would I wear a dress like that?"

"It's stunning, though," Renie allowed. "I saw it when I got off the elevator. That color is good on you."

"Stop it," Judith ordered tersely. "I absolutely cannot go around buying Mr. Artemis dresses."

The cousins went through the revolving door which led to one of the city's most legendary watering holes. "I did," Renie said in a small voice as they emerged into the bar.

"What?" Judith gaped at her cousin. "You spent twenty-five hundred dollars on a dress? Are you nuts?"

"It wasn't twenty-five hundred dollars," Renie replied hurriedly. "It was only a grand. I have to admit, it wasn't on sale. It just came in. They featured it in the fashion show."

"They also featured a murder victim," Judith said grimly, sitting down at a table for two in the middle of the big bar. On a late Tuesday afternoon, Ron's was already filling up with workers who apparently had sneaked out of the office early. "I used Daphne's phone to call Joe and tell him to talk to Tara Novotny. She was the bride."

"Ah!" Renie looked relieved, though Judith didn't know if it was caused by the confirmation of Tara's presence on the hotel roof or the change of subject. "What did Joe say?"

"He wasn't in," Judith answered, one hand on the black- and white-striped I. Magnifique box. She felt a need to guard it as if it were the family jewels. Which, she thought fleetingly, it was. Judith owned no gems that cost as much. "Joe and Woody were both out. Where is that radio station, anyway?"

Renie tried to get the attention of a nearby server, failed, and fingered her short chin. "KRAS and KORN are in one of those new office buildings at the bottom of Heraldsgate Hill. I've never been in their offices, but I've worked with an ad agency on the floor above them.''

Judith glanced at her watch. "It's not quite four. Why don't we skip drinks and call on KRAS?"

Renie made a face. "To what point? This is Joe's case. Let him at it. My mouth's all set for the biggest vodka martini in town.''

"But Joe doesn't even know who got killed," Judith pointed out. "He and Woody are stumbling around, trying to identify the victim through that tux.''

"So maybe they've done it by now," Renie shrugged, finally making eye contact with their server. She ordered with a hand signal, two fingers for two martinis, two more fingers for one of vodka, one finger for gin. Had the cousins wanted something other than the bartender's special, Renie would have had to speak out loud. Anything that wasn't a martini was considered exotic at Ron's.

Judith was on her feet, the big dress box clutched to her bosom. "I'm going to try to call Joe again.''

Renie started to argue, then threw up her hands. "Okay, but leave the damned box. I've got my own to guard.'' She gulped. "I bought three of the sale items, too. I don't think I'll show all of them to Bill right away. I'll tuck them away in the closet and wait until he's in a really good mood.''

Heading for the hallway where the pay phones were located, Judith's attention was diverted by a group of customers who were coming through the revolving doors. There was much animated conversation emanating from the half-dozen men and women, though their leader was stony-faced. Judith looked more closely. It was Mr. Artemis.

The designer was greeted by an effusive maitre d' who ushered the party into the bar. Judith abandoned her quest for the phone and hurried back to rejoin Renie.

"That's Mr. Artemis," Judith whispered as the tall,

thin bald man in the exquisitely cut suit slipped onto a chair at the head of a table in the rear. "I met him when Kristin was choosing her wedding gown."

Renie exhibited mild interest. "I've seen pictures. That's Tara Novotny on his left."

Judith reached into her purse, took out her glasses, and patted the I. Magnifique box in reassurance. "He's very temperamental."

"He's very rich." Renie grimaced. "Richer now than he was an hour ago. We just paid for his next three trips to Europe."

"You did," Judith retorted. "I'm getting my money back. Besides, he doesn't work out of Europe. His clothes are made somewhere in the Caribbean." Trying to be discreet, Judith focused on Tara Novotny. "That *could* be the woman I saw. She was dark-haired, but with the big veil, I couldn't see her face. And it happened so fast."

"If she landed on that balcony, she didn't get hurt," Renie noted as their server arrived with the drinks. "She didn't walk in here, she floated."

Judith turned to her martini. "Maybe she'll have to go to the rest room." Judith wiggled her eyebrows at Renie.

Renie sighed. "You're not going to . . . ? Yes, of course you are." Renie drank deeply.

"Maybe they were in love," Judith speculated. "Maybe they quarreled. I don't really know what Harley looked like, but she's obviously spectacularly beautiful. I'll bet Harley was bowled over, only she wasn't interested in a mere rock 'n' roll DJ, so his heart was broken and . . ."

"He couldn't see her." Renie took another, smaller sip.

Judith's eyes widened. "He couldn't see her *what*?"

"Her anything." Renie's voice was calm though raised slightly as the bar began to fill up and the noise level grew. "Didn't I tell you? Kerri said that Harley Davidson is blind."

*　　*　　*

Judith wanted to punch Renie in the stomach again, but she couldn't reach her cousin under the table. "*Blind*?" she repeated. "As in, 'as a bat'?"

Renie nodded. "Nobody knew. Outside of the station, I mean. Teenagers and young adults who listen to KRAS might be turned off by a blind DJ. Oh, it sounds kind of callous, but we're talking commercial radio here. Handicaps scare the young. It makes them stop and think about their own mortality."

"But . . ." Judith rubbed at her temples. "That means that Harley couldn't have seen what he was doing on that hotel roof."

Now it was Renie whose brown eyes grew wide. "You're right. I didn't think of that. How very strange."

Judith darted a quick look over her shoulder. Artemis Bohl's party was being served, and everyone, with the possible exception of Tara Novotny, seemed to be acting in a most deferential manner toward the great designer.

"I wonder," Judith said, chewing thoughtfully on her olive, "if an autopsy shows that a person's blind. If whoever is doing it has no reason to wonder, would they know?"

Again, Renie shrugged. "He wasn't stabbed through the eye. But aren't medical examiners pretty thorough?"

"Yes," Judith replied. "Joe did mention that the victim wasn't in very good health. But that could have meant almost anything. I gather Harley had poor eating habits. That's not surprising with a show biz type." Once more, she was on her feet. "I'm still going to give Joe another ring."

This time, Joe was in. Upon hearing her husband's voice, Judith made a swift decision regarding her demeanor: She didn't want to admit that she had been actively sleuthing. Joe would resent his wife's intrusion on his case. Thus, she tried to walk a fine line between girlish amazement and wifely duty:

"Joe! Guess what—Renie and I've just come from I.

Magnifique's spring clearance, and we made the most astonishing discovery! I wanted to pass it on to you and Woody as soon as . . .''

"You mean about Harley Davidson and the Novotny woman?" Joe's tone was flat. "Right, Woody and I are checking that out now. In fact, I may be late getting home tonight. We've already called on the radio station, but we have to interview the model and a few other people. Don't hold dinner. See you." Joe hung up.

Judith went back into the bar and ordered a second martini.

SIX

"IT MUST HAVE been the tux," Judith muttered. "Joe and Woody must have traced it to the fashion show."

"If you drink that second double," Renie warned, "you're not driving. You'll have to let me take you home and come back to get your car later."

Judith gave her cousin a bleak look. "I've been through a lot these past few days."

"Who hasn't?" Renie shot back. "That's life. I'm canceling your order." With a snap of her fingers and a thumbs-down signal, Renie conveyed the message to their server. "What about your guests? Do you really want them to see you crawling through the entry hall on your hands and knees?"

Judith scowled at Renie. "Two doubles wouldn't do that to me."

Renie didn't respond directly. "You're just miffed because Joe and Woody are way ahead of you on this one. Face it, coz, they get paid to be detectives. You don't."

"He's been to the radio station," Judith said, pawing at her empty glass. "I suppose somebody from there IDed the body. Or maybe Joe and Woody will have Tara do it." Turning in her chair, Judith gazed at the rear of the bar. Artemis Bohl's party was gone.

"They left while you were on the phone," Renie said calmly. "They drank fast. Maybe Tara knows the cops are on her trail."

Judith was on her feet. "Let's go. We should follow them."

"Oh, for . . ." Though annoyed, Renie also stood up. "Hold it, I have to get my packages."

Judith was already at the revolving door. Indeed, she had exited so hurriedly that one of the doors smacked Renie right in the face. Renie was still swearing when she joined her cousin on the sidewalk.

"I don't see them," Judith said vexedly, her eyes raking the street in all directions. "Do you suppose they went to Artemis Bohl's salon? It's only a half-block from I. Magnifique."

"Could be," Renie allowed, juggling black- and white-striped packages and trying to rub her forehead with her arm. "Which way?"

"In the building next to I. Magnifique, where they're putting in the new celebrity café and the sportswear store," Judith replied, now moving smartly down the sidewalk.

Renie scooted along behind, then yelled at Judith in alarm: "Hey! You forgot your dress!"

Judith stopped at the corner and whirled around to face her cousin. "Oh, my God! How could I?" She began galloping back towards Ron's Bar and Grill. Renie waited by a row of newspaper boxes.

The table that the cousins had occupied had been commandeered by a couple in their thirties who looked as if they were in love. It took Judith a few moments to catch their attention. She explained her small dilemma, then reached under the table to retrieve the twenty-five-hundred-dollar evening gown.

The box was gone.

The couple hadn't noticed it when they sat down. Panicking, Judith approached their server. He had no knowledge of an I. Magnifique parcel. Nor did the maitre d' at the front of the restaurant. Judith was beginning to feel sick. She checked the pay phones to see if she might have taken the package with her, but there was no sign of the black- and white-striped box. Then she wandered up and down the bar to see if someone might have moved it, or picked it up by accident—or by design. At last, she wandered back out onto the sidewalk. Renie was still at the corner, leaning on a *Wall Street Journal* box. Disconsolately, Judith approached her cousin.

"It's gone," she said in a hollow voice. "I've lost the most expensive dress I never intended to buy. What'll I do?"

"You can't have lost it," Renie insisted. "It'll turn up. Somebody probably gave it to a different server. Call when you get home, after the cocktail hour is over and they're not so rushed. By then, whoever is in charge of lost items will have it."

The advice was of minor consolation, but Judith didn't see what else she could do. Halfway up the block stood a large, ornate pedestal clock. It was going on four-thirty. For once, Judith's investigative thirst was quenched.

"I'm going home," she announced morosely. "I'll call you after I've committed suicide."

"You do that," Renie said, reorganizing her packages and giving Judith an encouraging smile. To cheer her cousin, Renie offered a small sacrifice: "If you want to snoop around KRAS tomorrow, I'll see if Kip can get us an entree."

Judith brightened only fractionally. It was very hot under the late afternoon sun, and traffic, both pedestrian and vehicular, had intensified in the last hour. "Okay. That sounds nice," Judith said weakly.

Having parked in separate garages, the cousins parted company. The drive home was aggravating. Like Judith, her fellow Pacific Northwesterners didn't take kindly to the heat. Most of them seemed determined to work out their frustrations with their cars. Judith used her horn four

times and mouthed a shocking obscenity twice on the
short drive from downtown to Heraldsgate Hill.

After serving her guests their punch and hors d'oeuvres,
Judith called Ron's Bar and Grill. The staff still hadn't
seen her package. Perhaps she'd care to call back tomorrow? She would, but hope was fading. Nursing a too-tart
lemonade, she wondered whether or not her homeowners'
insurance covered lost designer dresses.

It was after eight when Joe got home. It had been a
long, hot, tiring day for him, too. He was on his second
beer before he deigned to discuss what had now become
the Harley Davidson case.

"I told you that tux would be easy to trace," Joe said
as he and Judith sat outside in the long summer evening.
"It was some high-priced brand that's only carried in I.
Magnifique's men's department. From there, it was easy.
Davidson had worn one for the fashion show Friday. The
model who wore the wedding dress was Tara Novotny.
Woody and I checked with the radio station first, and
found out that Davidson hadn't shown up for his Monday
morning gig. We got a gofer at KRAS, name of Darrell
Mims, to ID the body. He went to pieces, but he did it.
Then, after you called this afternoon, we tracked down
Tara who was at that designer's shop—you know, the one
who made Kristin's dress." Joe's gaze slid in Judith's
direction. "I'm sure you accidentally heard about that
connection, too."

"Well, yes," Judith answered vaguely. She might as
well admit it, but she certainly wasn't going to tell Joe
about her extravagant purchase—and subsequent loss.

"Tara went into shock," Joe recounted, batting with
his hand at a flurry of gnats. "She wasn't much help. That
Bohl guy was a real pain. He swore that Tara didn't really
know Davidson, and demanded that we leave until she
recovered. We'll get back to her tomorrow."

Judith had long ago traded her sour lemonade for a diet
soda. Taking a big sip, she tried to focus on Joe's recital.

It wasn't easy, not with Lavender Dreams giving her nightmares.

"Did Harley Davidson have family?" Judith asked.

"Not around here," Joe replied as Sweetums trotted across the patio. "He's from the Midwest. Indiana, I think. Thirty-three, unmarried, worked all over the country, been here two years. Blind. But I suppose you unwittingly discovered that, too."

Judith avoided Joe's gaze. "Renie told me. Bill's nephew, Kip, works for . . ."

Joe nodded. "Yes, Kip Sherman. He wasn't around when Woody and I were there, but somebody said he was filling in for Davidson. I remember Kip from some of the Jones family get-togethers."

A few feet away from the patio, Gertrude appeared at the door to the toolshed. She leaned on her walker and peered at Joe. "Judith Anne!" Gertrude called sharply. "Who's that man you're entertaining?"

Judith tensed. "What?"

"I said," Gertrude repeated, banging her walker for emphasis, "who's your gentleman caller?"

Judith glanced at Joe, but he had lowered his head and was staring at the birdbath. "It's Joe, Mother," Judith finally answered.

"Joe who? I don't know any Joe. Tell him he's got to go home by ten o'clock. We keep proper hours around here." Gertrude slammed her walker one more time, then laboriously turned around and went back indoors.

"Oh, dear," Judith sighed. "Is she kidding? Is she gaga? Or is she going to drive me as crazy as she may or may not be?"

"No comment," Joe murmured. "My mother died young. It was my father who was impossible. Luckily, in his later years, he didn't want to see me any more than I wanted to see him."

Sweetums was weaving in and out between Judith's feet. He paused just long enough to brush up against her

leg in an uncharacteristic gesture of affection. Then, as
she reached down to pet him, he threw up a hairball on
her hand.

Repulsed, Judith jumped out of the lawn chair and went
into the house to wash. It had been that kind of day.
Standing at the kitchen sink, she stared out into the hedge.
Uncle Gurd's home away from home was undetectable in
the laurel's thick branches and glossy leaves. There had
to be a way to get the old man back to Deep Denial, Idaho
or Trenchant, Montana, or whichever isolated dot on the
map he claimed as his legal address. Maybe Herself could
coax him into leaving.

Maybe the I. Magnifique box would turn up tomorrow.
Maybe Gertrude's apparent memory loss would stop both-
ering Judith so much. Maybe, after the wedding and the
reception and the out-of-town company, life would settle
down at Hillside Manor.

Maybe Judith was kidding herself.

The morning mail brought more wedding-related bills,
but also the contact prints from Morris Mitchell's photographs. Judith excitedly opened the thick package and began perusing the dozens of proofs that Morris had clicked
off over the two-day period. As ever, her heart sang when
she saw her son's wide, infectious smile; she was enveloped by a sense of completion when the camera captured
her husband's magic eyes. There they were together, Mike
and Joe, shoulder-to-shoulder. Except for their coloring,
there wasn't much of a resemblance. That was good, Judith thought. And yet . . . she really should have talked to
Mike before he went off on his honeymoon.

She was studying the pictures inside Our Lady, Star of
the Sea when Phyliss came to stand at her elbow.

"Gaudy," the cleaning woman remarked, pointing to
the altar with its life-sized crucified Christ and statues of
the Blessed Virgin and St. Joseph. "Idolatry. Don't you
Catholics feel like pagans in such an ungodly place? And

that Lutheran fellow—he didn't seem the least put out by all the flim-flam. I'd hope for better from one of his kind.''

"We don't worship statues," Judith said firmly. "I've told you that before, Phyliss. The images are reminders—like these photographs.''

Phyliss snorted. "Did you ever see Our Savior taking snapshots? 'Course not. He didn't make sketches, either. It's blasphemy, if you ask me.''

"I didn't ask," Judith said dryly, moving on to the reception photos. "You were at the wedding. Didn't you think it was a lovely ceremony?''

"It was all right, as such things go," Phyliss allowed. "But where were the hymns? Why didn't you have joyful voices raised to the Lord? All that slow stuff on the organ didn't move me one bit.''

Judith knew it was useless to argue religion with Phyliss—or anybody else, for that matter. Fortunately, she was spared by the telephone. It was Renie, asking when her cousin wanted to call on KRAS. Judith said any time was fine, but would Renie like to stop in first and see the wedding proofs? Renie said she would.

Half an hour later the cousins were sitting in the living room, poring over the pictures. Judith now had fixated on the first set, taken at the rehearsal dinner.

"I know these aren't very big," she said, "but when they're blown up, some of them will show the roof of the Naples Hotel. Do you suppose we'll be able to see Harley and Tara?''

Renie wrinkled her pug nose. "And if we did?''

"Well . . ." Judith fidgeted a bit on the sofa. "We might be able to tell something from their facial expressions. You know, if they were angry or happy or . . . whatever.''

Renie wagged a finger at Judith. "Look, you'd have to get those things blown up about three hundred percent to see anything that far away. Morris wasn't using a telephoto lens, he was shooting subjects in the same room. I'm perfectly willing to go along with this gag and take you to the radio station, but that's it. Joe and Woody seem to be doing just fine with the investigation. After today, let it ride, coz. You'll only get in the way.''

It was useless trying to defend herself. Indeed, if Judith had to be honest, she didn't have a leg to stand on. Unlike other situations where she had had some personal involvement with either the victim or the suspects, Judith had been witness to a nonevent. Or so it appeared. Joe, she realized, hadn't yet quizzed her closely about what she had seen on the hotel roof. It was obvious that he didn't believe she had seen anything, at least not anything of importance.

''Nobody at Ron's has seen my dress box,'' Judith finally said, evading the issue at hand. ''I called just a few minutes ago.''

''It's got to show up,'' Renie said with conviction. ''If somebody had taken it, the server or the maitre d' would have noticed. Besides, we hadn't been away from the table more than a minute or two when I saw that you didn't have the box.''

Judith tried to take comfort from Renie's words. On the way down the hill to KRAS-FM, Judith also tried to put the lavender dress out of her mind. There was no point in worrying over something she couldn't do anything about; or so she kept telling herself.

The offices of KRAS and KORN were divided by a long, carpeted corridor on the main floor of an almost new six-story office building. Through the glass entrance to KORN, Judith could glimpse large photos of the station's radio personalities. She recognized the laughing, freckled face of Kip Sherman.

Renie nodded. ''Morris Mitchell took those pictures. I think he also did the ones for KRAS.''

Sure enough, the photos that lined the walls of the FM station bore a stylistic resemblance to their AM affiliate's

portraits. As the cousins entered the reception area, Judith
nudged Renie.

"Is that Harley?" she whispered, pointing to a photo
that showed a bearded man in dark glasses.

Renie studied the photo. "I think so. To tell the truth,
I haven't any idea what he looks—looked—like. But the
dark glasses are a clue, right?"

Behind the curving mahogany desk, a piquant, spike-
haired receptionist offered to help the cousins. Renie mentioned Kip Sherman's name, and was informed that
Revolution Man was on the air. Except, the punk-rock
receptionist went on, he was known as Rappin' Rip on
KRAS.

"Rappin' Rip, huh?" Renie said in an aside to Judith.
"Kerri must love that." Renie turned back to the desk.
"We're actually here to see Darrell Mims."

"Darrell?" The bleached blond spikes quivered and a
look of disapproval passed across the piquant face. "Oh,
why not?" The receptionist pressed a button and re-
quested Darrell Mims's presence up front.

The young man who came bounding out through the
long, narrow hall was no more than twenty-two, and his
appearance was a far cry from the rockin', rappin', jam-
min' image that KRAS presented to its listening public.
Darrell Mims wore a pale blue dress shirt, neatly pressed
gray slacks, and a muted, striped tie. His fair hair was
cropped in a neat crewcut and his fine features were set
in a face that looked as if it only had to be shaved twice
a week. Patches of color stood out on his smooth cheeks.

Renie introduced herself as Kip Sherman's Aunt Serena, then offered up her cousin as Aunt Judith, which
wasn't exactly true but served the purpose.

"Judith," Renie explained with a bogus mournful air,
"was one of the last people to see Harley Davidson
alive."

If Darrell saw through Renie's phony manner, he didn't

let it show. In fact, the color faded from his cheeks, and he staggered slightly.

"No! Really?" His blue eyes widened, then he blinked several times before steadying himself against the reception desk. "Maybe we'd better sit down somewhere," he said in a weak voice.

Darrell's choice of a private spot was the employee coffee room, a cluttered, windowless area down the hall. The walls were adorned not with Morris Mitchell portraits, but posters and glossy photos of various bands and other performers. The room reeked of coffee grounds, cigarette smoke, and a tinge of marijuana.

"Excuse the mess," Darrell said, indicating plastic molded chairs. "It's my job to keep this place tidy, but frankly, it's a losing battle. These people are animals."

Noting that Darrell seemed to have recovered himself, Judith gingerly sat down in one of the chairs. "You identified the body?" she inquired in what she hoped was a pleasant, conversational tone.

Darrell jumped. "Is there some problem?"

Judith assured him there was not. "I'm just curious how you got stuck with such a repugnant duty," she said.

"Well, I did." Darrell looked pained. "The police came to the station yesterday and asked if someone could go to the morgue. Naturally, they sent me. I always get the jobs around here that nobody else wants." The young man looked much put upon.

"That was tough, I'll bet," Judith remarked with a sympathetic little smile.

"It sure was," Darrell responded. "I was just stunned. I mean, I knew what to expect, but somehow, when I saw poor Harley lying there, I almost blacked out. It took me awhile before I could speak."

Judith nodded solemnly. "That was very brave of you, Darrell. Have you any idea who might have wanted to kill Harley?"

Over time, Judith had come to expect a standard response to the question: The usual answer was a flat no. But Darrell Mims's face screwed up in an agonized expression. "Yes, I do. There must be at least a half-dozen people who would have loved to kill Harley. He was that kind of person. Despicable."

Judith damped down her elation. "Did you tell this to the police?"

"You bet," Darrell said earnestly, "but I don't know if they believed me. One of the detectives, an older guy with reddish hair, acted as if I were a head case. His partner, a younger black man with a big mustache, took notes. I couldn't tell much from his attitude, though. He was kind of . . ."

"Stoic?" Judith suggested, well aware of how Woody Price operated. Joe's partner always kept his own counsel.

"That's the word," Darrell nodded. "Still, they've got to check the names I gave them, right?" Now Darrell was not only earnest, but eager. The spots of color had returned to his cheeks.

"I'm sure they will," Judith said. Even if Joe and Woody might be skeptical, they'd never default on a lead. "Just who in particular would have wanted to get rid of Mr. Davidson?"

Darrell folded his hands on the marred tabletop. "First, there's his producer, Chuck Rawls, Jr. Mr. Rawls and Harley never got along. I'm not sure why, but I think it was something personal. Sometimes they came to blows and had to be pulled apart. It was amazing to see how a sight-impaired person could engage in hand-to-hand combat. He usually went for Mr. Rawls's nose. Once, Mr. Rawls knocked Harley right off the air." Darrell blanched at the violent memory.

"What did they fight about?" asked Judith.

"Mostly Harley's pro-drug attitude," Darrell answered with an expression of deep dismay. "Even he couldn't come right out and say that it was okay to do drugs. But he sure didn't speak out against them. It was more subtle, like always taking a stand on personal freedom. In fact, one time that he and Mr. Rawls came to blows was over that Ruby Ridge incident, with the survivalists. Harley supported Randy Weaver, and Mr. Rawls said that people couldn't twist the law to suit themselves.''

Judith recalled the high-profile standoff which had held the nation spellbound a few years earlier. "There were terrible mistakes on both sides," she allowed, then tried to put Darrell back on track: "What about the rest of the people at KRAS?"

"Well, there's Ms. Highcastle, who owns the station," Darrell replied in his earnest manner. "She'd had to warn him about his language a million times. I don't blame her—he gets really raw in his broadcasts. There's no place for that kind of talk on radio. You can get your FCC license pulled if you go too far. Besides, KRAS is aimed at young people, and it's wrong to present a crude image. Oh, some of the music is pretty gross, but a lot of it is wonderful. Why not cater to our listeners' better natures instead of all this dirty talk? It makes me mad.''

Noting that Darrell was now completely red in the face, Judith put out a restraining hand. "Your attitude is commendable," she murmured. "But you were saying about . . . suspects?"

Adjusting his tie and taking a deep breath, Darrell gave Judith an apologetic look. "Sorry. I jumped on my favorite soapbox there for a minute. You see, I'd like to be a DJ myself some day. I'd call myself Blip Man, the DJ with a conscience. What do you think?"

"That's good. I think that's good," Judith said hastily. "Now about those suspects . . ."

Darrell held up a hand. "Sorry, I got sidetracked again." He paused as two young women in very short skirts and very tall boots came into the coffee room. Chatting and giggling, they paid no attention to Darrell or the cousins. When they sat down at the far end of the table, Darrell lowered his voice:

"Ms. Highcastle's husband couldn't stand Harley, either," Darrell said almost in a whisper. "That may be the one thing they agreed on."

"They don't agree on other things?" Judith queried.

Darrell shook his head. "They're getting a divorce. But they both hated Harley."

"Does Mr. Highcastle work at the station?" Judith asked, noting that Renie was staring off into space.

Darrell shook his head some more. "It's not Mr. Highcastle. It's Tino Tenino. You know, TNT Tenino, the boxer. He's Ms. Highcastle's fourth husband. She's had bad luck with men. Like Nero and Ethelred the Unready and Karl Marx."

"What?" Judith thought she'd misunderstood.

Darrell smiled weakly. "I know, it sounds weird, but Ms. Highcastle believes she's lived several lives before this one."

"Goodness," Judith breathed, kicking Renie under the table. "What do you think of that, Coz?"

Renie jumped. "Huh? Esperanza married a Marx brother? Which one?"

Judith's face tightened. "Never mind. She also married TNT Tenino. Did you know that, coz?"

"The boxer?" Renie's expression was still vague. "Middleweight, decent record, coulda been a contendah. Broke his hand on some lummox's head." She shrugged. "Bill follows boxing. I don't, but I follow Bill." She turned away and again stared at the wall.

"And?" Judith coaxed Darrell.

"Who's Bill?" The young man's forehead furrowed in puzzlement.

"Never mind," said Judith. "He's not a suspect, he's a husband. Who else hated Harley?"

"Oh. Well, just about everybody here at the station. The manager, the other DJs, the advertising salespeople, the engineers, the support staff—you name it. Harley wasn't very popular. Except on the air. His fans were loyal, I'll say that. If they hadn't been, he'd have been gone a long time ago. Harley's share was huge, and he got paid accordingly." A bitter note crept into Darrell's soft voice.

Judith glanced at the two young women. They were utterly self-absorbed, as young women often are. She turned back to Darrell. "He made good money, then?"

Darrell put a hand to his close-cropped head. "You bet!" Realizing that he'd raised his voice, he moved the hand to his mouth. "Tons," he whispered between his fingers. "And not all of it in a KRAS check."

"You mean . . . ?" Judith tried to resurrect the term. "Payola?"

The quaint reference to what had amounted to bribery in days of radio yore caused Darrell to smile. "Yes, I guess that's what they used to call it. Whatever it is, it's not honest. You know, under the table stuff. It's usually the raunchiest promoters and distributors who pay off unprincipled people like Harley. He asked for trouble. No wonder he had premonitions."

"Really?" Judith edged closer in her chair. "What kind?"

"Oh," Darrell replied, fingering the collar of his crisp blue shirt, "like telling me lately how he might not be around much longer. I didn't take it seriously, because I thought he was hinting about job offers to sweeten the pot when his next contract came up. I sure didn't think he was talking about getting killed." The young man shook his head in an incredulous manner.

"Interesting," Judith said thoughtfully, then gave Darrell a grateful smile. "Thanks for your help. My cousin and I appreciate your candor." Another kick was aimed at Renie.

For the first time since arriving in the coffee room, Darrell looked at the woman who had introduced herself as Kip Sherman's aunt. "Excuse me," he said in an embarrassed manner. "A few minutes ago I told you that everybody at KRAS would have liked to kill Harley Davidson, but I didn't mean your nephew. You see, he's really with KORN. That is, he was. Right now, he's helping us by filling in for . . ."

Renie waved a dismissive hand. "I know, skip it. Kip's not a homicidal maniac, even when he has a motive. Which he sometimes has. After all, I see him at family parties. Who doesn't have a motive for murder with fifty relatives trying to outshout and outeat each other?"

"But . . . ?" Darrell was now looking bewildered. "I thought you came here because of Kip."

"Kip?" Renie laughed. "No. We came here because of Drip." She nodded at Judith. "My cousin is sleuthing. Thanks for all the suspects. See you, Darrell." Renie started out of the coffee room.

Judith's smile was now fixed on her face. "It's a long story," she said hastily as she, too, made for the door. "I'll tell you about it some time. Thanks again, Darrell. 'Bye."

The cousins were half-running down the hall when they crashed into Esperanza Highcastle. The heiress to Highcastle Hot Dogs and owner of KRAS and KORN didn't take kindly to the collision. She righted herself quickly, stood her ground, and summoned security. Before Judith and Renie could explain themselves, they were out on the sidewalk.

"Are you sure that was Esperanza?" Judith asked as she tried to catch her breath.

Renie nodded. "I met her once at some charity bash. You couldn't forget her easily, could you?"

Judith recalled the brief encounter with the fortyish woman who looked more like a gypsy queen and less like a hot dog heiress. Long curly black hair, bangles at ears, throat, and wrists, a flowing dress and several scarves proclaimed a penchant for flamboyance. The bare feet, one of which Renie had stepped on, were evidence of a free spirit. Or so Judith assumed.

"Does she always dress like that?" Judith asked as the cousins trudged off down the street to Renie's big blue Chevrolet.

"No. The time I met her she was an Indian princess. India Indian, complete with gold sari and red caste mark. She's also been an African warrior queen, an Egyptian sphinx, and a rather unconvincing Christian martyr." Renie sighed as she unlocked the car. "Esperanza believes in living all sorts of lives, in all kinds of eras. I'm waiting for her to go into outer space."

"A good place for her," Judith murmured, still smarting from their precipitous exit. "What did you think of Darrell Mims?"

Renie waited to answer until after the cousins were both in the car. "He's ambitious, sincere, and a young man on a mission, part of which may be to discredit Harley Davidson."

Judith couldn't help but grin at Renie. "So you were listening? I thought you'd zoned out."

"I did, a little." Renie revved up the big engine and hurtled into traffic. "Frankly, I think he was exaggerating. There may be a lot of people who didn't like Harley, but I doubt most of them would want to kill him."

"True," Judith replied, blanching as her cousin whipped around a corner, narrowly missed hitting an old man in the crosswalk, and just barely got through an amber light before roaring up Heraldsgate Hill. "The fact is, you only need one."

Renie turned to look at Judith. "One what?"

Judith wished Renie would keep her eyes on the road. "One killer. That's all it took to stab Harley Davidson."

Renie took the corner to the cul-de-sac on two wheels. Judith went home and took two aspirin.

It was turning out to be another one of those days.

SEVEN

DESPITE RENIE'S DISMISSAL of Darrell's suspect list, Judith made notes. When Joe got off work, she'd ask if he and Woody had followed up on any of the young gofer's leads. It had occurred to her that alibis would be hard to fix in this particular case: The time of death could not be pinpointed, therefore, the suspects had some leeway in accounting for their whereabouts.

It also dawned on Judith that there were at least two suspects whose names hadn't been mentioned during the session in the coffee room at KRAS: One was Tara Novotny, the other was Darrell Mims himself. Judith sat at the kitchen table and wished she had been able to talk to Esperanza and Chuck Rawls Jr. and even TNT Tenino.

But that wasn't her job. Joe would handle the interrogation. Judith tried to console herself. Her husband and Woody were veteran detectives. Between them, they had solved many cases. However, Judith believed that her chatty, personal method of talking to suspects could sometimes elicit more revealing information than the professional techniques employed by even the most assiduous policemen.

There was, of course, more to Judith's life than murder. As was usually the case during the summer months, the B&B would be full on Wednesday night. Phyliss had finished her housecleaning duties by one o'clock, and was getting ready to leave for her next client.

"It's somebody new," Phyliss said as she yanked her housedress down to cover a row of slightly bedraggled lace on her slip. "You know those fancy new condos above the cul-de-sac?"

Judith knew them well. Above her shrubbery and between the trees on the hillside, she could catch a glimpse of their balconies. The architecture conveyed a European air, and it was rumored that each unit took up an entire floor and cost close to a million dollars. Judith and Joe had jokingly told each other that some day they'd retire to one of the condos and spend the rest of their lives admiring the spectacular view.

"Have you been inside yet?" Judith asked eagerly. "I've heard that some of them are decorated in the most fabulous styles."

This was Phyliss's first foray into what was known as Belgravia Gardens. "I'll give you a full report tomorrow morning," she promised. "I'll even let you know what color undies Mr. Deetooleyville wears."

"Mr. Deetooleyville?" Judith echoed as she escorted Phyliss to the door. "What kind of a name is that?"

Phyliss rummaged in her worn imitation leather purse. "Here, this is his business card. Does it say Mr. Deetooleyville or doesn't it?"

It didn't. The tasteful if exotic gold printing read "Bascombe de Tourville." His address, telephone, fax, and cable numbers appeared in smaller letters.

"I think it's pronounced de Tourville," Judith said, giving the name a French twist. "What does he do for a living? It doesn't say here."

"I don't know," Phyliss admitted, tucking the card back into her purse. "I've never met the man. He moved in a while back and needs somebody to do for him. I got the referral through that fancy-pants dress designer who did your daughter-in-law's wedding gown.''

Judith's eyes widened. "You did? How? I didn't know you knew Artemis Bohl.''

"Is that his name?" Phyliss sniffed. "Peculiar thing to call yourself, if you ask me. Mr. Bowl, Mr. Plate, Mr. Soup Tureen—what next? All I did was answer the phone one day when he called a couple of weeks ago about the wedding dress. One thing led to another, and I could tell he was a soul in torment. Anybody who talks that snooty isn't talking to the Lord. The Lord wouldn't stand for it. So I told him what he needed was to be washed in the Blood of the Lamb. He said he needed to hang up. Imagine! Then I got filled with the Holy Spirit, and kept right on evangelizing, telling him about our church cruise on the *Good Fellowship*, and how we have all this fine food, like vegetable dip and Velveeta cheese in two colors and three kinds of potato chips and my favorite raspberry-lemon punch. But the Evil One's got a tight hold on that poor lost soul. Finally, I kind of ran out of steam. But after he swore he didn't want to be saved for about the tenth time, he asked if I knew of a cleaning woman. Praise the Lord, I said, I am one. Who wants me? And then he gave me this Deetooleyville's phone number. The Almighty works in mysterious ways, I said, and this Mr. Bowl hung up. Did I ever tell you he called?''

"Maybe," Judith said faintly. "It doesn't matter now.''

"Good," said Phyliss as she trotted off down the walk.

Judith was still standing on the porch when Arlene Rankers appeared from around the end of the laurel hedge. "We have to talk," she whispered in a dark tone and went straight inside the house. "Uncle Gurd is causing some problems. I think Carl and I have been too nice to him. Somebody has got to tell him that the hedge is *not* a bathroom.''

Judith looked horrified. "You mean . . . ?''

Arlene nodded, her red-gold curls in uncharacteristic disarray. "Yes, that's what I mean. I offered to let him use one of ours, preferably the one in the basement, but he said he was afraid of toilets. Apparently, he had an unfortunate experience in the Korean War, something to do with a hand grenade in a latrine. Really, Judith, something must be done about him. Carl is losing patience."

"I don't blame him." Judith said, feeling a need to sit down at the kitchen table. "We have to get him out of here. He's a real nuisance."

Arlene also sat down. "I do feel sorry for him, but there are limits."

Judith, whose kind heart rivaled Arlene's, nodded slowly. "Yes, I do, too, but I'm not sure why. He has a home and family. I don't understand why he insists on staying here. He hates cities."

"It's that woman," Arlene said in a conspiratorial tone. "You know who." The red-gold eyebrows lifted.

"Vivian?" Judith sighed. "I hope she's not leading him on. I'll have Joe talk to her. If anybody can convince Uncle Gurd to leave, it'd be Herself."

"Good." Arlene stood up, but Judith put out a hand.

"Say, what do you know about those lavish new condos on the next street up?" Judith asked. Arlene's network of news, gossip, and rumor was legendary on Heraldsgate Hill.

"I went through them before they started selling," Arlene said, very serious. With a daughter in real estate, Arlene had a lock on who was buying what property on the hill. "I've only seen two units since the new owners moved in. One was very modern, all white and gold, a retired air force general and his third wife. I didn't much care for it. The other was too fussy—lots of chintz, flounces, frills. A couple of interior decorators, and I'd certainly never hire them. Busy, busy, busy. Would you like a peek? There's one still on the market."

Judith hedged. "Maybe. The building is certainly handsome. But I was mainly interested in Phyliss's new client, Bascombe de Tourville."

"Ah!" Arlene snapped her fingers. "Now there's an interesting personality. Our Cathy didn't handle that sale, but she knows who did. Bascombe is a very mysterious fellow. His life is an open book."

Accustomed to Arlene's contradictions, Judith was only mildly fazed. "You mean . . .?"

Arlene nodded. "Exactly. Rumors galore. International intrigue."

Now Judith was becoming confused. "De Tourville's a spy?"

"No, no." Arlene shook her red-gold girls. "He looks mysterious. Cathy was fascinated."

"Oh." Judith's head was swimming. "Well, you can't always tell by looks."

"It depends on what you see." Arlene's expression was very knowing.

"I . . . guess," said Judith. There were times when it wasn't possible to follow Arlene's convoluted thought processes. "I hope Phyliss finds him easy to work for."

"Phyliss," Arlene asserted as she rose from the kitchen chair, "can take care of herself. She's virtually helpless."

"Yes," Judith said vaguely; then, not to be outdone, she added, "and no."

"Maybe," said Arlene, and was gone.

Joe merely glanced at the suspect list Judith had made. "Right, young Mr. Stoolie," he said, referring to Darrell Mims. "There's one in every office." Joe headed outside with a pair of hedge-clippers.

"What are you doing with those?" Judith asked, hurrying after her husband. It was late Wednesday, another warm evening with virtually no breeze.

"You wanted me to prune some of those bushes up against the fence," Joe answered reasonably. "You said you almost couldn't see Dooleys' house any more."

"True," Judith allowed. "I thought you were going

after Uncle Gurd and the Rankers's hedge. Somebody should. He's become a pest.''

Joe positioned himself in the flower bed and began whacking away at a Japanese quince. "Do you want me to talk to him?" Joe called over his shoulder.

Judith stirred the dying barbecue coals which she'd used to cook hamburgers for dinner. "I was thinking that Vivian might have better luck. Gurd seems quite taken with her.''

"Vivian left for Florida this morning," Joe replied. "She still has some business to wind up there. Her condo has been leased this past year and a half, but now she wants to sell it.''

"Oh.'' Sometimes it bothered Judith that there was a lingering intimacy between Joe and his first wife. It especially bothered her when he neglected to share details concerning Herself. "So she's no help," Judith murmured. "Big surprise."

"What?" Joe was tossing branches out onto the grass. As far as Judith could tell, there was no method to his pruning. The quince was beginning to look as if it had been butchered, rather than trimmed.

"Joe—could you make the shrub more symmetrical?" Judith asked in what she hoped was a humble wifely tone.

"Symmetrical?" Joe chopped a big piece right out of the middle. "I'm not a tree surgeon, I'm a cop." He cut off another chunk, at the bottom. The quince definitely looked skewed.

"Then maybe you should do it. Talk to Uncle Gurd, I mean." Judith tried not to wince as the gap in the shrub grew to alarming proportions.

"I'll try," Joe agreed, now plundering the honeysuckle. "What time does he curl up into a ball and go to sleep with the slugs?"

"I've no idea. Joe, could you be careful with that honeysuckle vine? If you cut it near the bottom, the whole thing will . . .''

It was too late. Joe had already chopped off the entire clump of sturdy, twisting growth that anchored the honeysuckle. "What?" He turned to look over his shoulder at Judith.

"Dammit, you've killed it! Honeysuckle almost never comes back after you whack it like that! We've had that vine since I was a girl!" Judith was close to tears.

"Hey," Joe yelled back, his face now a deep crimson from exertion, "you wanted me to prune, so I'm pruning. What does it matter how I do it as long as it gets done?"

Judith knew it was useless to explain that pruning wasn't the same as slashing. In her experience, husbands didn't understand the subtleties of gardening. Clippers, shears, pruners—whatever the implement, it wasn't a tool in a man's hand, it was a weapon. That was bad enough, but what really irked Judith was that from year to year, she didn't remember the carnage that Joe—or Bill or Carl or whichever other husband came to mind—could wreak on shrubs and bushes. This summer, she'd put a reminder in her computer to hire a professional. Cost be damned, Judith didn't want to lose the landscaping that she and other Grovers had tended for three generations.

She was still angry when Joe finally joined her in the kitchen. "So you and Renie went sleuthing at KRAS," he remarked as he washed his hands. "You never give up, do you?"

"I didn't even know who was dead until today," Judith replied in annoyance. "*You* hadn't told me anything."

"I didn't know anything," Joe replied reasonably.

"You must have known he was blind," Judith asserted. "Why didn't you say so?"

Joe made a face. "I thought I did."

"You did not. You mentioned that he wasn't in very good health, but not that he was blind. What," Judith pressed, as relentless as Joe himself inside the interrogation box, "did you mean by that?"

"By what?" Joe ruffled his thinning red hair. "How do you feel about a combover?"

"Repulsed. Come on, Joseph, tell me about Harley's health."

Joe sighed. "The ME said the guy suffered from some form of malnutrition. I gather that's not uncommon among radio personalities. They don't eat right, they chug down uppers and downers, they generally abuse themselves. Their idea of two major food groups are coffee and cigarettes. Worse, in many cases. Did you meet Esperanza Highcastle?"

Judith started to balk at the change of subject, then decided not to further aggravate her husband. "No, not exactly," she answered, recalling the collision with the station owner. "We talked only to Darrell Mims. I suppose you know all about Esperanza's marital breakup with TNT Tenino."

"Woody and I'll question them tomorrow," Joe said, pouring himself a glass of lemonade. "We'll zero in on Chuck Rawls Jr. and the rest of the crew, too. We tried to see Tara Novotny again, but she was unreachable. Or so that hoity-toity dress designer told us."

"Artemis Bohl?" Judith's anger began to fade, replaced by apprehension. The designer's name evoked more than curiosity; Judith still hadn't heard any word of her missing dress.

"Right," Joe replied as Judith fidgeted by the stove. "What a pain in the butt. He acted as if Woody and I were vermin."

"You went to his studio?" Judith asked in an unusually meek voice.

Joe cast his eyes to furthest reaches of the kitchen's high ceiling. "You bet. What a place! All white and steel chrome and those damned floating draperies—but you've seen it. Didn't you go there when Kristin was picking out her wedding dress?"

"Oh, yes, I was there two or three times," Judith said,

nodding vaguely. She recalled the designer's atelier very well. While the furnishings might seem stark, Judith knew they must also be expensive. Artemis Bohl could afford them, however; at twenty-five-hundred dollars for an evening gown, he could just as well have accented his studio in gold leaf. Judith reminded herself to call their insurance agent in the morning.

Judith figured that Joe probably noticed that she was unusually quiet for the rest of the evening. She was fairly sure he'd ascribe her frame of mind to his foray in the shrubbery. She might as well; the truth was even more depressing.

Nor did Judith's mood lighten in the morning. Her insurance agent informed her that loss of apparel wasn't covered under her homeowners' policy. Unless Judith was sure that the item had been stolen. If that's what she believed, then she'd have to file a police report before the insurance company could act.

"I don't think I want to do that," Judith said in an anguished voice. "I mean . . . well, I'll wait."

Twenty minutes later, Phyliss was reporting on her tour of duty at Belgravia Gardens. "Lots of antique stuff, or at least stuff that's supposed to be old. You can't put your feet up on any of it. Why do people have to show off? But Mr. Deetooleyville keeps it pretty clean, I'll give him that."

"What's he like?" Judith inquired.

"Couldn't tell you," Phyliss replied, shaking up a bottle of furniture polish. "I never saw him. He left a key, and didn't come back while I was there. I suppose he was at work."

"There's no work number on his card," Judith pointed out.

"Then he was out somewhere not working." Phyliss dismissed her new employer with a swish of her housedress and the flounce of pink slip that showed below the hem. "Maybe he's one of them idle rich."

Phyliss was upstairs in the guest bedrooms when Arlene came to the back door. "You've pruned your shrubs," she said in a cheery voice. "I'm going to nag Carl to clip the hedge. Maybe that'll discourage Uncle Gurd."

"It's a thought," Judith said hopefully, then indicated a stack of mail which had just arrived. "Almost all of the wedding bills are in—except yours and Morris Mitchell's. We can't do anything about his until Mike and Kristin get back and make their choices from the proofs. But I'd like to send your invoice on to Kristin's folks, so you can get paid."

Arlene shook her head. "I'm not charging you. We're partners, for heavens' sake! Just consider the reception as part of my wedding gift."

"But Arlene," Judith protested, "that's far too generous, even for you. At least submit a bill for your expenditures."

Arlene, however, remained firm. "You have only one child. We have five, and by the time we've married them all off—if we ever do—you will have spent as much on presents for them as I did on Mike's reception. Just forget it. When do you want to see the condos? You've certainly got a much better view of them now that Joe has cleared out most of your bushes."

Judith sighed. "Yes, it's wonderful—in a way." While delivering Gertrude's breakfast, Judith had noticed that she could not only see more of the Dutch colonial that housed the Dooley brood on the other side of the fence, but that her expanded view took in almost all of the balconies on the south side of Belgravia Gardens. However, the augmented vista had been achieved at an upsetting price—the once lush growth of quince, forsythia, honeysuckle, and cotoneaster had been hacked and whacked until it was virtually decimated. "I don't know," she murmured, comforting herself with the thought that the bushes and shrubs eventually would grow back, "maybe we

could go up to Belgravia Gardens tomorrow. Are you free
in the early afternoon?''

Arlene said that late afternoon on Friday would be better. With a vow to get Carl's rear in gear and into the
hedge, Arlene sailed out of the kitchen and through the
back door. Judith immediately picked up the telephone
and called Renie.

"Can Kip arrange a meeting with Chuck Rawls Jr.?"
Judith asked without preamble.

Renie groaned. "The correct question is, 'Are you
busy?' The correct answer is, 'Yes, I'm working on another fall catalogue, for DOA, the outdoor equipment sup-
pliers.' However, you flunked, so I must ask why in the
world are you pursuing this Harley Davidson thing? I've
humored you twice, and that's plenty. Back off, let Joe
and Woody do their jobs.''

"I know, I'm asking for trouble," Judith admitted.
"But I feel very proprietary about this case. I guess I need
to vindicate myself about what I saw on the Belmont roof.
It's not that I think Joe and Woody can't find the killer,
it's that I need to know what happened on that blasted
roof. Since Joe doesn't believe me—no matter what he
says—I have to figure out how that little scene fit into
Harley's death. And Joe and Woody will never discover
the truth because they think I was hallucinating. Tell me
this—do you agree with them?''

"No," Renie responded with conviction. "I don't. You
only make things up when it's a necessity. But . . ."

"Then you have to help me," Judith interrupted. "You
always do.''

"Rats." Renie could be heard rummaging through papers. "I don't want to pester Kip any more. Maybe we
could fake something, like a conference with this Rawls
about a promotion for DOA. He's not really the person
who'd handle such a thing, but it'd give us an excuse.
Rats," Renie repeated.

"That's brilliant," Judith enthused. "When can you set it up?"

Reluctantly, Renie said she'd aim for Friday afternoon. Half an hour later she called back to say that they had an appointment for one-thirty the following day. Judith was pleased.

She was less pleased when the phone rang again as soon as Renie hung up. This time it was Merle Rundberg, calling from the family's wheat ranch across the state.

"I'm in shock," Merle declared in a strained voice. "I've received the wedding bills you forwarded, and Sig and I had no idea how extravagant you'd been. Judith, we really didn't intend to spend this kind of money. Do you realize that the total now comes to over twelve thousand dollars?"

Judith was taken aback. "It was Kristin who made most of the decisions. She had very fixed ideas of what she wanted."

"But she needed guidance, Judith," Merle insisted. "Young people these days often have no concept of what things cost. You should have set limits. Kristin operates very well within parameters. I would have expected you to let her benefit from your experience. After all, you were married quite recently. Again." Merle made it sound as if Judith took trips to the altar as often as doctors played golf.

"Since it was your money Kristin was spending, I assumed you and Sig had already set parameters," Judith said, planting her feet firmly on the kitchen floor and staring stonily through the window above the sink. "By the way, you won't be charged for the reception, which is a huge savings. My neighbor has very kindly donated not only her time and labor, but all the food and drink as well."

"I never thought we would pay for the reception," Merle huffed. "Wasn't it put on by one of your sidelines?

Goodness, I can't imagine paying *you* for your own son's reception!''

Judith realized that she really didn't know Merle and Sig Rundberg. Like so many people, they appeared pleasant and congenial on the surface. But when the issue of money was raised, their true colors showed up in neon lights.

"I'm sorry," Judith said, her tone now as chilly as Merle's. "Weddings are terribly expensive, especially the kind that Kristin wanted. If you feel you've been cheated, you should discuss it with your daughter. Maybe she can help shoulder some of the cost."

"Nonsense," Merle snapped. "That's out of the question. I suspect that because you only have a son, you were living vicariously through Kristin, and filling her head with all sorts of ridiculous and extravagant ideas."

At that moment, Judith could see Uncle Gurd through the window as he emerged from the Rankers's hedge. He was wearing a blue dress and red patent leather pumps.

"One other thing," Judith said between gritted teeth. "We still have your uncle staying here. Shall I send you the bill for that, too?"

"Gurd?" Merle sounded startled. "He's not *my* uncle. Talk to Sig." She hung up.

EIGHT

JUDITH REMAINED IRATE and indignant for almost
twenty minutes. Then she began to lecture herself: *The
Rundbergs eventually would see reason. When the
newlyweds returned from their honeymoon, Kristin
would exert some influence on her parents. Everyone
knew that the bride's family paid for most of the wedding expenses. Merle and Sig would realize that they
had an obligation, not only to their creditors, but to
their daughter.*

Judith had to stop fussing about Merle's reluctance
to pony up. But of course it was Judith who had signed
all the bills.

To take her mind off the latest imminent disaster,
Judith decided to go downtown. So far there had been
three duplications among the wedding gifts, and Judith
had told Mike and Kristin that she'd return the un-
wanted items and get store credit. The task would, she
hoped, take her mind off of the Rundbergs' stinginess,
the lost evening gown, and Uncle Gurd's unusual attire. Judith didn't want to know where he'd gone or
what he was doing in the blue dress and red patent
leather pumps.

It took almost an hour for Judith to make the returns
at the Belle Epoch and Donner & Blitzen department

stores. Since Donner and Blitzen was located catercorner
from I. Magnifique, Judith felt her feet carry her across
the intersection, past the store's elegant wrought-iron entrance, beyond Ron's Bar and Grill, and through the door
that led to the lobby of the building that housed Artemis
Bohl's atelier.

Even as she stepped out onto the plush white carpet on
the top floor, Judith wasn't sure why she had come to the
designer's lair. *Do I think he somehow retrieved my evening gown from Ron's? Am I gullible enough to believe
I might be able to talk down the price-tag on Kristin's
wedding dress? Or am I here to ask questions of Tara
Novotny?*

The first two tasks struck Judith as impossible. Thus,
when she approached the young man at the chrome desk,
Judith inquired of Tara.

"Mrs. Flynn?" The young man smiled broadly, revealing perfect teeth that had probably cost his parents
more than the price of an Artemis Bohl dress. "I remember you—Kristin was your daughter's name, right?"

"My daughter-in-law," Judith said as her signature on
the bridal gown receipt rose to haunt her.

"Oh. Yes." The excellent teeth flashed some more.
"How was the wedding?"

"Wonderful," Judith answered, though it seemed that
more than a month had passed instead of less than a week
since the big event. "Thanks for asking, Rodney. Now
about Ms. Novotny . . ."

The teeth all but disappeared. "I'm afraid she hasn't
been in today." Rodney pawed nervously at the desktop,
then tugged at his gold earring. "I really think we should
call the police."

Judith edged closer. "The police? Why?"

Rodney turned an anxious face up to Judith. "Mr. Artemis pooh-poohs the idea, but Tara hasn't been here since
Tuesday, and after that very peculiar situation with Harley

Davidson, I can't help but wonder if something's happened to her, too.''

Swiftly, Judith glanced around the reception area, which was cut off from the main part of the atelier by double chrome doors. Large photographs, mostly of Tara in Artemis Bohl's creations, lined the white walls. But there was no one else in sight.

''You mean,'' Judith said, lowering her voice despite the fact that no one could overhear, ''Tara really was involved with Harley?''

''Oh, no!'' The suggestion shocked the young man. ''Tara would never date a *disc jockey*! But it does seem strange that he gets killed and suddenly Tara disappears.''

''Well . . .'' Judith fingered her chin. ''Perhaps she saw something or somebody at the Belmont Hotel. Is that what you mean?''

Rodney nodded vigorously. ''She's been very high-strung since Friday. That is, she's always high-strung, models are like that, it's their peculiar diet and all the stress. But Monday and Tuesday Tara was practically a wreck. I can't believe how much Evian she drank.''

Judith's eyes strayed to the largest of the color photographs which showed Tara in a flowing satin evening gown with emeralds at her throat and ears. She looked incredibly beautiful and stultifyingly bored.

''Where does she live?'' Judith asked.

Rodney gestured in a direction that indicated the hospital district. ''Tara has an apartment in one of the newer high-rises, a block from St. Fabiola's. But Mr. Artemis says no one has seen her for the last couple of days. Her Mercedes 280 SL is in the building's garage, but her mail hasn't been picked up, and UPS has left notices of several parcels that she has to sign for. Mr. Artemis has a key so he let himself in, but there was no sign of her. Don't you think someone ought to call the police?''

Judith recalled that Joe had tried to see Tara on Wednesday, and had failed to find her. Twenty-four hours later, he and Woody had probably grown suspicious.

"Wait until tomorrow," Judith cautioned. "Does she travel a lot?"

"She certainly does," Rodney responded, looking piqued. "Tara is supposed to have an exclusive arrangement with Mr. Artemis, but she's often on the East Coast or in Europe or South America. I can't help but think that she's freelancing when Mr. Artemis's back is turned."

"But there'd be pictures to prove it," Judith pointed out.

"Not if she's doing runway work," Rodney said, still piqued. "Mr. Artemis never looks at the competition's tapes or photos."

"I see," Judith said, though she was less concerned with Tara's career than her whereabouts. "Well, she might have left town."

Rodney didn't appear convinced. "She shouldn't have. The police came by to question her the other day. Wouldn't they have warned her to stay in the city?"

Judith considered. "Maybe." Joe hadn't mentioned warning Tara Novotny or anyone else, but then he hadn't been forthcoming about any details concerning the investigation. "How did Harley get involved in that fashion show in the first place?" Judith queried.

Rodney twirled a pencil in his long, slim fingers. "The show was sponsored by I. Magnifique and KRAS-FM. It was geared to cultivate younger customers. Apparently Harley Davidson and some of the other radio personalities modeled menswear."

Judith pounced on the information. "Were other male models wearing tuxedos?"

Rodney didn't think so. "I gather there were only a few outfits for men—business suits and sport coats and some casual wear. Harley Davidson wore the tuxedo because he was the groom in the closing sequence."

"Yes, so I heard." Judith saw the chrome doors open

to reveal Artemis Bohl. He noticed Judith and gave her a questioning look.

"Mr. Bohl," Judith smiled. "I mean, Mr. Artemis. I just wanted to let you know how everyone admired my daughter-in-law's wedding gown. I'm sure you'll get some new customers now that they've seen your wonderful work."

Artemis Bohl's long, lean face exhibited disdain. "I don't shop my designs around, like some peddler with a pushcart. If a potential client is seeking the best, he or she will find me. Are you here to pay the bill or are you interested in something new?"

Judith gulped. "I . . . um . . . ah . . . Well, yes. Something new. For fall. An evening gown, in lavender. My husband thinks I look my best in lavender."

Sadly, Mr. Artemis shook his bald head. "No, no. Not for you. Crimson, that's your color. In any event, I have no more lavender gowns. They've all been purchased or shipped." He snapped his fingers. "Flames of Desire! Rodney, ask Tara to model the gown for Mrs. . . . ?" The long face again wore a questioning air.

"Flynn," Judith said hastily. "But . . ."

She was interrupted by a diffident Rodney. "Tara isn't here today, Mr. Artemis. I mentioned it earlier, I believe."

A pulse suddenly throbbed in Mr. Artemis's bald skull. "What? She's *still* not here? I left a most emphatic note at her flat. Send for her at once." The designer gestured at Judith. "Come, perhaps Deirdre can show you the dress. Her coloring is all wrong, but you'll be able to see how it flows, how it moves, how it catches fire." With long, quick steps, Mr. Artemis led Judith into his inner sanctum, where she had previously waited during Kristin's fittings.

Judith cleared her throat. "Actually, you needn't go to any trouble, Mr . . . Artemis. My husband hates me in red." It was a lie, but Judith was beginning to feel desperate.

"Nonsense!" Mr. Artemis snapped his fingers again. "Deirdre! At once!"

A willowy blond appeared from behind the gauzy pearl-white curtains that cordoned off one end of the show room. The designer gave his orders, then indicated that Judith should sit in a white armless modular chair. With a sigh of resignation, Judith sat. A Saint-Saëns symphony played softly in the background, and a hint of incense floated on the air. At the far end of the room a large muted TV screen showed Mr. Artemis's latest collection. Judith recognized Tara Novotny in a pumpkin orange suit. Her dark hair was very short and her graceful stride was very long. Judith cudgeled her brain for a tactful way of asking Mr. Artemis about Harley Davidson's connection with the designer's favorite model.

"Tara must have made a beautiful bride in last week's show at I. Magnifique," Judith said at last. "Did Kristin and I see the gown she modeled?"

"No, no," Mr. Artemis replied, adjusting the fawn-colored ascot he wore with his ecru shirt and slacks. "The bridal gown in last week's show had never been seen by anyone. It had only just arrived from my shop in Santa Teresa del Fiore Thursday afternoon."

"I see," Judith said, still working her brain overtime. "Did you also design Mr. Davidson's tuxedo?"

Mr. Artemis looked grave. "Yes, I have a limited menswear line. But after what happened Friday, I feel like stopping it. Such an outrage!"

Judith nodded solemnly. "Yes, it was terrible. Did you know him well?"

"*Him*?" Mr. Artemis seemed puzzled. "Oh, you mean that disc jockey? Certainly not. I was referring to the tuxedo. Someone removed my labels. I was infuriated when the police told me about it. Imagine! Cutting out a Mr. Artemis label! Whatever is the point?"

"The point of . . . ?" But the question went unfinished

as Deirdre appeared in a crimson satin gown with a gathered waist and décolleté neckline.

"Excellent, Deirdre!" Mr. Artemis applauded gently. "Yes, move forward, step back, sway a little. You see," he said in a confidential tone to Judith, "the motion of the dress is like liquid fire, a molten force that rises up out of nature and consumes not only the wearer, but the observer. It's not a design for the faint-hearted, let me tell you! Have you courage, Mrs. Flynn?" A faint smirk played at Mr. Artemis's thin lips.

I have some courage but no money, Judith wanted to say. Instead, she murmured that the gown was lovely. Deirdre paraded back and forth across the room, posing and preening. Mr. Artemis applauded some more.

"Enough!" he declared. "You'll give us the vapors, my dear. Shoo, away with you."

Deirdre slipped between the pearl-white draperies, a tongue of fire enveloped by an avalanche of snow. Or so Judith imagined. It was a much safer fantasy than picturing herself in the crimson gown.

"Tara didn't know Mr. Davidson either, I guess," Judith said as Mr. Artemis opened a white oak armoire to pour the ritual glasses of champagne.

"I shouldn't think so," the designer replied, though his words lacked their usual certainty. Indeed, as he handed Judith a tulip-shaped glass, his very green eyes showed a trace of doubt. "Why do you ask?"

Judith started to think of a plausible fib, then realized there was no point in hiding the truth. "Because I saw them together Friday evening after the fashion show. They were on the roof of the Belmont Hotel."

Mr. Artemis had taken a sip of champagne; he suddenly looked as if he'd swallowed poison. "No! Never! You're referring to that dilapidated old building where my poor mutilated tuxedo was found in such incredibly shabby surroundings?"

"Yes," Judith replied, thinking that it was pointless to

remind Mr. Artemis that a dead man had been discovered inside the tuxedo. "I was attending the rehearsal dinner for Kristin and my son. It was early evening, around eight. What time was the show over?"

"Sevenish." Mr. Artemis frowned. "Or later. Time is of no importance."

"When did Tara return the wedding dress?" Judith inquired casually.

"Later. She and that dreadful radio man were to meet us in Ron's Bar and Grill for a celebratory bottle of champagne." Expectantly, the designer kept his eye on the draperies, awaiting Deirdre's return.

"They didn't come?" Judith hoped she still sounded casual.

"No. So unpredictable, these models. I didn't see Tara again until we returned here. Really, what can be taking Deirdre so long to change?" Mr. Artemis made a fretful gesture with his long, thin fingers.

"Was Tara still wearing the wedding gown when she finally got here?" Out of the corner of her eye, Judith saw Deirdre come through the draperies with the crimson gown on a satin-covered hanger.

"Certainly," Mr. Artemis replied, turning to Deirdre. "You looked marvelous, my dear. But of course that color is meant for someone darker, such as Mrs. Flynn." The designer sketched a little bow.

"Did Harley come back, too?" Judith asked, wishing that the pearl-white carpet would open up and swallow Deirdre and the crimson dress.

"No," Mr. Artemis answered, "which vexed me. He was to return the tuxedo immediately. Of course he did *not*, and look what happened to my marvelous creation!" Once again, the designer's expression conveyed extreme distress. "Deirdre, you helped Tara out of the wedding gown, did you not? It was pinned in ever so many places."

Deirdre nodded her sleek blond head. "Yes, it took

forever. And the hem and train were quite soiled." Deirdre pouted at Mr. Artemis. "Tara can be very careless. She'd torn the hem right out of the Amber Autumn suit and ripped an entire seam in the Winter Wonderland coat. She should never be allowed to take your lovely garments home with her from Santa Teresa del Fiore instead of bringing them straight to the salon."

Mr. Artemis didn't take well to the implied criticism. "I depend on her to transport my very special creations. Tara understands workmanship. If there's even the slightest imperfection, she can have it tended to on site. You, my dear," he added with caressing sarcasm, "haven't got the eye for such detail."

Deirdre sniffed and gave a toss of her blond head. "I know damage when I see it. I still say Tara is careless. I wouldn't doubt that she wears your garments before she brings them here."

Afraid that the conversation was not only getting off-track, but out of hand, Judith smiled ingratiatingly at Deirdre. "While you were helping Tara out of the wedding gown the other night, did she seem . . . upset?"

"Oh, very!" Deirdre's slender hands fluttered. "She adores that gown! It broke her heart to take it off."

"Oh." Judith's face fell. "That's why she was upset?"

Mr. Artemis nodded in his languid fashion. "Tara has a genuine affinity for my creations. Which," he continued with a cold stare for Deirdre, "is why I permit her a few minor aberrations." He glanced at the double chrome doors. "I certainly hope Rodney has gotten hold of her by now. This absenteeism has lost its charm. I need her tomorrow for the show at Nordquist's."

It seemed to Judith that Tara's employer didn't understand the enormity of his model's defection. Perhaps he had not been fully informed. Or maybe he didn't want to know. Judith had the feeling that Mr. Artemis believed only in what suited him.

"I don't suppose," Judith said in a rather whimsical

voice, "that you'd know why Tara was on the Belmont Hotel roof with Harley Davidson?" She gazed first at Mr. Artemis, then at Deirdre.

Mr. Artemis shrugged. "I've no idea. Indeed, I doubt very much that you saw Tara. This time of year, there are brides here, there, and everywhere. Tell me, Mrs. Flynn, do you have a particularly active imagination?" The designer's smile was somewhat smug.

"Not really," Judith answered a bit more sharply than she'd intended. "Doesn't it strike you as unlikely that Harley Davidson would show up on the Belmont roof with a woman in a wedding dress who wasn't Tara?"

"Not at all." Mr. Artemis poured himself some more champagne. "There's no accounting for what people like this disc jockey will do. Radio personalities are highly volatile, extremely unpredictable, and often addicted to drugs. Come, let us try on Flames of Desire."

Judith jumped. "No! That is—I can't! I broke my ribs. I'm in a cast. I mean, a brace. You can't see it, but it's there, all big and bulky. I'll call you when I'm healed." Judith practically galloped out of the salon.

She slowed her pace when she reached the sidewalk. Just before reaching the entrance to Ron's Bar and Grill, Judith spotted a familiar figure leaning against the building: It was Uncle Gurd, still wearing the blue dress and red patent leather pumps. He was holding a hand-lettered sign that said, "Will protest U. S. pig-faced government for cash. No checks accepted."

Judith wanted to turn tail and flee, but Gurd had seen her. "Hey," he yelled, "you got a spare dollar?"

"It's illegal in this city to verbally solicit," Judith informed Uncle Gurd as she approached him warily. "You can get arrested."

"Ha! I'll bet I can! The government arrests anybody for anything." He paused as a well-dressed young man dropped a quarter in the cardboard box that lay next to Uncle Gurd's red pumps. "I'm testin' city ways," he said. "Folks dress mighty strange around here, so I'm tryin' out some different duds. So far, it ain't workin'— I been here ten minutes, and I only got ninety cents."

"Maybe it's the dress," Judith said through tight lips. "City fashions can be extreme, but there are some limits. How did you get here?"

"On the bus." He shrugged, then nodded in the direction of Donner & Blitzen. "Judgin' from the other passengers, I fit right in, dress or no dress. There's some mighty peculiar people ridin' the bus in this town." He shook his bald head. "I wanted to sit across the street by that big swanky department store, but they told me that spot's reserved for some other guy. Does the government regulate the beggars in this city, too?"

Judith had followed Gurd's gaze across the street to the corner display window where Billy Big Horn had sat for the past few years. At the moment, his usual panhandling post was vacant. But Billy moved around, as Judith recalled from seeing him in front of the Naples Hotel the night of the wedding rehearsal dinner.

"It's a courtesy," Judith explained, trying to ignore the stares of passersby. "I've seen Billy Big Horn outside of Donner & Blitzen for a long time, and I've often given him a donation. Everyone acknowledges that corner as his spot. The government—the city—only regulates how panhandling is conducted, not where."

"Well, I'm conductin' it real slow." Uncle Gurd's leathery face showed disgust. "Maybe I'll go home. Can you give me a lift?"

To Judith's horror, she lied: "No, I'm not headed that way yet. You can catch a bus two blocks over and one block down. See you in the hedge."

With a frantic step, she turned into Ron's Bar and Grill. Chastising herself for refusing a ride to Uncle Gurd just because he was dressed like a woman, she asked the bartender if her I. Magnifique box had shown up. It hadn't. The bartender was young, perhaps working his way through graduate school, and seemed to sense Judith's distress.

"Would you care for something?" he asked in a kind voice.

Judith had also been a bartender, working nights at the Meat & Mingle three blocks from the McMonigle rental on Thurlow Street in the south end of town. During the day, she had served as head librarian in the local branch. Meanwhile, Dan had stayed home on the sofa, watching TV, napping, and eating and drinking and drinking and eating.

"I really shouldn't," Judith said, gazing at the clock above the bar which indicated it was shortly before noon. She remembered the last time she'd had a drink alone in a bar. It had been the night when she'd waited for Joe, and he'd never shown up. Over twenty years had passed before she saw him again. The mere thought of all that lost time changed her mind.

"Oh, what the heck," she said with an uncertain smile. "I'll have a Scotch—rocks." The bartender struck Judith as very sweet. She'd always had a weakness for bartenders, not because she liked to drink, but because they were kindred spirits. Judith shared their enjoyment of other people's company, the ability to listen, and the capacity for compassion. Indeed, Dan had been a bartender when she met him, before he became permanently underemployed and grossly overweight.

"My name's Barry," the bartender said, deftly serving the drink. "What was in your missing box?"

"A dress," Judith replied. "A very expensive dress. In fact, it was an Artemis Bohl design. I believe he comes in here now and then."

Barry chuckled. "He does, usually with his entourage. He holds court at that table down there." The bartender nodded in the direction where Judith had seen Mr. Artemis and Tara earlier in the week. "We call it our designer table; he tips well."

"That's the main thing," Judith said, recalling how meager her tips had been with the crowd of riff-raff at the Meat & Mingle. "I don't suppose you've seen Tara Novotny in here the past couple of days?"

"The model?" Barry chuckled again. "No, not since Tuesday. I think it was Tuesday. She's something, isn't she? I've never seen her eat, though. How do those super-thin models keep alive? One glass of white wine, that's it."

"I wouldn't know about being thin," Judith said with a lame little laugh. "Keeping from being fat has always been my problem. You were here Tuesday? Then you must have been on duty when I lost that blasted dress."

Barry looked thoughtful. "That's right, one of the servers asked me about it. Wow, that's really too bad. I hope you find it." Barry now seemed a bit distracted as the lunch trade began arriving. "Excuse me, I've got orders to fill."

Judith sipped at her drink and watched the influx of customers. The tables were filling up, mostly with office workers. A half-dozen older men in three-piece suits were scattered around the room, looking as if they were getting down to serious business, or serious drinking, or both. The stools at the bar were also becoming occupied. Judith moved her purse over a notch as a muscular man in shorts and tank top sat down next to her.

"Barry," the newcomer called, "throw me a Cuervo. I've had a rough morning."

Barry, who was mixing screwdrivers, nodded. "I got it, TNT. One tequila, straight up."

Catching the name, Judith couldn't resist swerving on the stool to get a better look. The muscular man was in his thirties, and his ears and nose definitely showed signs of wear and tear. There were a couple of scars, too, on his lower lip and near his left eye.

"You're the boxer," Judith said, and then lied: "I've seen you fight."

The man put out a beefy hand. "TNT Tenino. Who are you, Dark Eyes?"

Judith was so flattered that she giggled. "Nobody. I mean, I'm Judith Flynn. Is it true that you're retired?"

"You bet." TNT nodded at Barry as the shot of tequila was produced. "I did all right in the ring. Now I run clinics and check out new talent."

"That's wonderful," Judith said. "Is that why you had a rough morning? All aspects of the boxing profession must be a challenge."

Barry pointed to Judith's now-empty glass. She didn't want another drink, but needed an excuse to stay at the bar and talk to Esperanza Highcastle's estranged husband. Reluctantly, she gave a thumbs-up sign to Barry.

"Teaching, my butt!" TNT growled, downing the tequila in one gulp. "It's women. Or woman." He sketched a right cross at Barry, apparently the signal for another round. "You're not the kind who'd try to screw your old man, are you? I mean when it came to money, not . . ."

"No, no," Judith answered hastily. "I'm very fond of my husband. Is your wife causing you trouble?"

TNT put his curly dark head in his hands. "Brother! You don't know the half of it! You marry a rich dame and figure you got it made. Just keep her happy in the sack, and no more worries, right? But not this one. It'd take an entire fight card to satisfy Espy. You know what?" His close-set brown eyes zeroed in on Judith. "I think she's one of those nymphos."

"Really." Judith sipped decorously at her second Scotch. "Your wife, you mean?"

TNT had now polished off his second tequila. "That's right, my wife. Some wife. She can't cook, she hates sports, she makes fun of my friends, she thinks she used to be married to Napoleon." He feigned a left hook at Barry. "She doesn't drink, either. She's no damned fun. Except between the sheets or on the sofa or the rug or . . .

Hey, Bartender, you down for the count? Where's my Cuervo?''

Barry apologized, saying he had to mix a couple of martinis first. Judith cleared her throat, then reached for her purse. She couldn't possibly finish her second drink, not this early in the day.

''I take it you're separated?'' Judith said, placing a ten-dollar bill and two ones on the bar.

TNT nodded as he accepted his third tequila. ''She threw me out last Friday. I've been living at the Cascadia Hotel, but I had to get out. Espy canceled my credit cards. She's a bitch on wheels. You know a good lawyer?''

''Not really.'' Somehow Judith didn't think that the fuddy-duddy Grover family attorney, William Ewart Gladstone Whiffel, would make a match with TNT Tenino. ''Try the Yellow Pages. They list lawyers who specialize in divorce.''

''I need a real barracuda,'' TNT declared, swallowing his third Jose Cuervo in one gulp. He lowered his head and his voice. ''Hey, Mrs. Flynn, can I go home with you?''

NINE

JUDITH REALLY WASN'T sure how she ended up bringing TNT Tenino to Hillside Manor. Barry had tactfully refused to serve the ex-boxer another tequila, and after Judith had departed Ron's Bar and Grill, she realized she was being followed. At first, she thought it must be Uncle Gurd. But the old man had vacated the front of the restaurant and was nowhere in sight. Moments later TNT caught up with her while she waited to cross the street between I. Magnifique and the Donner & Blitzen parking garage. By that time, he was virtually in tears. Down to his last fifty dollars, he had nowhere to go. Did Mrs. Flynn know of a cheap motel?

She did, but wouldn't recommend such a seedy establishment to anyone, not even TNT Tenino. The B&B was full on this Thursday night, but Mike's bedroom on the third floor was available. Judith's soft heart melted. Maybe fate was paying her back for ditching Uncle Gurd. If she could put up with him in the hedge, she could suffer through a night with TNT. Besides, she really wanted to know more about Esperanza Highcastle and her employee, Harley Davidson.

"Has your wife had a lot of problems with Harley?" she'd asked TNT as they drove up the south side of Heraldsgate Hill.

TNT, who was now exhibiting the effects of his three shots of tequila, had mumbled that Esperanza had problems with everyone and everything. As for Harley, he had a dirty mouth; he'd get the station's license yanked. "Punk. Radio punk," he muttered. "Rocker punk. I hate him."

"But he's dead," Judith had pointed out.

"Good," TNT had said, and passed out.

Half an hour later, TNT was still sleeping it off in the Subaru while Judith questioned her sanity.

"You *what*?" Renie demanded over the phone. "Never mind, I'm coming over. I have to drop off a casserole for the funeral freezer."

Arlene Rankers and a couple of other SOTS, as Our Lady, Star of the Sea's parishioners were known, were in charge of keeping the church supplied with food for funeral receptions. Judith did her share, but the rotation was alphabetical. Last names beginning with F wouldn't be called on until the first week of September.

Renie arrived shortly before two. When she pulled the big blue Chev into the driveway, she saw TNT Tenino's head lolling against the passenger seat's upholstery.

"You better give him an eight count," Renie advised Judith as the cousins sat down in the living room. "How long has he been out?"

Judith considered. "An hour? Hour and a half? Really, I think he was tired. It sounds as if he's been through a rough patch with Esperanza. Or Espy, as he calls her."

"I don't doubt that," Renie allowed. "But I honestly can't see how you could . . ." She stopped, a hand at her tousled chestnut curls. "Yes, I can. You do some of the weirdest things, just because you can't say no."

"I said no to Uncle Gurd," Judith declared, recounting the meeting on the sidewalk. "But I felt bad about it. Why do I care what people think?"

"Because you own your own business and have to keep up a public image? That's good enough for me," Renie asserted, then changed the subject. "What about your visit to Artemis Bohl?"

Judith related what had happened, and in the process, tried to sort through the exchange for anything that might clarify the mystery. "Tara came back with the dress, so we know she was seen that night after I spotted her with Harley on the roof. We also know that she and Harley were not a romantic duo—though I thought I detected a note of doubt in Mr. Artemis's manner. What I'd like to find out is who stood to gain by Harley's death. Did you ask Kip about family or friends?"

"I asked Kerri to ask him," Renie replied, sipping a large Pepsi. "Kip told her that Harley was an orphan. He was born blind and abandoned by his unwed mother. Finding adoptive parents for a blind child is pretty hard. Harley went from orphanage to foster home and back again until he ran away when he was about fifteen. That was in the Midwest, Indiana, I think. He was fascinated with radio, and sort of bummed his way west, working for small stations. Eventually, he landed in L.A., and finally got a shot at being on the air. Harley was a big deal down there, but came a cropper and headed north. He'd been with KRAS-FM for almost five years, which is almost a record in radio. And yes," Renie added with a smirk, "his real name is John Smith."

"So," Judith sighed, "no relatives. Friends? Girlfriends? Wives? Ex-wives?"

"He never married, though there have been girlfriends," Renie answered. "And I do mean *girl* friends. Harley rarely went out with any female who was old enough to drive. He had a penchant for fifteen-year-olds."

"Oh, dear." Judith grimaced. "That's illegal. Groupies, I suppose."

"No doubt." Renie drank thirstily. The afternoon had grown very warm, and though the doors and windows were open, the living room felt stuffy. "I don't envy Joe and Woody trying to track down all those teenaged girls and then interviewing them." Despite the heat, Renie shuddered.

"Hmmm," Judith murmured. "Yes, that could be a pain. So who gets his money? According to Darrell, Harley had pots of it, especially under-the-table payoffs."

"If that's true, the IRS will get most of it," Renie said. "Don't they always?"

"They sure do," Judith said with bitterness. And then she launched into her conversation with Merle Rundberg.

Renie was appalled, as well as sympathetic. "Try Sig. Men are often more reasonable about money than women," Renie counseled. "Or maybe it's that they have a better sense of fair play."

"Maybe." Judith couldn't help but sound dubious. "Drat. I was hoping that money could be a motive. But under the circumstances, I don't see how."

"Maybe it is, in a different way," Renie suggested. "You know, someone who wanted to take over from Harley."

Judith only half heard Renie. "I don't believe that Harley and Tara were strangers to each other. Maybe they weren't lovers, but nobody pulls a stunt like that one on the Belmont roof unless there's some sort of history."

Renie inclined her head. "You're right. Why were they there in the first place? Has Joe asked that question?"

"I don't know," Judith admitted. "Maybe not, since he didn't believe I saw them in the first place."

Renie put her feet up on the coffee table. "*I* believe you saw Harley and Tara. Where do you suppose she's gone?"

"Where isn't as important as why," Judith responded, nibbling on her forefinger. "She's the key."

"Maybe," Renie allowed as Sweetums sauntered in from the parlor and collapsed in front of the empty fireplace. "But why the Belmont? What was the attraction?"

Judith's dark eyes lighted on Renie's face. "I've wondered. We know it wasn't locked up tight. Apparently, anyone could have gone inside. But to what purpose? All I can think of are transients, looking for an empty bed.''

Renie got to her feet. ''Speaking of transients, I'd better scoot. I had a rush project dumped on me by the local council of churches this morning. They're putting out a brochure to make the public more aware of the homeless. Unfortunately, they had to fire the first two designers. So guess who has to bail them out?'' Renie made a self-deprecating face.

''You could start with TNT Tenino,'' Judith said dryly, as she walked her cousin through the open French doors. ''How about a picture of him sleeping in my car?''

But TNT wasn't sleeping. Gertrude was standing beside the Subaru, using her walker as a weapon.

''Hey, you bum!'' she yelled. ''Get the hell out of my daughter's car! Come on, or I'm calling the cops!''

''Hi, Aunt Gertrude, bye, Aunt Gertrude.'' Renie raced for the Chev.

TNT was struggling to sit up. ''Where am I? What happened? Did I lose the fight?''

''You lost your mind, you moron!'' shouted Gertrude. ''It's bad enough we've got some crazy old fart living in the hedge, now we got some knothead sleeping in the driveway!'' As soon as TNT stuck his legs outside of the car, Gertrude hit him with the walker.

''Stop that!'' Judith rushed to restrain her mother. ''Mr. Tenino is a guest. Leave him alone, he's . . . tired.''

''What?'' Gertrude's small eyes got even smaller. ''This is one of your lame-brained B&B guests? So why isn't he sleeping in a bed or eating breakfast?''

''He should be. He will be.'' Judith beckoned to TNT. ''Come on, Mr. Tenino, I'll show you to your room.''

A bleary-eyed TNT shot Gertrude a wary glance, then followed Judith into the house. ''I could eat a horse,'' he announced as he stepped into the hallway that led to the kitchen.

"I'll make you some lunch," Judith said wearily. "There, sit at the table. How about ham and cheese?"

"A ham would be great," TNT said, flopping into a chair. "You can skip the cheese."

Judith began slicing slabs of ham, added bread, and despite TNT's exhortation, threw in some Havarti for good measure. The ex-boxer ate ravenously.

"I'm so sorry about your marital problems," Judith said, sitting down on the opposite side of the table. "What caused the break-up?"

"Huh?" TNT looked up from his third slice of ham. "Sex. Money. The usual stuff. Espy liked to get it on with other guys, like George Washington and Admiral Byrd. There are limits to what a man should put up with, right?" TNT stuffed a piece of bread in his mouth. "I wondered about her and that Davidson sometimes, but I don't know for sure. I threatened to deck him once, but it didn't seem fair, him being blind. So I just shook him a little. He laughed. Boy, did that tick me off!"

"Oh? When was that?" Judith proffered a jar of dill pickles.

Digging around inside the pickle jar, TNT considered. "What's today?"

Judith said it was Thursday.

"Last Friday," TNT asserted, crunching a pickle between his teeth. "Around noon. Harley had wound up his stupid show, and started needling me about Espy. I told him if he ever touched her, I'd kill him."

"So," Judith said slowly, "you were sort of . . . ah . . . gratified when you heard Harley had been killed."

TNT seemed puzzled by the remark. "Gratified? You mean as in grateful? Well, yeah, I guess so, but that won't stop Espy from getting her hooks into some other poor sap, like Chuck Rawls or Julius Caesar."

It occurred to Judith that no one showed any regret over Harley's demise. Despite the fact that the late disc jockey sounded like a reprehensible person, she was starting to feel sorry for him.

"Do you have any idea who might have stabbed Harley?" she inquired in what she hoped was a conversational tone.

TNT was eating more ham. "Naw. It could have been anybody with a creep like him. Maybe it was the drugs. It usually is."

Judith tried to conceal her surprise. "What drugs?"

"I heard he got busted in L.A. for selling drugs to teenagers." TNT had finally gotten around to the Havarti cheese. "That's why he came up here. Somebody at the station told me that. I forget who."

"Did Harley do drugs?" Judith asked.

TNT shrugged. "Maybe. All those radio guys act like they're high, at least when they're on the air. You got any ice cream? I really like ice cream."

Judith had rocky road, blackberry ribbon, and french vanilla. TNT said he'd try all of them. She was dishing each variety into separate bowls when Uncle Gurd came into the kitchen. He was now wearing only plaid boxer shorts.

"Ice cream!" Gurd exclaimed, his eyes lighting up. "Now I'm one for ice cream. Why didn't you tell me you had all these fancy kinds?"

Judith cleaned out the cartons of rocky road and french vanilla. She had just enough blackberry ribbon left over for Gertrude's dessert. "Are you going to eat it here or in the hedge?" Judith asked somewhat sharply.

Uncle Gurd considered. "The hedge. It's real nice in there, except for the bees." Carrying his two bowls, he exited the kitchen.

"Is that your father?" TNT inquired with mild interest.

"No!" Judith was horrified. "I hardly know him. He just . . . showed up, with some other people."

"You've got some real characters around here," TNT mused. "That old lady with the walker, this bald guy in his underwear—who else is wandering around this place?''

Judith declined to answer.

Joe was wild. He couldn't understand how Judith had been soft-hearted enough or sufficiently gullible or just plain stupid to let TNT Tenino stay at Hillside Manor. It wasn't merely that Joe felt an insolvent hard-drinking ex-boxer who'd been thrown out by his wife could cause some problems: Joe pointedly reminded Judith that TNT was also a suspect in the murder investigation.

''You never said he was a suspect,'' Judith asserted as Joe paced the kitchen. ''If you'd tell me these things, I'd be able to . . .''

Joe stomped off through the narrow hallway that led to the back porch. ''I'm going for a walk. Don't hold dinner.'' The screen slammed behind him.

''I don't think the case is going well,'' Judith confided to Renie an hour later on the phone. ''Joe's really crabby.''

''Will TNT leave tomorrow?'' Renie asked, raising her voice over the shouts of various Jones offspring who wanted to use the phone.

''I hope so,'' Judith said in a worried tone. ''But if he's only got fifty dollars, where can he go?''

''He must have access to money,'' Renie said after an aside to her children to shut up or she'd yank the phone out of the wall. ''Bill says he made a good living as a boxer. Unless he's blown it. Even so, this is a community property state. TNT ought to be able to get his hands on some cash. Esperanza Highcastle is stinking rich.''

''Maybe they had a pre-nup,'' Judith suggested. ''Wealthy people know how to tie up their money. I really have to get him out of here by tomorrow or Joe will blow a gasket.''

''Don't look at me,'' Renie warned. ''With the kids home for the summer, we're full up. How about putting

TNT in the hedge with Uncle Gurd? Just think, coz, before the summer is over, you could have an entire colony living in there.''

''Very funny,'' Judith snarled. Then she paused, and her voice softened. ''Will you go with me to take a look at the Belmont tomorrow before we meet with Chuck Rawls?''

''Ohhh . . .'' Renie was sounding irked. ''I've got this damned brochure design to finish. If I work late tonight . . . Dammit, coz, it's a stupid idea. What's the point?''

''Please? I'm drowning in dilemmas. There's Uncle Gurd and TNT and the Rundbergs trying to stiff me for the wedding bills and the lost evening gown and Joe acting like a jerk and . . . Mother. There's always Mother.''

''Yes, there is,'' Renie said, calming down. ''Mine had me driving all over town this morning trying to find a certain color of tan thread. Not a true tan, not a deep tan, not a light tan, but one with just a hint of gold. And do you know why? She wanted to mend her nylons. Who the hell wears nylon stockings these days? Who the hell *mends* nylons?''

''Your mother?'' said Judith meekly.

''Aaargh,'' said Renie, and hung up.

When Joe returned from his long walk around seven-thirty, he was in a slightly better mood. Though she had a million questions, Judith decided not to mention the murder investigation. Fortunately, Uncle Gurd had settled in for the night, and TNT hadn't reappeared since Judith had shown him to his third-floor room and provided him with a huge plate of food.

In the morning, Judith couldn't resist posing one query for her husband: ''Have you and Woody talked to Tara Novotny again?'' she inquired after Joe had finished his second cup of coffee.

''The model?'' Joe looked up from the morning paper. ''No. She's playing hard to get.''

"Isn't she an important witness?" Judith hoped she wasn't pushing her luck.

"Maybe." Joe seemed absorbed in the sports page. "We didn't get much the first time we interviewed her."

"You don't think she's a serious suspect then?" Judith obligingly poured more coffee for Joe.

Joe didn't look up from the paper. "No. That wedding dress had some dirt on it, but there weren't any bloodstains. She couldn't have stabbed Davidson and not gotten blood on that white dress."

"Do you think she's in danger?" Judith inquired, hearing some of her guests arrive in the adjacent dining room.

"What? No, why should she be? I doubt that she was around when the murder took place. Now what kind of an ERA is 5.86?" Joe demanded, finally lifting his head. "You don't win baseball games with hitting, you win with pitching, dammit."

Judith decided not to ask any more questions. Instead, she took a basket of hot scones into the dining room, and played the gracious hostess. It was a job she understood. Joe was the detective, Judith was the innkeeper. She had to keep remembering those facts of life.

Renie picked up Judith at twelve-thirty. "We're meeting Rawls first," she told her cousin. "He wants to see us on his lunch break. We'll do a quick trip to the Belmont afterwards, but I can only spare you ninety minutes, tops. How's TNT this morning? Did he get up at the bell?"

"He left," Judith said, exuding a sigh of relief. "When I tapped on his door around nine, there wasn't any response. I assumed he was still asleep, so I peeked inside. He wasn't there. I guess he went out via the back stairs while I was with Phyliss in the living room."

"He might have thanked you," Renie noted as she eased the big Chev down the steep south side of Heraldsgate Hill. Clouds were moving in over the bay, and the temperature had dropped. Much to the relief of the natives, the forecast called for possible showers.

"I don't care if he didn't thank me," Judith said. "I'm just glad he's gone. Now to get rid of Uncle Gurd."

"Send the Rundbergs a bill for his keep," Renie proposed. "That will put them on the defensive. You *are* in the hostelry business, after all."

"I suppose I could," Judith admitted. "It seems kind of crass, though. I mean, it isn't even our hedge."

"Don't get soft," Renie warned. "Knowing you, you'll let those Rundbergs walk all over your ever-so-willing carcass. Stick it to them, every chance you get. I marvel you stay in business, coz, I really do."

Judith marveled at her cousin's toughness. Judith could always find excuses, and thus, reasons, for bad behavior. Renie's rules were more rigid: one strike, and you were out. Both attitudes got them into trouble.

"So what's our gig?" Judith asked, anxious to change the subject, and, as Renie would have put it, bury her head in the sand. "Something to do with a DOA promotion?"

"No. I went for the truth," Renie said with a little sigh. "I couldn't put Kip on the spot. I told him to tell Chuck Rawls Jr. that you were assisting your husband in the homicide investigation."

Judith was dismayed. "But that's not the truth. I'm just trying to . . ."

"Solve it on your own?" Renie shot Judith a swift glance, then cut the corner perilously close on a right-hand turn. "I'd like to think otherwise."

"Well . . ." Judith chewed on her index finger. "I guess you're right. But Joe doesn't want my help."

"Surprise," Renie said dryly, honking at a car that was taking its time pulling out of a parking space. "By the way, we're not meeting Chuck at the station. We're going across the street to Foozle's."

Foozle's was a local watering hole with stiff drinks and mediocre food. Despite the establishment's proximity to Hillside Manor, Judith had been in the place only once, to rescue a guest who had passed out in the bar.

"Is Foozle's a hangout for the radio people?" Judith asked as Renie maneuvered the big Chev into the parking spot.

"I guess," Renie answered. "We're supposed to meet Rawls in the bar."

"Oh." Judith was growing leery of bars. In her two recent visits to Ron's, she had lost a designer dress and found a homeless boxer. "I'm drinking pop," she declared.

"I'm eating lunch," said Renie as the cousins waited for the traffic signal to change. "I got so busy on that blasted church council project that I didn't get to eat much this morning."

"Wow," Judith murmured, as always awed not so much by her cousin's prodigious appetite as by Renie's metabolism, which kept off the extra pounds. "I'm going to have a look at Belgravia Gardens later this afternoon. Arlene's taking me. Want to come?"

The cousins hurried across the busy intersection. "No, thanks," Renie replied. "I told you, I'm really under the gun. I have to turn in my design first thing Monday morning, and I hate working weekends."

Foozle's was old, evincing not charm but neglect. The red and black carpeting was worn, the walls needed paint, the booths sagged, and the waitresses looked as if they were counting not tips, but the days until they became eligible for Social Security. In the bar, the lights were dim and the tables were tiny. Renie gazed around the tawdry room, trying to pick out Chuck Rawls Jr.

Rawls picked out the cousins instead. "You must be Mrs. Jones," he said, rising from one of the tiny tables. "Kip described you. Chuck Rawls here." He shook hands, while Renie introduced Judith.

The producer was a short, burly man with a deep voice that at one time had probably been heard over the airways. At close to fifty, he was balding and looked as if he needed a shave. When he sat back down at the table, there wasn't much room left over for Judith and Renie.

"Explain this to me," Rawls said, gripping the table edges with his beefy hands. "You're a cop, Mrs. Flynn? Or some sort of consultant?"

Judith's smile felt like a grimace. "A . . . consultant. That is, I sometimes interview witnesses. The woman's touch, you know. And the city is so short-handed with all the budget cuts. It's helpful to my husband to . . . have someone he can trust. I'm not . . . official." Aware that she was babbling, Judith shut up.

But her explanation seemed to satisfy Rawls, who was nursing a beer. "I don't know much, so I can't tell you much. Your husband and his partner already asked all the serious questions."

"Yes, Joe and Woody are very good at their jobs," Judith said with enthusiasm. "I'm sure they inquired into Harley's background, and how he got in trouble in L.A. for selling drugs."

"Oh, that." Rawls tugged at his ear. "Those kind of stories always follow radio people whenever they make a move. Dope, alcohol, sex with groupies, stalker fans, law suits, whatever. If Harley'd had a record, we wouldn't have hired him. Ms. Highcastle's strict about our employees. It's okay to be outrageous, but you can't be illegal."

"I see," Judith said, somehow disappointed. "But he wasn't well-liked among his colleagues, was he?"

A waitress with frizzy gray hair and wing-tipped glasses trudged to the table. Renie asked for a beef dip, rare, fries, a salad with Roquefort dressing, and a large Pepsi. Judith ordered a bowl of clam chowder and a diet 7-UP. Rawls declined another beer.

"Harley was a pain in the ass, excuse my French," Rawls said with a sigh. "He had this huge ego, and because his ratings were so good, he thought he was God. You couldn't tell him anything, even when he was going off the deep end. He knew it all."

Judith wore a politely curious expression. "You mean Harley took risks on the radio?"

"God yes!" Rawls uttered an exasperated laugh. "Talk about pushing the envelope! I kept warning him we'd get our FCC license yanked if he didn't watch his mouth. But he'd just jeer at me, and say that kids these days talk exactly the same way, so why the big sweat? And his ratings would go up another notch. He was getting a strong following among listeners in their twenties, because he played their kind of music, too."

"What about sponsors?" Renie inquired, keeping an eye out for the return of the waitress with her food.

"They were in a bind," Rawls responded, lighting a cigarette. "His morning share was huge and it crossed over from the teenage to the young adult market. They couldn't afford not to advertise, even if they privately deplored his radio persona." The producer waggled his cigarette. "Do you mind?"

Judith shook her head. "I quit several years ago, but I still spend a lot of time thinking about it."

"If the waitress doesn't hurry with my order, I'll eat that cigarette," Renie vowed, sounding cross.

Judith sniffed at the smoke-tainted air, then posed another question: "Who, in your opinion, benefits from Harley's death?"

Rawls examined his square-cut fingernails. "Nobody. He's literally irreplaceable. We're going on a talent search to find somebody, but whoever we hire will automatically lose half the audience. Good-bye listeners, good-bye sponsors, good-bye promotional opportunities, good-bye big profits."

"Does that mean the station is going to find itself in financial trouble?" Judith asked.

Rawls considered. "Red ink by the end of the year, maybe. Ms. Highcastle won't want to pour money into a leaky boat. KORN's ratings have slipped this past year, because country and western isn't as big as it was." Rawls glanced at Renie. "Losing your nephew didn't help. He had a loyal following in KORN's morning drive-to slot. Lots of radio and TV stations are being taken over by conglomerates. That's what I see happening to KRAS and KORN down the road."

"So," Judith mused, "from a business point of view, it was in everybody's best interests to keep Harley alive."

Rawls nodded. "Alive and on the air. Instead, we've got a memorial service for his fans this weekend. A lot of the ghouls wanted an open casket, but I put a stop to that. Harley might not have had or wanted much dignity in life, but he's going to have some in death, dammit."

The waitress delivered the cousins' orders. Renie pounced. Judith toyed with her soup spoon and waited for the chowder to cool. "So you don't have any idea who might have killed Harley?" Judith finally asked.

"Not a glimmer," Rawls answered, stubbing out his cigarette. "That's what I told your husband and his partner."

"Did Harley act afraid or nervous the last few days before he died?" Judith's question was rushed; she was afraid that Chuck Rawls was preparing to leave.

"Hell no," Rawls replied. "He was always antsy, you know, on a perpetual high. That's the way it is in radio, at least on the rock stations. But he was the same old Harley, maybe more so."

"More so?" Judith paused with the spoon at her mouth.

"Well . . ." The producer grew thoughtful, fingering the stubble on his chin. "I sort of threw that out, and yet there *was* something different about him. I really hadn't considered it until now. He was always excited and excitable. But last week, he . . . how can I put it?" Rawls frowned. "Harley acted as if he was anticipating something. In retrospect, it might have been a job offer from a bigger market, like Chicago or New York."

Renie dribbled Roquefort dressing on her sleeveless top. "Was it?"

Rawls shrugged his brawny shoulders. "I couldn't tell you. Though if that had been the case, there should have been some followup. As far as I know, nobody's called from out of town to see what happened to him."

"Do you have any idea why Harley and Tara went to the Belmont Hotel after the fashion show?" Judith asked.

Rawls shook his head. "Maybe Harley thought he'd get laid. Look, I told you—and your husband—I've no idea why Harley did what he did or why he got killed. A deranged fan is my best guess. It happens."

The clam chowder was mediocre. Judith ate it anyway. "I understand Harley didn't want his listeners to know that he was blind. Yet he took part in special promotions. How did he disguise his lack of sight?"

Rawls made a face, and turned ruminative. "You know, when he first came to KRAS, I admired him a whole lot. He'd overcome this handicap, and made a successful career for himself. But when you got to know what an egomaniac he was, you forgot he was blind. It's a funny thing, how we categorize people, whether it's their race or their religion or whatever—then we get to know them and that stuff on the surface doesn't matter, shouldn't have mattered in the first place. A jerk is a jerk."

Renie looked up from stuffing her face with her beef dip. "Nice homily. But you got sidetracked. Promotions? Public appearances?"

"Oh, right." Rawls fingered a matchbook that bore Foozle's outmoded logo. "He was pretty sly about that stuff. Take that fashion show—I gather all he had to do was hang onto Tara Novotny and walk down the runway. Who could guess he couldn't see? The same thing at rock concerts he emceed—once he got into his place on stage, he faced the audience and screamed his head off. You don't have to have eyes to do that, you just follow the sound. That was Harley's thing, sound, noise, voices, music. He used them all to his advantage. I hate to admit it, but it was something to watch him do his show. Everything's done by computer these days, and he played that board like a piano. I never heard him make a slip.''

Judith inclined her head. ''Harley must have been quite smart. Is it true that he had a lot of enemies, especially at work?''

Getting to his feet, Rawls chuckled. ''Enemies, rivals, people he'd offended—they'd fill a phone book. But none of the ones I could name would kill him. They wouldn't have the guts. Sorry to be such a washout. I've got to find a DJ who can get at least a five market share.''

Twenty minutes later, the cousins were cruising for a parking place by the Belmont Hotel. As they passed the Naples for the third time, Renie tapped her temple.

''Billy Big Horn,'' she said. ''He'd make a perfect photo for the homeless brochure. If he's not sitting outside the hotel fountain, I'll have to try Donner & Blitzen. That's his usual spot.''

''He wasn't there yesterday,'' Judith noted. ''Try the Cascadia Hotel. I've seen him there once or twice.''

''I'll do that,'' Renie said, turning once more into the street that led to the Belmont's entrance. ''Actually, I'll tell Morris Mitchell. He's the photographer who's doing the shoot.''

Ahead of them, a white sedan was pulling out of a parking space. Renie applied the brakes, just a little too late. The big Chev's bumper nudged the rear of the other car.

''Yikes!'' Renie cried. ''I told Bill we needed a brake job. He always thinks I'm imagining things.''

''You didn't allow enough time,'' Judith said. ''You were going kind of fast.''

''Oh, hush!'' Renie was glaring at the other car, the door of which was now being thrust open. ''I couldn't have been doing more than twenty-five.''

"On these narrow streets, that's still . . ." Judith swallowed the next words.

The driver emerging from the white sedan was Joe Flynn, and he was very angry.

TEN

IT APPEARED THAT Joe didn't recognize Judith and
Renie until he was within five feet of the Chev. He
was reaching for his badge when Renie poked her head
out of the window. A split second later, Joe saw Judith
in the passenger seat.

"Hi, Joe," Renie said in what sounded like a fal-
setto. "What's up?"

"Jeez." Joe held his head. "I'm not asking. I don't
want to know." He gave Renie a hard stare. "Maybe
I should arrest both of you. Then I could do my job
and not feel as if I'm being followed by a pair of doofus amateur sleuths."

"*Sleuths*?" Renie exclaimed.

"*Doofus*?" Judith blurted.

Joe looked grim. "That's what I said." Turning his
back on the cousins, he examined the rear of the unmarked city car. "You're lucky," he called to Renie.
"I don't see any damage."

"What about *my* car?" Renie demanded, her own
temper resurfacing.

Joe didn't bother looking. He started back towards
the white sedan, but Woody was getting out of the
passenger side.

"Is that . . . ?" Woody began, and then stopped.

"Hello, Judith, Serena. Nice to see you. I think."

"It's not nice," Joe snapped, swerving on his heel. "It's damned annoying. Look," he said, reapproaching the Chev, "Woody and I are here for one last look at the crime scene. The demolition people and the builders and the contractors want to get moving again on this old dump come Monday. We want to shut down our part. Now go home. I mean it."

Judith was leaning out of the Chev. "If you're going to take a look around, why can't we come with you? We won't get in your way, we won't let out a peep."

Joe shook his head. "That's against police procedure. We don't allow citizens to tag along on a homicide investigation. You heard me, go home."

"Hey, Woody," Renie called out. "Did you see that the local opera company is going to do *Trovatore* set in Iraq? Manrico and Azucena will be Kuwaiti spies."

Woody, who was now standing by the white sedan, gave a start. His passion for opera was as great as Renie's and had helped forge a bond between Joe's partner and Judith's cousin. "What? They can't be serious!"

"That's what I hear," Renie said, nodding sagely. "You won't believe what they plan for *Tristan und Isolde*."

Horrified, Woody walked up to the Chev. "Now wait a minute—nobody should mess around with Wagner, especially not *Tristan*. Oh, I know they do some peculiar things with the *Ring*, but . . ."

"Isolde is on a bus," Renie interrupted. "She's going to Salinas to meet her future husband, who's a wealthy lettuce farmer. The bus driver is . . ."

"Stop!" Woody put his hands over his ears. "You've got to be making this up!"

"Would I?" Renie wore her middle-aged ingenue's expression.

With his arms folded across his chest, Joe regarded his partner, his wife, and his cousin-in-law with exasperation.

"Come on, let's go. We've got work to do."

Renie jumped out of the car. "I'll tell you about it while we go inside the hotel, Woody. According to Melissa Bargroom, the local music critic, who just happens to be a dear friend of mine, from now on, all the operas will be presented in a different setting and time period. Faust becomes a dentist in Milwaukee, and Mephistopheles is a patient who needs a root canal . . ." Renie and Woody headed for the hotel entrance.

Joe glared at Judith. "You win. I didn't think Renie would pull such a cheap stunt."

"I didn't either," Judith agreed, falling in step with her husband. "But I'm glad she did. It's really silly of you to keep us from having a peek inside. After all, how else can I figure out what happened to Tara when she was pushed off the roof?"

"Oh, *that!*" Joe's voice was full of disgust. "I'd hoped you'd forgotten that nonsense."

Judith felt it was best not to argue. She kept quiet as they entered a much-abused freight elevator. While Renie and Woody lamented the state into which the local opera company allegedly had fallen, the cables groaned and the car creaked. At last they reached the top floor.

Joe led the way down a dingy corridor where the aged carpet was torn and the walls showed water damage. Electrical wiring dangled from the ceiling, piles of plaster littered the floor, and at least two doors had been ripped off of their hinges.

The door marked with crime scene tape was padlocked, however. The lock looked new, and Judith assumed it had been put in place by Joe and Woody. Sure enough, Joe unlocked it with a key that he had taken out of his pocket.

The room itself was spacious, with furnishings that had once been stylish and comfortable. But a patina of age and dust and decay had settled in over what Judith figured had once been a penthouse. Two bedrooms led from the sitting room which looked out onto a balcony. Judith had to restrain herself to keep from checking to see if it was the same balcony onto which Tara had been pushed.

"In here," Joe said, going into the bedroom on the left. "Harley was lying on that double bed. Half-lying, as if he'd fallen after he was stabbed."

"He never saw it coming," Judith murmured, suddenly overcome by the disc jockey's helplessness. "Dear me."

The bedroom was in approximately the same state of disintegration as the rest of the building, though the ceiling and walls were still intact. A couple of empty places where the rug looked cleaner and less worn indicated that someone had removed furniture.

"Did you take something out of here?" Judith asked, wincing at the dark stains on the carpet which she assumed were dried blood.

Joe shook his head. "Thieves, maybe. Whatever was in those spots was gone when we got here."

"The dust, the fallen plaster," Judith commented, studying the bed with its moth-eaten blanket. "Could you get footprints?"

"Dozens," Joe replied. "Transients, the demolition crew, whoever else has been around in the past month. We're still sorting through them."

"Where's the bedspread?" Renie was leaning against the wall next to a window that was covered by a tattered blue drape.

"We took that with us," Woody answered from his kneeling position by the bed. He held a powerful flashlight, which he played around the floor. "Possible hair and fibers, bloodstains. Not much help, though. Too many people over too long a time period have been here."

Judith moved quietly around the room, inspecting a dressing table, the closet, the bathroom. She found nothing unusual, only signs of deterioration and a hint of long-ago luxury. One item, however, caught her eye: It was an ordinary galvanized bucket that was almost filled with a gray, mushy substance.

"Plaster?" she asked as Joe joined her by the doors that led to the balcony.

Joe peered into the ten-gallon bucket. "No. It's some kind of ash. We noticed that earlier."

"Burning evidence?" Judith inquired, her eyes wide.

"Not likely," Joe responded, straightening up. "Some bum probably was trying to cook something and started a fire by accident. Whatever it is—was—it's completely destroyed."

Renie had returned to the sitting room. "Are you done?" she asked Judith with a trace of impatience. "I've got to get back to work. You can't say I haven't done my share by finessing Woody into a free pass."

"I appreciate it," Judith said and meant it. "But I'm afraid it hasn't done much good. It looks as if Joe and Woody are just going through the motions before they sign off on the building. I'm sure they made a thorough search of this place earlier."

"Of course." Renie made a fidgety gesture with one hand. "Let's hit it then. We *are* parked illegally."

"I think we're safe from being arrested," Judith responded, going to the Fench doors that led onto the balcony. "I wonder . . ."

Joe and Woody came out of the bedroom. "Okay, it's a wrap," Joe announced, then eyed his partner questioningly. "Unless you want to check the other bedroom one last time?"

Woody, who was still looking pained over Renie's operatic report, glumly allowed that he'd have a look. "It never hurts to be sure," he said in a morose tone that would have done a spurned baritone proud.

Judith pointed to the balcony. "You looked out there?"

Joe nodded. "We didn't find anything. We didn't expect to. It was latched from the inside. We checked the roof, too." He avoided Judith's eyes. "Nothing, except what you'd expect to find on an old roof."

The latch to the balcony was simple. Judith opened one

of the two doors and stepped outside. As she'd figured, the Naples Hotel rose a couple of floors above the Belmont on the far side. This was the balcony where Tara had fallen; it was a remarkably short drop.

"So the doors were latched when you came here Monday to find the body?" Judith inquired, still standing on the balcony.

"Yes." Joe was pacing the sitting room. Renie was halfway out into the hall. Woody remained in the second bedroom. "We don't think Harley came in through the balcony, if that's what you're implying," Joe added.

"Why not?" Judith asked the question while poking around in the rubble on the balcony floor.

"Because it doesn't make sense," Joe replied easily. "Would a blind man jump off a roof onto a balcony and get inside that way? Or would he come through the main entrance, which apparently wasn't secure?"

"Why come in at all?" Judith called over her shoulder.

"It has the makings of a drug deal gone wrong," Joe answered and then swore under his breath. "Pretend you didn't hear that."

Judith didn't have to pretend. Something had caught her eye among the pieces of tar paper and bird droppings and dirt. It wasn't much, just a chunk of dull green glass. On a whim, she slipped it into the pocket of her slacks and came back inside.

"Okay, I'm done," she declared just as Woody returned from the second bedroom.

"So am I," he said.

The quartet headed for the elevator. Joe didn't bother to lock up, and instead pocketed the padlock. "We're finished. That's official. They can wreck the damned place now." He poked Judith in the ribs. "Are you satisfied?"

Judith smiled, albeit a trifle weakly. "Oh, yes. Thank you. My curiosity must have gotten the better of me."

"No kidding," Joe said drolly, getting into the rickety elevator. "You don't want a souvenir?"

Judith patted the pocket of her blue cotton slacks. "I've got one."

"What is it?" Joe looked faintly amused.

"This." Judith removed the chunk of glass and held it out in front of her. "It was on the balcony."

Joe, Woody, and Renie all gave the fragment a cursory look. "A piece of a cheap wine bottle?" Joe remarked with a glance at Woody.

"Maybe," Woody replied. "It looks old and dirty. It might have come off of a paperweight or it could be one of those electrical transformer things."

Joe chuckled. "Whatever it is, it belongs to my dear wife. She's had her fun, now she can go home and run the B&B."

Judith heard the condescending note in Joe's voice and started to bristle. Instead, she put the glass back in her pocket and patted it again. The rugged bulge felt comforting, though Judith didn't know why. Maybe it was a symbol of her small victory over Joe. Maybe it was a sop to her sentimental nature.

Maybe it was nothing at all.

Maybe it was much more.

"Wow!" Judith exclaimed, admiring the view from the sixth floor of Belgravia Gardens. "You can see all over the city and across the bay and to the mountains on the other side."

"You could see more if it weren't so cloudy," Arlene noted. "It's going to rain. I suppose our summer is over."

Arlene was not a native Pacific Northwesterner, and didn't share Judith's aversion to warm weather. "It'll clear off in a couple of days," Judith said idly as she explored the master bedroom with its fireplace and sunken Jacuzzi. "These condos have everything. No wonder the asking price is a million dollars."

"It's nine hundred thousand for this one," Arlene said. "Of course the annual maintenance fee isn't included in the asking price. The only unit that actually went for a million was the penthouse Bascombe de Tourville bought.''

''The view would be even better up there on the tenth floor,'' Judith remarked as they wandered into the state-of-the-art kitchen with its marble countertops and hardwood floor. ''Did you say you don't know how de Tourville made his money?''

''That's right, I don't.'' Arlene flipped on the recessed lights. ''Regular oven, convection oven, microwave, dishwasher, trash compactor, garbage disposal, dishwasher, security monitor.'' She poked a button and turned on a small screen that was discreetly placed by the telephone. ''Look, you can see the lobby.''

Judith peered at the monitor. The color transmission was excellent. ''This is better than the one at the bank. Everybody there looks like they're standing in front of a funhouse mirror. I always feel like I weigh three hundred pounds and I'm deformed.''

''Yes, it's no wonder they never catch the bank robbers,'' Arlene agreed. ''They don't look the least like they do in real life. Oh, see there—someone is coming in.''

Judith watched the screen, which showed a woman entering the lobby. She was tall and dark and slim with a graceful, confident walk. Judith gasped.

''That's Tara Novotny! Come on, Arlene, let's head her off!'' Judith dashed for the front door.

''What?'' Arlene was still at the monitor. ''Here, you can see an exterior of the building. There's a cab pulling away, and here comes Corinne Dooley down the street in her van with some of the kids. Now which ones are with her . . . ?''

Judith was at the elevators, willing one of the two cars to hurry. Noiselessly, one set of gilded doors slid open. No one was inside. Judith swore under her breath. Tara must have taken the other elevator.

The lobby was empty, as Judith had feared. There was

no indicator to show at which floors the cars stopped. The elevators opened directly into each condo unit. Feeling forlorn, Judith spotted the mailboxes, two rows of five, set into the wall above a brocade-covered bench.

The only name she recognized was that of Bascombe de Tourville in Unit Ten. Mentally, she crossed off the retired military man and the two interior decorators. That left six other possibilities, not counting de Tourville.

Arlene came out of the elevator, wearing a frown. "Really, Judith, I can't think why you tore off in such a hurry! You hadn't seen the storage space."

Judith started to explain, then thought better of it. Arlene would ask a million questions, which Judith didn't feel like answering. Instead, Judith asked one of her own:

"Do you know if any of these residents have a connection with the fashion or apparel business?" She waved a hand at the mailboxes.

Dutifully, Arlene scanned the names. Judith's long-time friend and neighbor's knowledge of Heraldsgate Hill was legendary. Arlene's grapevine was so all-encompassing and her manner of dispensing information so efficient that Judith referred to this carefully cultivated network as the ABS—or Arlene's Broadcasting System.

"The Blumes on four are both lawyers, Devlin and Keel on two have something to do with computers and may or may not be married, here's General and Mrs. Bidwell, the interior designers—oh, I didn't realize it was Kain with a K—and this Witherspoon on nine is a retired broker who supposedly was a bookie on the side." Arlene grimaced. "I'm sorry, I don't know the other three. They may have moved here from somewhere else."

"You left out de Tourville," Judith noted. "I still don't understand. Did you say you knew how he made his money?"

Arlene ran an agitated hand through her red-gold curls. "Did I? Did I say—well. I'm not sure. Oh!" Her blue eyes lighted up. "He travels! That was it!"

Judith was growing impatient. "That's not a career, it's an avocation. What do you mean?"

"He's gone a lot," Arlene replied breezily. "Or so I hear. Does it matter as long as he keeps up the payments?"

"I guess not." Judith went over to the phone which was installed in an alcove near the door. "I have to call Joe."

Arlene looked at her watch. "Couldn't you do that at home? I really should run. I need to get the condo key back to Cathy before they close the real estate office. It's going on five now."

Judith hesitated. "Okay, go ahead. I'll walk. It's downhill."

Arlene's protests were feeble. A minute later, she was on her way, while Judith dialed Joe's number at work.

"I've found Tara," she said excitedly into the phone.

"There's no Ivan Taro here," the harsh voice said at the other end, and slammed down the receiver.

Judith made a face, then dialed Joe's number again. The same man answered. Judith asked if Joe was in. He wasn't. Judith decided to wait for Tara, and took up her watch on the brocade-covered bench. It was a quarter to five; she could spend a half-hour at Belgravia Gardens without detriment to her guests or the dinner hour. With any luck, Joe might get home early. She'd try to call him at Hillside Manor before she left the condos.

For the next thirty minutes, the only person Judith saw in the lobby was an older woman with a Dandie Dinmont on a leash. At five-twenty, Judith dialed her own number. The standard recording reached her ear. Apparently, Joe wasn't home yet. Torn between her household duties and abandoning her post in the lobby, Judith fretted. On a whim, she picked up the private condo line and dialed Unit Ten.

A man with a smooth, faintly accented voice answered.

Judith asked if Tara was available. The man hesitated, then said that there was no Tara at that number.

"Is this Mr. de Tourville?" Judith inquired.

"Yes," the man responded with what Judith thought was a trace of wariness. "Who is this, please?"

"This is Mrs. Flynn," Judith said in her friendliest manner. "I'm trying to reach my cleaning woman, Mrs. Rackley. I believe she also works for you. She accidentally left my house the other day with my address book. Is she there now by any chance?"

"No," de Tourville replied, no longer wary but aloof. "She comes but once a week, on Thursday."

"Oh!" Judith tried to sound both excited and pitiable. "She was there yesterday! I'm sure she must have left the address book then. That's when I missed it. Would you mind if I came up?"

"Yes," de Tourville answered. "I'm quite busy. Nor have I seen this lost address book. Tell me this—if you believed that the cleaning woman left this item, why did you ask for a person named Tara?"

"Tara?" Judith was flummoxed. "Well . . . Ah, did I say *Tara*? That was the name of my previous cleaning woman, Tara . . ." Judith glanced at her surroundings for inspiration. "Tara Brocade. Goodness, my mind must have been playing tricks on me!"

"It was playing tricks, yes," de Tourville remarked dryly. "If, by some remote chance, this address book turns up, I shall have a messenger deliver it. Where do you live? And how did you get into the condominium lobby?"

Nervously, Judith glanced around, trying to find the security camera. Now subdued, she recited her address. "I came with a realtor," Judith said, telling yet another lie. "My husband and I may buy the vacant condo on the sixth floor."

There was a slight pause on the other end. Judith figured that Bascombe de Tourville was trying to decide whether or not Judith was telling the truth—or if she was just plain wacko. "I see," he finally said. "Good luck to you. And goodbye." He clicked off.

Aware that she was probably still being observed on the security monitor, Judith forced herself to exit Belgravia Gardens at a leisurely pace. But as soon as she got out of range on the sidewalk, she half-ran to the corner, slowing only when she started the steep downhill descent. Turning onto her own street and then into the cul-de-sac, she saw no sign of Joe's MG. When she reached the kitchen, she tried to call him again at work. This time she was told that he had just left. Judith gritted her teeth in annoyance and faced the stove.

She was tossing a green salad when the front doorbell rang. Assuming it was some of her B&B guests, Judith put on her brightest smile. It dimmed when she recognized Esperanza Highcastle, dressed in an Argentinean gaucho costume.

"Where's my husband?" Esperanza demanded in an autocratic tone, barging into the entry hall.

Taken aback, Judith stammered, "You mean T-T-TNT?"

"I mean my husband," Esperanza repeated, scrutinizing the Victorian hat rack, the maple stand with the B&B guest book, the staircase, the door that led to the downstairs bathroom. "I know he's here. He called from this number this morning."

"He's gone," Judith replied, recovering her aplomb. "He left fairly early. I haven't seen him since yesterday."

Esperanza prowled the hallway, frowning under the brim of her hat. Black trousers billowed over black boots, and a brightly striped poncho swung from her shoulders. Judith guessed that the wide silver belt that flashed at her visitor's waist was made of real coins.

"Do you mean you don't know where he is now?" Esperanza wheeled on Judith. In her high-heeled boots, she stood close to six feet, a strapping, handsome woman with hard gray eyes and prematurely gray hair.

"No, I don't know where he is," Judith said firmly. "He spent the night and left, as I told you."

"A bed and breakfast," Esperanza said, not looking at Judith, but shaking her head. "He refused to stay in B&Bs while we were together. Too 'femmy,' he called them. Why here? Why now?" She spoke as if Judith weren't present.

Judith kept quiet. Esperanza continued to roam around the entry hall, then went into the living room. "Books. A piano. A jigsaw puzzle. A bay window with floral cushions. All the things that Tino hates. Who would have thought it?"

The doorbell rang again. This time it was two of Judith's expected guests, a middle-aged couple from Oregon. Judith murmured her excuses to an unresponsive Esperanza and went through the ritual of welcome. Ten minutes later, after the Oregonians had been shown to their room, Judith rejoined Esperanza in the living room.

"Would you care for some punch?" Judith asked, indicating the glasses and bowl on the gate-leg table. "I'm serving hors d'oeuvres in ten minutes."

"What?" Esperanza looked up sharply from the book cases she'd been inspecting. "Oh—no, certainly not. I must go." She sailed past Judith, heading for the entry hall.

Seeing the guest book, Esperanza waved a gloved hand. "He didn't sign in. How like him! How were you paid? His credit cards have been canceled and he has no money."

"Actually, he—" Judith began, but her visitor interrupted.

"Never mind." Esperanza opened the front door with a sweeping gesture. She snapped her fingers, the effect almost lost because of the kidskin gloves. "The Belmont! Maybe he's there!"

With a flash of silver coins and a click of high-heeled leather boots, Esperanza was gone.

ELEVEN

JUDITH HAD CHASED after Esperanza, but the other woman refused to turn around and had driven off in a sleek pearl-colored Lexus. Standing at the edge of the cul-de-sac, Judith was still panting a bit when Joe pulled into the driveway.

"Esperanza Highcastle was here looking for TNT and she says he's gone to the Belmont and I saw Tara Novotny come into Belgravia Gardens where I think she's staying with Bascombe de Tourville." The words tumbled out so fast that Joe drew back and put up his hands.

"Jude-girl! Is this a riddle? What's a Bascombe Etc.? How many times do I have to tell you to let me get inside the house and unwind before you hit me with a bunch of crazy stuff?" Shaking his head, he turned towards the back porch just as the first drops of rain began to fall.

"It's not crazy," Judith called after her husband. "Don't you want to find Tara?"

"At six o'clock after a long, hard day?" Joe was now inside the house with Judith on his heels. He got as far as the shelf that held the liquor before he spoke again. "Damn. Yes, I do." Carefully, he closed the cupboard door. "Okay. Where is she?"

"At Belgravia Gardens. At least she was there less than an hour ago." Judith tried to look apologetic. "I went there with Arlene to see the vacant condo, and by chance, I . . ."

Joe put a finger against Judith's lips. "I'm going."

"Can I come?" Judith tried not to sound too eager.

"No." Joe was emphatic. "What about your guests?"

"Oh!" Judith winced. "I forgot. The hors d'oeuvres."

During the next twenty minutes, Judith served her guests their appetizers and delivered Gertrude's dinner. Gertrude declared that green salad and tacos weren't dinner, but animal fodder. What next, Judith's mother demanded? Frozen borscht on a stick? Judith tried to be patient, then made an obligatory pass by the hedge, but saw no sign of Uncle Gurd. Maybe Arlene was feeding him. Over the weekend, a solution would have to be found for the unwelcome guest.

When Joe returned just before six-thirty, Judith had poured him a Scotch on the rocks. Joe needed it. He hadn't made contact with Bascombe de Tourville nor had he found Tara Novotny.

"So who's this Bascombe guy?" Joe asked, hanging his holster on the back of the kitchen chair. "I never heard of him."

Judith made herself a small drink while she explained the connection with Phyliss and the tour by Arlene. "It was pure chance. Arlene says de Tourville travels a lot. Maybe he's involved with the fashion industry."

Joe looked thoughtful. "That might make sense. Now Tara's holed up with this guy instead of living in her own place up by the hospitals. Maybe they're lovers, maybe they're in business, maybe . . . who knows? I've contacted the squad, and they'll stake out the condos."

"So you are interested in Tara as a witness," Judith remarked in what she hoped was a casual tone.

Joe grimaced. "It could be that she was the last person to see Harley alive—besides the murderer."

Judith kept her expression impassive. It wouldn't do to let Joe know that she felt a sense of victory. Her husband appeared to be acknowledging that she had actually seen Harley and Tara on the roof of the Belmont.

"At least she hasn't left town," Judith said encouragingly. She waited a few moments while Joe sipped his drink. "Let me tell you what Esperanza said about where she thought TNT had gone."

Joe held his head as Judith recited the part about the possibility that the ex-boxer had gone to the Belmont. "Why?" Joe moaned. "Why the Belmont?"

"There must be something . . . that was overlooked," Judith gulped, not wanting to suggest that her husband and his partner had been derelict in their duty. "It seems that the hotel is a magnet."

"The hotel is history, as of Monday," Joe sighed. "We gave the go-ahead for them to use the wrecking ball. Damn!"

"Can't you rescind it?" Judith asked quietly.

"I suppose." Joe drummed his nails on the table. "The last thing the city needs is a lawsuit because we held up a big bucks construction project."

"You have tomorrow and Sunday," Judith pointed out.

"Great. There goes the weekend." Joe took a big swallow of Scotch.

"We had no plans." Judith smiled thinly. "It's raining."

"It's raining all over my investigation." Wearily, Joe stood up. "I'll call Woody. *He* planned to take Sondra and the kids to the zoo."

"The zoo's not much fun in the rain," Judith said with what she hoped was a note of consolation.

Joe was at the phone. "This case is a zoo."

Judith kept mum, arranging the taco condiments in small bowls. Even if she had tried, she couldn't help but overhear her husband's half of the telephone conversation.

"I'll check out de Tourville . . . You finish up with the

banks? What? I'll be damned . . . How much? I wonder
. . . Yeah, I went through his apartment again this afternoon . . . Nothing of interest in today's mail . . . No, definitely no dog. That Mims kid said Harley refused to use
a seeing-eye dog . . . No, nothing. So much nothing that
it makes me suspicious . . . Okay, see you tomorrow
around nine. Yeah, tell Sondra I'm sorry, too.''

"Banks?" Judith said innocently. "Harley's banks?"

"Two of them." With a slight groan, Joe sat down at
the kitchen table and rescued his Scotch. "Both accounts
were cleaned out Thursday. That's odd in and of itself,
but what's really strange is that Harley had only a total
of four grand in the two accounts." Joe seemed to be
speaking more to himself than to Judith.

"That's not odd by *my* standards," Judith noted. "We
don't have four grand in the bank right now, not after
paying the June income tax quarterly."

Joe's response was to bury his nose in the evening paper. Judith served dinner, and refrained from discussing
the case until the end of the meal.

"Were you planning to go on the stakeout at Belgravia
Gardens this evening?" she asked in the same tone of
voice she would have used to inquire if her husband intended to watch TV.

"No." Joe handed his empty plate to Judith. "We can
ID Tara, but not this de Tourville. You haven't seen him,
I take it?"

Judith admitted that she had not. "But," she added
hopefully, "Phyliss has. Shall I call her and get a description?"

Reluctantly, Joe admitted it was probably a good idea.
Phyliss, however, proved a dubious witness:

"He's kind of tall, but not as tall as my cousin, Klepto.
He's not really fat, in fact, he's sort of skinny, except on
top. His hair is dark—well, not dark, maybe, so much as
gray streaks. I didn't notice his eyes. He wore sunglasses.''

Judith rubbed at her temple. "In other words . . ." If there were other words, they failed her. "There's nothing unusual about him? Nothing . . . noticeable?"

"He's spiffy," Phyliss replied. "I mean, I *guess* he's spiffy. I'm not one for these big, baggy suits. But he wears a tie, one of them big wide kinds with all the flowers. Oh, he has a mustache and a funny little beard."

"A goatee?" Judith suggested.

"That's it. I think."

Judith relayed the scanty information to Joe, who winced. "I'll pass it along to the stakeout crew. The goatee helps, if it is a goatee."

Twenty minutes later, Judith had finished clearing away the dinner things as well as the remnants of her guests' appetizer hour. Joe, who again had been in contact with the officers at Belgravia Gardens, remained at the kitchen table reading the paper.

Judith put an affectionate hand on her husband's shoulder. "Let's go for a walk. I could use some fresh air."

Joe twisted around to regard his wife with suspicion. "We never go for a walk. There're too many hills in this neighborhood."

"That's why it'd be fun." Judith gave Joe's shoulder a little squeeze. "Not the hilly part, but just looking around our own neighborhood and . . ."

"We're not going to Belgravia Gardens." Joe resumed reading the paper.

Judith put both hands on Joe's shoulders. "Uncle Gurd is missing. We should look for him."

"He's not our responsibility." Joe didn't move.

Judith gently massaged Joe's neck and shoulders. "We could take Sweetums for a run. He needs the exercise."

"Sweetums is a cat. He prowls all over the place." Joe sighed and put the paper down. "I'm going to watch the baseball game. I'm tired and I have to work tomorrow. Lay off, Jude-Girl."

During the top of the second inning, Judith quietly exited the cozy family retreat on the third floor, descended the backstairs, and went outside. The rain was soft yet steady, typical Pacific Northwest weather that made "damp" not merely a description, but an element. Judith, as a typical native, didn't bother with a jacket or an umbrella. It was warm, perhaps in the high sixties, and she wouldn't really get wet. Thus, she stood on the small patio, gazing up at the face of Heraldsgate Hill and Belgravia Gardens.

There were no lights in the penthouse, but at seven-thirty in late June, the sun wouldn't set for another two hours. Judith was about to head down the drive when her mother appeared in the doorway of the converted tool-shed.

"Where's my ice cream?" Gertrude demanded.

"Oh!" Judith put a hand to her mouth. "We're out. I forgot to get more at the store." She had given the last of the blackberry ribbon to her mother the previous evening.

"*What*?" Gertrude shrieked. "*No ice cream?* First I get grass clippings and a bunch of junk piled in a big cracker, and now there's *no ice cream*? Why don't you just put me in a home and throw away the key?"

"I'll drive up to Falstaff's right now," Judith promised. "What kind would you like?"

"Tutti-frutti," Gertrude answered promptly, her outrage evaporating. "Sometimes it makes me more tutti than frutti, but what the hey? Say," she said, her small eyes narrowing, "you didn't feed my ice cream to that goofy old coot in the hedge, did you?"

"Ahhh . . ." Judith could tell all sorts of fibs to other people, her husband included, but she often stalled when confronted by her mother. "There wasn't much left yesterday. I saved the blackberry ribbon for you."

"Hunh." Gertrude tapped a carpet-slippered foot. "You better get that nut case out of here. I saw him running around in his underwear the other day, and it wasn't a pretty sight, I can tell you.''

"I'd like to get rid of him," Judith admitted. "Have you seen him this afternoon?"

Gertrude shook her head. "Not since yesterday. In fact, I could sit here in this piano crate of an apartment all day and never see anybody, now that Vivian's out of town."

Judith always marveled at the friendship that had developed between her mother and Joe's ex-wife. Perhaps it was perversity on Gertrude's part, perhaps it was genuine affection—either way, Herself provided occasional companionship for the older woman, and Judith was grudgingly grateful.

"She's in Florida," Judith said absently, scanning the hedge anew for any sign of Uncle Gurd. "I don't think she'll be gone too long."

"Florida!" harumphed Gertrude. "Why would she go there with all the alligators and crocodiles and dope smugglers? I know, I watch TV."

"It's something to do with her condo," Judith responded, starting for the garage. "I'll be back in a few minutes. Is there anything else you need at the store?"

"Can you buy me a new gizzard? Or some good legs or better ears or eyes that can see farther than my bazooms?" Gertrude gave a sad shake of her head. "Never mind, kiddo. Ice cream and maybe some of those chocolate-covered peanuts. I'm not fussing over *my* figure. Who'd want to look like that bean pole who was here this morning?"

Pivoting on her heel, Judith stared at her mother. "What bean pole?"

Gertrude shrugged the hunched shoulders that were covered by a blue and orange cardigan. "One of your guests, who else? She and that knothead who was sleeping in your car took off at the crack of dawn. Didn't you see 'em leave?"

"No," Judith said in wonder as she took a quick mental

inventory of the visitors who had stayed at Hillside Manor Thursday night. None of the women could be described as a bean pole. "I must have been upstairs on the second floor. Did this woman have short black hair?"

"What?" Gertrude had turned vague. "What woman?"

"The bean pole." Judith exuded patience. "The woman who left with Mr. Tenino."

"Mr. Tenino?" Gertrude looked genuinely puzzled. "Is he the weirdo who runs around in his imagination?"

"No," Judith said, hanging onto her now-ebbing patience. "That's Uncle Gurd. Mr. Tenino is the man who was resting in my car. Now tell me about the bean pole."

"What bean pole?" Gertrude scowled at her daughter. "I don't know siccum about any bean poles. Where's my ice cream?"

Judith emitted a big sigh. "Okay, I'm off to the store." Maybe Gertrude would remember more by the time Judith got back.

After pulling onto the main thoroughfare, Judith took a short detour past Belgravia Gardens. To the right of the main entrance, she saw the grillwork of the basement garage. Across the street and almost at the corner, she noticed a man and a woman in an unmarked city car. After going around the next block, she again drove slowly by the elegant condos. As far as she could tell, there were only two ways to get out of the building, through the main entrance or from the basement garage. Tara Novotny and Bascombe de Tourville couldn't possibly come or go without being seen by the stakeout duo. Judith felt reassured, but she couldn't resist pulling into a loading zone across from Belgravia Gardens.

Through the rain that spattered the windshield, she peered upwards to the condos' top floor. All seemed quiet. Had Tara and de Tourville left during the hour interval after she had gone home and before the plainclothes officers had arrived? It was possible, of course. Or perhaps they weren't answering either the phone or the intercom.

"My call from the lobby may have spooked them," Judith told Renie over the pay phone at Falstaff's. She had explained her visit with Arlene, and the subsequent sighting of Tara. "What really bothers me is that blasted Belmont. I think it holds the answer to this whole, crazy mystery."

"So let Joe figure it out," Renie said, sounding exasperated. "I'm working, coz. I have a deadline, remember?"

"I thought you might ride with me to the Belmont so we could take another look," Judith said in her meekest voice.

"No!" Renie exploded. "Absolutely *not*. I've had enough of the Belmont. I thought you did, too. What good did it do to go there this afternoon?"

"That was before Esperanza showed up at the B&B," Judith said, turning mulish. "She thought TNT had gone there. Why?"

"Because it's a free flop," Renie responded. "Now hang up and let me finish this wretched project."

Judith had no choice. When she returned with the ice cream, Gertrude still couldn't remember anything about a bean pole. Judith gave up on her mother, too. Feeling futile, she crept upstairs to the third floor and joined Joe in watching the ball game. If he'd noticed that his wife had been gone for awhile, he didn't mention it. Judith was beginning to feel like a cipher.

And then she thought of O. P. Dooley, and her spirits rose. Oliver Plunkett Dooley was a younger brother of Judith's former paper boy and erstwhile sleuth-in-training. The large, extended family not only lived in back of Hillside Manor, but just under the brick and granite eminence of Belgravia Gardens. When Dooley, as Aloysius Gonzaga was more familiarly known, had gone away to college, he had bequeathed his telescope to his brother. On a previous occasion, O. P.'s aptitude for spying on the neighbors had proved beneficial in tracking down a murderer. Judith decided it was time to put O. P. back to work.

Calling on the Dooley ménage required walking to the entrance of the cul-de-sac, going around the west side of the block, and ending up at the far corner. As ever, the Dooleys' front yard was strewn with trikes, bikes, and all manner of playthings. Corinne Dooley, an amazingly placid woman who never seemed disturbed or dismayed by domestic crises, was swaying gently in a lawn swing on the front porch.

"Judith," she said with genuine pleasure. "How are you? I didn't get a chance to really talk to you at Mike's wedding reception. It was lovely."

"Thanks," Judith replied as two small children zipped out through the front door and chased each other around the yard. "Is O. P. home?"

"I think so," Corinne replied, paying no heed to the little boy and little girl who were now rolling around in an uncovered sandbox that had been turned to mud. "Try the downstairs den. Or his room." O. P.'s mother evinced no curiosity over Judith's reason for calling on the boy. No doubt, Judith thought as she made her way through the cluttered house, Corinne's children and grandchildren had been called upon by many people throughout the years. If it was trouble, Corinne would hear about it later. If it wasn't, then it didn't matter. Either way, the Dooley matriarch took whatever came in stride. Her equanimity amazed Judith.

There were several children in the downstairs den, but none of them was O. P. Judith trudged back up the stairs and made her way to the second floor. Zigzagging between piles of laundry, both dirty and clean, Judith stepped over a wary hamster and peeked into the open door that she had figured must belong to O. P. Sure enough, the boy was sitting on his bed, playing a video game.

"Mrs. Flynn!" O. P. exclaimed in a startled voice. "What's up?"

"How would you like to do some detective work?" Judith asked with a conspiratorial air.

O. P.'s blue eyes grew wide. "Like that other time, when Mrs. Goodrich got whacked with the axe?"

The reference to a grisly neighborhood murder that Judith had helped solve made her grimace. "Like that. Except this time it wasn't an axe."

"Wow!" O. P. popped off the video game and perched on his knees. "Who was it? Somebody around here?"

Judith shook her head. "It was that disc jockey, Harley Davidson. Did you ever listen to him on KRAS-FM?"

At thirteen, O. P. was into the local music scene. "Sure. I heard he got killed, but not exactly how. What happened?"

Judith started to explain, but was interrupted by the arrival of Dooley himself. "I didn't realize you were home from college," Judith exclaimed, giving the older boy a hug.

Dooley, who was now well over six feet and beginning to fill out, gamely hugged Judith back. "I got out of school a couple of weeks ago, but I went camping with some friends for a few days. I got home Wednesday. Don't tell me you're tracking down another killer?"

Somewhat to her chagrin, Judith admitted that indeed she was. "Mr. Flynn's working on it, too," she clarified. "But some of the suspects may be in this neighborhood."

Clearly intrigued, the Dooley brothers eyed each other. "Wild," Dooley breathed. "Who is it this time? Mr. and Mrs. Rankers?"

Judith couldn't help but laugh. "No, but Arlene—Mrs. Rankers—was with me today when I spotted one of the witnesses. We were at Belgravia Gardens, going through the vacant condo, and . . ."

As Judith's tale unfolded, her eyes strayed to O. P.'s windows. He had a corner room, and while one window looked out over the cul-de-sac, the other faced the hill behind the Dooley and Flynn houses. Belgravia Gardens' imposing facade looked straight down onto the Dooley property.

"So what I was wondering," Judith concluded after a lengthy recital that was interrupted by many questions from both boys, "is if you could see into the top floor of those condos with your telescope."

O. P. jumped off the bed and went over to the telescope which was positioned in front of the back window. "The angle's going to be tough," he said, peering through the lens and making some adjustments. "Gee, I think the building's too tall. Maybe if we moved the telescope into the attic, we could see better."

"That's a lot of trouble," Judith said, but her quibble ceased when O. P. and Dooley insisted on giving it a try.

"Some of the littler kids sleep up here," Dooley noted as they ascended a narrow wooden staircase that smelled of camphor wood. "Don't trip over anything. It might be one of the kids."

As far as Judith could tell, there were no children rolling around on the attic floor. The dormer room that looked up onto Belgravia Gardens was filled with clothes, toys, and unmade beds. The brothers eased the telescope into place, and O. P. took a look.

"Way cool," O. P. murmured. "All these people must be rich. I watched this place being built, and that was pretty cool, too. Mrs. Rankers came over to look through it a couple of times. She said she was keeping track of stuff for her daughter, the real estate lady."

"That's what she said, huh?" Judith smirked, then caught herself. She, too, was snooping, and had no right to criticize Arlene. "Well? What about the penthouse?"

"You mean the top floor?" O. P. still had his eye glued to the telescope. "I can see in—sort of. The angle's still not real good. Lots of fancy furniture, but no people. Here, have a look."

Judith affixed her eye to the lens. She saw the antiques or antique reproductions that Phyliss had mentioned. The living room appeared beautifully, if lavishly, decorated. Two other, smaller windows also faced south, but the drapes were pulled. Like O. P., she saw no activity of any kind.

"I'll bet they left," Judith said, more to herself than to the boys. "But they'll have to come back. Or will they?" She stood by the telescope, tapping a finger against her cheek.

"Do you want us to keep a watch on the place?" O. P. asked eagerly. "Now that school's out, I've got lots of time."

"Sure," Judith replied, though she wasn't certain what good it would do. The stakeout was in effect. But after the initial rush of freedom, no doubt O. P. was already growing bored with summer vacation. "The man who lives there is named Bascombe de Tourville, and although I haven't seen him . . ." Judith did her best with Phyliss's sketchy description, but painted a more precise picture of Tara Novotny. For good measure, she threw in TNT Tenino. "There are two officers watching the condos," Judith noted. "If Tara and de Tourville left before the stakeout personnel arrived, they'll be intercepted when they try to get back inside."

O. P. nodded solemnly. "Got it," he said.

Judith and Dooley left O. P. at his post. "I used to listen to Harley Davidson all the time before I went away to college," Dooley said as they maneuvered the narrow stairway. "He was one wild guy."

"Did you ever see him in person?" Judith inquired.

"Once. It was a rock concert at one of the downtown theaters. Harley was outrageous. It was great." Dooley smiled at the memory.

Judith and Dooley were now heading for the main floor. "Did you know he was blind?" she asked.

"Blind? No! Wow, that's the bomb! He sure didn't act

like he was blind." Dooley stood on the landing, running a hand through his fair hair. "But then he didn't do anything except stand there and get down with the bass. After he surfaced on stage in the submarine, that is."

"I understand he was well paid for those gigs," Judith said as one of the two children who had been rolling around in the sandbox charged through the front door screaming.

"I guess," Dooley said, scooping up the screaming child. "Hey, Pius X, what's wrong? Did you hurt something, little buddy? Come on, Pix, tell your uncle all about it."

Never ceasing to be amazed at the saintly names and peculiar nicknames given to the Dooley brood, Judith exited to the front porch. Corinne was still swaying in the swing, looking blissfully unperturbed and seemingly unaware that the other small child was now naked and riding the dog around out on the sidewalk.

"Did you find O. P.?" she inquired with only a slight move of her head.

"Yes, thanks. Um . . ." Judith hesitated, one hand gesturing vaguely at the street. "Is it okay if . . . ?" Wincing, she let the words trail away.

"Everything's okay," Corinne replied, turning neither head nor hair. "Everything's always okay. See you in church, Judith."

Judith left. The child and the dog followed her to the corner, then stopped and turned back. Apparently, even the Dooleys had some sort of limits.

Or maybe the dog was better trained than the family.

Saturday morning, Joe left for work while Judith was serving breakfast to her guests. Ordinarily, he would have been out of the house for at least half an hour before the eight-thirty dining room call. But this was a weekend, and Joe wasn't inclined to push himself.

Neither he nor Judith had heard any news from their

respective lookouts. Consequently, Judith had to assume that de Tourville and Tara hadn't returned.

After her guests had left for the day, Judith felt at loose ends. She didn't dare pester Renie, in case her cousin was still working. It was still drizzling, which meant working in the yard was off-limits. Trying to track down the lost lavender dress after nearly a week seemed hopeless. Checking in with the Rundbergs about the wedding bills was daunting. Aside from the usual cleanup, Judith had nothing to do. She wandered around the long living room, pausing to put in a couple of jigsaw puzzle pieces.

Her eye strayed to the chunky envelope that held Mike and Kristin's wedding proofs. Maybe she should check some of her favorites now, before the honeymooners returned on Tuesday. Judith carried the packet over to one of the matching sofas and sat down.

There were at least two dozen photos that she felt she must keep. Some were at the rehearsal dinner, several were at the church, and most came from the reception. Judith smiled fondly at the shot of her son and his bride as they toasted each other over the family dining room table.

On a faintly wicked whim, she dialed Morris Mitchell's number. To her surprise, the photographer himself answered.

"My weekend receptionist's sick," he said tersely. "She gets sick every time it rains. She should never have moved here from California."

Briefly, Judith commiserated. "Say, Morris, could you send the bill to Kristin's parents? They're paying, and it seems silly that it should have to be forwarded through me."

"You signed for it," Morris pointed out, not unreasonably.

"Of course I did," Judith agreed. "But it's such a nuisance, and this way, you'll get your money sooner. I'll give you their address."

After the photographer had taken down the address of the Rundberg wheat ranch, Judith posed a question. "On the night of the rehearsal dinner, did you see anything unusual on the roof of the Belmont Hotel?"

"The Belmont Hotel?" Morris echoed, sounding surprised. "Is that what's next to the Naples? Hunh. Let me think. Why do you ask?"

Judith swallowed hard before offering her candid explanation. "Please don't think I'm crazy, Morris, but the night of the rehearsal dinner, I saw Tara Novotny and Harley Davidson on the Belmont roof. Some people—such as my husband—don't believe me. But they were there, still wearing their bridal gear from Mr. Artemis's fashion show at I. Magnifique."

"No kidding." To Judith's relief, Morris didn't sound surprised. "And not long after that, Harley gets whacked in Mr. Artemis's tux. You didn't see *that*, did you?" The photographer seemed amused.

"No," Judith admitted. "Did *you* see them?"

"Afraid not. I must have been shooting away from the windows. Damn, it would have made a good picture," Morris lamented. "You know, wedding couple inside, wedding couple outside. A double image. I wish you'd told me at the time."

"It all happened so quickly," Judith said, deciding it was pointless to mention having seen Harley push Tara off the roof. "I mean, they weren't there for more than a minute."

"Another photo op down the drain. Oh, well." Morris chuckled. "All I saw on that roof was a bunch of pigeon doo and some cigars."

Judith's grip on the phone tightened. "Cigars?"

"Yeah, about a half-dozen brand new cigars scattered around," Morris replied. "I've got an eye for detail, it's part of my work. But they didn't *say* anything, you know what I mean?"

"Yes, I think so," Judith said though she wondered if

the cigars said something that had nothing to do with visual aesthetics. "Why cigars? Where did they come from?"

"Maybe from Harley," Morris answered. "He liked cigars. He must have dropped them. Got to run, Mrs. Flynn. I'll send the bill to the Rundbergs. Meanwhile, try to get your bride and groom to return the proofs by Friday, okay? I'm off to Europe week after next and won't be back until the end of the month. See you."

Judith's mind flashed back to the rehearsal dinner. She heard herself nagging Joe about his inquiry outside of the Naples and Belmont hotels. She saw him shrugging off the queries, then lighting up a big fat cigar. He'd gotten it from Kobe, the Naples parking attendant. But where had Kobe gotten the cigar in the first place? And why hadn't the cigars still been on the Belmont roof when she and Renie had gone there with Joe and Woody?

Judith sensed that the cigar played some part in her little mystery. She was determined to find out how before everything went up in smoke.

TWELVE

FUELED BY A six-pack of Pepsi, Renie was hard at work in the basement den. "Go away," she mumbled when Judith appeared on the basement steps. "I'm busy."

"You need a break," Judith said, crossing through the one-time playroom that was now used mainly for storage. "Bill told me so."

"Bill would never say any such thing," Renie declared, still not looking up from her drawing board. "Good-bye."

"Morris Mitchell saw cigars," said Judith as Clarence, the Holland dwarf lop, sniffed at her shoes.

"Morris Mitchell can see visions of cigars, stars, and men on Mars for all I care," Renie snapped, glaring at her cousin. "Are you nuts? This is the first time you've ever barged in here to pester me while I'm up against a deadline. I'm about to get very angry."

"Don't. Please." Judith put on her most pathetic face. "I need to talk to somebody. Just for five minutes. Joe's working this weekend."

"So am I," Renie retorted, though her expression had softened a bit. "I don't know why you can't let this thing go. Joe and Woody are pros. If you keep meddling, Joe's going to blow a gasket."

"I've told you I have to vindicate myself," Judith said doggedly. "You *seemed* to understand. And if that vindication comes through figuring out who killed Harley, so be it."

Renie didn't look convinced. With a huge sigh of reluctance, she swiveled around in her chair. "Okay, you've got five minutes. But watch out for Clarence. He likes to get under foot."

Judith began by telling Renie that Joe and Woody were going through the Belmont one more time, trying to figure out what seemed to make it such a magnet to various persons involved in the murder case. She touched lightly on her visit to the Dooley house, but emphasized Morris Mitchell's cigar sighting on the old hotel roof.

"That's the part that puzzles me most," Judith said in conclusion. "It suggests something, but I don't know what."

A casual listener might have dismissed Judith's statement, but Renie instinctively understood. If Judith felt the cigars were important, then they probably were. On several occasions Judith had figured out important clues from seemingly trivial items. Renie would give her cousin the benefit of a doubt.

"And Joe actually smoked one of these cigars the night of the rehearsal dinner?" Renie finally inquired.

As Clarence sat on her left foot, Judith nodded. "That is, he smoked *a* cigar. Kobe, the parking attendant, gave it to him."

Renie fiddled with a couple of drafting pencils. "Usually, cigars are handed out at the birth of babies or at bachelor parties. But not at rehearsal dinners, which, I understand, is what the Naples was hosting for much of June. No tie-in with cigars there. You haven't asked Joe, I take it?"

"I haven't seen him since I talked to Morris." Trying gently to shake Clarence loose, Judith leaned up against a tall filing cabinet. The bunny resisted, planting his own oversized hind paws firmly on each of Judith's shoes. "I suppose it's silly—Kobe had probably been given the cigar, and doesn't smoke, so he passed it on to Joe. But that doesn't explain why Morris saw several of them on the Belmont roof. Why were they there and where did they go?"

Renie was fingering her short chin. "The homeless don't bring cigars to their self-proclaimed shelter. But somebody like Harley or TNT or even Tara might. Women are into cigars these days."

"True." Judith glanced down at Clarence, who had finally hopped off of her person and was now circling her feet. His small, fluffy beige fur stood slightly on end, and he had one ear up and one ear down. "So Joe and Woody are going through the Belmont one last time, with a fine-toothed comb."

"Looking for cigars," Renie remarked rather absently. "Or something. Is that it?" She gazed up at Judith with narrowed brown eyes.

"You mean . . . Oh, am I done? Well, I guess so. You don't have any ideas?"

"Not about your little mystery. All my ideas are here." Renie tapped her drawing board. "The only thing I can say is that you actually have two mysteries, which may or may not have anything to do with each other. One is Harley's murder. The other is the Belmont itself."

Judith nodded eagerly. "That's so. But it's too much of a coincidence for the murder and whatever has been happening at the Belmont *not* to be tied in, right?"

"The people involved are tied in, yes," Renie replied somewhat impatiently. "Maybe Harley discovered what was going on at the old hotel. He had to be silenced."

Judith clapped her hands. "Yes! I hadn't thought of that slant. Brilliant, coz!" She reached out to grasp Renie's hand, and in the process, stepped on Clarence.

The rabbit let out a terrified cry, rolled over, and

thrashed about. Renie leaped from her chair and dove for Clarence, who had gone completely limp.

"Baby boy!" Renie shrieked in horror. "Darling bunny! Oh, Clarence! You're hurt! Help!"

Next to the filing cabinet, Judith stood as if frozen. "Coz! I feel terrible! I didn't mean to . . ."

But Renie had grabbed her cordless phone and was dialing frantically. "Get Bill," she ordered Judith. "Hurry!"

With a last glance at the motionless Clarence, Judith dashed upstairs. Bill, however, was nowhere to be found. A quick look outside showed that the Jones's Chev, which had been parked in front of the house when Judith arrived, was now gone. A shout up the stairs that led to the bedrooms brought no response. Apparently none of the Jones children were home. Judith hurried back to the basement where an agitated Renie was carefully placing the injured rabbit into a cardboard pet carrier.

"The regular vet is closed today," Renie moaned, almost in tears. "We'll have to take him to the emergency clinic across the canal."

" 'We'll'?" Judith echoed.

Renie's face hardened. "You got it. Bill's gone, right? You're the one who stepped on Clarence, you clumsy moron. You're the designated ambulance driver. Let's hit it."

Renie cradled the carrier all the way to the emergency pet clinic, meanwhile making soothing, cooing noises which were interspersed with heartfelt lamentations: "Clarence may have a broken back." "Clarence may be paralyzed." "Clarence may be dead."

Grimly, Judith remained silent. She felt wretched about hurting the bunny, but the poor thing wasn't exactly irreplaceable. Rabbits being what they were, there must be at least a thousand more Clarences in the city. By tomorrow, there'd be another thousand. They weren't an endangered species. Or, Judith thought with a guilty pang, maybe they were, with careless people stepping on them.

The receptionist said they could take Clarence right away, but tactfully told Renie and Judith to wait outside. It was very unusual for a rabbit to cry out, and often signaled the worst. Looking stricken, Renie began to pace the small waiting room.

"Coz," Judith finally said in a miserable voice, "I can't tell you how awful I feel. I remember when Sweetums was attacked by that dreadful dog, and I was afraid that he might not make it. But I kept telling myself that maybe we could find another cat. I realized then that even Sweetums isn't . . . um . . . ah . . . er . . ."

While Judith fumbled for words and Renie gave her cousin a baleful stare, a white-coated woman veterinarian came out of the examining room. "I'm Dr. Leone," she said in hushed tones. "I'm afraid I have bad news."

Renie blanched and gripped Judith's hand. "No! Oh, please!"

The vet nodded solemnly. "We can't find Clarence. He jumped off the examining table and he's hiding. Could you come back with us and see if you can lure him out into the open? He's extremely frisky. What have you been feeding him?"

Renie's expression changed from grief to pique. "Everything," she snapped. "That rabbit eats like a pig." Releasing Judith's hand, she marched off to the examining room.

Judith collapsed on the brown vinyl couch. She was experiencing the first wave of relief when the door opened and Darrell Mims appeared with a black and white mutt in his arms. Judith and Darrell exchanged startled looks.

"Ms. Flynn, right?" Darrell said. "Gee, what a surprise." His smile was thin as he proceeded to the reception desk.

His dog, Sound Bite, had gotten into a fight with a German Shepherd. A badly torn ear, an injured neck, and a chewed-up leg were the unfortunate results. Darrell explained this to the receptionist who made sympathetic noises, as much for the benefit of the owner as for the dog, and said it would be only a few minutes before Dr. Leone could see Sound Bite.

"Do you live around here?" Darrell asked as he sat down next to Judith on the couch.

Judith explained that she didn't, but that she and her cousin had come to the nearest emergency clinic. Darrell responded that he had an apartment just four blocks away, near one of the bridges that spanned the canal.

"This is where I usually bring Sound Bite," he added, gazing down at the dog, who was lying in his lap and whimpering. "Gosh, wouldn't you know it? Just when I was thinking that everything was going my way!"

"Oh?" Judith said with interest. "How is that?"

Despite his pet's discomfort, Darrell managed a grin. "I'm going on air Monday. They're giving me a trial run as Harley's replacement. Isn't that something?"

"That's wonderful," Judith declared with a warm smile of her own. "Were you surprised?"

Patting the dog, Darrell nodded. "I sure was. I'd begged Chuck Rawls for the chance, and he finally took my case to Ms. Highcastle. She gave the go-ahead, so now it's up to me."

Judith tried to imagine the drastic change from Harley Davidson to Blip Man. "You'll be doing a different . . . what do you call it? Format?"

Darrell nodded again, this time with so much vigor that Sound Bite began to howl. "You bet. I'm going in for a much softer sound, and none of that nasty, suggestive stuff. Boy, I can hardly wait."

The wait was over for Sound Bite. Dr. Leone reappeared with Renie in tow, holding the pet carrier and looking vexed.

"Clarence is fine," Renie announced. "Like most of our family, he tends to overdramatize himself."

"Where was he?" Judith asked, rising to her feet.

"In Dr. Leone's purse." Renie set the carrier down on the floor. It immediately began to move.

Feeling vaguely cross-eyed, Judith kept one eye on the carrier and the other on Renie, who was waiting for the bill. The receptionist whispered the amount softly, as if it were a secret password.

"Seventy-five dollars?" Renie shrieked. "What for? Clarence didn't require treatment. Are you crazy?"

The receptionist's expression was bland. "We still have to charge for an office call, and since this is an emergency situation, it's somewhat extra."

"*Somewhat?*" Renie was practically hopping up and down. So was the pet carrier, which had almost reached the front door. "A regular visit to Dr. Fine is ten bucks."

"This isn't Dr. Fine's clinic, it's Dr. Leone's," the receptionist replied with a touch of spirit. "If I were you, Mrs. Jones, I'd be thankful that you weren't charged for damages. Apparently, Clarence chewed through the strap on Dr. Leone's Gucci purse."

"Gucci!" Renie cried. "Sure, the vet can afford Gucci purses while I'm going to be reduced to carrying my stuff around in a paper sack."

Judith could see that the argument was going nowhere, but that Clarence was. The carrier had reached the door, and anyone coming through from outside would slam into the rabbit's transportation.

"Clarence is leaving," Judith announced, going over to the entrance to grab the cardboard box.

Renie swerved on her heels. "Oh, damn!" Sighing heavily, she rummaged in her handbag. "Okay, okay. I'll pay, but I'm not happy about it."

The receptionist looked smug. "Thank you, Mrs. Jones. I knew you'd see reason. By the way, Dr. Leone mentioned that your rabbit is overweight. He's in grave danger of becoming morbidly obese. I suggest you put him on an alfalfa diet."

Renie's mouth clamped into a straight line. "He hates

alfalfa. He loves his Fat Boy food, and he'll only drink Evian water. Do you want his whole personality ruined? Do you want me even more upset? How can we engage Clarence in family fun when he's grumpy?''

"We have counseling," the receptionist responded.

"I don't need counseling," Renie said. "My husband's a psychologist."

"I don't mean you," the receptionist said with a slight smirk. "I mean the rabbit."

The rest of the weekend passed without any sign of Tara and de Tourville, Uncle Gurd, or the lavender dress. Joe and Woody had spent both Saturday and Sunday combing the Belmont Hotel. The only thing they had found of interest was in the room below the one where Harley Davidson had been killed.

"It showed signs of occupancy," Joe told Judith late Sunday night as they prepared for bed. "Not the kind you'd expect from vagrants, but of ordinary activity. There was a fairly new padlock to keep people out. The nightstand and dresser drawers had been left open, as if somebody had conducted a hurried search. The twin beds were rumpled, and the water in the bathroom sink and toilet ran clear. The pipes into that unit hadn't been allowed to collect rust."

Judith, who was shrugging out of her summer-weight cotton robe, asked Joe about fingerprints. Joe replied that there were plenty.

"The dust seeped in there, just like it did all over the rest of the hotel," he informed his wife. "We'll see what we can get from the lab."

"Was anything left behind? You know, like a newspaper or cigarette butts or fast-food bags?"

Joe shook his head. "Not a trace. That's what bugged Woody and me. Whoever used that room was damned careful to clean up afterward."

Folding back the bedclothes, Judith smiled to herself.

It sounded as if Joe was beginning to take her theory seriously. On Saturday night, she had carefully backed off from discussing the case, not even bringing up the cigars on the Belmont roof. Joe had been tired and out of sorts by the time he got home. But tonight, with the search apparently concluded, he was in a much better mood, and had willingly talked about the two-day canvass of the Belmont.

"A love nest," Judith suggested as she slipped between the sheets. "Esperanza and her latest conquest. TNT and whoever. Harley and Tara?"

But Joe, who was putting on his pajama bottoms, chuckled and shook his head. "I've seen plenty of so-called love nests," he asserted. "This wasn't one of them. I'd say this was strictly business. Or politics."

"Politics?" Judith was startled.

"Sure. Some secret organization." Joe came around to his side of the bed. It was still drizzling, and the soft splatter could be heard through the partially open window. "Far left, far right, religious cranks, a cult, whatever. There are a lot of wackos out there, Jude-Girl."

Judith turned off the bedside lamp. "I suppose. Like the Rundberg relations, and their survivalist mentality."

"Like that," Joe agreed, gathering Judith in his arms. "But no love nest. Not like this." He kissed her temple.

"You don't seem too disappointed in not finding out what went on at the hotel," Judith noted, snuggling closer.

"It'll come together," Joe replied carelessly as his hands began their magic exploration. "We need to start questioning possible suspects all over again, with this new line of inquiry."

Judith gently bit Joe's earlobe. "Good. I was afraid you'd be upset because you came away empty-handed."

Joe buried his face in Judith's hair. "I didn't quite," he said in a muffled voice. "I found a Cuban cigar."

Judith stiffened in her husband's arms. Then she relaxed. The cigar could wait. There was a time and a place for everything. The room grew quiet, except for the patter of gentle rain and the sighs of marital bliss.

Back in May, Renie had volunteered to host the family Fourth of July celebration. Judith had known then that not only would she be worn out from the wedding preparations and festivities, but the honeymooners were due home on the day itself. It would be a zoo at the airport, the flight would be late, and Judith didn't need the added aggravation of putting on a picnic.

"So," Renie said as she and Judith pushed their huge carts in tandem through the wide aisles of the local BulkBusters warehouse, "you'll have Mike and Kristin staying with you for a couple of days, huh?"

"Til Friday," Judith replied, distracted by a vast display of dill pickles in two-gallon jars. "Then they'll head for the Rundbergs, and stay overnight. After that, they'll go on to Idaho, and Mike'll return to work. Kristin's new posting isn't expected to come through until late July."

While Mike had worked in the Idaho Panhandle's Nez Perce National Park, Kristin had served as a ranger at Craters of the Moon National Monument two hundred miles away in the southern part of the state. But upon her marriage, Kristin had asked for a transfer. There was no assurance that she, too, would receive an assignment at the Nez Perce site. Still, the newlyweds were young and optimistic.

Renie paused at a relish display, then put a half-gallon jug in her cart. "Mike and Kristin won't be here long. You won't have much time to talk to him," she said in a musing tone. "Assuming you plan to."

"Yes, well I . . ." Judith interrupted herself to pick up a quart of mustard. "Maybe I can make the time. That is, if . . . um . . ." She gathered a gallon of ketchup to her bosom. "We'll see."

The cousins turned the corner, gazing up into the rafters

at the tall shelves ladened with huge cartons and packing crates. "You're not going to tell Mike," Renie stated flatly. "Chicken, cluck, cluck."

Judith turned to glare at Renie. "I didn't say that. But it's hard. Real hard. How do you tell your son, who has always believed he knew who his father was, that he'd been wrong? How do you admit that you made a mistake—if a well-intentioned one, given the fact that Joe and I were engaged at the time? How do you say, 'Hey, Mike, meet Dad. He isn't dead after all, he's been here all along. Ha-ha.' "

Small worry lines crimped Renie's forehead. "Yeah, right, it's tough. And for all his faults, Dan was a good father. Or so you've said. The rest of the family never saw much of the interaction, because Dan wouldn't come near us except for major events like funerals and food fights."

"I know." Judith spoke quietly, her shadowy gaze traveling down the row of gigantic cereal boxes. "Crazy as it sounds, I get kind of nostalgic when I come to BulkBusters. Dan really loved it here. Once he bought a ham that was the size of Oregon. We could hardly push it around the store. My, but he was happy that day."

"I'm sure it stands out," Renie said with sarcasm. "Dan was happy about four times in the eighteen years you guys were married."

"Oh, coz . . ." Judith's voice trailed away, and in what appeared to be a rebellious gesture, she scooped up mammoth boxes of Cheerios, Wheaties, Corn Flakes, and Grape Nuts.

Aware that her cousin was upset, Renie changed topics. "So what about this cigar that Joe found at the Belmont?"

The shadows began to lift from Judith's face as the cousins trundled toward soda pop and juice. "It was Cuban, just like the one Kobe gave him. Of course they're still illegal in this country."

Renie was struggling with a forty-eight-can case of

Pepsi. "So maybe whoever used the room was smuggling cigars?"

Judith hauled down a four-gallon plastic container of orange juice. "Joe and Woody considered the idea. But Joe says that in recent years, Cuban cigars aren't as great as they used to be. The Jamaicans and at least one other country import much better quality."

"Good cigars are terribly expensive," Renie pointed out. "Bill's practically quit smoking them."

Now in the household section, Judith and Renie stared at the hundred-pound boxes of laundry detergent. Between them, they each managed to load a carton onto the bottom of their carts. However, they gasped for breath as soon as they began to shove off towards wine and beer.

"Just . . . a . . . couple . . . more items," Judith panted. "Batteries, film."

"Okay. Kleenex . . . napkins . . . toilet paper," Renie groaned. "They aren't . . . so . . . heavy. Oh, and the hot dogs and buns for tomorrow."

Ten minutes later, the cousins stood in line at the checkout stands. Their purchases were piled so high that neither could see the other. Judith leaned against the cart, still out of breath.

The tab came to two hundred and forty dollars for Renie, and almost three hundred for Judith.

"Good grief!" Judith cried after they reached Renie's Chev. "That's my household budget for the month! I always forget that while I come here to save, I spend a bundle. Drat!"

"But you did save," Renie pointed out, unloading the twenty-pound pack of hot dogs and the six dozen buns. Hey, look at these hot dogs—they're the Highcastle brand, but underneath the regular label it says 'Manufactured and distributed by Pork Barrel Meats, Chicago, Illinois.' "

Judith also stared at the label. "You're right. Esperanza must have sold out. I suppose I missed reading about it in the business section. Let's face it, I usually skip that part of the paper."

"I don't," Renie said. "In my business, I have to keep up. Of course," she went on in a thoughtful voice, "I might have seen the article and not paid attention. It wouldn't have meant anything to me until now."

"We need to talk to the radio station people again," Judith murmured after she and Renie had finally finished loading the car. "Let's turn on KRAS. Darrell Mims is making his debut today. He should still be on. It's not yet noon."

The music that came out of the speakers was mild compared to what Harley Davidson had offered. At the commercial break, Darrell merely announced the time and gave the station identification. A second song, equally tame, played through. Then Darrell spoke again.

"This is Blip Man, the D. J. with a conscience. Teenagers, if you're listening to me, you should be in school, so turn off that dial and get back to class. Dropouts have no future."

The Beatles sang "Yellow Submarine." Judith and Renie exchanged curious glances.

"He won't last," Renie declared.

"I suppose not." Judith sighed. "Why did they let him go on the air?"

In the vicinity of the downtown ferry docks, Renie braked for a red light. "I don't know. I wonder what's going on with Esperanza. Maybe the real question is, will KRAS last?"

Judith gave Renie a sidelong glance. "As I was saying . . . We should call on KRAS."

"Call Kip," Renie responded. "He'll know something."

"First-hand information is better." Judith's jaw had set in a stubborn line.

"Look, just because I'm almost done with that homeless project doesn't mean I don't have work to do," Renie argued as they cruised along the waterfront. "I've got to get in touch with Morris Mitchell this afternoon about the photos."

"We're heading right for KRAS," Judith pointed out. "We go by their building on the way to Hillside Manor."

"Then that's what we'll do," Renie countered. "We'll go right by it."

"Coz . . ."

"Damn . . ."

"Thanks."

The cousins arrived at KRAS just behind the fire department.

THIRTEEN

AT EXACTLY ELEVEN-FIFTY, a small explosive device had been thrown into the lobby of the Heraldsgate 400 building. Luckily, no one had been injured, though damage was considerable. Passersby had seen four teenagers race away, shouting, "Blip Man sucks!"

The cousins heard the news from Chuck Rawls, who was standing out on the sidewalk, rubbing the stubble on his chin. "Damned kids," he muttered. "Can't they give Mims a chance? He's never been on the air before."

Near the entrance, the firefighters were debating the necessity of evacuating the building while they waited for the bomb squad. At least two dozen spectators now congregated nearby, some of them in the street where they were blocking traffic. Horns began to honk, and motorists shouted. Judith, Renie, and Rawls moved toward the corner.

"Where were you when it happened?" Judith asked Rawls.

The producer gestured across the street. "At Foozle's. I had an early lunch today." His gaze didn't quite meet Judith's.

"That bad, huh?" Renie murmured.

Rawls apparently didn't hear her, which was no

wonder, with all the commotion going on around the Heraldsgate 400 building. Police cars were arriving, complete with wailing sirens.

"Did anyone get a good look at the kids who did this?" Judith asked as she waved in the direction of the smoke-filled entrance.

Rawls's high forehead puckered. "I don't know. Somebody said the car was an older model, dark green, maybe a GM make." He looked back across the street toward Foozle's. "I'd better call Ms. Highcastle from there. Access to the building is cut off for now. Excuse me."

Renie was sniggering. "So much for questioning the radio people today. I wonder if Darrell Mims is still broadcasting."

Judith glanced at her watch; it was two minutes before noon. "He's probably winding up his show. At least he's got a hot news flash."

"Literally." Renie started for the Chev. "Let's go."

Judith started to protest, but despite the urging of the firefighters to disperse, the area around the building was getting crowded. With an aura of defeat, Judith followed Renie to the car.

"I'm frustrated," Judith declared, fastening her seatbelt. "I pride myself on getting people to open up and talk to me. But I can't even meet with Tara or de Tourville, Esperanza was a washout, Chuck Rawls hasn't been much help, and TNT Tenino was drunk."

"So give it up," Renie said as the Chev roared up the steep hill that led away from the lower Heraldsgate business district. "I told you that earlier. It isn't worth all the effort and energy you're putting into this case."

Judith didn't respond. Maybe Renie was right. What was she trying to prove? That she wasn't delusional or drunk or as daffy as her mother? It really wasn't important to show Joe that she had seen a couple in wedding attire on the Belmont roof. And it certainly wasn't necessary to get involved in Joe's investigation.

Renie pulled into the cul-de-sac. "Okay, here you go," she said, giving Judith a little nudge. "Hey, coz! Wake up! You're zoned out."

Judith gave a start. "Huh? Oh! Right, we're here. It's stopped raining. I didn't notice that at the bottom of the hill."

"Maybe it'll clear up for the Fourth," Renie said. "I don't want to cram all the relatives and friends of relatives inside the house."

"I don't blame you." Judith opened the passenger door, then turned back to Renie. "You're right. I've been very foolish. Harley's death has nothing to do with me. I'd never even heard of him until a week or so ago. It's just that . . . well, I guess it's the proximity of Tara and de Tourville and the fact that Kip works for the radio stations and that I actually saw Harley and Tara on the hotel roof and that . . ."

"Which way are you arguing?" Renie demanded with a wry expression.

Judith bit her lip. "I don't know. Against, I think."

"I hope so. Go inside. Have lunch. Forget it." Renie gave Judith another nudge.

"I will." Judith got out of the car, took five minutes to unload the trunk, then returned to wave her cousin off. Halfway up the drive, she saw Phyliss Rackley coming around the corner from the back porch.

"All done," Phyliss announced. "And a good thing— my sciatica's giving me fits. It's this unseasonable damp weather. If the pain keeps up, I may not be able to come tomorrow."

"You weren't coming anyway," Judith pointed out. "It's a holiday."

Phyliss's pale blue eyes widened. "Oh. That's so. Well, then maybe I can't make it Wednesday. Though I'd hate to put you out. I wouldn't mind standing up that snooty Mrs. Rumplemeyer over on the bluff, though. I'll have to pray for a cure by Thursday. It's too soon to miss a session with that de Tooleyville fella."

On impulse, Judith put a hand on Phyliss's shoulder. "Do you have a key to the condo?"

Phyliss's eyes now narrowed. "Yep, I sure do. Why do you want to know?"

Torn between candor and deception, Judith walked the fence. "He's a witness in Joe's current case. Access to the condo would be very helpful. It would save the trouble of getting a search warrant." Wincing, Judith avoided Phyliss's curious gaze, and hoped that the cleaning woman was ignorant of police procedure. When it came to Bascombe de Tourville, Joe had no probable cause to ask for a search warrant.

"I don't know," Phyliss said slowly. "It's not something I ever do, handing out keys like peppermint sticks. How soon would I get it back?"

"Tomorrow," Judith replied quickly. "I mean Wednesday. If you feel like coming to work."

Phyliss considered. "A witness, huh? To what?"

"Ah . . . to contraband." It seemed safer than murder. "Smuggling of illegal goods."

"Hmmm." Phyliss's gaze darted along the driveway and through the flower beds, as if she expected to see drugs, guns, and any manner of illicit items spring up around Hillside Manor. "Sinful stuff, huh? Dirty pictures, maybe?" Phyliss seemed hopeful, but Judith shook her head. "Okay," Phyliss agreed, "I won't stand in the way of righteousness." Digging into her faux leather purse, she removed not a key but a slim plastic card. "Here you go. But don't let Mr. Flynn tell where he got it."

"I won't, Phyliss," Judith promised with a straight face. "It's as safe a secret as if Joe never knew."

Half an hour later, Judith was on the phone to Renie, begging her to join the search of de Tourville's condo. Renie refused. She was busy and Judith was nuts. What if de Tourville was there?

"He can't be." Judith said. "The place is still under surveillance."

"Are you sure?" Renie countered.

"Well, no. I mean, I haven't checked today," Judith admitted.

"So how do you know the place is empty?" Renie asked in a vexed voice. "It's not as if this de Tourville is a homicide suspect. It costs money to maintain a stakeout."

"He may not be, but Tara is directly involved," Judith reasoned. "She's the one Joe and Woody want to question."

"And all they have is your word for it that she was ever there." Renie sounded skeptical.

"Well, she was," Judith said in annoyance. Then she reshuffled her options. "Never mind, go back to work."

"Thanks, I will," said Renie and hung up.

Ten minutes later, Judith was at Belgravia Gardens. She couldn't spot the stakeout car and wondered if the officers had been pulled from duty. It was possible, of course, that the personnel had been changed, and so had their mode of operations. They might be in the phone company or city utility trucks that were parked along the street. They could even be in a vacant apartment in the big old handsome brick building across from the elegant condos.

The plastic card let Judith into the building without a hitch. The elevator glided up to the top floor, and again the card-key provided easy access. Judith stepped into the condo's entry hall and came face-to-face with Bascombe de Tourville.

Judith let out a small shriek. "Mr. de Bascombe!" she cried. "I mean, Mr. de Tourville! I didn't expect you to be at home."

"I am," de Tourville replied smoothly, though one dark eyebrow was slightly raised. "Please—tell me who you are or I shall have to call the police."

"The police?" Judith's eyes grew large. The police were probably within shouting distance. In which case, why hadn't they spotted de Tourville? Judith's brain moved at a frenetic pace. "No, you don't need to do that. I'm . . . the cleaning woman."

"No, you are not," de Tourville replied calmly. He vaguely resembled Phyliss's description, with a graying mustache, a neatly trimmed Vandyke beard, and a thick head of hair. "The cleaning woman is older, uglier, and comes on Thursday. This is Monday." He turned to pick up the gold- and ivory-encased telephone.

"She's sick," Judith said hurriedly. "Mrs. Rackley is very ill, and may have to have an operation. She's in the hospital. That's why she can't come Thursday, and I only had this afternoon available. I'm booked." *I'm cooked*, Judith thought, watching de Tourville's narrowed gray eyes to see if he believed her.

"You are somehow familiar. Your name?" he inquired, now arching the other eyebrow.

"Mrs . . . McMonigle," Judith fibbed. "Do you mind if I get started? I really am pressed for time. Of course if it's not convenient, I can come back later . . ."

De Tourville brushed a long finger against his mustache. He was tall, well over six feet, and trim of build. Judith figured him to be in his forties, and he would have been handsome if there wasn't something sinister in his manner.

"No, I think not today," he finally said in his faintly accented voice. "I have been away since Friday, returning only this morning. My home is in good order. The cleaning may wait until next Monday. I shall not be entertaining for awhile."

Judith's gaze took in the living room with its elaborate Louis XV decor. One wall was mirrored, making the space look vast, endless—and almost overwhelming. Marble, pillars, draperies, and decorated paneling set off reproductions of chairs, tables, couches, cabinets, and a huge armoire. Or, Judith thought fleetingly, maybe the furniture was original. Certainly the sense of wealth and luxury was real.

"Then I guess I'll be running along," Judith said in a
meek voice. She turned towards the elevators, but suddenly snapped her fingers. "Oh! Do you mind? Mrs.
Rackley mentioned an address book she may have left
here. It belongs to one of her other clients, a Mrs. Flynn."

"I have no such address book," de Tourville replied
flatly. "There has already been an inquiry, by Mrs. . . . ."

"Oh, well!" Judith didn't want de Tourville conjuring
up her voice on the phone. "Mrs. Rackley must not have
known. She was partially sedated when I last spoke with
her. I'll be going now."

At the elevator, Judith pressed the button. Her back was
turned to de Tourville, who made no sound as she waited.
Had he remembered what was familiar about her? Did he
believe her flimsy story? Would he let her out of the
condo without mishap? Judith felt her nerves grow taut
as she listened for the hum of the elevator cables.

But the car arrived and the doors slid open. Judith was
inside and poking the button for the main floor when Tara
Novotny raced into the living room.

"Stop! My taxi must be here by now! Wait!" She ran
past de Tourville as if he were part of the decor.

Fumbling around the control panel, Judith found the
"open door" button just in time. Tara, who was carrying
a small suitcase, rushed inside and leaned against the elegant gilded paneling.

"Thank you! I'm so hurried today. Everything goes
bing-bang, zip-zap. Now I must catch an airplane. Life is
very hard."

The supermodel seemed unfazed to find a stranger in
the elevator. Perhaps her calling in life caused her to be
self-absorbed, Judith thought, to show interest only in a
mirror's reflection or the camera's eye. For the first time,
Judith had a chance to observe Tara Novotny up close:
nearing thirty with dark brown hair, green eyes that
matched the emeralds in her ears, and a classic profile.
She was tall, maybe six feet, and too thin, but beautiful.

The brown silk pantsuit was perfectly cut, the low-heeled alligator shoes looked new, and the matching purse was slung over one slim shoulder. Tara reached into the bag and removed a pair of huge sunglasses.

"You're going away?" Judith asked as they reached the main floor.

Tara nodded. "Here, there, everywhere." Like de Tourville, she also had a slight accent. "Yesterday, New York. Today, San Francisco. It is a hard life, this super-modeling."

Judith wondered if Tara assumed that everyone would know who she was and what she did. Or perhaps it was merely a passing comment. The classic profile was thrust upwards, as if Tara could read her itinerary on the elevator ceiling.

"Where do you stay in San Francisco?" Judith inquired as they stepped out into the foyer.

"The St. Francis," Tara replied, as if on cue. Though her movements were graceful, there was something of the automaton in her manner. "Always the St. Francis. So old, so chic, so San Francisco. Taxi!" The supermodel breezed through the double doors towards the waiting Yellow Cab.

"Hold it!" Judith was at Tara's heels, frantically searching for a means to detain her. "You're wanted by the police."

Tara turned, but because she had now put on the big sunglasses, Judith couldn't read her expression. "Certainly not. I have done nothing wrong, not in my whole life."

"That's not the point," Judith countered, trying to scan the street to see if she could pick out a surveillance vehicle. "It's about Harley Davidson. The police want to ask you some questions."

"They already did." Tara got into the cab. "Stupid questions, such as 'Was he my lover?' Bah! I take only the richest, most handsome men as my lovers. Harley Da-

vidson was a blind man, a vulgar person, *a disc jockey*!"
She slammed the door and the cab took off.

Feeling a headache coming on, Judith rubbed at her
temples. The phone company van had gone, but the city
utility vehicle was still parked at the end of the block.
Judith marched down the street and yelled at the driver
who was eating a sandwich.

"Are you a cop?" she asked.

The driver looked startled, then wary. "Are you a
nut?" he responded.

Judith went home.

After almost fifty nonproductive hours, the stakeout had
been canceled Monday at 6 A.M. Joe's superiors refused
to authorize any more time and money to watch a private
citizen who wasn't a suspect in the Davidson homicide
investigation.

"What about Tara?" Judith asked after Joe had settled
in with a beer and the evening paper.

Joe avoided his wife's gaze. "Tara's not a suspect, only
a possible witness. She doesn't live at Belgravia Gardens.
It's hearsay that she was ever there. Or so the chief says."

Judith could imagine Joe's portly superior snorting in
derision. "Your *wife* says she saw this Novotny woman?
Where? How? Come on, Flynn—gimme a break." No
doubt the chief had burst into uproarious, mocking laughter.

But Judith knew it was pointless to argue with her husband. She had told him about seeing Tara again—by accident, of course—and that the supermodel was heading
for San Francisco. The news had mildly perturbed Joe,
but he had come home early from work, and was determined to put the case on the backburner until after the
holiday. Judith decided she might as well do the same.

Unfortunately for Renie and Bill, the Fourth brought
more rain. The twenty-plus guests were forced to remain
inside the Jones house, stuffing themselves on hamburg-

ers, Highcastle hot dogs, and Gertrude's legendary potato salad. Mike and Kristin had arrived in time for the festivities, though their flight had been predictably late. Both were deeply tanned and seemed very happy.

As Judith had foreseen, there was no time to talk to Mike alone Tuesday night. By the time Judith, Joe, Gertrude, and the newlyweds got home, the fireworks display was beginning out in the harbor. The family and some of the B&B guests gathered at the edge of the cul-de-sac, where they had an almost unobstructed view of the pyrotechnics. To the accompaniment of much oohing and aahing, they joined their neighbors in watching the spectacular show. When it concluded just before eleven, everyone agreed that it was the best ever—except Gertrude, who insisted that she preferred the old days when Uncle Cliff put cherry bombs in Aunt Deb's oven, and Uncle Al shot off Roman candles that set fire to the neighbor's garage.

The rain continued through Wednesday. Mike and Kristin chose their wedding pictures, then headed off to Morris Mitchell's studio. Phyliss showed up for work, though full of bodily complaints. For once, Judith didn't try to interrupt. She was stalling for time, trying to think of a plausible excuse for lying to Bascombe de Tourville about the cleaning woman's condition.

Finally, as Phyliss was about to cart a load of laundry to the basement, Judith blurted out the truth:

"I used that plastic key to get into Mr. de Tourville's condo. He was home, and I had to think up a reason for being there, Phyliss. I told him you were very ill."

Phyliss blinked. "I was. I am. What was I just telling you?"

"I mean . . ." Judith began, then thought better of it. If de Tourville questioned Phyliss when she showed up for work on Thursday, the cleaning woman would be only too glad to recite the details of her current ailments. De Tourville would phase out at some point and wish he'd never asked. "Just don't mention who I am," Judith finally said. "I was operating sort of undercover . . . for Joe."

"Did you find that cummerbund?" Phyllis inquired, hefting the laundry basket.

Judith gave a small start. "What? Oh—the contraband. No. I didn't get a chance to look, since de Tourville was there."

"I'll look tomorrow." Phyliss cocked an eye at Judith. "What am I looking for? I should know, I guess, so that I can act in a righteous manner."

"Don't act," Judith urged hastily. "But if you see anything unusual, tell me. The truth is, Phyllis, I don't know what we're looking for. It might be . . . cigars."

"Cigars!" Phyliss's unruly white eyebrows shot up in horror. "Tobacco! Did you know why Satan is in the Hot Spot? It's because he *smoked*."

"Really," Judith said in a mild tone. "No, I didn't know that." Making appropriate musing noises, she returned to scrubbing the kitchen sink.

By late afternoon, the rain had stopped and the clouds were beginning to lift. Judith went outside to check the hedge. Uncle Gurd had been gone now for almost five days. Undoubtedly, he had headed back to Idaho or Montana or wherever he lived with the rest of his oddball clan.

But the Austrian canvas military pack in which he carried his possessions was still under the laurel leaves. It contained underwear, a fatigue jacket, socks, and road maps of the western states. The bedroll was still on the ground, as were some of Judith's eating utensils. Perplexed, Judith retrieved the kitchenware and went back into the house.

She caught the phone just before it trunked over to the answering machine. "Guess what!" exclaimed Renie. "Bill and I won a free dinner at the Naples Hotel. Except Bill can't go. Want to come?"

Judith started to say yes, then reconsidered. "Can't you wait until Bill can make it?"

Renie explained that they'd actually been awarded the freebie a month ago, but that she'd forgotten about it until she was cleaning out a drawer. "It expires July fifth, which is today. Bill is attending a lecture by some weirdo psychiatrist from Bulgaria. I refuse to offer a free dinner to any of our kids, because it's for two and they'd fight over it. What do you say?"

Joe was working late to make up for the holiday. Still, Judith had to take care of her guests—and Gertrude. She hemmed and hawed while Renie coaxed and cajoled.

"Since it's the Naples," Judith finally relented, "I won't beg off. If we didn't go until seven-thirty, maybe Arlene could fill in here at the B&B."

Arlene could—at first. Then she called back and said she couldn't after all. Judith was about to dial Renie's number when the phone rang again in her hand. Arlene would be glad to help out. Judith asked if she was certain; what about her previous refusal? Had her plans changed?

"What plans?" Arlene asked in a dumbfounded voice. "Why would I have plans?"

As was often the case in dealing with Arlene, Judith's brain felt as if it were on the spin cycle. Then, in a typical gesture of generosity, Arlene invited Gertrude to dinner. "It's always such fun to entertain your mother," Arlene enthused. "She keeps Carl and me in stitches."

Mystified as ever by Gertrude's ability to amuse the neighbors, Judith thanked Arlene. Then she called Joe at work to tell him of her plans. He was out, so she left a note on the bulletin board that a baked potato was in the oven, green beans were on the stove, and a T-bone steak was in the fridge.

After preparing the guests' punch and hors d'oeuvres, Judith brought in the evening paper. The previous day's edition had contained a four-inch story on the bombing at the Heraldsgate 400 building. Though Judith carefully scanned both the front page and the local section, she could find nothing more on the incident. It was the first thing she mentioned to Renie as the cousins set out for the Naples Hotel shortly after seven.

"Sometimes," Renie responded thoughtfully, "the media bands together to protect their own. The local newspapers might feel that by publicizing the explosion they'd be inviting more of the same, only next time it might be directed at them, instead of a radio or TV station."

"I'll have to ask Joe about it," Judith said. "He must have heard something at work. After all, there is a connection with the homicide case. I mean, Harley Davidson worked for the station that was targeted by the bomb."

In the Naples's circular drive, Judith and Renie were met by Kobe. Renie gave him a jaunty wave, but Judith practically backed him up against the Italian fountain.

"Kobe, you're just the man I want to see," she said, employing a big, friendly smile. "Have you got a minute?"

Anxiously, Kobe looked at the drive and the street beyond. No other cars were approaching. "I guess. The night after a holiday is usually kind of slow."

"Okay." Judith kept smiling. "I'm Detective Flynn's wife, remember? The rehearsal dinner, the body in the Belmont, the cigar?"

Kobe's earnest young face grew puzzled. "I remember most of that, sure. What about the cigar?"

"You gave one to Mr. Flynn the night we were here for dinner," Judith explained as Renie stood by the entrance, tapping her foot. "You know, when he came down to ask if you'd heard or seen anything odd?"

"Oh!" Kobe grinned and put a hand to his head. "Right, I don't smoke, so I gave it to Mr. Flynn."

The smile deserted Judith's eyes and tightened on her lips. "Where did you get it?"

Kobe frowned briefly, then wagged a finger toward the sidewalk. "From that guy who panhandles around here sometimes. Billy Something-or-other. He's not supposed to hang out by the hotel, but he doesn't cause any trouble and I don't hassle him. I guess that's why he gave me the cigar.''

Judith glanced at the empty corner where she had last seen Billy Big Horn. ''Where did he get it?''

Kobe shrugged. ''Somebody gave it to him, I suppose. You'd be surprised at what people give a panhandler besides money. Of course Billy uses a cigar box for his donations, which may be why he ends up with cigars sometimes. But he doesn't smoke, and I didn't want to hurt his feelings which is why I took the cigar from him.''

''Have you seen Billy lately?'' Judith asked.

Kobe shook his head. ''Not since that night, now that you mention it, but he isn't a regular fixture. Once a week, maybe.''

Judith grew silent while Renie loudly cleared her throat. ''Kobe,'' Judith began at last, ''do you recall anything— anything at all—unusual about the Friday that we were here for the rehearsal dinner?''

Kobe took the question seriously. ''I didn't at the time,'' he said slowly, ''but since then, when I heard that the body they found in the Belmont was that disc jockey I listen to sometimes, I remembered that he'd come here for lunch that day.''

Judith stared at Kobe. Even Renie took a step forward. ''Harley Davidson was *here*?'' Judith asked in a breathless voice.

''Right,'' Kobe answered. ''He comes pretty often. But that day, one of the other valets got sick, so I had to fill in. I got here just before one, Davidson came a few minutes later with some recording types. I've seen them around before, but not with Davidson. They own a studio downtown.''

Judith could barely control her eagerness to encourage more information from Kobe. ''Do you know them? What are their names? Which studio?''

Kobe seemed a trifle overwhelmed by Judith's enthusiasm. "I . . . yes, I've seen them here several times, including with one of the rock groups they have under contract. But I don't know their names. The rock group was Mud Bath, which I think records for the Red Fog label. I've got a couple of their CDs."

Judith turned to Renie, who appeared sufficiently interested to remain patient. "Do you know them, coz?"

Renie scrunched up her face in the effort of recollection. "They sound vaguely familiar. Yes, I think they're local."

Judith started to pump Kobe's hand in gratitude, then thought of something else: "How did you recognize Harley Davidson the first time you saw him?"

"He came with some other radio types in a car that had the KRAS logo plastered all over it," Kobe answered. "Besides, I'd seen his picture around town." The parking valet's tone accelerated as a sleek white Cadillac pulled into the drive. "Mr. Davidson seemed like a nice guy— he gave Billy Big Horn a twenty that Friday. Excuse me, I've got to get back to work."

Renie had saved her consternation until dessert. Throughout the meal, she'd let Judith meander through theories, ideas, and conjecture concerning Harley Davidson's demise and the possibility that someone was involved in contraband. When Judith seemed to run down just as the crème brûlée was presented, Renie took over the conversation.

"Okay, you were going to back off the last I heard, and let Joe and Woody do their jobs. Now you're . . ."

"I wouldn't have gotten involved again if you hadn't offered me a free dinner at . . ."

"Shut up." Renie knew Judith was lying. "You haven't been idle these past two days or you wouldn't have gone to de Tourville's condo. And where on earth did this stupid contraband idea come from? A bunch of Cuban cigars?"

"It's not just the cigars," Judith said in defense of her theory. "It's the Belmont itself. It looks as if it were being used for some sort of rendezvous. The cigars may be just a peripheral item being brought in. I suspect that drugs are the real contraband."

Renie had paused to taste her crème brûlée, and it had pleased her greatly. "I'm sick of drugs," she declared. "Why can't it be something more glamorous, like Russian sables or Canadian fisher?"

Judith started to make a flippant retort, but suddenly stopped, one hand poised over her ramekin. "That may be it, coz," she said excitedly. "Not furs, but clothes. Mr. Artemis has his clothes made on an island in the Caribbean—Santa Teresa del Fiore. He'd received a shipment the day before the fashion show at I. Magnifique. What if parts of that shipment were filled with illegal drugs? Tara often brought the garments into this country and took them straight to her apartment. I remember Deirdre, one of Mr. Artemis's other models, accusing Tara of ripping out hems and seams in some of the latest shipment. What if she did that to get at the drugs?"

Renie's eyes roved around the dining room's gesso ceiling. "Could be. So who's in on this scam beside Tara and Mr. Artemis?"

"We can't be sure about him, but Tara has to know if she's tearing up designer outfits." Judith was making notes on her cocktail napkin. "Then there's TNT. Esperanza thought she could find him at the Belmont. Why else would he go there?"

"Because," Renie offered, "she'd thrown him out and it was a place to flop?"

Judith's sanguine manner faded. "It's possible. But why did he come home with me? He said he had no place to stay. Admittedly, he was drunk. That's all the more reason why—if he associated the Belmont with something else—like smuggling—he wouldn't have thought of it as a home away from home. He was muddled."

The waiter came to take away their dessert dishes and inquire about after-dinner drinks. Judith chose Galliano on the rocks; Renie opted for Drambuie, straight up. Though there were empty tables on this Wednesday night, the hotel dining room's simulated English hunting lodge hummed with the sound of contented customers. Judith consulted her cocktail napkin.

"I doubt if anyone at the radio station was in on this," she said. "I see it emanating from de Tourville, Tara, TNT, and maybe Mr. Artemis."

"What about Harley?" Renie asked, placing her free coupon next to her water glass.

"You said it." Judith gave Renie a knowing look. "Remember, just before I . . . ran afoul of Clarence? Harley was killed to keep him quiet. He must have found out about the smuggling ring that night at the Belmont. It was dangerous knowledge, and the gang couldn't afford to let him live."

A slight nod, the parting of lips, and then a peal of laughter erupted from Renie. "How, coz?"

Judith frowned. "What do you mean, how? If Tara had brought the drugs with her that night she'd have to take them out and put them . . ." A horrified expression crossed Judith's face. "Oh! I see what you mean!"

Renie nodded sagely. "Of course you do. You see that Harley couldn't see. Return to go, coz. Excuse the pun, but I just blindsided your theory."

FOURTEEN

JUDITH WASN'T WILLING to quite let go of the premise she'd built out of a Caribbean workshop, Cuban cigars, and a dead disc jockey. "He may have heard something," she argued as the cousins waited for Kobe to fetch their car. "If Tara didn't kill him, somebody else was there. They talked. Harley listened. And that's why he's dead."

"Uh-huh." Renie yawned. "So why don't you let Joe figure it out?"

Judith didn't answer because Kobe appeared just then with the big Chev. The cousins both tipped him. "Thank you for being so helpful," Judith said as she slipped a ten-dollar bill into the parking valet's hand along with her phone number. "If Billy Big Horn shows up here, call me. Please."

As they circled the fountain and turned into the street, Judith craned her neck for a look at the Belmont. It loomed large and dark behind the Naples.

"I don't think they've started tearing it down yet," she said.

"The holiday probably interfered," Renie replied without much interest. "Once you screw with schedules, things get put on the back burner."

"Maybe it's just as well," Judith mused. "That

place could still be evidence. Want to visit Red Fog recording studios tomorrow?"

"Not particularly," Renie responded as they skirted the
downtown area where the city's commerce melded into
the hospital and apartment district.

Coming off the hill of high-rises, Judith glimpsed I.
Magnifique a block away. "I wonder . . . what if there's
some kind of . . . I'm not sure what . . . residue, or whatever from the drugs left in the garments that are being
sold? Maybe Joe and Woody should check out Mr. Artemis's inventory there and at his studio."

"Maybe they have," Renie said absently. "Their job,
you know."

"I suppose that drugs are carefully packaged. At least
they are on TV, in heavy plastic." Judith stroked her chin.
"Still, you could tell if the seams had been altered. I wonder if . . . Ohmigod!" She gave such a start that the seatbelt cut into her midsection.

"What now?" Renie asked without turning to look at
her cousin.

"Lavender Dreams! I didn't lose it, it was stolen!"
Despite the fact that Renie was negotiating a corner, Judith grabbed her cousin's arm. "I'll bet that dress was
worth a lot more than twenty-five hundred dollars! I'll bet
somebody thought it was loaded with cocaine!"

Renie disengaged her arm and tugged at the steering
wheel to keep the car from hitting the curb. "Do that
again and I'll smack you."

"Smack!" Judith exclaimed. "Isn't that a drug term?"

At the next stop light, Renie smacked her anyway.

Judith had kept her cocktail napkin. On Thursday morning, she studied the scribbled names once more. Bascombe de Tourville. Tara Novotny. TNT Tenino. Mr.
Artemis, with a question mark. Then she reproached herself for not asking TNT more questions while he was
under her roof. What did he actually do as a boxing coach

and scout? Did he travel? Who were his friends? It was one thing not to be able to quiz the suspects; it was quite another to neglect questioning them when she had the opportunity. Judith felt that she was slipping.

"Hey, Mom, you're slipping," Mike said as he breezed into the kitchen.   Judith jumped. "What?"

Mike grinned and sat down on the counter where Judith had been cogitating. "Never mind," he consoled his mother. "What's up?"

Judith glanced toward the backstairs where Mike had just descended. "Where's Kristin?"

"In the shower. We've opened all the wedding presents, and we're getting the bigger ones ready to ship to Idaho. We'll take the rest in my Wrangler."

Judith barely heard the last of her son's words. Kristin was in the shower. Phyllis was upstairs cleaning the guest rooms. Gertrude was out in the toolshed. Judith was alone at last with Mike.

"Mike," she said, clearing her throat, "we're overdue for a talk."

Mike's grin grew even wider. "Isn't it kind of late for that, Mom? I mean, Kristin and I are married. You should've talked to me about fifteen years ago."

"I don't mean that." Judith moved around nervously in her chair. "Besides," she added, stalling to find the right words, "I *did* talk to you about that sort of thing. You were in sixth grade."

"It was Dad," Mike said. "And I was in fourth grade. Sometimes I think you forget how much time I spent with Dad while you were working."

Sometimes Judith did forget. It was easy to do in the blur of years. While she'd held both a day and an evening job, Dan had stayed home with Mike. Dan would have stayed home if there'd been no Mike, but the truth was that father and son had forged a close, if sometimes uneasy, bond. Dan had been there for Mike, and Judith hadn't. It wasn't her fault, but it was a fact.

"Yes . . . well . . . of course." Judith stumbled over the words. "What I'm trying to say is that sometimes people do things that seem right at the time, but in the long run they may regret them. Do you know what I mean?"

Mike turned serious. "Oh. So you did notice. I should have guessed."

Mystified, Judith frowned at her son. Then he held out his left arm. "So what do you really think? I had it done in Mexico. I like it." Mike's tone was proud and defensive.

Tattooed inside his upper arm in discreet but easily read letters was "Daniel Neal McMonigle, 1937–1986."

Judith bit her lip. "I didn't notice." She felt her eyes fill with tears. "That's . . . very moving, Mike. What does Kristin think?"

Mike rubbed at the tattoo, as if it were a talisman. "She thinks it's nice. She's always said she wished she'd known my dad. This makes him a little more real to her."

And keeps him real for you, Judith thought with a pang. Judith might not have loved Dan, at least not the way a wife should love a husband, but Mike had loved him like a son loves his father. Judith reached up and hugged Mike.

"Your . . . dad would be proud," she murmured.

"I think so," Mike said quietly. Then giving Judith a tight squeeze, he drew back. "Hey, I thought you were talking about the tattoo a minute ago. What did you want to tell me?"

"Oh." Judith stepped back, falling over the chair. She caught herself and giggled. "Just that . . . ah . . . I never really got to wish you and Kristin all the happiness in the world. Things got so hectic around here before the wedding, and I know I must have said something, maybe often, but not one-on-one, when everything was calm." The heartfelt words finally came tumbling out, though they were not what Judith originally had intended. "I hope that the two of you will be as happy as . . ."

The phone rang, cutting Judith off. But as she picked up the receiver, Mike grinned and finished for her:

"As you and Dad were. Thanks, Mom. I'm going to the basement to get some cartons."

It wasn't, Judith thought fleetingly as she answered the phone, what she was going to say. She wanted to wish Mike and Kristin to be as happy as she and Joe were. But if her son thought that she and Dan had been happy, why spoil his illusion? Why spoil anything and everything? Judith would never bring up the subject of Mike's parentage again.

"Coz," Judith said, relieved that it was Renie on the other end of the line. "I've got something to tell you."

"My turn first, I called," Renie said. "What did Kobe say last night about Billy Big Horn? I need to find him for Morris Mitchell. We want to use him in the homeless photographs. He's very picturesque, especially with that harmonica."

Judith explained that Billy hadn't been around the Naples since the night of the rehearsal dinner. "I told him to call me if he does show up. Did you check the corner by Donner & Blitzen?"

"Morris did," Renie replied. "Nobody's seen Billy there for the last two weeks. One of the other panhandlers told Morris that he might be in jail. Sometimes the cops make a sweep of the bums, especially during tourist season. Could you check with Joe?"

The request seemed harmless enough. Agreeing, Judith started to tell Renie about Mike's tattoo, but Phyliss had come down from the second floor. "I'll talk to you later," Judith said, and hung up.

"I'll put in a load of laundry and then I'm off to de Tooleyville's," Phyliss called from the hallway.

"Look for drugs," Judith told the cleaning woman.

"Drugs?" The sausage curls danced on Phyliss's head. "Think he's got something I can take for my sciatica?"

Judith tried to explain the difference between medicinal

and recreational drugs. Phyliss thought that cocaine sounded just fine.

"If it's that powerful," she said, heading down to the basement, "it might cure bunions, too."

Judith had some trouble finding Red Fog recording studios. Although she had gotten the address out of the phone book, the site was unmarked by any kind of sign. After going around the block four times in search of a parking place, she ended up leaving the Subaru in a loading zone and taking her chances with the meter maids.

While the exterior was unadorned and painted an institutional brown, the reception area was ablaze with colorful photographs and posters of various recording artists. The furnishings were less obtrusive, however, with soft mauve predominating.

Judith's excuse for calling on the record executives was flimsy at best. Without Renie's graphic design cachet, the only guise she could assume was that of Renie herself.

"I'm Serena Jones," Judith announced, hoisting a worn briefcase onto the reception desk. The leather case had belonged to her father, and was presently filled with old income tax statements. "I'm a graphic designer. I had an appointment for one-thirty today."

The pert African-American woman with the head full of cornrows consulted the day book. "Ms. Jones? I don't have you down. Who were you seeing?"

"Mr. . . . ." Judith feigned a coughing fit. "Sorry. Is he in?"

"Mr. Kerr? Is that what you said?" The receptionist, whose nameplate read Aisha Barnes, looked puzzled.

Judith nodded. "That's right, Mr. Kerr."

"He's in, but he's busy." Aisha Barnes glanced at a paneled door next to the desk. "Maybe you should re-schedule." She flipped through the day book. "Next Tuesday at ten?"

Judith let out a vexed sigh. "I can't. I'll be in Boston

then. In fact, I leave tomorrow, and won't return until the end of the month.''

Aisha looked perturbed. "My, my—I don't know what I can do. Mr. Kerr had other unexpected visitors this afternoon, and I've no idea how long they'll take. If you'd like to wait, I'll check with him when the others leave.''

Judith smiled broadly. "That would be wonderful, Ms. Barnes. I appreciate . . .''

The paneled door opened, and a short leather-clad man in his mid-thirties ushered out his visitors. "Sorry I can't be more help, fellas," said the man whom Judith assumed was Mr. Kerr. "As far is Red Fog is concerned, Harley Davidson was just another DJ on the make. Or take, depending on how you look at it.''

Judith barely heard the words. She was fixated on Mr. Kerr's departing guests. Joe Flynn and Woody Price entered the reception area and stopped in their tracks.

"Hi," said Judith in a small voice.

Woody offered a small, if startled, smile from under his walrus mustache. Joe simply stared.

"I was just leaving," Judith finally gulped.

"That part's right," Joe said under his breath, taking Judith's elbow and marching her to the door.

"But Ms. Jones," Aisha called after the trio, "Mr. Kerr can see you now for about fifteen minutes.''

Judith flinched as Joe turned to look at the receptionist. "Ms. Jones is having an identity crisis. Apparently, when I changed her name, it didn't take. She insists on trying out new ones. So long.''

"Joe," Judith said miserably as they reached the sidewalk. "I can explain. I didn't realize you knew about the recording executives lunching with Harley at . . .''

Joe was very red in the face, but he took a deep breath and reined in his temper. "Look, Woody and I actually know our jobs. We follow procedures, we work as a team, within a team. We've got assistance from the M.E., the forensic pathologist, the crime lab, a whole battery of

skilled professionals. We don't go by appearances or as-
sumptions or hunches. We dig and interview and dig and
interrogate and dig some more. Maybe we don't jump
from Point A to Point D like amateurs do. But we get
there eventually. Our success rate is damned good, so we
don't need outside help. By the way, your car is being
towed. See you around, Jude-girl. Let's go, Woody.''

Swerving on her heel, Judith saw a green and white
towtruck putting the hook onto her Subaru. "Wait!" she
cried, turning back to Joe who was calmly walking away
with Woody. "Joe! You can stop this! Tell them I'm your
wife!''

Joe kept walking, though Judith could hear him as he
spoke to Woody. "Now how can I say she's my wife
when she thinks she's Ms. Jones?''

Somehow, Judith managed to talk the towtruck driver
out of taking her car. She was still stuck with the sixty-
five-dollar parking ticket, however. Chastened, mortified,
and incensed, though not necessarily in that order, Judith
went home.

"Do you know what I've done besides make a fool of
myself?" Judith asked of Renie as the cousins sat on the
Jones's deck that Thursday afternoon. "The reason I got
so involved trying to solve the murder case was because
I didn't want to think about Mike and Dan and Joe. It's
always been hard for me to look back at my first marriage.''

"Painful," Renie said between quaffs of pink lemonade. The skies were clearing, and the temperature was
rising again. Beyond the ornamental cherry trees, the silver spruce, and the hawthorns that enclosed the Jones's
backyard, the mountain range to the east was emerging
from the clouds. The aroma of charcoal burning in the
barbecue melded with the rose bushes that grew around
the deck. Here on the north slope of Heraldsgate Hill, the
atmosphere was pleasant, quiet, and, for Judith, soothing.

"It's going on ten years since Dan died," Renie continued. "I'm guessing you've forgotten some of the bad stuff."

Judith made a face. "I think I've forgotten some of the good stuff, too. Like how Dan and Mike actually got along pretty well. I spent a lot of time feeling sorry for myself, both while I was married, and then after Dan died. When Joe came back into my life, I sort of erased everything that had gone before. It was as if my marriage to Dan was an intermission between the first and second acts with Joe."

Dodging a bee, Renie gave a little sigh. "It's true, Dan spent more time raising Mike than you did. It had to be that way, of course. None of the rest of the family knew what was going on—except what you told us—because Dan wouldn't let us commingle. What we heard was when you were upset and he'd done something awful, like when he 'allowed' "—Renie made quote marks with her fingers—"you to come to the family Thanksgiving as long as you made him his own dinner complete with all the trimmings, and when you got back, you found the turkey in the birdbath."

"It was the mailbox," Judith corrected. "We were too poor to have a birdbath. The birds used to bring *us* food."

Renie poked her cousin in the arm. "See? There you go—I mean, it's basically true, but you're making it out to be worse than it really was. *Ergo*, our sympathy mounts for you, and our antipathy escalates for Dan."

"That's so," Judith admitted. "I needed all the sympathy I could get—then. But I don't now. That's where I've been unfair. That's why I'm letting Dan keep the one thing he did well—raising Mike. It's like a memorial, and I don't think it will matter that much to Joe. After all, he went along for over twenty years not even knowing he had a son."

"So you haven't told Joe about your decision not to tell Mike?" Renie inquired.

Judith shook her head. "I haven't had a chance. Mike showed me the tattoo this morning. The only time I've seen Joe since is at Red Fog studios. It wasn't exactly a propitious moment."

Renie inclined her head in tacit agreement. "What about the dress? Did you decide to report it as stolen?"

Judith grimaced. "Do I dare? Then I have to admit I bought it."

"Well . . ." Renie rubbed her short chin. "It could be evidence, if you're right about the smuggling."

Judith brightened. "You don't think I'm crazy?"

Renie tugged at the short, shapeless shift that served as part of her rag-tag stay-at-home wardrobe. "Not exactly. There has to be something clandestine going on to tie Tara and TNT and de Tourville together. I doubt if it's a prayer group."

Glancing at her watch, Judith saw that it was almost five. Discovering that she was low on rum, she had made an emergency run to the liquor store on top of the hill. Since she was halfway to Renie's at that point, she decided to chance calling on her cousin. Judith had definitely felt the need for a convivial ear.

"I'd better head home," she said, rising from the chaise longue. "I'm glad I didn't interrupt you today."

Renie wrinkled her pug nose. "I'm stuck until we find a bum. Morris has an underling out looking. I suppose you didn't ask Joe about Billy Big Horn being in the slammer?"

Judith snapped her fingers. "I don't have to bother him about that. We can call. Here, give me the phone."

Renie handed over the cordless model that had been resting next to her lawn chair. It took Judith so long to get through to someone who could give her the information that Renie began arranging shish-kabobs in the kitchen. Following her cousin inside, Judith finally made contact just as Renie was drizzling melted butter on top of the prawns, mushrooms, baby tomatoes, green peppers, and onions.

"Yes, that's right, Billy Big Horn . . . It's the only name I know him by . . . Well, I suppose it would be loitering or vagrancy or whatever they call that new law where you can't sit or lie down on the sidewalk . . . But if you don't enforce it often, what good is . . . ? Oh—yes, thank you. Yes, that's it. He what? I see. Okay, thank you very much."

Judith put the phone down on the kitchen counter and beamed at Renie. "It's true—Billy was picked up a week ago Saturday for violating that new sidewalk ordinance. He spent ten days in jail, and was released Monday."

Renie looked up from the roll of aluminum foil she was using to wrap the shish-kabobs. "Hunh. I didn't think they really arrested homeless people for that."

"They don't, unless they're making a pest of themselves," Judith replied. "Which, I gather, is what Billy Big Horn did. It sounded as if he was lying around all over the place, creating quite a nuisance. Maybe they wanted to make an example."

"Poor Billy," Renie remarked. "He seems such a harmless sort. Did you say he got out Monday?"

Judith nodded. "It's now Thursday. He hasn't been at the Naples, and nobody's seen him at his usual spot downtown. I wonder where he went?"

"He might have gotten disgusted and left town," Renie suggested. "I suppose Morris can find another bum. Let's face it, to the general public, all homeless people look alike."

"That's because we don't see them as individuals," Judith pointed out, "only as a symptom of society's ills."

"And," Renie added, getting out a kettle from the cupboard under the counter, "it's a problem the rest of us don't want to think about. It's hard to be reminded that you have a snug home and enough to eat while hungry people are sleeping under a bridge."

"Which," Judith said in wispy voice as she headed for the front door, "is where I used to think I'd end up when I was married to Dan."

Renie paused in the act of opening a canister of rice. "Hey—there you go again. You were never homeless."

"That's because after Dan died I came back to live with Mother." Judith waved goodbye from the doorway. "For awhile there were times when the bridge looked good."

To Judith's surprise, Phyliss was waiting for her in the driveway. In her long black raincoat and matching gloves, she looked overdressed for what had become a warm, sunny afternoon.

"Where've you been?" the cleaning woman demanded. "I got here half an hour ago. Your crabby old mother told me you were out picking up sailors, but I doubted that. Or were you? She's kind of convincing when she takes out her teeth."

"I had to go to the . . ." Judith cut herself off. Even though Phyliss knew that the Flynns kept alcohol in the house, it didn't do to advertise the fact. ". . . store," Judith gulped. "What is it, Phyliss? Did you forget something this morning?"

Phyliss shook her head. "No. It's that de Tooleyville. He had some crazy notion that I'd been in the hospital. I didn't set him straight, 'cause that's where I should have been the past couple of days. I could see that he was sorry for me, which was kind of surprising, him being such a hoity-toity foreigner and all. He asked a trillion questions, and you can be sure I answered every one and then some, right down to my liver complaint and the uncertainty of my bowels. Then he had to go out all of a sudden, so I started looking for that cummerbund stuff. Though how you can figure what's cummerbund and what isn't with all them fancy doo-dads and fripperies and whatnot, I don't know. So," Phyliss went on, pausing only for a deep breath, "I sort of kept my eye out for cigars. Lo and behold,'' she declared, reaching into the pocket of her raincoat, ''I found a couple. They were in the guest bedroom, under the brocade dust ruffle.'' In triumph, Phyliss held out two fat, brown cigars.

''I'll be darned,'' Judith murmured. ''Good work, Phyliss. Thank you very much.''

Phyliss bestowed a sour look on Judith. ''You won't be smoking these, I hope?''

''Of course not, Phyliss.'' She gave the cleaning woman's bony shoulder a grateful squeeze. ''Thank you. Ah . . . do you want a ride home?''

Phyliss shook her head. ''I can take the bus, like I always do. I got nobody waiting for me. Except Jesus.'' She tromped off down the drive, the black coat swinging behind her.

If the temperature had grown warmer, the atmosphere inside Hillside Manor had gotten cooler. When Joe arrived home shortly after six, he greeted his wife with a cursory peck on the cheek, and headed straight upstairs to change. Busy serving her guests, Judith tried to put her husband's aloof manner out of her mind. But when he remained detached throughout dinner and even after they had adjourned to the third-floor family quarters, she could stand it no longer. Judith unleashed an avalanche of explanations, excuses, and apologies.

''So it was because I was upset about you and Mike,'' she concluded, wringing her hands. ''I had to focus on something else. The wedding was over, so the murder was it. Did I do the right thing?'' She turned a tearful face to Joe, who was sitting next to her on the sofa in the family room.

After a long day, Joe was understandably worn out. The last thing he needed was an emotional outburst from his wife. But it had been building, ever since the wedding, and it would be cowardly to dismiss either Judith's dilemma or her contrition.

On the other hand, he, too, had feelings, though they were often kept under wraps. "I have a daughter," he said slowly. "Caitlin means the world to me. She was the one good thing that came out of my marriage to Vivian. For a long time, I thought she was my sole claim to immortality. Then, when I met you again six years ago, I found out that wasn't so. I had a son, a son I didn't know existed—a son I just plain didn't know." Joe passed a hand over his graying red hair. "I still don't know him, not really. He's been away at college or working in Idaho all the time we've been together. I've tried . . ." Joe paused, cleared his throat, and shifted his gaze to the blank TV set across the room. "I tried to get to know him, man-to-man. Not father-to-son, you'll note. Maybe I made some inroads, maybe not. Frankly, I don't feel any closer to him than I do to Bill and Renie's kids. We pass like ships in the night, at family gatherings, in and out of town, whenever."

As Joe hesitated with his green eyes in shadow, Judith put a hand on his arm. "He likes you. I know he does. Mike admires you and respects you. What more could you ask?"

It was a stupid question, and Judith immediately regretted it. "Love," Joe said simply, finally meeting his wife's anxious gaze. "Caitlin loves me. It's natural for a child to love a parent. It's not natural to love a stepfather. It has to be cultivated. I resent that."

Judith bit her lip. "Oh, Joe! I'm so sorry!"

"You made your decision," he said quietly. "It was probably the right thing to do. The truth would upset Mike, put him in therapy, screw up his marriage, his career, whatever. That's the way it is with kids today, isn't it?"

"Are you saying Mike's not man enough to handle it?"

Joe stood up, making for the door. "No. I didn't say it—you did." He left Judith alone in the family room.

*   *   *

She hadn't had a chance to ask him about new developments in the case or what he and Woody had learned at Red Fog studios or if he'd enjoy a cigar. Maybe he didn't intend to talk about the Harley Davidson investigation any more. Certainly there were things, lots of things, he hadn't been telling her along the way. Judith turned on the TV, gazed with unseeing eyes at a series of banal, meaningless programs as she channel-surfed, and finally clicked off the remote control.

She'd blown it. Lacking the courage to tell Mike the truth, she'd forever condemned her husband and his son to casual friendship. And all for Dan, that big, worthless lump who'd made her miserable for most of their eighteen years together.

Except she hadn't done it only for Dan. She'd done it for Mike, too. When Mike needed a father, Dan was there. To Mike, Dan *was* his father. Joe didn't even know Mike existed. He was living with Herself, doting on Caitlin, and playing stepfather to the sons that his first wife had borne to previous mates.

Life had no easy answers. Judith reached into the cloisonne candy box on the sidetable where she'd put the cigars Phyliss had confiscated from Bascombe de Tourville. She juggled what she assumed was first-rate Cuban quality in her hands. "Firm and fully packed"—the phrase from a radio commercial of her youth tripped through her brain.

But the cigars were no such thing. They felt light and lumpy. Carefully, Judith peeled back a layer of dark brown tobacco leaf. She peeled some more.

Three small objects fell in her lap. It was growing dark in the family room, and she switched on the table lamp. At first, the objects looked dull and rocklike. Then she held them up to the light.

They were green, like glass, and under the murky exterior, a dazzling fire struck her eye. She was reminded of the glass chunk she'd collected from the Belmont balcony. A bottle, Woody had suggested, or something equally innocuous.

They were neither.

Upon close inspection, Judith knew an emerald when she saw one.

FIFTEEN

THE MOMENT OF madness had passed. Judith had caressed the uncut stones, held them under a three-way bulb, laid them against her bare throat and on her finger. The smallest of the emeralds would make a brilliant ring. Chips from any of the gems would look heavenly at her ears. Who would miss one little piece of unpolished rock? Someone with a Uzi, Judith decided, and went downstairs to tell Joe about the emeralds.

She found him outside on the patio, sitting in a lawn chair and listening to the soft sounds of summer. Approaching quietly, she juggled the three stones she'd found in the first cigar, the four smaller ones from the second, and the chunk she'd saved from the Belmont roof. Judith was about to rouse Joe from his reverie when she heard the phone ring.

Of course she could let it switch over to the answering machine, but it might be a reservation or a cancellation. Judith darted back into the house and picked up the phone where she'd left it on the kitchen counter next to the computer. If Joe heard or saw her, he didn't move.

"I'm in the soup," Renie declared in a frazzled voice. "I told Morris Mitchell that Billy Big Horn was still around, and now he insists that I find him. Any old bum won't do for our Morris. Where should we go to hustle the homeless? Bill's coming with me."

The old schoolhouse clock on the kitchen wall said it was almost eight-thirty. "You're going now?" Judith said in surprise.

"Immediately," Renie answered, now sounding testy. "Morris can't wait. I told him it was useless, because Billy will be holed up for the night, probably under some bridge or maybe the viaduct."

"That could be dangerous," Judith pointed out.

"I know," Renie responded. "Which is why we won't go there. We're just going to take a swing through downtown, and maybe the hospital district by the Naples. It'll stay light for another hour, so we can spot Billy if he's around. At least I can tell Morris that I tried."

"Donner & Blitzen's corner and the Naples are the main places where Billy hung out," Judith said as she heard Joe come through the back door and go upstairs. "The Belle Epoch, Nordquist's, and the Cascadia Hotel are popular with panhandlers, too."

"I thought of them," Renie said as her husband's voice rang out from somewhere in the Jones's household. "Got to go, Bill's ready and roaring."

Judith clicked off the phone and sank into the chair by the computer. She should take the emeralds to Joe at once. But Renie's interruption had given her time to think. Maybe this wasn't the moment to spring the uncut stones on her husband. He had plenty on his mind right now, and his job wasn't what was troubling him.

Picking up the phone book, Judith searched for Chuck Rawls's number. She found Charles Rawls Jr. in a suburb east of the lake. He answered on the first ring.

"No," he said after Judith had expressed her dismay about the bombing, "there was no damage except to the lobby. The company that owns the building had insurance, and they've just about got everything fixed. There're a lot of other businesses besides KRAS and KORN at Heraldsgate 400, including the Highcastle Hot Dog administrative offices. If that bomb had been a biggie, there'd be some serious pissing and moaning. Excuse the expression.''

Somewhere in the back of her mind, Judith recalled the Highcastle Hot Dog sign featuring Willie, the Winking Wienie, atop the actual plant in the city's industrial section south of downtown. It also occurred to her that she hadn't seen Willie wink at her lately as she traveled the freeway.

''I understand that Pork Barrel Meats in Chicago bought Highcastle Hot Dogs,'' Judith said in a casual tone. ''Did that happen recently?''

''Oh—about six months ago,'' Rawls answered. ''Not long after the first of the year. Ms. Highcastle thought they'd keep the operation here going, but all they wanted was the name. So she had to make it up to her employees, buy-outs, severance, all that stuff. That's why she keeps an office in the 400 building. She's still writing checks.''

''All the same,'' Judith said in what she hoped was envious amazement, ''Ms. Highcastle must have made a bundle off the sale.''

''You'd figure as much,'' Rawls allowed, ''but it actually turned into a headache. She owned the building south of town, but not the land. Now that there's talk of building a new sports stadium in that area, she's responsible for razing the place. Lately, Ms. Highcastle seems to be in the business of wrack and ruin instead of rock 'n' roll.''

''Are you saying that she's going through hard times?'' Judith suggested tentatively.

''Who knows?'' Rawls replied with what sounded like a yawn. ''With rich people, it's tough to tell. When they say they're broke, they mean they're down to their last few millions. It's a funny thing—that's as hard for them as it is for working stiffs like me who figure we're broke when the old checking account is overdrawn by a couple of hundred bucks, and the so-called reserves were never there in the first place.''

''True,'' Judith murmured, then changed the subject. ''I haven't heard if the kids who tossed the bomb have been caught. The newspapers have been very quiet on the subject since the initial article.''

''Right,'' Rawls agreed. ''No deaths, no serious damage, no real news. We're just as bad in radio. Heck, we only follow up on stories if it's a major war, major plane crash, or some major gets caught in bed with another major.'' Rawls chuckled at his own twisted humor.

Judith forced a truncated giggle, but her mind was elsewhere. ''Are you keeping Darrell Mims on the air?''

''We have to.'' Rawls now sounded glum. ''Our talent search hasn't turned up anyone else, at least nobody we can afford. And Mims may be pretty bland, but he's a hell of a lot cheaper than Harley.''

''What did Harley do with his money?'' Judith inquired in a musing tone. ''That is, I'm told he didn't have any sizable savings.''

''He didn't?'' Rawls sounded genuinely surprised. ''He must have. He made big six figures, maybe more.''

''As a DJ?''

''Not from KRAS,'' Rawls responded slowly. ''Oh, he had a good salary, that's for damned sure, but according to inside-the-industry rumors, the real money came from . . . other sources.'' The producer's voice lowered a notch.

''Yes, so I understand,'' Judith said in a conspiratorial tone. ''So where did it go? Women? Drugs?''

There was a pause at the other end of the line. ''I really don't know,'' Rawls finally answered with what sounded a bit like wonderment. ''There were women, sure, but mostly groupies. I've been to his apartment, and it was okay, but nothing special. He wasn't a collector. You know, when a guy can't see, there isn't much point in hanging Old Masters on the wall or putting rare stamps in an album. And, as you might have guessed, he didn't spend it on cars.''

It hadn't fully occurred to Judith until now that having impaired sight or no sight at all was bound to limit life's pleasures. A wave of compassion for Harley Davidson swept over her. As if to prove what he was missing, she rose from the chair and gazed out the window. Dusk was settling in over Heraldsgate Hill, creating a gray-gold glow behind the maple and evergreen trees. Judith smiled at the often unappreciated sight.

"So Harley couldn't see at all?" she asked in a soft voice.

"Actually, he could see a little. Sort of extreme tunnel vision, just enough that he could get around familiar places by himself. Maybe," Rawls added in a speculative tone, "that's why he never had a guide dog."

"How did he lose his sight?" Judith inquired, hearing Joe on the stairs.

"I don't know," Rawls admitted. "I gathered it was a birth defect."

"Poor man." Judith turned to see Joe in the hallway. "Thank you. I appreciate your help. I really must run now."

Joe went to the refrigerator where he got out a can of diet soda. "Still sleuthing, huh?" His voice held no inflection.

"Yes," Judith confessed. "It's like an addiction. I wanted to stop, I really did, but . . . I can't." She hung her head. "I'm sorry."

Joe popped the top of his soda can, gave Judith a pensive look, and went upstairs.

As expected, Renie and Bill had had no luck searching for Billy Big Horn. They had, however, learned more about what had happened to the harmonica-playing homeless man.

"It's a real grapevine among those people," Renie told

Judith Friday morning as the cousins sat at sidewalk tables outside of Moonbeam's coffee house. The newlyweds had taken off early, long before Judith's B&B guests had risen. Judith had shed a tear or two as she kissed her son and his bride goodbye. Joe had shaken hands with Mike and bestowed a paternal peck on Kristin's cheek. The rental car they'd picked up the day before had disappeared out of the cul-de-sac and faded into the gold and purple haze of the summer sunrise. Judith had stayed out on the curb for several minutes, wondering if she'd done the right thing by not doing anything at all.

"They have their own world," Renie was saying, and Judith realized she might have missed part of her cousin's conversation. "The members of the homeless community all know each other. Anyway, it seems that Saturday morning—the day Mike and Kristin were married—somebody from St. Fabiola's Hospital reported Billy lying across the main entrance. Whoever it was recognized him, and after he—or she, I'm not sure which—figured out that Billy wasn't sick, he—or she—tried to move him, or get him to move. Billy refused. So he—or she—called the cops. They trotted out the anti-sidewalk sitting ordinance, and hauled Billy away."

"He—or she—must be a hard case," Judith remarked with a puckish smile. "Couldn't you just have said 'hospital staffer'?"

Renie gave a swipe at the mocha mustache she'd created. "Never mind. I have to do all this P.C. crap in my work these days, and it gets to be a habit. Somebody objected to 'history' in some text a couple of weeks ago, and insisted on calling it 'herstory.' The writer got so mad, he changed it to 'ustory.' I didn't much blame him, except that the typesetter thought it was supposed to be 'usury' and the client had a fit, since it was a bank."

" 'It'?" Judith lifted her eyebrows.

"Them. They. Screw it." Renie took another swig of her mocha. "I'm a designer, not a writer. Anyway, Billy was carted off to jail, and he went most meekly. I suppose those homeless folks don't mind sometimes, because they get a bed and food and a roof over their heads.''

''So where is he now?'' Judith asked, sipping her latte.

Renie shook her head. ''Nobody's seen him since. They—the other bums—figure he left town. Though that's not like him, I gather. He's been a fixture around here for the last four or five years.''

For a few moments, Judith sipped her beverage and kept quiet. As usual, the corner on which Moonbeam's was located hosted a horde of passersby. The constant parade included mothers pushing babies, couples with dogs on leashes, grocery shoppers carrying Falstaff bags, teenagers on summer break, and children heading for the rec center two blocks away. Judith was an inveterate people-watcher, but on this warm morning in July, she was distracted by her thoughts.

''How?'' she finally asked.

''How what?'' Renie frowned and accidentally sloshed mocha on the table.

''How would Billy leave town? He's blind. Wouldn't that make hitchhiking especially dangerous?''

Renie used a napkin to wipe up the small puddle. ''Look—for all we know, Billy's a very successful panhandler. Maybe he saved. He could have flown some place, or taken a bus or train. What do sheltered middle-class people like us really know about the homeless?''

Judith allowed that Renie was right. The subculture comprised of the homeless was as foreign as an African tribe. ''So what are you going to do now about your brochure photos?'' Judith asked.

Renie sighed. ''Morris insists I spend this afternoon looking for a bum. His underling came up wanting, so I'm stuck. Care to join me?''

Judith's hand strayed to her purse, which was resting at her feet. ''Well . . . I was thinking of going to the jeweler's at the bottom of the hill.'' Casting around the vicinity to make sure that no one was watching, Judith dug into her purse and pulled out one of the smaller emeralds. Renie's eyes grew huge as Judith told her about the discovery in the cigars.

"But you haven't shown these to Joe?" Renie asked when Judith had completed her tale.

"No. I didn't have a chance." In a woebegone voice, Judith told her cousin about the previous evening. "I don't blame Joe, but it makes me unhappy."

Elbows on the table and resting her chin on her hands, Renie regarded Judith quite seriously. "Our kids are young enough to still believe in black and white. We know better. It's very gray out there."

"I realize that," Judith said, still forlorn. "It doesn't stop me from wanting to make it better."

"Yes," Renie said, now gazing beyond Judith to Begelman's Bakery across the street. "We don't want anyone we love to be hurt or sad or upset. But sometimes they are, and there's not much we can do about it. At some point when Mike was small, you and Dan could have told him the truth. But you chose not to—or maybe, knowing you, dear coz, you let it drift." Renie was again looking at Judith, and saw her cousin bristle. "Whichever, it doesn't matter now. The moment passed. You and Joe are both going to have to live with what didn't happen."

"I don't like it," Judith said in a flat voice.

"We don't like lots of things that we have to live with," Renie replied, still wearing what Judith called her cousin's boardroom face. "Joe was the one who ran off. Of course he didn't know you were pregnant, you didn't know it, either. So this is the price he pays for a moment of drunken folly. You found Dan on a very hard rebound. I'll admit that his offer of marriage was uncharacteristically kind, but he had his reasons, which included a meal ticket. Still, before that had to happen, why didn't Joe come to his senses and get his marriage annulled? Did you ever ask him?"

"No. Yes. Sort of," Judith hedged.

"And?"

"First of all," Judith said, taking a deep breath, "he tried to call me from Vegas, but Mother wouldn't let him talk to me. She told him I hated him, or some such thing, which wasn't exactly true. I never knew he'd called until after we met each other again six years ago. I told you all about that."

"So your mother sabotaged everything?" Renie made a face. "She's capable of it, but Joe gave up too easily. Gave in too easily as well. I've never understood why he stayed married to a woman he hardly knew, and who was a lush even then. I'm sorry, I hold Joe at fault. If he's unhappy about the outcome after all these years, that's too bad. You did the best you could at the time, given the circumstances. That's all anybody can do. Regrets stink."

Judith knew Renie was right, though it didn't make her feel better. "I don't like having this between us," she said with a feeble wave for Cecil the mailman who was emptying the storage box on the corner by Moonbeam's. "It's like a big, ugly weight."

To Judith's surprise, Renie laughed. "You mean it's like Dan?"

Judith bristled. "You told me not to think negative thoughts about him all the time."

"This isn't all the time, this is now." Renie was still grinning. "Sorry. But all married couples have baggage they'd like to dump. You and Joe haven't been married long enough to acquire much. Get used to it. Maybe you've been living in a false paradise."

"We quarrel," Judith pointed out. "You know that."

"That's different." Renie finished her mocha and dabbed at her mouth. "You can make up quarrels and forget about them. Marriage is about more than wrangling. It's about big hurts and old wounds. You can ignore chronic problems in good weather, but when things get chilly, they're just like physical aches and pains that keep coming back.'' With a wry little smile, Renie stood up. ''Got to run, coz. I need a bum. See you.''

Judith remained at the small table, sipping her latte, which had now grown cold. Despite the morning sun, she too felt cold. Yes, it was okay to suffer the little flaws, the irksome habits, the minor breakdowns in communication, the disagreements about which TV shows to watch. But heavy, disturbing burdens were another matter. Renie might blame Joe, but Judith blamed herself.

''Hey, Mrs. Flynn,'' said Cecil, coming out of Moonbeam's with a steaming cup in his hand, ''you're still getting mail for that Mrs. Rackley at your address. Why doesn't she tell whoever is writing to her where she lives? Is it a secret?''

Judith knew that Phyliss had received another letter from the Rundberg clan on Monday. ''Is it from Idaho or Montana?''

''I think so.'' Cecil patted his mail pouch with his free hand.

''I suspect she forgot to give them her address,'' Judith said. ''She's probably too wrapped up in exchanging tall tales about the Lord.''

Cecil looked puzzled. ''Excuse me?''

Judith smiled, summoning up good cheer from her reserves. ''Never mind, Cecil. I'll remind her. Just drop the letter off with the rest of our stuff and I'll give it to her.''

Cecil went off on his route while Judith gathered up her purse, then headed for her car, which was parked a few doors down the street. Ten minutes later she was in the Gem Shop, placing the uncut emeralds on a chamois cloth.

''Good grief,'' gasped Donna Weick, who owned the store with her husband, Arnold. ''Where on earth did you get *these*?''

Judith winced. ''If I said I found them, would you believe me?''

Donna, however, had served Judith and other Grover

family members for almost twenty years. "I guess I'd have to," she said in an awed tone. "Dare I ask where?"

"No." Judith flushed a bit. "It has to do with a police investigation. My husband, you know. But they're authentic?"

To Judith's surprise, Donna came out from behind the counter, locked the front door, and hung up the "Closed" sign. "I'm not taking any chances," she said in a more normal tone. "You might have been followed. Putting these things in a sandwich bag isn't the proper way to transport them."

"It was all I had," Judith gulped.

Donna, a big, handsome woman in her late forties, nodded with indulgent good humor. "Okay. Let's go to the back of the shop. Arnie and I are both certified gemologists, so we've got equipment. You know—a refractive index, a polariscope, a special dark field illuminator."

Judith had no idea what Donna was talking about but docilely followed the store owner. The back room looked like part laboratory, part workshop, and part storage. While Donna examined the stones, Judith stood quietly, with her hands clasped in front of her.

Twenty minutes passed before Donna sat back in her chair, rubbed her eyes, and then put a hand over her heart. "Beautiful," she breathed. "I can't test for hardness, because we don't have a dichroscope or a spectroscope. You never test cut stones, which is all that Arnie and I usually see. These are really excellent quality. I'd guess that they come from Colombia. Most emeralds do these days, though some have been found in North Carolina. The largest stones are Siberian."

Judith carefully leaned against the work counter. "Can you give me any idea of what they'd be worth?"

Donna fingered her full upper lip. "Not specifically. But offhand—and this is a very conservative estimate— I'd say that you're looking at close to two million dollars, wholesale."

"Yikes!" Judith staggered at the sum. "You mean . . .
I've been carrying two million bucks worth of emeralds
around in a sandwich bag?"

Donna nodded. "That's why I was so astonished. If I
were you, I'd get a police escort to take me home. Or put
them in a bank right now. Unless, of course, the police
want them back." Donna's voice sounded dubious.

"Goodness!" Judith paced the small open area. "I
don't know what to do." She glanced at her watch, which
told her it was not quite noon. If she had any sense, she'd
go straight to headquarters and hand the emeralds over to
Joe. "Yes," she said, more to herself than to Donna, "I'm
going to get rid of these right away. Thanks, Donna. I
really appreciate your help."

Donna seemed loathe to part with the uncut stones. "If
you—or whoever—wants to unload one or two of those,
call me. I'd mortgage the kids to get my hands on emeralds like that. The market's very good. Arnie's been
hearing about some big sales in the Bay Area."

Judith's ears tingled. "Cut or uncut?"

"Both." Donna was now eyeing the emeralds speculatively. "I wonder."

So did Judith. But Donna knew nothing more, except
that a handful of San Francisco jewelers, both wholesale
and retail, had been selling more emeralds than usual.
"Not enough to flood the market and devalue the price,"
Donna added, "but sufficient to make shop-owners like
Arnie and me green with envy. Excuse the expression."

As Judith headed downtown, she could have sworn that
every car that pulled up alongside of her, every pedestrian
walking in a crosswalk, every person gazing out of a
store-front window was hatching a plan to accost her and
steal the emeralds. A gypsy cab with a bearded driver
seemed to be following her from the bottom of Heraldsgate Hill, though he finally turned off near Nordquist's.
At one long stoplight in midtown, a rowdy group of teenagers pounded on her hood as they danced through the

intersection. They continued on, however, laughing and shouting. Judith arrived at the municipal building safely.

Parking, however, was another matter. The city, in its infinite lack of wisdom, had allotted only a couple of dozen parking places in the small open area between the street and the building itself. Visitors were expected to find a nearby garage or drive around in circles until something opened up on a meter. Judith had always figured it was a cunning plan to discourage citizens from making pests of themselves.

Judith was not going to go around in circles while she had two million dollars worth of emeralds in her purse. Noting a vacant space marked "Deputy Mayor" next to the main entrance, she pulled in and got out of the car. Then, recalling her near-disaster outside of Red Fog recording studios, she scribbled a note and left it on her windshield. "Delivering vital homicide–smuggling evidence," the note said. She had underlined "vital" three times.

The air-conditioning in the city building never worked properly, or so Joe often complained. Judith noticed that the halls seemed stale, stuffy, and fractionally overwarm. She got into an elevator with a dozen other people, all of whom looked like purse-snatchers or pickpockets, but were probably ordinary city employees who lacked sufficient ambition to commit a felony. Clutching her purse as if it were a newborn baby, she headed for the homicide division.

Joe and Woody were out. Gritting her teeth, Judith said she'd wait. The reception area was a busy place, and Judith recognized several of the police and city personnel who passed by. She was not, however, in a mood to chat. Her fingers dug into the purse's black leather; tension, if not the inadequate air-conditioning, was making her perspire.

"I know you!" exclaimed a vaguely familiar voice.

Judith looked up to see TNT Tenino, wearing shorts

and a tank top that exposed his impressive muscles. "Hello, Mr. Tenino," she responded nervously. "What are you doing here?"

"I don't know," TNT answered, gazing vaguely up at the fluorescent lighting that turned him and everyone else a sickly shade of chartreuse. "I was trying to find the divorce filings. But that's the county, not the city, right?"

"I think so," Judith replied. "Is . . . are you and your wife divorcing?"

TNT sat down in the chair next to Judith. "I heard she filed yesterday," he said in a weary voice. "But I haven't been served with any papers. I'd like to know before I leave town."

"You're going away?" Judith asked in surprise.

TNT nodded. "Business. I'll be gone a couple of weeks. It's a good thing my expenses are covered. Otherwise, I'd be out of luck."

"I see," Judith said, though she didn't quite. Still, a glimmer of an idea flickered through her brain. "Where are you going?"

"San Jose," TNT responded. "There's a good boxing club in the area. I check out promising kids for a couple of local promoters."

Judith was disappointed. Somehow, she'd expected TNT to say that he was heading for Colombia or Santa Teresa del Fiore or even Siberia. "How interesting," she said, hoping she sounded more enthusiastic than she felt. "I was wondering—where did you stay after you left Hillside Manor last week?"

"Hillside Manor?" TNT seemed puzzled. "Oh—is that your place? I bunked with a pal for a few days."

"Ms. Novotny?" Judith murmured.

TNT shook his head. "She picked me up, but that was only because I needed a ride. The pal's a guy who works at KRAS. Darrell Mims—he's filling in for Harley Davidson, I guess. But he doesn't have Harley's style. Style's really important, in boxing, and everything else.

Espy has style. Class, too. It's a shame she can't afford to keep me.''

"I thought she'd been unfaithful," Judith said, then took in the import of TNT's words. "Are you saying she's no longer rich?"

TNT drooped in the chair, as if his wife's cash flow and his energy were synonymous. "That's what she tells me. Sometimes I don't think she's too bright. At least not when it comes to business stuff. You got to be savvy to be in business, right? I mean, it's like boxing—your fists'll only get you so far. You got to be savvy in the ring. Espy's got a glass jaw when it comes to swimming with the money sharks."

The mixed metaphor was a little hazy, but Judith knew what TNT was trying to say. As she recalled, Esperanza Highcastle had inherited the hot dog empire. Her father— or maybe it was her grandfather, Judith couldn't remember which—had founded the company and built it into a successful regional concern. Perhaps Esperanza had inherited the business, but not the business sense.

"Surely she must have investments," Judith offered as more familiar faces trudged past, though none of them belonged to Joe or Woody. "The radio stations are doing okay, aren't they?"

"So-so." TNT seemed dejected by his wife's broadcasting enterprises. "Without Harley, KRAS'll lose money. Like I said, Darrell's a good guy, but he's no teenage-type DJ. Maybe Espy should switch to a call-in format. A sports show—that'd be good." TNT brightened at the idea. "I could call in with boxing questions."

Though not concentrating on the ring, Judith's mind was dancing around in circles. Caught offguard, she noticed that TNT was rising from his chair. "I'd better go across the street to the county building," he said. "I wish Espy'd just sit down and talk to me about all this. Maybe she could explain about those other guys. I really get confused when she talks about getting it on with Babe Ruth and King Tut.''

''Maybe they're just friends,'' Judith suggested with a straight face. ''By the way, did you know she came to get you at Hillside Manor?''

TNT's close-set eyes sparked with interest. ''She did? Was she mad? Or glad?''

Judith thought back to her brief encounter with Esperanza Highcastle. ''Neither. She was disappointed, I think. Because you'd left.'' Noting that TNT seemed touched by the news, Judith couldn't help but smile kindly. ''I doubt that she would have come if she didn't care. But she indicated that she knew where to find you. She said you must have gone to the Belmont. Why would she have thought that?''

TNT rubbed at his low forehead. ''Maybe because I told her I'd keep a look-out on that demolition crew. They're stalling, and it bugs Espy. Maybe it's because of the cops.'' His eyes darted warily around the waiting room, as if he expected to be arrested for mentioning the police in anything but a laudatory manner.

Judith was puzzled. ''Why should your wife care about the Belmont's demolition?''

Edging toward the elevators, TNT's attention seemed to be wandering from Judith. ''Huh? Oh, because she owns it. See you around.'' He hurried off as two sets of elevator doors opened.

Judith realized that she should have known. Chuck Rawls had mentioned that Esperanza Highcastle seemed to be in the business of tearing things down. The hot dog plant couldn't have been the only edifice that was doomed to the wrecking ball.

Anxiously, Judith checked her purse. The emeralds were still in place, tucked into the flimsy sandwich bag. She was about to resume her vigil when Joe and Woody stepped out from one of the elevators.

They had Bascombe de Tourville with them, and he was wearing handcuffs.

SIXTEEN

JUDITH DIDN'T KNOW what to do. She could hardly wave the emeralds at her husband while he had the alleged owner in custody. Besides, Joe looked grim and very businesslike. Both he and Woody appeared not to notice her, but walked briskly by the row of visitors' chairs. A moment later, they had disappeared behind the reception desk and down the hall that led to the booking and interrogation rooms.

She supposed she could wait some more, but one pair of B&B guests had announced their intention of arriving before the usual check-in time. Judith felt she should get home.

Approaching the reception desk, she smiled at the uniformed young woman whose nameplate indicated that she was Officer Mariana Reyes. "I've an unusual request," Judith said after identifying herself as Joe Flynn's wife. "I think I have some evidence concerning a case my husband is working on."

Mariana Reyes's brown eyes flickered. "Is that so?" she said in a smooth, calm voice. "May I see your identification, please?"

"My . . . ?" Judith gaped at the officer, then fumbled in her purse. The sandwich bag fell to the floor. One of the emeralds rolled out, heading toward the

Grecian-sandaled feet of an oncoming visitor. "Look out!" Judith cried, diving after the stone. Her arm darted between trim ankles, upsetting the newcomer who fell on top of Judith.

"My leg!" the victim cried. "My arm! My back! I'll sue!"

Immobilized, Judith could see only one sandaled foot and the soft pleats of a Grecian chiton. "Ooof!" Judith exclaimed, trying to maneuver just enough to breathe. "Uhnh . . ."

Apparently Officer Reyes had come around to the other side of the reception counter. "Let me help you," she offered, still sounding calm. At last, amid protests and warnings from her victim, Judith felt the other woman's weight being removed.

"Do you know who I am?" Esperanza Highcastle demanded, straightening the pleats of her diaphanous gown.

"Athena?" Officer Reyes suggested.

"Saucy! I'll have your badge!" Esperanza glared down at Judith who had miraculously recovered the stray emerald and was trying to get up. "And you! I'll see that . . ." She stopped. "*You*! This isn't the first time you've tried to kill me! A week or two ago, at the radio station . . ." She stopped again, narrowing her eyes at Judith's struggling figure. "The bed and breakfast! You were the one harboring TNT! Why are you stalking me?" Esperanza whirled on Officer Reyes. "Arrest this woman! I want to file a complaint!"

The minor fracas had drawn a small crowd. City workers, private citizens, and perhaps a crook or two had gathered between the elevators and the reception desk, creating a bottleneck. Now on her feet, but feeling wobbly, Judith surreptitiously counted the emeralds. Though her fingers shook, the stones were all accounted for. Anxiously, Judith looked at Officer Reyes.

"Excuse me," the policewoman said in that same calm voice, "but I saw what happened. Mrs. . . ." She glanced at Judith for confirmation. "Flynn? Mrs. Flynn didn't intend to trip you. She's here to see her husband, who she claims is a homicide detective."

Judith didn't care for the word "claims." Did Officer Reyes mean that Judith "claimed" to be Joe's wife, or that Joe "claimed" to be a homicide detective? Neither boded well for Judith.

But Mariana Reyes wasn't through with Esperanza Highcastle. "How may I help you?" The calm manner discouraged further nonsense and somehow conveyed to the onlookers that they should disperse.

Esperanza seemed taken aback. "Well! Now that you mention it, I was summoned here to press charges." The disheveled curls tumbled around Esperanza's shoulders as she turned to glower at Judith. "Not with regard to *her*, but some juvenile delinquents who tried to blow up my radio stations."

Officer Reyes checked her computer screen. "Yes, I believe they've been IDed by passersby at the scene. Lucky for you. Someone actually got a partial on the license plate. I'll get a bomb squad officer to assist you."

To Judith's relief, Esperanza now seemed completely caught up in seeking justice for the damage done to the Heraldsgate 400 building. Indeed, she looked both worried and distracted. Perhaps she thought the perpetrators still had a bomb or two on their persons.

After Esperanza had departed with a member of the bomb squad, Officer Reyes returned her attention to Judith. "You were about to show me your driver's license?" Still the same even, unflappable tone. Judith wondered if a large bomb going off in the reception area might cause the young woman to bat an eye.

Her credentials having proved acceptable, Judith was informed that Detective Flynn was in the interrogation room. There was no telling when he might be free. Would Mrs. Flynn care to wait?

Judith already had waited half an hour. She hemmed

and hawed, and was about to leave when Woody Price appeared. This time he noticed Judith and smiled warmly.

"What are you doing here?" he asked in his mellifluous baritone. "Joe's tied up right now."

"I know," Judith said, so relieved to see a friendly face that she kissed Woody twice. "I have something for him. And for you. Here." Again fumbling in her purse, she brought out the emeralds. "I found this one on the Belmont balcony—remember? The others were in a cigar."

Woody frowned at the stones. "They're not . . . glass?"

Judith shook her head. "No," she said in hushed tones. "They're honest-to-God uncut emeralds. I had them checked by a certified gemologist."

Woody let out a low whistle. "This is incredible," he murmured. "Where did you get the cigar?"

Judith wrestled with the truth, and, for once, fell victim to virtue. "My cleaning woman, Phyliss Rackley, found the cigar at Bascombe de Tourville's condo. She works for him, too."

By reflex, Woody turned back toward what Judith assumed was the interrogation room. "I'll be darned," he said mildly. "So de Tourville *is* mixed up in all this."

"Of course." Judith couldn't help but feel a bit smug. Then Woody's meaning dawned on her. "You knew that, though—I mean, why else would you and Joe bring de Tourville here in handcuffs?"

"You saw that?" Woody's smile tensed a bit as he leaned closer to Judith and lowered his voice. "Actually, de Tourville may be guilty of several crimes, including immigration fraud. He's been using a phony passport to avoid extradition, but the original charges didn't involve theft or smuggling. He's a con artist, though, specializing in bilking wealthy tourists." Woody now held the emeralds in his hand and eyed them appreciatively.

"Really." Judith tried to look ingenuous. "Goodness, how did he do that?"

Woody, however, remained discreet. "Let's just say

he's a real pro. The fact is, we don't know all the details, which is why Joe and I are questioning him. Excuse me, but I'd better get that coffee I promised your husband. We may be in for a long haul.''

Judith pointed to the emeralds. ''What will you do with them? I'm told they're worth a small fortune.''

''Don't worry. We'll put them in the evidence room. They'll be safe.'' Woody grinned. ''We have a stash of coke in there that would buy these emeralds and much, much more.''

As Woody walked away, Judith's shoulders slumped. The emeralds were in good hands, proper hands. She needn't fuss about them any more. ''Thank you,'' she called to Officer Reyes. With a lightened step, she headed for the elevators.

It took almost three full minutes before a down elevator arrived. It was jammed, and Judith had to wedge herself in between two burly city workers who grumbled at the inconvenience. The doors began to close just as Esperanza Highcastle rushed through the reception area.

''Hold, please!'' she commanded in her imperious voice.

Amazingly, someone hit the right button and the doors reopened. There were no protests when Esperanza squeezed into the elevator. Apparently her manner, which was accustomed to sacrifice on the part of others, had negated any complaints. She and Judith stood so close that their shoulders were pressing against each other. Judith felt compelled to say something to mitigate the awkwardness.

''Did everything go well for you?'' she asked in an undertone.

Esperanza, apparently not used to being addressed so casually, gave a little start. ''Yes. Certainly.''

''Good.'' The elevator stopped and the burly men got out, easing the crush. ''Let's hope those youngsters learn a lesson.''

"Oh, no!" Esperanza sounded shocked. "They didn't do it. I spoke with them, and they're quite innocent. I insisted they be released."

The elevator had arrived on the main floor. Judith kept step with Esperanza in her flowing Grecian chiton. "But I thought they were IDed and that somebody caught part of the license . . ."

"A mistake," Esperanza responded. "People make very poor observers."

Judith felt like asking *as opposed to what*? but Esperanza was already out the door and headed for her pearl-gray Lexus. With a sigh, Judith trudged into the small parking area to seek out her blue Subaru.

The car was gone.

Not having enough cash on her, Judith was forced to take the bus home. Not familiar with the schedule, she had to walk three blocks uphill to find the stop for the Heraldsgate Hill numbers 1, 2, 3, 4, and 13. Not feeling terribly lucky at this point, it was only natural that the 13 would be the first to come along. Judith got on, only to discover that the 13 didn't go all the way up the hill. She had to walk the last six blocks under a sweltering sun.

"Hey, nitwit," called Gertrude from the door of the toolshed, "where've you been? I didn't get my lunch."

Frazzled, Judith paused to catch her breath and check her temper. "I'm sorry, Mother," she finally said in measured tones. "I had to go downtown. Would you like a tuna sandwich?"

"I had tuna yesterday," Gertrude replied. "I'm in the mood for tongue."

"I don't have any tongue," Judith answered, still clutching at her patience. "What about egg salad?"

"Ugh." Gertrude made a face. "The last egg salad you made was all squishy and slimy and icky and there were shells in it. I practically puked. Why can't you make *good* egg salad, like I used to?"

Judith didn't recall ever having made an egg salad sandwich the way her mother so loathsomely described. "Baloney?"

"The same to you," Gertrude said, flipping Judith off. "Boy, are you ornery!" She leaned on her walker and clumped back into the toolshed.

"Mother . . ." The cry was weary, and Judith started to follow Gertrude but thought better of it. Instead, she went inside and opened a can of Spam. It was the closest thing to tongue that she had on hand.

Five minutes later, she was at the toolshed door, carrying a tray which included a Spam sandwich, three kinds of sliced fresh fruit, a mound of potato chips, and a glass of lemonade. "Here's your lunch," she called when there was no response to her knock. "Mother?"

Nothing but silence met Judith's ears. "Mother?" she repeated, as a note of worry crept into her voice. "Mother?"

"Go away," Gertrude rasped. "I already ate."

Judith clenched her teeth. "You told me you had no lunch."

"No, I didn't," came the muffled response. "I said you didn't bring me my lunch."

Trying to calm herself under the hot sun, Judith forced herself to reflect. "You did not. You said *you didn't get your lunch.*"

There was a pause while Gertrude presumably thought through her daughter's words. "Right, I didn't *get it from you.* So I got it myself."

"What did you have?" Judith inquired, fully expecting the Spam to start sizzling on the plate.

"Candy," Gertrude replied. "Lots of candy. It filled me up."

"Swell." Judith sighed. Gertrude always kept a large stash of sweets in her apartment. She nibbled constantly on an assortment of chocolate-covered peanuts, chocolate creams, chocolate truffles, and chocolate bars. Her mother's sweet tooth drove Judith crazy. "That's not wholesome. You need something more nourishing. Open the door and let me give you this tray."

"Nope. I'm full." Gertrude let out an artificial belch to prove the point.

Argument was useless. Judith started back for the house. She was putting the fruit and the Spam away when her early visitors arrived. They had started out at 4 A.M. to beat the heat, and had driven all the way from southern Oregon. Both husband and wife, who were about Judith's age, were in a cantankerous mood.

"This place isn't air-conditioned?" the wife asked in shocked tones. "We're from Chula Vista where everything is air-conditioned. What's wrong with you people?"

"Stairs?" the husband gasped, gazing up to the second landing. "How come you don't put in an elevator? Do you expect us to haul these bags to our rooms?"

The bags included three large suitcases and two sets of golf clubs. With an inward groan, Judith offered to help. The guests responded by going upstairs empty-handed. It took Judith three trips to deliver their luggage.

At last, she sat down to call about her car. The name of the towing company had been posted in the city hall lot. Yes, they had Judith's Subaru. It would cost her eighty-five dollars to claim it. The parking fine was extra. To add insult to injury, their holding area was located clear across town in a slightly seedy neighborhood.

Judith called Renie, who was not in a charitable mood. "I found six bums, but Morris doesn't like any of them. 'Too prosaic,' 'too nondescript,' 'no visible character.' What does he want, some USC film grad out of central casting? I told him to go hustle his own damned bums. It's too hot to be combing the streets for people who are even more miserable than I am."

"Poor coz," Judith said in a meek voice. "I guess you won't be taking me to Tow 'N' Stow. Maybe I can work up enough courage to ask Joe when he gets home. That is, if he's speaking to me yet.''

''Ohhh . . .'' Renie sounded as if she might be beating her head against her desk. ''All right, I'll pick you up in ten minutes. I've done all I can on this blasted design until Morris gets his bum and sorts out his photos.''

On the way across town, Judith regaled Renie with her emerald adventure. Renie was suitably impressed. In fact, she almost wiped out two pedestrians in a crosswalk when she heard the value that Donna Weick had put on the uncut stones.

''So de Tourville was smuggling emeralds inside the Cuban cigars,'' Renie mused after the pedestrians had scattered and their obscene shouts hung on the air. ''Clever.''

''Maybe not,'' Judith responded. ''That is, Woody isn't sure that de Tourville is a smuggler or if he's just a con man. It'll be interesting to hear what he and Joe find out after they question him. If,'' she added wanly, ''Joe will deign to tell me.''

''He'd better,'' Renie said darkly. ''You were the one who found the emeralds.''

''I'm not sure Joe's in a grateful mood,'' Judith said as they began to wend their way through some of the city's meaner streets. Boarded-up buildings, clusters of restless young people on street corners, wary and weary adults pushing grocery carts earmarked the less prosperous neighborhood. And though Renie had turned the Chev's air-conditioner on full blast, the crumbling vista looked, even if it didn't feel, hotter than Heraldsgate Hill.

''Joe'll get over his fit of pique,'' Renie asserted blithely. ''Is that Tow 'N' Stow a couple of blocks on the left beyond the mission sign?''

Judith leaned forward, straining against the seatbelt. ''I think so. Gee, look at all those poor men waiting outside that mission. It must be awful to be hot and hungry.''

''Not as awful as being cold and hungry,'' Renie remarked, glancing at the dozen or more homeless persons of every age, race, and state of despair. "Winter must be even . . . Yikes!" Renie hit the brakes, almost causing a rear-end collision with the green beater just behind the Chev. "Look!" she cried, ignoring the horn that was honking loudly. "Over there, at the mission! See the guy in the blue bathrobe? That's Uncle Gurd!"

Judith gaped. "That's my bathrobe! Let's get him!"

Renie pulled over, double-parking. Judith rolled down the window and shouted Gurd's name.

He ran.

The cousins cut off Uncle Gurd at the entrance to a dead-end alley. The old man danced around piles of trash, ducked behind a garbage can, and tried to climb into a dumpster.

"Cut it out, Uncle Gurd," Judith called through the open car window. "Please get in. We've been worried about you."

"You're the feds!" Gurd shouted, his back plastered against the dumpster. "Don't kid me! They always drive big blue cars like this!"

Judith was losing patience. "You know better," she snapped. "I'm Kristin's mother-in-law." The words struggled in Judith's throat; she had not yet taken in the concept of her new role: *Mother-in-law*. With Dan, she'd had Effie McMonigle, who wasn't inclined to venture beyond the well-manicured grounds of her Arizona retirement home. Joe's mother had died when he was in his teens. But the specter of Gertrude loomed over Judith's husband. It was not a pretty sight.

"Do you want us to run you down?" Judith asked in an unusually menacing voice. "We will, if you don't get in this car right now!"

Gurd's bony body seemed to collapse under Judith's soiled chenille bathrobe. "Okay, okay," he grumbled, trying to open the rear door before Renie could exercise the power locks. "But I need my stuff. I stashed it at the mission."

Backing the car out of the alley, Renie waited with uncharacteristic patience for an opening in traffic. After they had returned to the mission and Uncle Gurd had retrieved his belongings, which appeared to consist of a large grocery bag, the trio headed for the towing impound.

Since Uncle Gurd didn't smell exactly fresh, Renie had been forced to turn off the air-conditioning and roll down the windows. She was slowing to search for the correct address when a series of jarring musical notes came from the back seat.

Judith turned. Uncle Gurd was playing a harmonica. Badly. "Do you mind?" Judith winced, her good humor not yet regained.

"I mind a lot," Gurd replied, then gave four loud toots on the harmonica. "You don't like music?"

"I haven't heard any," Judith retorted. "Where did you get . . ."

Renie had pulled up in front of the towing company's office. "Here you go, coz," she said with forced cheer. "You can take your new best friend with you."

Halfway out of the car, Judith turned to glare at Renie. "You take him. *You're* the one who wanted a bum."

"I didn't want this one," Renie responded as Uncle Gurd played the opening bars of what might have been Beethoven's Fifth. Or "Dixie." "He lives in *your* hedge," Renie added darkly.

"It's Rankers's hedge," Judith retorted. "Drop him off at Arlene and Carl's. They seem to like him."

Put off-guard by Judith's unusually harsh tone, Renie gave in. "Okay, I'll meet you at your place." Tromping on the accelerator, Renie swung out from the curb and barreled up the hill that led away from the towing site.

After paying her fee and claiming her car, Judith drove home in a glum mood. Nothing seemed to be going right for her lately. Not with Joe, not with her mother, not with

her finances, not even with her feeble attempts at amateur
sleuthing. Discouragement covered her like the ruined
chenille bathrobe enveloped Uncle Gurd.

It was going on four, the hottest part of the day, when
Judith got out of the car in her driveway. Renie was sitting
on the back porch steps, tapping her foot.

"Morris wants Gurd to audition," Renie said, sounding
as morose as Judith felt. "I called from the Rankers's
house. Gurd's there now, eating left-over barbecued pork
ribs. Here," she added, handing Gurd's harmonica over
to Judith. "He left this in my car."

The instrument was worn and battered, with signs of
rust. "That's funny," Judith remarked. "I never saw this
or heard him play it while he was living in the hedge."
She paused, fingering the marred metal. "Does it look
familiar?"

Renie curled her lip. "Are you kidding? Why should
it? I don't hang out with Uncle Gurd at the mission."

Suddenly, Judith's eyes brightened. "Uncle Gurd can't
play this. It's not his. I wonder . . ." She got up from
where she had been sitting next to Renie and stared in the
direction of the Rankers house.

Just then, Uncle Gurd came through the hedge. He still
wore Judith's bathrobe but had a big red- and white-
checked napkin tied around his neck. "Yep, that woman
makes mighty fine pork ribs," Gurd asserted, then turned
to Renie. "When do I get my picture took?"

Renie let out a tortured sigh. "Tomorrow, at ten. I'll
pick you up around nine-thirty. Be ready, or become
dead."

Judith knew how much her cousin hated to work on a
Saturday, not to mention being forced to turn her brain
on before ten o'clock in the morning.

Gurd took umbrage with Renie. "Say, you're kind of
ornery." His eyes narrowed as his gaze took in Judith.
"You, too. You made it seem like I wore out my welcome. Over at that mission, they made me feel right at

home. Now where's that good-looker with the blond hair? I haven't seen her for quite a spell. That's one real pleasant female. Good figger, too, plenty of curves.''

"Vivian?" Judith tried not to blanch at Gurd's over-enthusiastic description. "She went to Florida."

"Florida, huh?" Gurd grimaced. "Never been there. Now why would anybody go to Florida for the *summer*?"

Judith started to reply, but suddenly changed topics. "Where did you get this harmonica, Gurd?" Her tone had softened.

Gurd turned defensive. "I found it. Why? You lose one?"

Judith shook her head. "No. *Where* did you find it?"

Gurd's wrinkled face grew wary. "Why you askin'?"

"Because," Judith said evenly, "I know who it belongs to. I've seen it before, many times."

Apparently assuaged by Judith's matter-of-fact manner, Gurd shrugged. "It was in that fish pond thing at the hotel where you folks had the big do."

Judith gazed questioningly at Renie, but her cousin's face was blank. She looked again at Gurd. "You found it the night of the rehearsal dinner?"

"Nope, I found it a couple of days ago. I was tryin' out Billy Big Horn's other spot."

Judith frowned. "Billy's other . . . ? What are you talking about?"

Both cousins were now on their feet, watching Gurd with interest. "That bum who used to hang out at the hotel and by the department store downtown," Uncle Gurd responded. "Some other bums told me he skipped town. I decided I'd try his spot, see if I could pick up some pin money. The department store was a bust, so I went up to the hotel. I didn't like that much either, but while I was hangin' around, I saw that harmonica in the fish pond. I'd heard Billy played such a thing, so I figgered it must be his. I took it out, but the water didn't do it no good. It sounds kinda sour. 'Course I'm no expert."

"That's correct," Renie breathed.

There was something wrong about Gurd's recital, Judith was certain of it. Not in the facts as he told them, but the actual discovery. "You say you heard Billy wasn't coming back? Do you mean from jail or not at all?"

For an alarming instant, the bathrobe fell open, and both cousins averted their eyes. But Gurd quickly retied the sash. "How do I know? I never knew this Billy guy. But it didn't seem right to leave his harmonica in that fish pond."

"It isn't," Judith said abruptly. "It's all wrong." She whirled on Renie who was drooping under the late afternoon sun. "Don't you see? Billy was arrested across the street at the hospital entrance. He would never have left his harmonica behind, let alone in the Naples Hotel fountain."

Understanding began to dawn on Renie. "You're right. Billy always had that thing with him. He played beautifully. Once, Bill gave him a twenty-dollar bill after he performed 'Danny Boy' for my mother-in-law."

Pacing the walkway, Judith tried to keep in the shade. "I've got to ask Joe about Billy's arrest. It just doesn't sound right. It never did."

Renie patted Judith's arm, then headed towards the driveway. "You do that. You've got evidence. Joe will really like having a harmonica thrown into the case. 'Bye, coz." She swerved on her heel and stared Uncle Gurd down. "Nine-thirty, remember? And don't wear that bathrobe. I never liked it, not even on my cousin."

Judith barely heard Renie's remark. She didn't care that Uncle Gurd was waggling his fingers in his ears and sticking his tongue out at Renie's retreating form. She was indifferent to the appearance of Gertrude, who was clumping her way out of the toolshed, yelling that Uncle Gurd was either a woman or a pervert, and that he'd better hightail it out of her back yard or she'd turn the hose on him. Didn't he know she was a life-long *Democrat*?

Judith ignored them all. For the first time since seeing the man push the woman off the roof of the Belmont Hotel, she had a real insight into the case.

Harley Davidson wasn't the only victim. Judith was sure that Billy Big Horn was dead, too.

Joe arrived home shortly before six-thirty looking hot, tired, and subdued. Judith greeted him with a tentative kiss and proffered cold beer. Her husband accepted and collapsed at the kitchen table. His tie had already come off and now he pulled his shirt out of confinement. With one ear attuned to her guests in the living room, Judith fussed over dinner preparations and waited for Joe to speak first.

At last, he did. "You're really something," he said in a strange tone that Judith found indecipherable.

"Ummm . . . You'd be speaking of the emeralds?" she said, hazarding a guess.

Joe nodded. "That, and Esperanza Highcastle filing a complaint against you. She says you attacked her at headquarters today."

Judith's jaw dropped. "That's absurd! She tripped. Besides, I thought she left after I talked to her."

"She came back. I guess she ran into TNT somewhere, and they got into it, which made her mad, so she stomped into the chief's office and claimed you were stalking her." Joe's tone was weary.

Judith slammed a package of boneless chicken breasts down on the kitchen counter. "She's a liar! I've seen the woman twice in my entire life. Well, three times, maybe. I . . . ah . . . ran into her one day at the radio station. Did you talk to the chief?"

Joe nodded slowly. "He really wishes you'd keep out of official investigations. Frankly, it's embarrassing."

Feeling suddenly weak at the knees, Judith sat down opposite Joe. "But . . . what about the emeralds? Aren't they a help?"

Taking a big swallow of beer, Joe clutched the glass stein as if it were an anchor—or maybe the remnants of his career. "Yes, they are. But Woody and I might have made the same discovery. The point is, the emeralds may have nothing to do with the murder investigation."

"But they must have something to do with Bascombe de Tourville," Judith countered. "Did you arrest him?"

"No. His scams aren't in our jurisdiction." Joe's expression was bleak. "He clammed up, claimed he knew nothing about cigars or emeralds. The most we can do is turn him over to Immigration and see if they can get him deported."

"I see." Judith had folded her hands in her lap and assumed a humble manner. "Joe, I have a big favor to ask. Just one, and then I won't ever bother you again." She finally had the temerity to seek Joe's face.

Joe slumped in the chair. "What?"

"Can you check with whoever handles vagrancy and find out exactly what happened when Billy Big Horn was arrested at St. Fabiola's Hospital?"

Joe was obviously surprised. "Billy was busted? When?"

"The Saturday that Mike and Kristin were married, the twenty-fourth of June." Judith hoped she looked appropriately meek. She certainly felt that way.

Joe expelled air from his round cheeks. "I could do that. I don't know why I should, but I could." He seemed to be wrestling with internal demons, most of whom Judith was sure looked like her. "Okay. Is Monday good enough?"

Regretfully, Judith shook her head. "No. Now is best."

It would take a simple phone call, and Judith knew it. "Okay," Joe agreed with as much enthusiasm as a man headed for a root canal. "Why not?" With a grunt, he rose from the chair and went to the phone.

Judith sat very quietly. In the living room, she could hear her guests, including the cranky couple from Chula

Vista, preparing to go off on their evening revels. The
chicken breasts still sat on the counter, oozing pink juice
onto the kitchen floor.

"Right," Joe was saying after a lull where he presumably was being transferred from pillar to post, "you can't
block a hospital entrance . . . Billy was hostile? That's
weird . . . Sure, he had to be booked . . . Right, I understand . . . Okay, that's . . . what?" Joe's usually rubicund
color faded a bit. "That's . . . odd." There was a long
pause, and Judith felt her scalp tingle. "No, you're right
. . . Most of those guys are whacked out on cheap wine
and God knows what else. Thanks, that's all I need to
know."

Joe set the phone down on the counter and returned to
his chair. The green eyes slid to the package of chicken
breasts. "Are we going to eat tonight? Despite the heat,
I'm kind of hungry."

Judith jumped up. "Oh! Yes, sure. I've already fed
Mother. She wanted a chop. The barbecue's going, I'll be
right back. There's a green salad and French bread
and . . ."

"Peanuts McGoohan said Billy wasn't the one who was
arrested." Joe's voice followed Judith down the hallway.

She stopped in mid-step and nodded. "I thought not.
Who's Peanuts?"

"A highly unreliable wino and pickpocket who was
doing a stretch at the city's expense around the same time
Billy was in jail." Joe looked vaguely intrigued as his
wife turned to face him. "I take it you believe Peanuts?"

"Definitely." Judith turned away and headed outside
to the barbecue. When she came back into the kitchen,
Joe was eyeing her speculatively.

"Okay," he said, "I'll bite. Why do you believe Peanuts?"

Judith sat down at the table where she explained about
Uncle Gurd and the harmonica in the Naples Hotel fountain. Joe seemed more shocked by the news that Gurd was

back than by his find. Judith, however, persevered.

"Billy Big Horn would never leave his harmonica, let alone in that fountain. Besides, when Renie told me he'd been arrested after making a scene at St. Fabiola's, it didn't ring true. Billy is a very gentle soul. If someone other than Billy was arrested," Judith added ominously, "then I'm afraid he's in danger. Or worse."

"Like dead?" Joe grew thoughtful. "Why would anyone harm Billy?

Judith sensed a condescending note in Joe's voice, but at least he was discussing the case. "He couldn't have seen anything because he's blind," she reminded her husband. "He had to have heard something. Maybe he heard whatever it was at the Belmont or the Naples that Friday night." Her voice grew uncertain, then she put a hand on Joe's arm. "You're absolutely sure that the Belmont has been searched top to bottom?"

Joe nodded. "Absolutely." He cocked an eyebrow at Judith. "You're thinking 'body'?"

"Yes. But I suppose it's not possible." She rested her face on her fists and concentrated. "The Naples? Did the police search there? Or at the hospital?"

"No. There was no reason." Joe winced. "There still isn't. Your hunch isn't probable cause."

Judith got up and began pacing the kitchen. She stopped by the counter where she kept her bills and reservations and correspondence, and snapped her fingers. "Joe—where's Harley's apartment?"

"At the bottom of the hill, about four blocks from the radio station, towards downtown." He finished his beer and leaned back in the captain's chair. "Why?"

Briefly, Judith looked disappointed. "It was just an idea." Then she brightened again. "But Tara has a highrise about a block from St. Fabiola's, which means it's a block or two from the Naples and the Belmont. Can you search it?"

Joe grimaced. "We already did. Woody and I got a

warrant this afternoon after we'd interrogated de Tourville and you gave Woody the emeralds. No dead body. No emeralds. No cigars.''

"You checked Tara's wardrobe?" Judith leaned against the counter, knocking over a stack of mail.

"We checked everything," Joe replied. "We're thorough, we go by the book. That's how we do our job."

"Yes," Judith murmured, bending down to pick the correspondence off the floor. "Oh—this is today's mail. Phyliss must have brought it in while I was gone. Good grief, more wedding bills. I hope the Rundbergs are shelling out for . . . Hmmm . . . Phyliss must not have seen this. It's another letter to her from the gang in Deep Denial. I forgot that Cecil said he was delivering it here. I'll give it to her when she comes to work on Monday."

Judith slipped the letter into the frame of her bulletin board.

She couldn't possibly guess that the answer to the mystery lay inside.

SEVENTEEN

"YOU'VE GOT TO do it," Renie declared when she arrived the next morning to pick up Uncle Gurd. "Joe or no Joe, you've got to report that designer dress as missing. It could be full of emeralds."

"But it wasn't," Judith protested. "I would have felt their weight. The dress was light as a feather."

"Whoever stole it from Ron's Bar and Grill didn't think so," Renie asserted. "Coz, you have to collect on the insurance, and the only way you can do that is to report it to the police."

"I know, I know," Judith said nervously as Uncle Gurd emerged from the hedge wearing U. S. Army combat fatigues. "More to the point, if we knew who stole it, we might know more about Harley's death. Though I still think it's fairly simple. Whoever is running the smuggling ring killed him to keep him quiet. But right now I hate to upset the apple cart. Joe seems in a much better mood today. We talked quite awhile last night about the emeralds. I honestly think he was impressed that I'd found them."

"He should be," Renie responded, then frowned at Gurd. "Couldn't you wear something that doesn't look like you're AWOL?"

"I was at Bastogne," Gurd growled, getting into the passenger's seat beside Renie.

"You smell like you're still there," Renie snarled. "Get out, sit in the back seat, you crazy old coot."

Despite a show of anger, Gurd obeyed. "Do I get paid for this?" he asked in a querulous tone.

"Talk to Morris Mitchell," Renie snapped. "I'm just the chauffeur. And graphic designer," she added under her breath.

Judith started to wave them off, but Uncle Gurd had rolled down the rear window. "*Where* in Florida?" he shouted.

"What?" Judith strained to catch his meaning. "Florida? Oh! Vivian! Panama City!" But she felt her words were lost on the warm summer air.

That afternoon, while Joe was checking out his fishing gear, Judith sat down at the big oak dining room table and tried to organize her thoughts about the Harley Davidson case. She began with what facts she knew, but they didn't seem to fall into any logical pattern. Instead, she wrote down the names of each person involved. She was studying her findings when Renie came through the back door.

"I lost Uncle Gurd," she announced cheerfully. "You got any Pepsi?"

Judith told her cousin to get a can out of the fridge. "Where did he go?" Judith asked when Renie came into the dining room.

"Who knows? Who cares? Morris and I got the pictures, which is all that matters." She sat down next to Judith. "We had to dress Gurd up in bum clothes, though. The fatigues just didn't do it for Morris."

"So what happened to Gurd?" Judith asked, finally looking up from the tablet on which she'd made her notations.

Renie shrugged. "He went to change and never came

back. Do you really want to know? I think he's caused
you enough problems.''

"True," Judith allowed. "He seems able to take care
of himself. But he must have left his belongings here.''

"They don't amount to much, from what you've said.''
Renie drank from her can, then looked over Judith's
shoulder. "What's that?''

Judith showed her cousin the tablet. "I started with
Harley. I've tried to put down anything about each individual that might pertain to his murder. See if you can
think of anything I've left out.''

Renie put on her glasses with the scratched and
smudged lenses, the efficacy of which Judith always
doubted. But despite the blemishes, Renie managed to
read aloud:

HARLEY DAVIDSON

Blind disc jockey.
Made excellent salary, much of it outside the studio
    and possibly under the table.
Made enemies easily, yet popular with listeners.
Rumors of drug use/peddling in L.A.
Seemingly not romantically involved with any par-
    ticular woman.
Last seen alive by me atop Belmont; also by Tara
    Novotny and by killer (assuming she and perp
    aren't the same).
May have gone to Belmont Hotel because he knew
    smuggling ring met there—killed because of dis-
    covery.

TARA NOVOTNY

Top model, working primarily, but not exclusively,
    for Artemis Bohl.

Travels extensively—could be smuggler, or at least part of ring.

For reasons unknown, moved out of her apt. and into de Tourville's condo. Connection with de Tourville? Lovers?

Until then, lived two blocks from Belmont; might have set up headquarters there for smugglers.

Could be Killer? Seems too high-strung to carry it off.

BASCOMBE DE TOURVILLE

Known to authorities; uses illegal visas, papers to travel under aliases.

Involved in various scams; wealthy tourist victims.

Claims not to know about smuggling.

What is connection to Tara? Smuggling? Lover? Blackmail?

Connection to Harley? None that we know of.

Possesses sinister quality that could make him a murderer.

ESPERANZA HIGHCASTLE

Highcastle Hot Dog heiress, owner of various properties including Belmont, owner of KRAS and KORN radio stations.

Accused of being unfaithful by husband; about to be divorced.

May be in financial trouble.

No apparent motive for killing Harley—ratings kept her in business.

CHUCK RAWLS JR.

Hated Harley, often got into it.

But Harley was job security.

Or was Harley a threat to same if he made known his antipathy to Rawls?

Emerald smuggling? Not that we can tell.

Where was he when killing occurred?

Doesn't seem capable of homicide, but often hard to tell.

ARTEMIS BOHL

Internationally-known designer, tied in with I. Magnifique stores.

Owns Caribbean sweat shop, or so it's alleged— drop-off point between Colombia (?) and U.S. for emerald-filled cigars? Bohl garments used for transport?

Mastermind—or dupe?

Could be killer if he's running the smuggling ring; ego, single-mindedness, arrogance often typical of killer.

Does he have an alibi for time of murder?

Why haven't Joe and Woody questioned him? (Or have they?)

DARRELL MIMS

KRAS gofer, aspiring DJ.

Didn't like Harley, loathed crude format and language.

Ambitious, crusader (crusaders can be dangerous).

Involved in smuggling? Dubious. Appears too principled.

Might have wanted rival DJ out of the way.

Doesn't seem right for the job—either as DJ or killer.

TNT TENINO

Estranged husband of Esperanza, retired boxer, does some kind of boxing-related work on occasion (and thus travels a bit).

Smuggler? Possibly.

As dumb as he seems? Maybe.

Motive? Only if involved in smuggling—unless he suspected Esperanza of cheating on him with Harley, which seems unlikely.

Have Joe and Woody talked to him?

BILLY BIG HORN

Well-known blind homeless person.

Allegedly arrested for loitering day after the murder; released from jail ten days later; hasn't been seen since—doubts have arisen as to whether it was really Billy who caused the disturbance.

Possible second murder victim? (No known connection to any of the above, but may have had intimate knowledge of Belmont which was sometimes used by homeless people.)

"Well?" Judith inquired when Renie had finished reading. "What do you think?"

Renie's air was apologetic. "Not much. It's pretty fragmentary, coz. One of the problems is that you don't have the time of the murder nailed down. Did Joe ever get more specific?"

"The ME figured between five and ten P.M. Friday, which narrows it a little," Judith said, taking the tablet from Renie. "We know it had to be after eight, because I saw Harley alive around that time."

Renie craned her neck to look at the final entry. "You really think Billy is dead?"

"I'm afraid I do." Judith underlined the phrase, "Second victim?" "Where was Billy between eight o'clock Friday night and early Saturday morning when he was supposedly arrested for loitering outside the hospital? If it was him, then he had to have stayed in the vicinity. Maybe he sneaked into the Belmont. The employees at the Naples wouldn't let him spend the night in the courtyard. Joe saw him when he went down to check on what I'd seen through the banquet room window. But by the time we left the hotel, he . . . wasn't . . . there." The color drained from Judith's face.

"What's wrong?" Renie asked in alarm.

Judith grabbed Renie by the short sleeves of her shapeless muu-muu. "Coz! It only dawned on me now—Billy was gone by nine o'clock, when we went home."

Renie was looking puzzled. "Meaning . . . what? He missed out on the late-night panhandling?"

Releasing Renie, Judith let out a big breath. "Meaning he may have gone to the Belmont then. He could have been there when Harley was killed! Ever since I saw that harmonica, I knew Billy had some part in this whole thing."

Renie cocked her head. "So Billy decides to hit the hay and toddles off to the Belmont. He can get there because he's done it before. By chance, he goes up to the top floor—because he enjoys the view even if he can't see—and stumbles in on Harley and his murderer. Meanwhile, he's pitched his beloved harmonica in the Naples fountain. Gee, coz, that's really *logical*."

Judith's face fell. "You're right. It doesn't make much sense. What am I missing?"

Naturally, Renie didn't know. "One thing," she finally offered, gazing thoughtfully at the bowl of yellow, pink, and red roses that sat in the middle of the dining room table, "if Billy was killed at the Belmont—and I'm not saying you're completely wrong about that—then where is his body?"

"I asked Joe if they'd searched the Naples or any of the other buildings, but he said they had no reason to. In fact," she added sheepishly, "I even called St. Fabiola's awhile ago and tried to find out if they could account for all the bodies in their morgue."

Renie couldn't suppress a grin. "What did they say?"

"They thought I was crazy, of course. But I did manage to learn that nobody died at the hospital between June twenty-first and July sixth, which washes out my theory."

For a few moments, the cousins fell silent. "Then Billy's body has to be at the Belmont," Renie said at last.

Judith shook her head. "Joe insists they searched everywhere."

"You miss my point," Renie said. "You can't cart a body around and not have someone notice. *Ergo*, if your premise is right, Billy was never taken out of the Belmont. Think about it, coz."

Frustrated, Judith held out her hands. "Then my premise is wrong. Billy is alive and well and missing his harmonica on a Greyhound bus bound for southern California. The truth is, the killer didn't care if Harley's body was found, so why would they care about a poor homeless man being discovered? The only precaution the murderer took was to remove all of Harley's ID and to cut Mr. Artemis's precious labels out of . . ."

The cousins' eyes met. "Are you thinking what I'm thinking?" Judith breathed.

"I think so," Renie answered in a weak voice. "But why?"

"I don't know." Judith chewed on her lower lip, then ripped off the pages of notes she'd made in the tablet and crumpled them into a ball. "We're back to square one."

Renie caressed her Pepsi can. "Are you going to tell Joe?"

Judith thought for a minute. "No. He wouldn't believe me. I haven't a shred of evidence, and no motive. Not a real motive, that is."

"So what do we—ah, I mean, *you*—do next?" Renie inquired.

Judith uttered a nervous laugh. "I haven't a clue. Literally."

What Judith actually did was fetch the mail, which brought yet more wedding bills, including a couple of courteous "reminders." She also received her I. Magnifique statement and an innocuous-looking envelope from the U. S. Treasury Department.

"I'm getting so I hate to bring in the mail," Judith declared to Renie who'd been about to leave. "Damn, if those Rundbergs don't start tending to some of these, I'm in big trouble." With apprehension, she tore open the I. Magnifique envelope. "Double damn! I'm in big trouble anyway. That lavender dress is charged to this statement. You're right, coz. I've got to report it as stolen."

"Do it now," Renie urged, "while Joe's not at work. Maybe he won't hear about it. He's always complaining about how one division doesn't know what the other is doing."

"That's so. I will." Judith sighed as she fingered the brown government envelope which was addressed to Joseph P. Flynn and Judith A. Flynn. "I don't like this. Dan and I used to get these and they were always bad news. Dare I?"

"You'd better," Renie said with reluctance.

Judith carefully tore the envelope open, removed the two-page missive, and collapsed against the oak credenza in the entrance hall. "Oh, God! We're being audited!"

"So?" Renie seemed unmoved by the announcement.

"We've been audited three times. It happens when you're in business for yourself. What's the problem? Expense deductions?"

Judith scanned the two pages. "No. It's . . . Mother."

"*Your mother*?" Renie was aghast. "What on earth . . . ?"

"We've been claiming Mother as a deduction. Our accountant said it was okay," Judith said, speaking nervously and rapidly, as if Renie herself were a vicious IRS agent. "She lives with us, you see. Sort of. I mean, she's on our property."

Renie shrugged. "Of course she is. There shouldn't be any problem. It's probably just a random check. People like you and me who are in business for ourselves automatically raise a red flag with the IRS. Don't worry about it. You'll have a hearing and you can explain. If they don't believe you, you have the perfect fall-back position."

Judith shot Renie a dubious look. "Like what?"

Renie grinned. "Take your mother with you to the audit interview. It'll serve the IRS right. If worse comes to worse, you can leave her there. See you, coz."

Renie left.

Joe wasn't as sanguine as Renie about the audit notice. To Judith's surprise, he recognized the envelope's significance even before he saw its contents.

"I told you we should have put your mother in a retirement home," he shouted as he stomped around the living room. "It isn't just whether or not she's living at the same address, but her net worth. Don't try to tell me she doesn't have money socked away some place. To claim her as a dependent, she has to be virtually broke."

"She may be," Judith said in a small voice. "I had to borrow from her quite a bit while Dan and I were married."

Joe stopped in the middle of the living room and stared

at Judith. "Are you trying to tell me that she still does her own books? How can she, when she's so addled?"

"She's still sharp about some things," Judith said in a defensive tone. "I wouldn't dream of offering to take over her finances. She has so little independence left, and it means so much to her."

Joe threw up his hands. "This is crazy! You've been claiming her when you don't even know what she's got stashed away? Do you realize what kind of trouble we can get into?"

Judith, who was sitting on the arm of one of the matching sofas, cast her eyes down at the Persian carpet. "We pay everything for her," she murmured. "Why doesn't that make her a dependent?"

Joe clapped his hand to his forehead. "Jeez! It doesn't work that way, that's why. And if you've been dumb enough to foot all her bills, she's probably got a big savings account. Social Security, your father's pension, whatever." He collapsed onto the windowseat and shook his head.

Judith swallowed hard. "Are you and Woody going fishing tomorrow?" It seemed prudent to change the subject.

"What?" Joe reacted as if he'd never heard of fishing. "Oh—fishing. Yeah, I think so. Woody wants to try out his new fly rig. We'll hit one of those lakes above the family cabin."

"That sounds nice." Judith teetered on the sofa arm. "If it's not too hot, I'll work in the garden."

Joe didn't comment. Rising from the windowseat, he scratched his head in a stupefied manner and headed out through the Fench doors. Judith slipped onto the sofa and stared at a wilting floral arrangement that had been part of the decor for Mike and Kristin's wedding reception. Five years earlier, she and Joe had been newlyweds. Early on, they had never quarreled, or so it seemed to Judith. Lately, tension existed between them on an almost daily basis. Maybe Renie was right: Marriage wasn't just about quarreling and making up; it was about deep-rooted mindsets and individual experiences and personality conflicts that could never be resolved, only ignored in order to make life bearable.

Judith's eyes traveled to a brochure for Hillside Manor. "Full-course breakfasts, cozy atmosphere, and comfortable accommodations," the copy read. Maybe "comfortable accommodations" were what marriage was all about. But you paid for them, Judith thought, not just at Hillside Manor, but in real life.

With an effort, Judith got up and went to the telephone on the cherrywood pedestal stand. She started to dial the number for police headquarters to report her stolen dress, but before she could enter the last digit, Joe came back into the living room.

"I'm going to five o'clock Mass," he said, "so Woody and I can get an early start in the morning."

Judith could never attend the Saturday evening service. She had to be at the B&B to serve her guests for their cocktail hour.

"Okay," she said in a tired voice. "We'll eat at six-thirty."

Joe continued through the living room, brushed past Judith, and went upstairs. Judith picked up the phone again, lost her nerve, and replaced the receiver.

Sunday, the ninth of July, was a long, hot day. Judith spent an hour weeding in the shade. But after her mother had interrupted to ask the whereabouts of her glasses, her solitaire deck, her jumble puzzle, her *TV Guide*, her dentures, and her Granny Goodness Chewy Caramels, Judith gave up and went into the house. She tried calling Renie, but nobody answered. Feeling bereft, she sat at her computer in the kitchen and tried to figure out what had really happened at the Belmont Hotel.

No fresh inspiration struck. She was thinking about

making a big gin and tonic when the phone rang.

It was Mike. "Hey, Mom," he said in a cheerful voice, "we're about to leave Kristin's folks and head for Idaho. Mrs. R. wanted me to tell you that they won't be paying any of the wedding bills for awhile because of some tax problems. I don't understand it, but it has something to do with the Rundbergs owning a wheat ranch. They pay differently than other people."

Judith snapped out of her doldrums. "We all have tax problems," she declared in an angry tone. "We also have bills, some of which aren't ours. You tell Mrs. R. to pony up before I get turned over to a collection agency. How dare she make you a patsy? Not only is she cheap, she's chicken!"

The cheer fled from Mike's voice. "Hey, cool it, Mom. You don't understand. They're in a bind. They explained it all to Kristin and me, but it's kind of confusing."

"No, it's not," Judith said, trying to rein in her temper. "It's very simple. The bride's family has an obligation for certain things. The Rundbergs know that. The only reason I signed for everything was because I was here in town and they were three hundred miles away on their ranch. Now they're trying to weasel out of paying their share. It's unconscionable."

"It's smut," Mike said.

"What?"

"That's the other thing—some of the crop that's supposed to be harvested later this summer has smut," Mike explained, trying to remain reasonable. "It's some disease that attacks wheat."

"Tough," Judith retorted. "I don't care if it's smut, mutt, or butt. If Kristin's parents don't come across in the next few days, I'm going to get an attorney to go after them. Or the bunco squad."

"Mom!" Mike sounded horrified. "You're talking about my in-laws!"

"To me, they're outlaws." Judith paused. "Is Merle there?"

"I'm not at the house," Mike replied. "I'm calling from a pay phone at the gas station down the road. Hey, don't put me in the middle of this!"

"Mrs. R. already put you in the middle," Judith growled. "Merle should do her own dirty work." For Mike's sake, Judith tried to simmer down. "Look, tell her that your . . . that Joe and I don't have the money to pay these bills. Tell her we've got our own tax problems. Tell her I'm sure she can make arrangements with most of the creditors, but she'll have to contact them herself. Their phone numbers and addresses are on the invoices."

"Gee, I don't know . . ." Mike's voice was skeptical. "Maybe Kristin should talk to them."

"Good idea," Judith replied. "She's the one who chose the dress, the flowers, the photos, and almost everything else. Just remember, this is the Rundbergs' responsibility, not the Flynns'. You needn't feel guilty."

"I'm not," Mike responded.

"That's fine. It's easy to feel guilty. I ought to know."

"I'm not talking about guilt," Mike said, his voice lower. "I meant, I'm not a Flynn."

For a long moment, Judith said nothing.

Joe returned from his fishing trip in a much happier frame of mind. He and Woody had actually managed to catch a half-dozen rainbow trout between them. By contemporary local fishing standards, they had had a successful outing.

Judith decided not to deflate Joe's good mood by telling him about the phone call from Mike. Though it cost her dearly, she put on a smile, and offered to clean and cook her husband's share of the catch.

"Say," Joe said, much later that night as he and Judith were preparing for bed, "I was kind of harsh about that

IRS notice. It sounds as if the CPA might have misled you. It's not your fault.''

"That we're going broke?'' Judith's mask finally fell away.

"That won't happen,'' Joe said. "We might have to pay something, but didn't you say the hearing wasn't scheduled until October? There's no point worrying about it between now and then.'' Getting into bed, Joe put his arm around Judith.

"I guess not,'' Judith replied dubiously. She snuggled closer. "Joe—do you love me?''

"What?'' He grinned at her before turning out the light. "Of course I do. Why would you ask such a silly question?''

"I think I've been a twerp lately,'' Judith said. "About a lot of things.''

"So?''

"Well, I'm sorry.''

Joe's arm squeezed Judith's middle. "Forget it. You just married off your only child. That's got to be hard.''

Judith's head popped up from the pillow. "I never thought of it like that,'' she said in wonder. "I mean, it's not just the expense and the busy work and the anxiety. It's . . . more.''

"Much more.'' Joe chuckled. "You know, Jude-girl, sometimes you get so caught up in things that you don't stop to reflect.''

Maybe, Judith thought to herself, *that's why I get so caught up in the first place. I don't want to reflect. Reflection can be painful.*

She fell back onto the pillow and relaxed. "You're awfully sweet—usually,'' Judith said in a soft voice.

"Usually.'' Joe yawned. "There's a breeze coming in tonight. Maybe we'll sleep okay. G'night, Jude-girl.''

"Goodnight, Joe.'' She patted his hip. He was right. The wind was ruffling the chintz curtains. The third floor family quarters, which always retained more heat than the rest of the house, were beginning to cool down.

"Joe?"

"Mmm?"

"I have one small favor to ask. Do you mind?"

"Mmm." Joe rolled over and yawned again. "No, what?"

"Can you dig up Harley Davidson?"

EIGHTEEN

JOE COULDN'T HONOR Judith's request, because, as he put it, the evidence had gone up in smoke. Harley had been cremated, and his ashes had been interred at a local mausoleum. But to Judith's immense relief, her husband had not become upset when she explained her reason for wanting the corpse exhumed.

"I wasn't going to tell him," she said to Renie Monday morning as the cousins sat at Judith's kitchen table drinking coffee. "But then I realized that if this case was ever going to be solved, that would be one way to do it."

"So what's another way?" asked Renie who was just barely awake at ten past ten and was dribbling coffee down the front of her frayed pocket tee.

"By getting hold of Darrell Mims and shaking him until his teeth rattle," Judith answered with a cunning expression. "I intend to do that when he goes off the air at noon. Want to join me?"

Though Renie looked puzzled, she didn't ask why Judith wanted to see the former gofer and apprentice disc jockey. "Sure, it beats cleaning my closet which is what I planned to do today. I'm all wrapped up on the homeless brochure."

Judith had left word at KRAS that she and Renie

would like to treat Darrell Mims to lunch at Foozle's. It was twelve-thirty when the cousins arrived. On this visit, they eschewed the bar, and settled into one of the vinyl-covered booths by the grimy front window.

"Do you think he'll come?" asked Renie, who was now wide awake and had figured out the reason for questioning Darrell.

"I don't see why not," Judith responded as she glanced at the menu. "He has no reason to suspect what we want to ask him."

"I suppose not." Renie grimaced at the luncheon listings. "Did I have the beef dip last time? Was it rare? Did I get ptomaine?"

"Yes. No. No. I'm going to get a hamburger. They're hard to screw up." Judith replaced the menu and stared across the street at the entrance to the Heraldsgate 400 building. "We should have turned the radio on in the car. I wonder if he's gotten any livelier."

"Dubious," Renie replied, still frowning at the menu. "I wonder what the chili would do to me? Sometimes dives like this make good chili."

"You might as well order Sterno," Judith counseled. "Play it safe, get a burger."

"I'm not in a burger mood," Renie said. "What could go wrong with fish and chips?"

"The fish? The chips? I believe the term is 'go bad,' not 'go wrong.' " Judith snickered but kept her gaze on the 400 building.

A weary waitress wearing fuzzy blue carpet slippers shuffled over, but Judith told her they were waiting for someone. The waitress poured coffee and left, her slippers flip-flopping on the worn carpeting. The restaurant clock, with hands that were the wings of a manic duck in a top hat, indicated that it was now twelve-forty-five. Judith kept watch.

"Darrell probably has things to do after he goes off the air," Renie said. "I know Kip always stays at the studio for several hours, usually getting ready for the next day's show.''

"Darrell still has to eat," Judith pointed out.

"DJs eat while the records are playing," Renie said, leaning out of the booth to examine an armload of orders that were being delivered to the customers across the aisle. "The hot turkey sandwich looks okay."

"You can't eat hot turkey in July," Judith pointed out.

"Yes, I actually could," countered Renie. "If Darrell doesn't show up pretty soon, I could eat your arm."

Judith was beginning to fidget. "It's ten to one. Maybe Darrell didn't get the message."

"Call him," Renie suggested.

"I'll wait until one," Judith said, fiddling with the salt and pepper shakers. "For all we know, he may not be doing the show this week."

Only a few seconds passed before Judith spotted Darrell hurrying out of the 400 building. He waited for the light to change, then walked quickly across the street and into the restaurant. Judith waved at Darrell; Renie waved at the waitress.

"It's really nice of you to invite me to lunch," Darrell said, sitting down next to Renie. "I appreciate it. Right about now, I'm not feeling very appreciated by anybody else." His youthful face grew poignant.

Judith immediately became sympathetic. "Isn't the program going well?"

"Oh . . ." Darrell cocked his head to one side. "I don't know. *I* think it is, but some of our advertisers aren't happy, and we're getting lots of calls and letters and faxes saying they want somebody more . . . more like Harley. Can you imagine?"

The waitress had returned, sparing the cousins an answer. Judith and Darrell both ordered hamburgers, but Renie hemmed and hawed and, to her cousin's surprise, finally chose the tuna melt.

Sitting opposite Darrell, Judith rested her chin on her

hands and assumed a confidential air. "You really wanted this chance to be on the radio, didn't you, Darrell?"

"Oh boy, I sure did." The spots of color in his boyish cheeks darkened. "It meant the world to me. That's why I feel so bad that it doesn't seem to be . . . working out."

"But Ms. Highcastle hasn't fired you, has she?" Judith's smile struck Renie as a trifle soupy.

Darrell's eyes widened. "No, not yet. Oh, there's been talk about interviewing other DJs, but so far, nothing's come of it."

"Why," Judith asked, dropping the cloying smile, "do you think that is?"

Darrell gave a shake of his head. "I honestly don't know. I mean, maybe Ms. Highcastle wants me to have a chance to show what I can do. A week or two doesn't prove anything, really."

"Then you're not losing money for KRAS?" Judith asked innocently.

"Not yet." Darrell smiled a polite refusal as the waitress came by with the coffee pot. "For one thing, I don't make nearly as much money as Harley did. And advertisers buy package deals, so they wouldn't pull out until their commercials have been used up."

"I see," said Judith with a glance at Renie whose eyes appeared glued to the kitchen area. "Does it really matter to Ms. Highcastle how much money the radio station makes?"

"Sure!" Darrell seemed surprised by the question. "It's her living. Or part of it."

"I just wondered," Judith said idly, then leaned forward and lowered her voice. "What I want to know most, Darrell, is why you identified the wrong man at the morgue. Why did you say it was Harley Davidson when you knew it was someone else?"

The color drained from Darrell's face and his hands began to shake. "That's not true!" he protested. "It was Harley! Didn't the medical examiner's report state it was a blind man in his early thirties? Who else could it have been?'' Darrell's voice had risen to such a shrill pitch that the customers across the aisle turned to stare.

''All that's true,'' Judith said calmly. ''But it wasn't Harley. It was Billy Big Horn, and you knew it. Why, Darrell? Why?''

The silence that fell over the booth was echoed by the sudden quiet throughout the restaurant. It was as if everyone in Foozle's had heard the exchange between Judith and Darrell, and now they were waiting for the dramatic denouement.

It never came. Darrell seemed to shrivel up and didn't utter a word. The waitress appeared with their orders, and it was Renie who broke the silence.

''What's this thing?'' she demanded, pointing to her plate. ''It looks like tuna melt. I never order tuna melt. I hate tuna melt.''

''You ordered it, honey,'' the waitress said in a husky voice.

Renie turned to Judith, who was looking vexed at the interruption. ''Did I order this glop?'' Renie asked in an indignant tone. ''Well? Did I?''

''Yes,'' Judith replied irritably. ''Now shut up and eat the damned thing.''

Renie let out a heavy sigh while the waitress gave her a smug look and trudged away. ''Tuna melt,'' muttered Renie. ''I'd rather eat cork.''

Ignoring Renie, Judith regarded Darrell with a stern expression. ''The police know what you did. Now you have to tell them *why* you did it.''

''I don't know what came over me,'' Darrell said in a miserable voice. ''Harley was missing, so it was possible that he was dead. The detectives—your husband and his partner—said they needed someone who knew Harley to make a positive ID.'' Darrell gulped. ''Or not. Anyway, they took me in to look at the body. I'd never seen a dead person before. It was upsetting. I could barely keep from closing my eyes. Then, when I finally worked up my courage, the . . . body didn't look like Harley. But I thought that was because he was dead. I mean, it had changed him.''

''Can somebody change this tuna melt into a beef dip?'' Renie interjected.

Judith shot her cousin a warning glance before speaking to Darrell. ''But you must have known better.'' The reproach was evident in her tone.

''Well . . . yes.'' The young man nodded slowly. ''I guess I did. But I was so upset, and then I remembered what had been going through my mind on the way to the morgue. That if Harley was dead, I might have a chance at his job. After all, Harley was missing. *Something* had happened to him. He told me that he wasn't going to be around, and it dawned on me that maybe he was saying that my big chance was coming up. So I thought, *What difference does it make?* Whoever this person is is dead anyway, and maybe Harley is, too, and if he isn't, he must not want to keep doing his show, because he hasn't even called the station. Do you see? All this went through my head in about a second.''

Watching Darrell's earnest, troubled face, Judith was moved. But she couldn't let her sympathy show. Not yet. ''So you . . . what?''

''I told your husband and his partner it was Harley.'' Darrell nodded as if confirming the statement. ''That was it. I honestly didn't recognize this Billy Whatsisname you mentioned. Anyway, they took me outside and asked some general questions and then they let me go.''

Judith sat back, resting her head on the worn vinyl. ''I understand why you did it, but you certainly created an impossible situation. The police have wasted a great deal of time and money on this case. You'll be very lucky if you aren't arrested for impeding justice.''

Darrell hung his head. ''I know. It's just that I saw my

big chance, and opportunities in radio don't come along very often. I was driven to clean up the airways and create a more wholesome listening environment for young people. Is that so wrong?''

Judith sighed. "No. But how you went about it is."

"I know." Darrell stared at his hamburger which was growing cold on the plate. "You must think I'm an awful person. It's no wonder I've lost my appetite."

Renie leaned into Darrell. "Really? Then I'll eat your burger. You can have the tuna melt." She whisked Darrell's plate in her direction.

He paid no heed as his sad eyes searched Judith's face. "Should I turn myself in now?" Darrell asked.

"Call my husband." Judith removed one of Joe's official cards from her handbag and passed it across the table to Darrell. "He probably gave you one of these, but in case you've misplaced it, here's a spare. Why don't you call from the pay phone by the rest rooms?"

Darrell obeyed, moving woodenly. "What will everybody say? What will Ms. Highcastle think?"

"We're wondering about that, too," Judith murmured. Then, after Darrell was out of earshot, she added, "I wonder about a lot of things when it comes to Ms. Highcastle. But most of all," she said, her features hardening as she watched Renie gobble up Darrell's burger, "I wonder what's really become of Harley Davidson?"

Woody had answered Darrell's phone call. He told the young man to stay put; they'd be out to pick him up at once. The cousins waited until Joe and Woody arrived. Darrell had become even more dejected, though his curiosity was piqued.

"How did you know I hadn't told the truth about Harley?" he asked, moving Renie's abandoned tuna melt to one side.

Judith wasn't sure she should level with Darrell, but decided she owed him an explanation. "Billy Big Horn was a blind homeless man who frequented the courtyard of the Naples Hotel and possibly the Belmont as well. According to the authorities, he was arrested early Saturday morning for obstructing traffic into St. Fabiola's Hospital. That didn't sound like Billy, who was a very gentle person. Then, Billy's harmonica was fished out of the Naples fountain. Billy would never have left his harmonica behind, which indicated that something had happened to him. It finally dawned on me that Harley and Billy were both blind, about the same age, and had beards. One might be mistaken for the other. The truth is, I should have guessed from the start, because Joe mentioned that the tux the victim was wearing didn't fit very well. Mr. Artemis would never have allowed a garment of his to fit badly at a fashion show. Then there was the missing label from the tux and the absence of Harley's ID. Why would the killer not want Harley recognized? To gain time, was the only answer I could think of. But if it wasn't Harley, what was the point? Was it the same? I think so. But I can't be sure, because *I don't know what's happened to Harley.*"

Looking both chagrined and flabbergasted, Darrell squirmed in the booth. "You mean—you think he's dead, too?" The young man seemed to brighten at the thought.

"No," Judith responded, with a firm shake of her head. "What I think is that . . ." She stopped as she saw Joe and Woody pull into a loading zone outside of Foozle's. "Never mind, I may be wrong." Judith gave Darrell an apologetic smile.

Renie greeted her cousin's husband and his partner with a big smile. "Want a tuna melt?"

"No thanks," said Joe. "We've eaten." He and Woody remained standing, a pair of intimidating figures looming over Darrell Mims. "We've been wondering for a week when you'd come around to telling us the truth, Mims. Let's take a ride down to headquarters."

Nervously Darrell got to his feet, but it was Judith who

was suddenly shaken. "You've been wondering . . . ? What do you mean? I only told you about Billy last night!"

Joe's expression was only faintly patronizing. "Jude-girl, do you think Woody and I didn't know what was going on with this guy?"

"*What?*" Judith rocked in the booth.

"Come on." Joe placed a hand on Darrell's shoulder, then turned to look at his stunned wife. "I knew what Billy Big Horn looked like. I saw him the night of the rehearsal dinner, remember? Mims here couldn't fool me. Let's go."

Judith sunk so deep into the booth that her chin almost touched the tabletop. "Oooh! I'm a moron! Oh, coz, shoot me now and get it over with!"

Renie was also looking upset. "Jeez, I can't believe it! Of course Joe would recognize Billy. But why the charade?"

"Which one?" Judith snapped. "The victim or Joe and Woody?"

"Both," Renie replied as the waitress reappeared. "But I meant Joe. Why did he string you along? Why did he and Woody and the rest of the department pretend it was Harley?" With an impatient motion, Renie turned to the waitress. "What?"

The waitress chuckled. "You folks sure are having a high old time this afternoon. How about some dessert?"

"No, thanks," Renie said. Despite her usual ravenous appetite, she wasn't particularly keen on sweets.

The waitress started to leave, but Judith called her back. "I think I'd like a . . . martini," she said weakly.

"Coz!" Renie exclaimed. "Since when did you start drinking *after* lunch?"

"Since now," Judith answered glumly.

Renie settled for a root beer. "I've got to clean that closet when I get home, and I don't want to be swizzled when I do it."

With unseeing eyes, Judith watched the waitress plod away in the direction of the bar. "Joe and Woody must have pretended to believe Darrell because they're hoping to lull the killer into a misstep."

"Do you think they know who did it?" Renie asked in an uneasy voice.

"Probably." Judith sounded bitter.

"Do you?"

"Yes." Judith eyed the now-cold tuna melt with distaste. "Don't you? It's obvious."

Phyliss Rackley was almost ready to leave when Judith returned to Hillside Manor. The cleaning woman took one whiff of Judith and let out a shriek.

"Spirits! I smell spirits! Have you been *imbibing*?"

Judith was in no mood for a temperance lecture. "Yes, Phyliss. I had a drink at lunch. I may have a drink before dinner. I'm in a drinking frame of mind."

Phyliss clenched her hands in a prayerful attitude. "Lord, Lord, Lordy! I never thought I'd see the day! Deliver me from sinful gin! Deliver Mrs. Flynn here from sinful ways! Deliver . . ."

"Speaking of delivering things," Judith interrupted in a weary voice, "did you get your letter from Idaho? Cecil left it last Friday. I put it on my bulletin board."

"No, I'll get it now. Such upstanding people," Phyliss asserted, bustling back into the kitchen. "I'll bet they don't drink spirits. 'Course I don't bet, gambling being as sinful as . . ." Her voice trailed off.

Judith was still standing in the hallway between the pantry and the basement stairs when the phone rang. Assuming it might be a prospective guest, she forced herself to answer in a gracious manner.

"Judith!" Vivian Flynn sounded ecstatic, a state no doubt induced by the very spirits that Phyliss had just denounced. Or so Judith thought. "I'm calling to say that I won't be home tomorrow as I'd planned." Judith

frowned, not recalling that Vivian had ever mentioned a
return date. Maybe she'd told Joe. It didn't matter; she let
Herself rattle on: "The weather here is gorgeous, none of
that nasty rain you have up there in the Northwest." Was
it raining when Vivian left? Judith couldn't remember
that, either. It certainly wasn't raining now; it must be
close to ninety. "I've closed the condo deal, and the new
owners will be down from Indianapolis at the end of the
month. But I've got to arrange to have my things shipped.
I've still got quite a few pieces of furniture and . . . Ah!
Stop that, you devil! What was I saying? Oh, paintings
and mementos and a rug I bought at . . . Silly! You
mustn't . . . !"

Judith made a face into the receiver. "Do you want me
to water your plants and the garden?" she inquired in a
tired voice.

Standing at the swinging doors, Phyliss let out a de-
lighted cackle. "They sent me a picture of the whole clan!
Didn't I say they were fine folks?"

Trying to catch Herself's reply, Judith nodded and
smiled at the cleaning woman.

"What?" Vivian was saying, also distracted. "Oh, yes,
if you would. I'm not really sure when I'll . . . Oh, that
tickles!"

Judith was becoming annoyed. "Vivian, could
you . . ."

Phyliss shouted farewell and departed.

"Oh my, you shouldn't . . ." Vivian gasped, her voice
barely audible. "Oh, that's too much, you naughty boy!
Oh, oh, oh, *Gurd* . . ."

The phone went dead.

Judith was as good as her word. By four-thirty, she was
fixing a martini when the phone rang again. This time it
was Renie.

"Coz! Guess what! Remember how I told you I was
going to wait until Bill was in a really good mood before

I showed him what I bought at I. Magnifique's?''

Judith said she did remember. Vaguely.

''Well, he came home this afternoon feeling terrific because one of his masochist patients has fallen in love with one of his sadists, and while I was cleaning my closet I hauled out my boxes from the store and told him we'd have a fashion show and when I opened the last box *I found your lavender dress*.'' Renie paused for breath.

Judith's indifference left her. ''You . . . *what*?''

Renie's laugh was truncated. ''I guess I grabbed your I. Magnifique box by mistake that day at Ron's Bar and Grill. Sorry, coz. It's been safe in my closet all along. Heh-heh.''

Judith slumped onto the kitchen counter. ''Oh my . . .''

''I'll bring it over tomorrow morning. By the way, you're right—there aren't any emeralds or cigars or anything else in the seams. It's just . . . a dress.''

I've been saved two thousand five hundred dollars, Judith thought. *A big fat credit on my I. Magnifique bill.* The initial desire to strangle Renie passed quickly.

''Thanks, coz,'' Judith gulped. The rattle of the screen door caused her to look up. ''Hey, here's Joe. Got to run. Thanks again. Thanks a couple of thousand.'' With hesitancy in her step, Judith moved down the narrow hallway to greet her husband. ''Well? You're home early.''

''Right.'' Joe hung his lightweight summer jacket on a peg. ''We took Mims's statement, but we're up against a stone wall. Now we have to go public to right the wrongful ID.'' He saw the gin bottle on the kitchen table and eyed Judith with curiosity. ''Are you drinking to forget— or to remember?''

''I don't know,'' Judith replied curtly. ''Do you want a martini?''

''Sure,'' Joe answered, sinking into the captain's chair. ''Hey—I'm sorry I had to fool you. But we need to smoke out a killer.''

"I understand." Judith's tone was still clipped. "So who did it?"

"You know." Joe stretched and yawned. "Do you know why?"

Judith was by the sink, shaking Joe's martini. "No." She turned, her eye caught by the notice from the IRS. A sinking feeling began in her stomach, but was suddenly replaced by a sense of enlightenment. She felt a bit like Buddha in his quest for Nirvana. "Yes."

Joe evinced only mild surprise. "It's not too hard to figure out, once you know the circumstances. But the big question is, where do we find our clever killer?"

Judith handed Joe his martini. "That I can't tell you. What I don't see is why you led me on. Couldn't you have confided the victim's identity to me?"

Joe shook his head. "You know better than that. When we work a case like this where we're trying to trick the killer into thinking we know much less than we really do, we don't dare tell anybody. Believe me, word leaks out."

Judith sat down and took a first sip from her own drink. "I would never have told . . ." She paused, hearing herself whisper the news to Renie, hearing Renie tell Bill, hearing Arlene listening out in the hedge. "Okay, I see your point. But you made such a big deal out of it, describing the victim, the circumstances, all the rest of it. You laid it on pretty thick."

The magic green eyes surveyed her over the rim of the martini glass. "I thought it was thick enough to give you a hint. I described Billy Big Horn perfectly, including his questionable health and poor nutrition."

Judith thought back to the evening at the Heraldsgate Pub. "It could have fit Harley, too. DJs are famous for eating junk food and keeping odd hours and taking pills and doing heaven-knows-what to ruin their health. Chuck Rawls mentioned how Harley was always hyper."

Joe lifted one shoulder in a guarded gesture. "I'm surprised you didn't recognize Billy yourself. You saw him in that body bag."

With deep chagrin, Judith sadly shook her head. "That's the pitiful part. I should have. But you don't really *look* at the homeless. You look *through* them. I'm ashamed of myself. As often as I'd seen him, I never really knew what Billy looked like. I knew his harmonica better than I knew him."

Joe sighed. "It's true, I'm afraid. If I hadn't talked to him outside the Naples that night, I might not have recognized him either."

They grew silent for a few moments, as if honoring the memory of Billy Big Horn. "Your ruse with the mistaken identity hasn't worked so far, has it?" Judith said in a melancholy tone.

"No. No, it hasn't." Joe's shoulders sagged as he gazed into his glass. "We lost track a week ago today."

"You and Woody are smart. You'll figure it out."

Joe gave Judith a bleak look. "Now you're the one who's being condescending."

Judith shook her head. "Not really. You and Woody were always one step ahead of me on this one. It's okay. Really. It's your job. It's just that you go through all the procedures, and you don't always know what's going on in the other divisions, things that might have a connection to the case, and you get stifled because the department doesn't encourage creativity and . . ." She stopped, rubbing at her forehead. "I've lost perspective. I'm not an investigator. Maybe it's just a game to me. To you, it's your job. It's who you are, what you are. I'm sorry I ever got involved in this one."

Joe gave Judith a half-smile. "Apology accepted. But," he went on, putting his hand on Judith's, "if you get any inspirations, let me know."

Judith smiled back. "Right, sure." She shook her head in a forlorn manner. "Don't hold your breath. I'm out of gas on this one."

The green eyes locked with her dark-eyed gaze. "Are you?" Joe chuckled. "Are you really?"

Judith doubted herself, but maybe Joe didn't. The thought was as surprising as it was comforting.

"Then you don't think I'm just another bungling amateur?" Judith asked with a touch of diffidence.

"There's nothing wrong with your amateur status," Joe asserted, his knee nudging her leg under the table.

"Bungling is bad," Judith said.

"Bundling is good," Joe grinned. "So is snuggling and hugging and . . ."

"It's dinnertime," Judith broke in.

Joe rose from his chair. "Put it on the back burner. We'll do the same with this case. Let's bundle ourselves upstairs."

They didn't bungle the bundling.

NINETEEN

JOE HAD LISTENED to the news of his ex-wife with barely a murmur. He didn't seem at all surprised that Uncle Gurd had joined Vivian in Panama City. If anything, Joe was amused.

"I'm going over to her house this evening," Judith said while cleaning up from the hors d'oeuvres hour. "She wants me to keep watering the garden and the house plants."

"I can do that," Joe volunteered. "I'll get the mail, too."

"No, let me," Judith protested as she wiped down Grandma Grover's sterling silver tray. "You've put in a hard day at work." Judith didn't care for the idea of Joe doing favors for his ex. It was bad enough that Herself had bought a house in the cul-de-sac in the first place.

"Whatever," he said with a shrug. "I'm going upstairs to watch ESPN. They should have some stuff on tomorrow's All Star baseball game."

But Joe was interrupted by a phone call. He spent most of it listening and saying little more than "Uh-huh," "Is that right?", and "Okay."

Judith had answered the phone, but wasn't able to identify the male voice at the other end. A colleague, she reasoned and felt a pang of sympathy for her husband. Ordinarily, Joe didn't like to be bothered at home. "Who was that?" she asked after he'd hung up.

"Bradley at Immigration," Joe replied, looking more pleased than aggrieved. "U.S. Customs has come in on the smuggling angle. De Tourville still swears he knows nothing about the ring." The green eyes sparked, and Judith paused in the act of loading the dishwasher. "But they've found the link with Tara Novotny."

"Lovers?" Judith asked.

Joe shook his head. "One of de Tourville's passports turned out to be the real thing. It was issued by the Cuban government, and his legal name is Basil Novotny."

Judith laughed. "They're married? Or brother and sister?"

"Neither," Joe replied, leaning against the refrigerator. "Got another guess?"

Judith went blank. Her usually logical mind seemed to have deserted her. "Cousins?" she offered, thinking of herself and Renie.

"Tara is Bascombe's—Basil's—daughter." Joe chuckled.

"Oh!" Judith laughed aloud. "Well, why not? She's in her twenties, and his age is hard to figure, but he could be closer to fifty than forty."

"It would explain why she fled to his place at Belgravia Gardens after Harley was supposedly murdered." Joe had become thoughtful. "Now if Bascombe was smuggling cigars out of Cuba, where did they end up? Santa Teresa del Fiore, maybe, which doesn't make him a crook. Not there anyway, because Cuban cigars are perfectly legal. But let's say Tara handles that part of the emerald smuggling at Mr. Artemis's sweat shop. She puts the emeralds into some of the cigars and then into selected garments. Maybe Tara brings these garments with her. Shipping them to Mr. Artemis's atelier would be risky. Anyway, she removes the cigars with the emeralds and trots the dresses or whatever over to Mr. Artemis. How does that sound?''

Judith had been listening with fascination. It seemed that Joe had gone from being virtually incommunicado to thinking out loud. ''It sounds fine. The next question is where did the cigars go?''

''To the Belmont,'' Joe replied, giving the refrigerator a thump. ''That's what was in the bucket of ashes. After the emeralds were removed, the cigars were burned.'' He paused, rubbing his chin. ''But Tara couldn't take the contraband there herself. She's a tall, stunning woman whose job in the real world is to be noticed, which is the last thing she wants at the Belmont.''

Judith, feeling fairly tall but not exactly stunning, put the last items into the dishwasher. ''She could go at night.''

Joe's index finger was drawing squiggly circles on the side of the refrigerator. ''No. That's when the bums would go there. Tara would be afraid.'' He looked up from his invisible doodling. ''Do you know when she'll be back from San Francisco?''

Judith tried to remember the brief conversation in the Belgravia Gardens elevator. ''No. But she did complain about so much traveling. She might have been going on to some other place.''

''Damn!'' Joe pounded his fist into his hand. ''Of course it's not our worry now. Still, I think there's a tie-in between Billy's murder and the emeralds.''

''You do?'' Judith was still marveling at her husband's immersion in the case during his off-hours. Maybe, she thought, he was trying to show his confidence in her ability to help. ''I'd begun to think they were two separate issues,'' she said in a less than certain voice.

''That'd be too big a coincidence,'' Joe responded. ''I don't believe in coincidence in a murder investigation.''

''I do,'' Judith said, giving a start. ''I just realized there's another motive for Billy's murder besides the possibility that he unwittingly discovered the smuggling ring.'' With mounting excitement, she grabbed her husband's arm.

Joe was skeptical. ''Like what?''

''Like Billy himself. Kobe, the parking valet at the Naples, said Billy used a cigar box to collect contributions, and that some people actually gave him cigars even though he didn't smoke. I'm betting those weren't ordinary cigars. The conduit between Mr. Artemis's atelier and the Belmont was Billy Big Horn.''

Joe whistled softly. ''It fits. Who'd suspect a poor homeless man of being an accomplice in an international smuggling ring? We also know who frequented the Naples Hotel restaurant. But how in hell are we going to bring that slippery customer in?''

Unfortunately, Judith didn't know. Joe's mood skidded into the doldrums. Judith wasn't far behind.

On Tuesday morning, Phyliss was late. The bus had had a problem, lost its trolley or its driver or its brakes. The explanation wasn't clear, though the Good Lord had played a large part in finally getting Phyliss to Hillside Manor. Maybe, Judith thought irreverently, He'd driven the bus. She let Phyliss rattle on, paying attention only when the cleaning woman pulled a snapshot out of her well-worn purse.

''Here's the whole bunch of 'em,'' she said, tapping the three-by-five color snapshot. ''There's Cousin Thorald and Aunt Tilda and Aunt Leota and . . .''

The Rundberg clan held no charm for Judith. Even if Sig and Merle didn't dwell in Deep Denial, the rest of the family still represented potential penury to Judith. They were all painted with the same brush.

''Later, Phyliss,'' Judith said. ''There's someone at the back door.''

O. P. Dooley was practically jumping up and down on the porch. ''Mrs. Flynn!'' he cried. ''Guess what!''

Judith opened the screen door to admit O. P., but he remained outside, pointing to the hill that swept up to Belgravia Gardens. "It's that condo," he said, out of breath. "I just remembered, there's a rear entrance. I used to see it when the place was being built. Then they planted a bunch of shrubs and stuff and you can't really see it now, at least not in the summer. That's how those people got in and out without being seen from the front of the condos." His fair face was flushed with excitement.

"That certainly explains it," Judith said. "Good work, O. P. Would you like to come in and . . ."

"That lady just went in there," O. P. continued in a rush. "I could see her walking down the path that goes around the side of the building. She had a suitcase and one of those . . . what do you call them? The long things you put clothes in."

Judith frowned in puzzlement. "A garment bag?"

"That's it." O. P. nodded vigorously. "Anyway, she's come back. Is that important?"

"Yes. Yes, it is." Judith's gaze traveled up the side hill to the impressive stone facade of Belgravia Gardens. She tapped her foot and considered. "I think I'll stop by."

"Can I come with you?" O. P.'s face was all boyish eagerness.

"Ah . . ." It didn't seem right to turn O. P. down. "Okay, hop in the car. We'll drive up there because I've got to go to the grocery store. But I think I'll have you wait in the lobby. Backup, you see."

"Oh, wow!" O. P. jumped into the Subaru. "This is totally cool!" Then, since even a twelve-year-old can have doubts, he turned a concerned face to Judith. "What are we doing? Is it dangerous?"

"I'm not sure. The main thing is to get inside." Phyliss had been scheduled to clean de Tourville's condo on Monday, but he had called to tell her to wait. His circumstances, he'd explained, had changed since their last communication. Pretending that she was Phyliss or Phyliss's

replacement wouldn't work. At this point, pretending she
was anybody but herself was virtually impossible.

"O. P., are you still a Boy Scout?" Judith inquired as
they turned out of the cul-de-sac and headed for Heraldsgate Avenue.

"Sure," O. P. replied. "I'm working to make first
class."

"Does that involve searching for lost children—like
your nephew, Pix?"

O. P. frowned. "Pix isn't lost. He just ate one of our
goldfish and got sent to his room."

"Let's pretend." Judith turned off of Heraldsgate Avenue and found a parking place at the far end of the block.
"Come on, I'll tell you what to say into the intercom."

Three minutes later, O. P. was speaking to Tara Novotny while Judith hid behind a large mountain laurel.
"He's just a little guy," O. P. said in an agitated voice
with his face pressed against the mesh grille. "I think
what must have happened is that somebody left the back
entrance unlocked within the last few minutes, and he
scooted inside. He really loves to ride elevators, and I
need to get in so I can see if he's going up and down.
Down and up. That's what he likes to do. Please, could I
come in and look? If he's not here, he must have tumbled
down the hill and he's lying all smashed up and bloody
in the bushes."

Peering through the mountain laurel, Judith marveled
at O. P.'s acting ability. There was a long pause before
Tara's accented voice came over the intercom: "Why are
you asking me this?"

"You're the first button I poked," O. P. answered, still
sounding distraught, but looking quite ingenuous.
"Please, ma'am, I'm so worried. My mother's sick and
my father's . . ."

"Very well." A buzzer sounded, indicating that Tara
had opened the front door. The intercom at her end
switched off.

As he'd been instructed, O. P. held the door open long enough to give Judith time to slip inside. "Okay," she said, "Tara probably stopped looking at the screen when you came in. Wait here in the lobby. If I don't come back in fifteen minutes, buzz de Tourville's unit again."

As the car glided noiselessly to the penthouse, Judith suddenly asked herself what on earth she planned to do. Perhaps Tara wasn't alone; maybe de Tourville was there, too. But the elevator doors slid open before she could figure out a scheme. Tara was standing by the big window, gazing out over the city and the bay. Apparently, she didn't hear Judith come in.

"Ms. Novotny," Judith said in what she hoped was a confident voice. "Where's your father?"

Tara whirled. "You! Who are you? What do you want?"

"I'm . . . a neighbor. I'm helping one of the Dooley children look for his little nephew."

"No," Tara breathed, advancing on Judith. "You are police. You warned me about police when I saw you in the elevator last week."

"No, I'm not." Judith had made up her mind that honesty was the best policy. "I live just below the condos, I run a bed and breakfast. You may have seen the sign. It's small and discreet."

"You are not small and you are not discreet." Tara drew herself up to her imposing height. "Get out."

Judith didn't budge. "I asked about your father. Is he here?"

"I have no father. He died many years ago in a slave labor camp." Tara was now standing only a foot away from Judith. "Go, go, go!"

Out of the corner of her eye, Judith saw the garment bag that O. P. had described. "Have you got some new Mr. Artemis fashions?"

Tara's green eyes flickered in the direction of a Louis XV armoire, where the garment bag hung from an ornate gold handle. "Yes." She spoke in clipped, impatient tones, obviously anxious to be rid of her uninvited guest. "There is a fall fashion show next week at Donner & Blitzen."

Something clicked in Judith's brain. "How long has he being doing that? I thought his merchandise was an I. Magnifique exclusive."

Tara gave an impatient shake of her head. "For a year or more he has permitted Donner & Blitzen as well as Nordquist's to feature a handful of his creations. But there must be no duplication between the stores. That would be a dreadful thing."

Judith assumed an awestruck expression. "He's such a brilliant couturier. Could I see the garments? It'd give me a huge thrill."

"No." Tara's perfect features hardened. "They are not to be viewed until the show. Now go, please. I have no small child here."

"Nor a father," Judith murmured, docilely heading for the elevator. "Well, thank you just the same."

In the lobby, O. P. was slouched against the mailboxes. "You're okay?" he inquired, sounding disappointed.

"More or less," Judith replied in a distracted tone. She was still in the elevator, pressing various buttons. At last she found the right one. "Call for the other car," she said to O. P. "I want both these elevators immobilized."

Looking intrigued, O. P. did as he was told. A moment later, the two cars stood frozen in place, with their doors open to the lobby. Judith rushed to the pay phone and called 911. She didn't want to waste time going through Joe; it would be much quicker to summon Corazon Perez and Ted Doyle in their patrol car.

Hanging up the phone, Judith scanned the lobby. "Where do you suppose the freight elevator is? There must be one."

"By that rear entrance?" O. P. suggested. "I remember

they used to haul stuff in that way when they were build-ing.''

Judith snapped her fingers. "Good thinking, O. P. Let's see if we can find it."

Their attempt was short-lived. The lobby dead-ended just past the elevators.

"It must be accessed only from that rear door and prob-ably through the underground parking," Judith said, try-ing to stay out of the surveillance camera's range. "Oh, well. We'll wait here for the police."

O. P. could hardly contain himself. "This is just like TV!" he exclaimed in a stage whisper. "Are the cops going to bust that Tara lady?"

"I hope so," Judith said. "At the very least, they want to take her in for questioning."

A vehicle was drawing up in front of Belgravia Gar-dens. At first glance, Judith thought it was Perez and Doyle, but realized it was a taxi. "Drat!" Judith cried. "I'll bet it's for Tara. She'll figure out the elevators aren't working and try the freight car. Where are those cops?"

"We could go around to the back and trap her," O. P. said, his eyes growing large at the thought.

Judith wavered. "You wait for the police. I'll go to the rear entrance." Seeing the disappointment on O. P.'s face, she handed over her shoulder bag. "Take this. I may need my hands free. You bring the officers to the back of the condos, just like a sheriff heading a posse. Okay?"

Reluctantly, O. P. agreed. Judith hurried outside, around the building, and down the path. The rear door was closed, and there was no sign of Tara. Flattening her-self against the stone facade, Judith waited.

No more than a minute passed before the door swung open. Tara appeared, carrying the garment bag and a Cha-nel purse. Judith jumped her from behind.

"Hold it!" Judith shouted, grappling with the other woman, who was impeded by her belongings. "Sorry, Tara, but you have to talk to the police."

"I knew you were police!" Tara cried. "Let me go! I have done nothing!"

"We'll . . . see . . . about . . . that." Despite the encumbrances, Tara was younger and more fit than Judith. The two women struggled on the narrow walk. Just as Judith seemed to be getting a firm grip, Tara dropped the garment bag and flung the purse into the shrubbery. She jerked free with such a violent motion that Judith was knocked to the ground. Before Tara could sprint off in her Chanel pumps, Judith clutched at one slim ankle. Tara also fell, and the grappling combatants rolled off the path and into a clump of prickly Oregon grape.

Judith and Tara began to slip and slide, ever downward. Digging in with the heels of her Keds, Judith tried to get a foothold while hanging onto Tara. The topsoil was too dry; no purchase could be gained. Judith felt herself falling faster, bumping past rhododendrons, azaleas, andromeda, and several varieties of fern. Halfway down, Tara managed to break free, but both women continued to tumble down the steep hillside. They didn't stop until they reached Judith's garden.

Trying to stand up, Tara let out a torrent of incomprehensible curses in what Judith assumed was her native language. Judith didn't much care. She was dazed and bruised and battered. Further pursuit seemed out of the question. Tara could run, but she couldn't hide. And the garment bag remained up on the hill, somewhere in the shrubbery outside of Belgravia Gardens.

Tara had lost one pump and was removing the other. She was standing like a stork by the toolshed when Gertrude opened the door.

"Hey!" Gertrude yelled. "What are you doing here? I saw you once before, hauling off that muscle-bound guy. He's not here now, so beat it."

Judith had finally gotten to her feet and was limping across the grass. Tara had turned to stare at Gertrude.

"Be quiet, old woman! You know nothing!" She started to move away.

"Watch your mouth, you scrawny twerp!" Gertrude rasped, shoving the walker at Tara who was thrown off-balance.

At that moment, Sweetums streaked out of the toolshed. He pounced on Tara's ankles and began to claw. Horrified, Tara reached down to pry the cat loose. Sweetums dug in deeper. Tara let out a howl of pain.

"My leg! My stockings! Help!"

Judith had finally reached the walkway. Gertrude turned to see her daughter staggering slightly and clutching her side.

"Well, dummy, where've you been? You're supposed to take Deb and me to bridge club today."

Judith had forgotten that Gertrude was supposed to play bridge. "Later, Mother," Judith said, attempting a half-hearted dive at Tara. "I'm trying to make a citizen's arrest."

Tara swung an elbow and caught Judith in the side, where her ribs had been bruised. Judith doubled over. Sweetums kept clawing.

"Now what's all this?" Gertrude demanded. "Is she a crook?"

"Yes," Judith retorted. "She's a . . . Republican."

With a mighty effort, Gertrude picked up the walker and brought it down on Tara. The blow wasn't severe, but the supermodel was now entangled in the walker with the cat at her ankles. Tara was still cursing and yelling and struggling when Corazon Perez and Ted Doyle came racing down the hill and into the backyard.

"Sorry," Perez shouted. "There was an accident on the bridge."

"Grab her," Judith shouted back, pointing at the beleaguered Tara. "The customs agents want her for smuggling."

It didn't take long for Perez and Doyle to subdue the

suspect. It took longer to make Sweetums give up his prey. At last the patrol officers brought their squad car down to the cul-de-sac and drove away with Tara. Under Judith's guidance, they also recovered the garment bag.

"I missed all the fun," O. P. complained after Judith had gone back to the condo to collect the boy, the Subaru, and the shoulder bag. "All I could see was you guys rolling around on the hillside."

"But you got Perez and Doyle there in time," Judith consoled him. "And you knew about that rear entrance which was the most important part of all."

"I guess." O. P. didn't sound convinced.

Putting a hand on the boy's shoulder, Judith bent down to speak into his ear. "You've helped capture an international jewel thief. If that doesn't get you a first class in scouting, it'll sure make you the envy of the rest of the troop."

O. P. brightened. "Can I tell my dad and mom?"

"Sure." Judith straightened up. "Well—I guess." She wasn't certain how the senior Dooleys would react to their son's brush with danger.

O. P. took off, vaulting over the fence as his older brother always did. Judith smiled to herself as she went into the house to check with Phyliss before taking Gertrude and Aunt Deb to bridge club and then heading for the grocery store. It occurred to her that catching crooks and chauffeuring mothers and supplying the B&B were all part of the fabric that made up her daily life. It was unusual, it was astonishing, it was, for some peculiar reason, part of being Judith.

Phyliss was scrubbing the kitchen floor. "What was all that commotion out in the yard just now? By the time I turned off the vacuum, I couldn't see much except your mother and that neighbor boy."

"It's a long story," Judith said, anxious to be on her way.

"Sometimes I wonder what goes on around this place,"

Phyliss said, wringing out the mop. "Frankly, you look like you've been dragged through a knot-hole. You're not doing anything godless, are you?"

"I hope not," Judith replied.

"Some people lead blameless lives—or try to." Phyliss went over to the kitchen counter and picked up her snapshot. "Like these Rundbergs. Here, take a minute, have a look. I want to.put it in my scrapbook."

Judith humored the cleaning woman, politely admiring the photo that showed the extended family posing in front of a sprawling structure set among the trees. The building looked as if it had been added onto at various stages to accommodate the growing number of survivalists. A huge American flag flew on the roof and a handmade sign in the foreground read, "Keep Out—Trespassers Will Be Annihilated."

"They're all armed," Judith exclaimed as her gaze traveled to the cluster of men, women, and children sitting on the front steps, leaning on the porch rail, and peering out from the recesses of open doors and windows. "Even the kids have guns."

" 'Course they do," Phyliss said. "They believe in the right to protect themselves. It's tough being a God-fearing sort and having all those wild-eyed liberals in Washington D.C. trying to take away your money and your freedom. I've learned a lot from them since we started writing . . ."

Judith snatched the photo from Phyliss's hand. "Ohmigod!" She moved closer to the kitchen window. "Phyliss, do you recognize the man in the doorway?"

Phyliss peered at the snapshot. "Nope. But I don't know half these fine folks. They didn't all come over here for the wedding, you know."

Opening the drawer under the counter, Judith pulled out a magnifying glass. Carefully, she examined the figure in the background. "Can I keep this for a little bit?"

Phyliss was reluctant. "It's the only group picture I got. How long?"

"Just today. In fact, I should be able to give it back to you by the time you're ready to go home. Okay?"

"Well . . . I guess so. Why do you want it?"

"I'll explain later, Phyliss," Judith said, heading for the back door. "Right now I have to take Mother to bridge and then go to police headquarters. I should be back by two." Slinging her handbag over her shoulder, Judith all but ran out of the house.

Judith loaded Gertrude into the car, then drove to the top of the hill to pick up Aunt Deb. Renie's mother noticed Judith's disheveled state immediately.

"Goodness, dear, did you have a fall? Your clothes are all torn and you have dirt just about everywhere. You look as disreputable as Renie."

Judith didn't feel like explaining. The bridge club was meeting only five blocks from Aunt Deb's apartment, so Judith managed to reach police headquarters before noon. According to Officer Reyes, who was again on duty behind the main desk, Joe and Woody were with Tara, waiting for the feds to take over. Judith cooled her sore heels in the reception area.

When Joe finally appeared almost an hour later, Judith was not only hurting, but hungry. Her husband hurried to envelop her in a hug.

"Hey, are you okay?" he asked in a worried tone. "Perez and Doyle told me you went to war with Tara."

"I'll be fine," Judith said, though she knew her voice was ragged. "Just don't hug too hard. My ribs are bruised."

Joe held her at arm's length. "You do look pretty rough. If I take you to a dark restaurant could you eat something?"

"I could," Judith answered. "But I've got something to show . . ."

"Where's Woody?" Joe scanned the reception area. Officer Reyes informed him that his partner was still filling out forms for the customs agents. "Tell him we'll be

at the Shanghai,'' Joe called, shielding Judith with an arm
as they headed for the elevators.

The down car was already crowded, but Judith and Joe
squeezed in. ''Tara's going to give somebody up in order
to cut a deal,'' Joe said into Judith's ear. ''It's you-know-
who.''

''That's what I wanted to . . .''

''Artemis Bohl is out of it—he's going to be one red-
faced dress designer.'' Joe chuckled. ''He never suspected
a thing. And TNT wasn't involved. He had access to the
Belmont, so Tara was thinking of him as a replacement
for the missing Billy. Then she changed her mind—not
enough smarts. But that's why she came to pick TNT up
at the B&B that day.''

''Phyliss got a snapshot from Deep Denial, and in the
background it shows . . .''

''Bascombe or Basil or whatever he's calling himself
wasn't to be trusted, not even by his own daughter.'' The
elevator stopped on the main floor. Judith and Joe got out
and headed for the street. ''She's fond of him, but she
knows him too well. That's okay, he'll be deported by
Immigration. The fraud charges will be filed in various
countries.''

Judith had given up trying to tell Joe about the photo-
graph. He was obviously flying high over the capture of
Tara and the garment bag which had indeed contained
emerald-filled cigars in the seams of Mr. Artemis's latest
designs. With a little sigh that hurt her ribs, Judith decided
to wait until they were at the restaurant.

''Meanwhile, we've been doing some digging into Esperanza Highcastle's finances,'' Joe went on as they continued south into the international district. ''She's got
some big money problems. The woman has no business
sense and she's the kind who won't listen to sound advice.
We're turning this case over to the bunco squad. Woody
and I think she hired those kids to blow up the Heralds-

gate 400 building. The insurance on that is way beyond its actual worth.''

''What about Darrell Mims?'' Judith asked meekly.

''Well . . . we could be in trouble along with Darrell for permitting the mistaken ID of the body to go public,'' Joe said as they began to pass shops and businesses where the facades featured Chinese characters instead of English words. ''But neither Billy Big Horn nor Harley Davidson have any relatives that we know of, so maybe we'll just figure Darrell's learned his lesson. I don't expect that either KRAS or KORN will be in business much longer anyway. Darrell's going to have to take his crusade somewhere else.''

''Goodness,'' Judith said, wishing her entire body didn't hurt so much. ''There's certainly been a lot of fallout from this case.''

''There sure has,'' Joe agreed as they approached the Shanghai's red and green marquee with its handsome gold dragon. ''That's one thing about police work—an investigation often reveals layers and layers of stuff you'd never otherwise find out.''

Since it was going on one o'clock, some of the diners in the busy restaurant were already leaving. Joe knew many of them, since the Shanghai was frequented by city employees.

''How about dim sum?'' Joe suggested. ''That's what Woody and I usually have here.''

''Good. Fine.'' Judith gave Joe a lame little smile.

''How about a drink?'' Joe said, scrutinizing Judith more closely. ''You're beginning to turn some funny colors. Black and blue don't become you as well as bright red.''

''Hot tea is fine,'' Judith said. ''I'll be fine. Honest.''

''You sure?'' Joe had grown serious, and Judith realized that the change in mood wasn't only due to his concern for her well-being. She knew that his professional euphoria never lasted long: Even when he'd closed one case, there were always loose ends and dead ends.

"I know where to find the killer." Judith spoke so matter-of-factly that at first her words didn't seem to register with Joe. She read the incomprehension on his face and dug into her shoulder bag. "Here. The Rundbergs sent this to Phyliss." As Joe studied the snapshot, Judith pointed to one of the open windows. "There he is. It's Harley Davidson, alive and well, and living in Deep Denial."

The standoff between the survivalists and the FBI and local law enforcement officials made headlines everywhere for over a week. When Harley was finally surrendered by his newfound friends, it was Aunt Leota who gave him up. She and Aunt Tilda had gotten into an argument over which one of their late husbands Harley most resembled, and when Leota put it to a vote, Tilda won. In a fit of pique, Leota hauled Harley outside the compound and turned him over to the feds. Because he was blind, Harley thought she was taking him into the bedroom, to what purpose he couldn't imagine. At that point, the feds seemed preferable to Aunt Leota.

On the last Saturday of July, Judith and Joe went downtown to have lunch at Ron's Bar and Grill. Judith wanted to celebrate the successful conclusion of the case, but Joe felt a sense of failure.

"I don't know if we've got enough real evidence," Joe told Judith for the dozenth time as they sat in the bar and sipped martinis. "Oh, Harley'll go to prison for income tax evasion and smuggling, but Woody and I aren't sure we can pin the murder rap on him."

"There's got to be a way," Judith said with fervor.

Joe gave a small shake of his head. "If Harley had stabbed Esperanza Highcastle or Tara Novotny or even Chuck Rawls, there'd be more urgency from my superiors. But a poor homeless bum like Billy Big Horn—nobody really cares. It's wrong, but it's true."

Judith and Joe had gone over the case so many times that they could recite it by heart: How Harley had run the smuggling ring with Tara, how they'd used TNT's connection with Esperanza to get into the Belmont, how they'd transferred the cigars from Mr. Artemis's designs to Billy Big Horn's cigar box. And then, when the IRS had come after Harley on suspicion of unreported income from his broadcasting career, the DJ had decided to cut his losses. Between his radio payoffs and the emerald profits, he apparently had millions stashed away. Joe and Woody had found the IRS letters in Harley's apartment, which Judith realized, had accounted for her husband's immediate recognition of their own audit notice. The only way Harley could avoid prosecution by the government was to become legally dead. Death and taxes were not merely inevitable, it seemed, but also linked in Harley's plan.

His attempt to kill Tara and thus eliminate one of his two potentially talkative partners had failed: Harley hadn't been able to see the balcony which had broken her fall. Nor had he realized that he'd dropped the emerald that Judith had later found on the balcony. But the encounter with Billy had gone off as planned. It was much easier for one blind man to kill a similarly handicapped victim. And Billy had to die not only because he was part of the smuggling ring, but because he could be mistaken for Harley.

There had been risks, of course: Harley had planted the idea of his disappearance in Darrell Mims's suggestible mind. Harley knew that Darrell would get stuck with the task of identifying the body. Even if Darrell hadn't seized the opportunity, Harley could still make a getaway. Getting himself arrested as Billy had given the wily DJ the means to hear what was going on with the police. After all, he couldn't read about it in the newspapers.

"You found Billy's cigar box and Harley's ID in the Naples fountain," Judith reminded Joe. "That's got to help finger Harley as the murderer. You know he impersonated Billy and deliberately got himself thrown in jail as the safest place to hide until he could make arrangements to get out of town.''

''Right, sure,'' Joe agreed, signaling the bartender for a second round. ''Customs can probably nail him on the smuggling, too. Now that Tara knows Harley's still alive, she's given him up. But everything else is circumstantial, which doesn't always go down in court.''

''Tara must be very angry about almost getting killed,'' Judith pointed out, then, because the first martini had made her rather bold, added, ''like I was with you when I found out Billy hadn't been cremated.''

''You should have known,'' Joe replied matter-of-factly. ''We always have to wait for next of kin, even when there aren't any. So far, no takers. Billy's still on ice.'' Judith grew temporarily silent. ''Well, there's one bright note on the personal side. The stand-off with their relatives scared—or maybe embarrassed—the Rundbergs so much that they're finally paying the wedding bills.''

''I'll drink to that,'' Joe said, raising his almost-empty glass.

''Me, too. What a relief!'' Judith smiled at her husband. ''By the way, I want to stop at I. Magnifique's after lunch.'' She nudged the big box under the table with her knee. ''I have something to return.''

''I was wondering what was in that box,'' Joe said with mild interest. ''Doesn't it fit?''

''It fits.'' Judith laughed feebly. ''But it's way too expensive. It's a Mr. Artemis evening dress.''

''Really?'' Joe's interest increased. ''Why didn't you show it to me?''

''It's a long story.'' Judith accepted a second martini from their server. She didn't want to admit that she had ended up with the dress as the result of her amateur sleuthing. Nor did she want to confess that it had gone missing for an unnerving length of time.

Joe didn't press Judith to explain. His mind was clearly still fixated on the homicide investigation.

"I guess you were right about coincidences," he finally said. "Who would have figured Harley would end up in Deep Denial?"

"Actually," Judith responded slowly, "we should have. I didn't remember until after the fact that Darrell Mims told me how Harley and Chuck Rawls got into a big fight over the Ruby Ridge debacle. Harley had strong feelings for survivalists. Maybe it was then that he got the idea to head for one of their refuges. The irony is that I'll bet he didn't realize he was having his picture taken. He couldn't have seen the camera."

After their server had jotted down their luncheon orders, Joe gave Judith a cockeyed grin. "I suppose Phyliss is taking credit for all this."

"Not really. She says the Lord works in mysterious ways. She's merely His instrument. But of course she knew nothing about how the Rundbergs had heard Harley on the radio while they were here, and had admired his political views."

"Harley didn't know that," Joe pointed out.

"No, but it made it much easier for him to talk them into taking him under their wing," Judith noted. "It was perfectly safe to call himself Harley Davidson. Didn't you say the IRS was looking for him under his real name?"

Joe nodded. "John Smith. Which complicated matters for the feds. He sold the emeralds as Harley Davidson when he rendezvoused with the buyers at concerts he MC'ed. Who'd bother looking for jewel smugglers during an event with whacked-out kids trying to trample each other to death? And that's just the performers. Thank God I never worked crowd control."

When their entrees arrived, Judith and Joe eventually spoke of other things. They were almost finished eating when Judith raised the topic she'd been reluctant to mention for weeks.

"You know, I think the reason I got so wrapped up in this case was because I didn't want to deal with talking to Mike about . . . you and Dan." She paused, waiting for Joe's reaction. But his expression was noncommittal, and Judith continued: "Then, after I did talk to him and got nowhere, you seemed upset. I didn't want to think about that, either. So I just kept slogging ahead, and it was very stupid of me, because you and Woody knew exactly where the case was going."

"It's what we do," Joe said simply.

"But I kept annoying you by meddling, and it didn't do me much good, because you must be still upset about Mike."

"I'm living with it," Joe said, fingering his coffee cup. "I always will."

"Yes." Judith stared at her empty plate. "And I'll always live with you living with it. That's okay, isn't it?"

"That's marriage." Joe put his hand on Judith's. "There are no easy answers. Not on the job, not in real life."

"That's true," Judith said softly. "That's the way it is."

"That's *us*," said Joe, and squeezed her hand.

The designer room at I. Magnifique conveyed an almost sepulchral air on a Saturday afternoon in mid-summer. Everything seemed hushed, as if the impeccably groomed saleswomen were waiting to view the body—or the fall collections.

Judith immediately spotted Portia, the sleek blond who had waited on Renie during the sale. "I'd like to return something," Judith said in a small voice. Carefully, she opened the box.

Portia recoiled slightly, as if Judith had let a snake out of a basket. "You want to return Lavender Dreams? Oh, my!"

"Yes," Judith replied, trying to sound firm. "It's . . . not me."

Joe had sidled over to the mahogany desk which served as a counter. "Hey—purple! You look good in purple, Jude-girl. Doesn't it fit?"

"It's not purple," Judith countered. "It's lavender. And it . . ."

"Let's see you in it," Joe said.

"But . . ." Judith tried to protest.

"The gentleman has exquisite taste," Portia purred. "Surely you'll let him be the judge." She simpered at Joe and patted her perfect French roll.

"Oooh . . ." Judith picked up the dress and trooped off in the direction of the fitting rooms. As before, the gown fit, and the lighter shade in the purple spectrum wasn't unflattering. But of course that was all beside the point. The price tag was still attached, and Judith would flash it at Joe. At twenty-five hundred dollars, he'd get the message.

Arranging the folds and slipping back into her shoes, Judith gazed out of the small, grilled window that looked out onto the hill above downtown. She could just catch the outline of the Naples Hotel. The Belmont was gone, having been finally pulled down the previous week. Judith paused, recalling what the old building had looked like, not only in its heyday, but on the night of the rehearsal dinner. Her eyes widened, and she practically ran out of the fitting room and into the salon where Joe was waiting in a plush armchair with a glass of champagne at his side.

"Joe!" she exclaimed, ignoring the fawning Portia. "I just realized something! I saw Harley try to kill Tara! That's attempted murder! I can be a witness! Surely she'll corroborate my statement! Between that and the evidence you already have, you can get Harley!"

Joe's high forehead creased. "You mean I finally have to believe what you saw on the Belmont roof?"

Judith nodded eagerly. "You bet! You know I saw it! Come on, it'll work."

"It might." Joe's brow cleared. "Yes, it might at that. Maybe Billy Big Horn will be avenged after all. And Woody and I can close this case."

"Great!" Judith couldn't help but twirl around in the lavender dress. Then she remembered the price tag, and leaned close to her husband. "What do you think?"

Joe didn't bat an eye. He looked at Portia and raised his champagne glass. "We'll take it," he said.